...Jeremy tensed, sensing something was wrong in the camp, but before he could move there came the triple shrill of a military whistle. Roughly releasing the startled Gwen, he rushed to the tent flap, throwing it open. Suddenly a bayonet flashed before his face, and he ducked back just in time. There was a shout of anger, and two burly Continentals in blue uniforms charged into the tent, cursing, and driving Jeremy backward as Gwen sprang up and screamed in fright.

Jeremy had a sword hanging at the rear of the tent, and he went for it as the Continentals shouted, "Surrender or die!"

Jeremy's fury caused him to lose his head, and as he reached for the weapon, one of the soldiers lunged forward, stabbing with the bayonet, narrowly slicing through his tunic. His attempt for the sword was nearly fatal, but the rebels were blocked by Gwen, who shrieked for them to stop. Almost at the same instant she threw herself at Jeremy before he tried again for his sword.

The rebels were wild with excitement. "Go on!" one yelled, jabbing his bayonet at Jeremy. "Get your steel! Give me a good reason to stick you!"

The other man menaced with a growl, "Don't need a reason. I'll kill him myself..."

# CONFLICT

The Fifth Powerful Novel
in the Northwest Territory Series

**THE REVOLUTION EXPLODES
INTO THE WILDERNESS,
AND THE MEN AND WOMEN
OF THE OLD NORTHWEST MUST
CHOOSE SIDES OR PERISH…**

**JEREMY BENTLY.** His calling is to save lives, but his honor demands that he go to war, even if it means losing the woman he loves…

✖

**GWEN HARDY.** She lives as a rebel outcast in a British wilderness stronghold…until even her lover becomes her enemy…

✖

**ANNIE ROSS.** Cheerful, loyal, and always a lady, she'll do anything to win one man—a man who is in love with her best friend…

✖

**OWEN SUTHERLAND.** His experience and steadfastness set an example to a young and inexperienced army fighting for its very survival . . .

**ELLA SUTHERLAND.** Without Owen by her side, she must lead her family on a flight through the wilderness, until they can run no farther . . .

**MANOTH.** Though the British try to control him, he will obey no orders that stand in the way of his bloodthirsty revenge . . .

**RICHARD WESTON.** Handsome, dashing, and confident, he is eager to fight for king and country—but not prepared for the savagery of wilderness warfare . . .

**BRADFORD CULLEN.** His money and influence make him the leading rebel in the northwest—and greed and ambition make him the most dangerous . . .

**HENRY HAMILTON.** To the British he is a brave and capable officer, a man of unbending honor; but to the rebels he is the devil himself . . .

*By Oliver Payne from Berkley*

## NORTHWEST TERRITORY SERIES

# NORTHWEST TERRITORY · BOOK 5
# CONFLICT
## OLIVER PAYNE

Created by the producers of
**Wagons West, The Australians,** and
**The Kent Family Chronicles.**

*Chairman of the Board: Lyle Kenyon Engel*

BERKLEY BOOKS, NEW YORK

CONFLICT

A Berkley Book / published by arrangement with
Book Creations, Inc.

PRINTING HISTORY
Berkley edition / July 1984

ISBN: 0-425-07021-2

Nine thousand Americans died fighting for freedom in the American Revolution; more than half of them died in the disastrous Canadian campaign of 1775–76. This book is dedicated to the memory of those five thousand who died. Their courage did not bring them victory, but their sacrifice made possible the triumph of those Americans who lived to fight again.

## AUTHOR'S NOTE

It should be mentioned here that Chief Joseph Brant was in England until August 1776 and was not involved in the action at the Cedars, which occurred in March. Also, Benjamin Franklin's clever though unscrupulous hoax in publishing a false report of the bundles of scalps said to be intercepted by rebel troops took place in 1781, not 1777. In addition, the Redcoats at the Cedars were led by a Captain Forster, not by the fictional Lieutenant Mark Davies.

For those readers who respect historical accuracy and also enjoy the fiction of historical novels, it is hoped these liberties are not only acceptable, but excusable for the sake of the tale.

Oliver Payne

July 1983

# THE
# OLD NORTHWEST
# AND THE
# NORTHERN
# COLONIES
## c. 1777

Fort
Michilimackinac

GEORGIAN
BAY

LAKE
HURON

LAKE ON

Ft Niag

LAKE ST.
CLAIR

Fort
Detroit

LAKE ERIE

ALLEGHENY RIVER

OHIO RIVER

MONONGAHELA
RIVER

Fort
Pitt

P

© BOOK CREATIONS INC. 1983

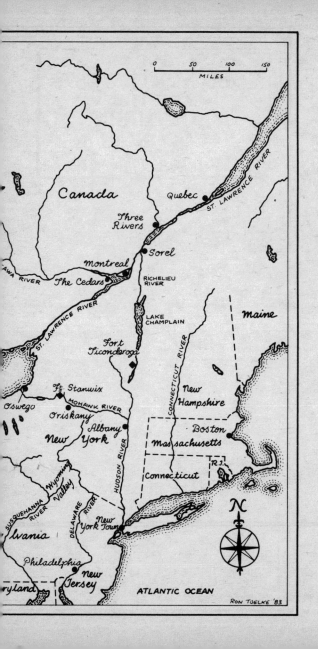

Every Tory is a coward, for servile, slavish, self-interested fear is the foundation of Toryism; and a man under such influence, though he may be cruel, never can be brave.

–Tom Paine
*The Crisis*
1776


These hardy knaves and stupid fools,
Some apish and pragmatic mules,
Some servile, acquiescing tools—
These, these compose the Congress!

When Jove resolved to send a curse,
And all the woes of life rehearse,
Not plague, not famine, but much worse—
He cursed us with a Congress!

–Tory ballad
1776

# PART ONE

# A Civil Conflict

## chapter 1

# THE MIST

It was Christmas morning in the year 1775, and a drizzling mist obscured the straits between Lake Erie and Lake Saint Clair. The pale light of wintry dawn merged water and sky into a gray mass, shrouding a birchbark canoe slipping upstream toward Fort Detroit, five miles ahead. The canoe's three paddlers were unaware of the danger that bore down on them silently from behind.

Only the dim yellow light of a bow lantern, invisible to the canoeists, signaled the approach of the last merchant ship on the straits before winter set in. Cutting through mist and water, the sloop *Trader* drove straight onward. The sloop's crew could just make out the dark outline of the eastern shore to the right, and they were taking advantage of a good following wind, impatient to reach their destination.

Unless someone on the sloop's deck spotted the canoe in time, it would be rammed like so much driftwood. There was even a chance that no one would hear the cries of the paddlers, who would be thrown into the icy water and lost. Mist darkened everything this morning, so it was no wonder a tall young man standing in the bow of the sloop could not see the canoe ahead.

Peering into the grayness, Jeremy Bently was alert for rocks and snags, not canoes. Wearing a thick scarlet stocking cap and a dark blue frock coat, Jeremy was a remarkably handsome young man, with long legs and arms. He had broad shoulders and a thick neck that told of immense physical strength. His blond hair, gathered in a club in back, hung over his collar, and drops of water gleamed on a scraggly beard of two weeks' growth. Jeremy's high cheekbones and square jaw caught the light of the lantern hanging before him on the bowsprit, and his eyes narrowed as he stared upriver. He could not penetrate the gloom far enough to see the canoe, however, now less than two hundred and fifty yards off.

A breeze steadily hurried the two-masted sloop along, and Jeremy took pleasure in the hushed atmosphere. He listened to the soothing rush of foam past the bow; overhead, spars creaked rhythmically. It was like floating through some dreamworld, and he found his mind wandering. Memories drew him away.

Though Jeremy appeared serene, lost in thought, within him there was a deep emptiness. His memories were visions of death and suffering, tragedy and loss. In his twenty-one years, he had never felt so alone.

The water was smooth, hardly ruffled by the breeze as the *Trader* pressed blindly on. Jeremy wondered whether that lovely island bluff where his young bride, Penelope, lay at rest was also shrouded in mist. He remembered the solitude there, and the sadness he had felt in leaving that place a few days ago. Standing at her grave, one had a wide view of the lake, and of the sunrise. Perhaps the sun was breaking over the horizon there, golden . . . Penelope would have loved that island, that beautiful hillside.

He opened his eyes and gazed ahead into the mist, still imagining Penelope, dark of hair and eyes, smiling at him the way she had the first time he knew he loved her. They had been riding together over an English meadow, and she had laughed often that day. How fortunate he had been to have had Penelope's love, if only for a few months.

He did not know how the words came into his mind, but it was as if Penelope had spoken them: "Have hope. Share that hope, and do good for your people in this difficult time."

*Have hope.* Indeed, hope was needed in this perilous time. Jeremy prayed that the bitter struggle between rebel Whigs and Tory loyalists in the eastern colonies would soon end. If it did not, the suffering in America would be appalling and might even spread into the wilderness, perhaps as far as Fort Detroit. Hardly an American or Briton would escape counting friends or relations among the casualties.

Something caught in Jeremy's throat. He sighed, feeling an uneasiness that did not belong. His duty now, he reminded himself, was to the ship. As they neared Detroit, there might be small craft on the straits. Perhaps, he thought, they should anchor until the drizzle lifted. But they had already lost two weeks because of the weather, and surely no one else would be on the water at this hour—particularly not on this holiday morning. He had almost forgotten what day it was!

To himself, Jeremy whispered, "Happy Christmas... peace on earth... goodwill—"

"Ahoy in the bow, Dr. Bently, sorr!"

Jeremy turned to look back at Simon Clancy, the wiry young Irishman at the helm. He called out that Jeremy should look lively for any sign of the river's swinging eastward. Jeremy waved in acknowledgment, glad to have Simon Clancy at the wheel. Clancy was the only real seaman in the crew, and the bandage wrapped around his head recalled the battle on Lake Erie three weeks back. Lake pirates had tried to seize the *Trader,* killing several of Jeremy's party—including most of the crew—before being defeated.

The Irishman stood beside an older man, whose homespun smock and red kerchief for a cap made him seem a common deckhand. But Dawson Merriwether, who sat on a barrel and calmly smoked a long-stemmed white pipe, was no ordinary seaman. He was the richest merchant in the northwest now that Owen Sutherland, Jeremy's stepfather, had been forced to leave for rebel country. As a staunch loyalist, the aging, paunchy Merriwether was a bulwark to others of his political sympathies, and his up-

bringing as a Virginia planter and gentleman suited him well
for the role of a leading Tory. This morning, however, he
was simply a sailor.

Clancy called once more. "There'll be no room for error,
Doc—not with our two landlubberly topmen down in the
cabin, shakin' rattles and throwin' bones to chase away bad
weather! Fog spooks 'em."

Jeremy waved again and thought about the two Indians
filling in for the lost sailors. For just a moment he thought
again of Penelope. She, too, had been killed in the fight
with the pirates. It was hard to believe that Penelope, so
vital and strong, was gone. That fierce conflict seemed an
eternity ago—unreal, a nightmare.

Jeremy sighed deeply and stared into the mist. He had
traveled these waters a thousand times, in boyhood rafts,
birchbark canoes, whaleboats, and fine ships like this one,
which belonged to his family's fur-trading company. Though
young, he was wise in the lore of the forest and rivers of
the vast frontier, having been taught by Indians and French,
Americans and Britons. Few his age were as experienced
in hunting and fighting in the shadowy depths of the woods
that dominated the land from the edge of the settlements in
the east to the Mississippi River in the distant west. And
no one that he knew of in all this wild country had the
university education or skill as a trained physician that he
had acquired in Philadelphia and Edinburgh.

After five years of study and practical application abroad,
Jeremy had cut short his education and hurried back to
America and the northwest. He had come with his bride
Penelope, who loved him enough to leave England for an
unknown wilderness, and to venture into colonies tormented
by rebellion and civil war.

Jeremy had returned to persuade his mother, Ella Bently
Sutherland, and his stepfather, the Scottish-born frontiersman and fur trader Owen Sutherland, to spurn the rebellion
and remain loyal to the king. But he had been unable to
convince them that the rebel cause would be overwhelmed
by the might of the British empire. Instead, they planned
to take refuge in rebel-held Montreal, having been forced
with their two young children from their fine home near

Fort Detroit. The wilderness community at the straits was so fiercely loyalist that it had compelled even its leading residents to abandon the lives and businesses they had built there, because they supported Congress.

Jeremy, though he counted himself a neutral, had some sympathy with Congress, which demanded more American rights and an equal partnership with Parliament in the government of the colonies. But he opposed the use of force to win those rights. He had too many friends in Britain, and he refused to take up arms against them. Peaceful, legal means would achieve America's political ends far better than taking on the army and navy in a death struggle.

But on that windswept island in Lake Erie, after the pirate attack, he and his parents had sadly parted—he as a neutral, they as sworn rebels. Penelope's death and the break with his beloved family had nearly torn his heart from him, but now he was returning to Valenya, the grand Sutherland home on the straits, to begin anew.

There came a hoarse shouting from aft, and Jeremy looked back to see Clancy and Merriwether laughing as they listened to the Indians argue down in the cabin. They were hotly debating whether Ottawa magic was more effective than Sioux spells when one had to travel on the threshold of winter.

Jeremy knew that in this season most northwestern Indians stayed close to the dozen scattered British trading posts, such as Detroit, and tried to keep from starving. Though living in a land of plenty, Indians were notoriously poor at providing for the cold months, and often only the charity of Redcoat commanders prevented whole villages from being wiped out. Of course, such generosity kept the redskins loyal to the king. The government and the white traders supplied all their needs, and thus year after year kept them trapping peltry for wealthy British merchants, who made huge profits each spring, when furs were shipped across the sea.

No, Indians would not be out so early on a winter's morning, and none would risk canoeing through such fog, which they considered a sign of demonic power, full of peril. Nor would the few hundred French and half-breed *habitants* of the straits be on the water. By now all were surely at mass in the Church of Sainte Anne's at the fort.

"Are you thinking about Valenya, little brother?"

The voice from behind spoke in Chippewa, deep and melodious. Jeremy turned as Tamano joined him in the bow. A lean, middle-aged warrior, Tamano was almost as tall as Jeremy; though past his prime, he more than made up for in intelligence and experience what he had lost in physical strength. Like Jeremy, he wore a heavy frock coat, but he had no hat, and his long black hair hung in two braids upon his chest. A single eagle feather flickered at his ear as he stared forward into the curtain of mist.

Jeremy turned to lean on the railing. In the softness of lantern light and gray drizzle, these two were sharp contrasts—the Indian dark, solemn, with eyes black and penetrating like some bird of prey; the white man fair, with delicate features and a firm mouth.

Tamano spoke again, his voice gentle and slow, once more using the tongue of his people, which Jeremy knew so well. Tamano had taught him much about the Indians and the forest and was like an uncle to him.

"I have no drawings or magic needle to guide me, but we are close to home, for I can smell my Lela's cooking fire." Tamano shut his eyes, raised his face, and breathed as though savoring a wonderful aroma. "Ahhh. Beaver tail, broiled and spiced! Lela knows her man is near."

Jeremy smiled. "Your little ones will be at it first if we don't get clear of this mist and catch a stronger breeze, my brother."

Jeremy's voice was of medium pitch, but he spoke the Chippewa language with all the throaty gutturals of a native son. His elegant friends back in Britain would have marveled at the transformation; they knew him only as a refined and educated gentleman, comfortable in the most sophisticated company. Jeremy had demonstrated that not all Americans from the forestlands were bumpkins, but they would have been confused to see him just then. He looked almost like a Chippewa as he spoke, hands moving freely, head tilted back.

"Aiee," Tamano replied with a grin and a nod. "The little

ones are not so little these days; you have not beheld them in five years, and you will be pleased to see how they grow like green corn and eat beaver tail like *carcajou,* the wolverine!"

Tamano proudly said that his twin children, a boy and a girl of six, favored the clothes of whites and longed to learn all they could in a white man's school.

"They will bring the best of your people to my people," he went on, gazing thoughtfully into the mist. "And they will assure my race a stronger position in the bad time to come, when this rebellion is past and the whites come to take our land. This no red man can prevent."

Jeremy considered his friend's words carefully. For years, Tamano had been the close companion of Owen Sutherland, and had taught Donoway—Donoway was Sutherland's Indian name—when the Scotsman first came to this land twenty years earlier.

Tamano, too, had bidden farewell to Sutherland after the battle with the pirates on the lake; like most northwestern Indians, Tamano opposed the rebel cause that Sutherland supported. Jeremy was about to ask Tamano who he thought would eventually prevail, but just then the ship lurched, momentarily losing headway, and the canvas snapped loudly.

Back on the quarterdeck, Simon Clancy shouted in his brogue to the cabin below. "Hands on deck, me hearties! We've some sailin' to do! Wind's swingin' round, me redskin boyos! We'll get home in style if you handle her right. On deck!"

Two figures came bounding out of the cabin door, both reeling awkwardly with the sudden roll of the ship.

"Steady, there! I'll make ye Jack Tars afore we reach anchorage!"

The first man, lumbering and portly, had long, braided hair and wore buckskin leggins and several layers of colorful trade shirts. This was Mawak, an aged Ottawa medicine man who was old enough to take his ease but insisted on helping to sail the ship. The other fellow was a slim and muscular Indian in his late twenties, who like Mawak had never before been a sailor. Little Hawk was a tall Santee Sioux from west of the Wees-konsan, a dashing brave determined to prove that no white man's skill was too difficult to master.

Clancy cried, "Sheet home the mains'l boom, and pay no mind to the gaff for now. Then lay forward and take in the—" Seeing that the Indians had stopped short with no idea what he meant, he cursed, pointed, and tried another approach. "Pull on that rope there behind me, Mawak. You, Little Hawk, unlash that line—" But before Clancy could finish, Little Hawk shrilled a savage cry and sprang into the rigging, scurrying up the foremast shrouds like a monkey. "Hoka hey! Blow, old woman wind! Hoka hey!"

"No! No!" Clancy yelled. "Not the forecourse, Little Hawk! The main topsail! Just help Mawak on the sheet tackle! Come down now, afore the wind throws you into the drink!"

In one fluid motion, Little Hawk stopped, leaped onto another rope, and slid lightly down to the deck. His reckless agility made even the hard-bitten Clancy whoop with admiration.

"Ye'd do for a dandy topman, me boyo!"

In the bow, Jeremy and Tamano watched, chuckling to see the Indians haul away in unison and sing a seaman's chant Clancy had taught them. The flapping mainsail caught the breeze and filled, billowing in the mist. The *Trader* leaned over, quickening its pace.

Jeremy settled back against the railing. He was home again. Here were his Indian companions of boyhood, and this was the country he knew and loved. He wished he could see the familiar, low-lying shore better. But the feel of the driving mist, the smell of the wind, and the sound of the Detroit River spoke to him. For the first time since Penelope's death, he knew there really was hope, and there was a future for him here.

Then he was distracted. He thought he heard singing in the distance. It was a beautiful sound, the sort that might be enchantment, like the voices of elusive, bewitched sirens luring sailors to doom. He listened, wondering whether he was the only one who heard it. But Tamano, too, hesitated. Yes, women were singing nearby. Was the ship too close to shore? Was the wind playing tricks, carrying the song far over the water? No lights from campfires or cabins were in sight.

It was an English song, melodious and gay, in perfect harmony. Jeremy glanced at Tamano, then at the dark eastern shore, before peering ahead into the distance.

"You hear it, my brother?" he asked.

"It is close," Tamano replied. "But where?"

The wind in the rigging and the creak of the ship mingled with the quiet surge of water under the bow, making the singers difficult to pinpoint. The other four men on deck continued their banter as the *Trader* drove onward. The song rose higher, closer now. It was the popular tune "Drum Major," about a young woman who enlists in the Redcoats to be with her sweetheart soldier.

Young men and maidens and bachelors sweet,
I'll sing you a song that is new and complete,
Concerning a damsel that followed the drum;
For the sake of her true love for a soldier she's gone.

The voices were pure, haunting in the mist. Jeremy knew suddenly the singers were on the water, and very near.

"Halloo!" he cried out, attracting the attention of the others on the *Trader*. "Halloo, out there! Where are you?"

The song died instantly. There was a shout of dismay, followed by the clatter of paddles on a canoe's gunwale.

"Where be ye, b'gad?" It was a rough, deep voice, just yards off, dead ahead. "This is Cole Ross! Who are you?"

"Sloop!" Jeremy roared, and then the mist gave up the canoe, revealing it almost under the ship's charging bow. "Helm to port! Helm aport!"

Simon Clancy spun the wheel over, but it was too late. Women in the canoe screamed, and the man bellowed in fury. The craft sprang aside as paddles flashed. Jeremy and Tamano gaped helplessly as the ship scraped the stern of the canoe, the wash raising the fragile vessel and slewing it sideways. Its paddlers—two women in scarlet cloaks, and a lanky, gray-bearded man in a floppy brown hat—

struggled to keep from capsizing. But water sloshed in, filling the canoe quickly. The rush of foam left the paddlers hip deep. The craft was sinking.

"Get the dinghy!" Jeremy yelled. Tamano sprang away to unlash the rowboat stowed on the sloop's deck. "Hold on!" Jeremy cried to the man in the birchbark canoe, but it was swamped. It could last only minutes.

The man below shook a fist at Jeremy. "Blackguard! Scoundrel! Save us! Save us so I can thrash you within an inch—"

"Uncle Cole!" shouted the woman in the center of the canoe. Her hood fell away, revealing honey-blond hair and a pretty face that seemed to radiate in the dusky light. "Just bail, Uncle Cole! Bail! Use your hat!"

Cole Ross yanked off his hat, dipping it into the canoe to battle with the river. The two women used wooden bowls to throw out the icy water, which already came almost to the canoe's gunwales, soaking gear and clothing. They worked quickly but without panic. Jeremy stripped off his frock coat and kicked off his shoes; the canoeists had no hope of surviving in the icy river unless someone came to their aid and soon.

By now the *Trader* had drifted past, but Clancy had turned her bow into the wind, and she was steadily losing headway, beginning to drift back downstream toward the canoe. But the canoe was also drifting downstream. Jeremy was joined in the bow by Little Hawk, whose black hair hung down over his shoulders. Both men were naked to the waist despite the chill of early winter. The canoe was already thirty yards away, nearly lost in the mist. The slightest gust of wind or trick of current would be enough to send it to the bottom.

"I should've been watching closer!" Jeremy declared. "They're done for if we can't get them aboard the *Trader!*"

Tamano and Mawak hurriedly unlashed the dinghy, which would be lowered over the side within a few moments. Almost naked, with only an undergarment over his loins, Jeremy snatched two coiled lines from the railing and gave one to Little Hawk. Dawson Merriwether, puffing and nervous, joined them at the bow.

"Help Tamano lower the dinghy!" Jeremy yelled at Merriwether. "We'll try to keep them afloat until you reach us!"

"Take care, lads." Merriwether called. "God speed you!" Then he scurried away to help with the boat. At the same moment, Jeremy and Little Hawk dived into the bitterly cold water. As they swam toward the canoe, it was as if the river clamped itself about them, holding them back as they labored to reach the birch boat in time.

Jeremy heard the defiant shout of the bearded man. "Come on, ye scoundrels! Come on so I can drag yer worthless hides down with me!" Then, apparently thinking better of it, he cried, "Save the ladies! Never mind me! Come for the girls! Oh... my end's surely sinking! Damned Injun boats! We should've took a whaleboat!"

His voice changing from anger to anxiety, Cole Ross spoke rapidly to the two women. "Grab one of these knaves, girls, and don't let go! Here they come! Don't panic! Oh... I'm done for! Annie, Gwendolyn, take care of yourselves!"

Jeremy reached the swamped canoe. Looking through water that streamed down over his eyes, he saw two very beautiful women—the blonde with the shining face, and a young woman with long auburn hair. The canoe was nearly under by now, but there was still a chance of saving it. Jeremy removed the coil from over his neck and threw part of it to the blond woman, who held on to it, seeming to understand her rescuer's intentions. Jeremy swam under the craft, no easy task in such freezing water. His strength was sapped with every passing moment, but he surfaced on the other side and took the end of the rope from the woman's hands. Tying a loop, he pulled the line taut around the canoe, which might be kept from sinking if the *Trader* came back soon enough.

Little Hawk tossed an end of his coil to the muttering Cole Ross. Then Jeremy's worst fears came to pass: The canoe tilted, stern down, and took in more water.

"Gwendolyn, Annie—grab hold of those fellows!" Ross clutched the blond woman by the shoulders. "Quick, now. Gwendolyn! Save yourself!"

"Not yet!" she cried, shaking her head. While the auburn-haired Annie sprang into the river and Jeremy's arms, Gwendolyn took up the line her uncle was holding and rammed it through an iron eyebolt fastened to the canoe's left gunwale. Water poured over her legs as she battled to secure the rope to another iron loop on the right side.

"Give it up!" Ross bellowed, ready to leave the canoe. "Gwen Hardy! I command you—"

Struggling to stay afloat in a mass of petticoats and the cloak of the other woman, Jeremy shouted, "Get overboard, you, or you'll be sucked down with it! Don't be a fool!"

For an instant, Gwen glared at Jeremy, with blue eyes that seemed to catch fire. He felt her tremendous force of character and courage, and knew she would not give up—not until it was too late.

Ross shouted, "We're lost . . ."

The canoe went completely below the surface. Sputtering and gagging, Ross fell out of the stern, flailing with arms and legs, obviously a poor swimmer.

The woman in Jeremy's arms screamed, "Papa! Help him! He can't swim! Help him, please!"

Little Hawk made for the panicky man, who went under and resurfaced twice before the Sioux got a grip on him. The fellow might have been too much even for Little Hawk had not Gwen swum to their side, calling for her uncle to calm down and stop struggling. With the Indian and the woman helping, Ross lay back in the water, gasping for air.

"All we have in the world . . ." he moaned, sputtering for air. "Lost! Oh, woe! Why should we have to suffer so?"

Gwen tried to soothe him and held up an end of the line she had lashed to the canoe. "It's not sunk yet, Uncle Cole! See, it's not all the way to the bottom. We still have the line! There's hope!"

Jeremy admired her bravery, but knew she soon would have to let go of the rope. He held on to his own line, but once it went taut, he would have to let go rather than be pulled under to certain death. If they tried to keep the canoe afloat without the aid of the *Trader*'s dinghy, they both would drown in the icy water.

Then he heard a welcome shout from nearby. Out of the

fog came the rowboat, Tamano and Simon Clancy pulling hard on the oars.

Annie Ross, the beauty in Jeremy's arms, called, "We're saved! Thank God! We're saved!" Then she screamed, "Gwen!"

Gwendolyn Hardy had been pulled under. Jeremy realized Gwen's line was far shorter than his, which was yet playing out. He was dismayed that she still had not let go. The dinghy was upon them, and Jeremy took the startled Annie by the waist and roughly pushed her up out of the water. She dangled half over the side, legs in the air. Little Hawk brought the woozy Cole Ross to the rowboat, barely keeping him afloat.

Jeremy threw his line aboard the dinghy. Clancy ran it over the bow, then lashed it to a thwart; but the tug of the canoe going down forced the Irishman to pay the line out gradually. Still there was no sign of Gwen.

In Chippewa, Little Hawk shouted to Jeremy, "The girl must let go! We can save her canoe, but she'll be dead before we get her back up!"

With a swift gulp of air, Jeremy dived for her through gray, chilly water, hardly able to see. Following the line from the dinghy, he swam downward, his anger at the brash young woman increasing every second. That fury drove him to the limit of endurance.

Lungs swelling as though to burst, he released air slowly and ached to breathe. Still no sign of Gwen. The water was dim and bleak as he hauled himself downward, hand over hand, lower and lower, amazed at how far the canoe had sunk. His chest felt slowly crushed as in some great vise.

He wanted to shout the girl's name, to surface for one quick breath. But lost seconds would cost her life. He fought his way down the rope, lower and lower. Where was she?

Then he saw a shadow, limp and unmoving. He grabbed for Gwen's body and immediately felt that the rope was wound around her waist. It would have held her under even if she had tried to escape.

Jeremy struggled to free the line. Gwen's hands touched his shoulders and went slowly about his neck, as though she were barely conscious, moving in a daze. He worked, but the line would not come loose. Bubbles drifted from her lips. She seemed to release them slowly, controlled. She was still alive, though not by much. The line was snug about her slim waist, twisted and tangled by her desperate attempt to save the canoe. He fumbled futilely, and then, with a fierce yank, he pulled the tangles loose. She was free.

Jeremy gave a tremendous kick and shot upward, the girl in his arms. He must have air. He could not hold his breath another second, and released it, his mouth spewing bubbles. Still the surface was not there. He kicked fiercely. He must breathe!

Then with a roar and a burst of water, he broke into sweet air, bobbing and gasping, hearing the cheers of the others in the boat nearby. Both he and Gwen coughed up water as they floated. She was in his arms, hands about his neck, eyes closed. After a moment, when he saw she was alive and would be all right, Jeremy exploded.

"You damned, pigheaded little fool!" His voice carried across the water, but Gwen seemed not to hear. Toward them came the dinghy, with the other two survivors huddled in its center. Cole Ross seemed unconscious; Annie was shivering and fearfully calling Gwen's name. Also in the boat were Little Hawk, Tamano, and Clancy. The Irishman stood up, ready to help get the swimmers aboard.

As Jeremy grasped a gunwale with one hand, Gwen opened her eyes languidly. She gazed up at the handsome Clancy and weakly said, "Who are you to call . . . me a . . . fool, sir?"

Clancy grinned, leaning over to pull her up. "Not I, my fair colleen! I'd never call ye a fool, not without saying 'beautiful' first!"

As Gwen came out of the water, which poured from her, she looked back down at Jeremy. His grim expression told her who had said she was a fool.

"It was I," he declared loudly, shaking water from his hair. "And I'd say it again, if I thought you able to comprehend my meaning!"

Clancy clucked, "Go easy there, Dr. Bently, sorr!" He gently and kindly covered Gwen with his coat and helped her sit down beside Annie, who embraced her and huddled close. "This here damsel's in distress, and it ain't chivalrous to abuse her so. There, there, pretty ones, we'll have ye aboard my fine ship in a moment... There, there." He whispered, "The doc's jest touchy these days."

In the center of the dinghy, Cole Ross came to as Tamano helped Jeremy aboard. Ross started to vent his anger at being rammed, but when Clancy said the canoe would be winched aboard the *Trader* within the hour, the man turned his attention to the two trembling women. Relieved to find them unhurt, he settled down, muttering that he should demand a hearing with the Detroit commissary to recover his losses.

Sniffing and wiping away water from his face, Jeremy said dully, "We'll pay for your losses, sir, but do me the favor of keeping your complaints to yourself. I've had a bellyful of late, and your troubles can easily be resolved with hard cash."

That seemed to mollify Ross, who harrumphed and turned to stare at the *Trader*, which grew larger as the dinghy approached. The women were gazing at Jeremy, who clenched his jaw to keep his teeth from chattering. The mist was lifting, and a cold sun tried to break through.

Angry at what had happened, Jeremy looked blankly at the dark water, refusing to speak. He was blue with cold. Then someone handed him a coat. It was Gwen Hardy. He looked up and saw soft eyes full of sympathy for him. He did not know what to say. When she smiled, all he could do was nod and return the coat, mumbling that she needed it more than he.

"Perhaps I am a fool, sir," she said gently, putting the coat over her shoulders.

Grumpily, Jeremy made no response. He felt sour that he and this woman had almost drowned for a canoeload of trade goods.

"But," the woman went on, only loud enough so that he and her cousin could hear, "what are you, to have come down after me? It's a greater fool who follows a fool through folly—Dr. Bently, is it?"

Jeremy again glanced up. Annoyance was hard to maintain in the light of this woman's good-natured teasing. Annie Ross tittered, hand to her mouth, then broke out laughing in spite of herself. Jeremy, too, grinned, at a loss for a scathing rejoinder. He realized that he liked these two saucy beauties, whoever they were, and whyever they were out here in the wilderness.

*chapter* **2**

# FORT DETROIT

The mist rose soon after the canoeists were brought, drenched and shivering, aboard the *Trader*. Cole Ross blustered and cursed as he was led to the center hatchway, where Merriwether had readied dry clothes for him. The women bore their misery in silence, and Jeremy, numb with cold, admired them for that. Merriwether gave them each a blanket, and as he escorted the women to the after cabin, the one named Annie tossed back her wet, shining hair and stared directly at Jeremy with an intimacy no man could miss. He met her large, dark eyes as she passed, arm in arm with Gwendolyn, who stared downward, exhausted.

Jeremy made no response to Annie's guarded sign of interest. He recognized it, having seen much of the world and its women, but Penelope was too warm in his mind for him to desire anyone else. He looked away from Annie, to see Mawak lumbering toward him, spare clothes in hand. Jeremy took them to the forecastle to dress.

Just then bright sunlight fell on the glistening deck. Standing at the helm, Simon Clancy gave a yell of delight as the women entered the cabin door below his feet.

"Yer canoe's about winched up, ladies!" He gallantly doffed his woolen cap and grinned. "Ye'll be good as new afore long! And arrivin' at the fort in company with Simon Clancy aboard the Frontier Company ship *Trader,* ye'll be treated with awe by red, white, black, and half-breed alike! At yer service, Mistress Hardy, Mistress Ross!"

From down in the hatchway, Cole Ross stuck up his balding head, dripping with long, stringy gray hair. "Frontier Company ship!" he shouted. "In the name of all that's holy, do ye mean to say we been sunk and rescued by rebels?" He began to storm out of the hold, but caught himself when he realized he was naked and that women were looking on.

Shaking a fist at Clancy, Ross bellowed, "I'll not be seen in company of traitors to the king! I'll be put ashore with my ladies and my goods afore we come in sight of the fort! Woe and damnation! Ye rascally scoundrels! How can ye boldly sail upon the king's trade routes and not be arrested and tossed in the clink?"

All the while, Ross was observed by Dawson Merriwether, who stood with the women at the cabin door. The ladies said nothing, but both were aware that the Frontier Company had been organized by Owen Sutherland, one of the leading rebels in America. Though his name had once been honored by the people of the northwest, it now signified turncoat, enemy of King George and all loyalists.

"I'll see you arrested!" Ross howled, face as red as the flannel shirt he pulled over his head. "Never in my life have I been so insulted, so abused! First rebel Whigs force me to flee my home in Montreal! Now they sink me and my—"

"Mr. Ross," said Dawson Merriwether, who was strolling slowly toward him, hands behind his back.

"Don't speak to me, rebel!" Ross shouted, waving his arms. By now Jeremy and Little Hawk, dressed in dry clothes, were up in the ship's rigging, unfurling sail, and the sunlight shone cheerfully on them. Ignoring Merriwether, Ross furiously yanked on a pair of Simon Clancy's breeches, far too short for him.

Merriwether said calmly, "I'm no rebel, Mr. Ross. Nor am I a Whig. I suggest you take some comfort in that, sir, for I fear your bile is getting the better of you."

Ross eyed the dignified Merriwether with contempt. His scathing glare had no effect on the wealthy merchant, however. Merriwether simply smiled pleasantly and bowed, introducing himself. Ross hardly heard the man's name and went on growling and snapping, tugging at his stockings.

Merriwether, seeing Ross would not return the courtesy of introducing himself, was about to move away when Gwen Hardy dashed to his side, her eyes wide.

"Forgive me, sir, but did I hear your name correctly? Dawson Merriwether . . . *the* Dawson—" As the merchant nodded and kissed Gwen's hand, she nearly fainted. "Oh, my heavens . . . Oh, Uncle Cole, Annie, did you hear?"

Annie put a hand to her open mouth; her father had just insulted one of the most important loyalists in the northwest. Not only was Merriwether's reputation almost as great as Owen Sutherland's, but he was the very man Cole Ross was to meet upon arrival at Fort Detroit. Merriwether could help Ross get started as a trader at Detroit; without the Virginian's aid, life would be hard for a newcomer to the fur country.

In the hatchway, Ross finally heard and went pale. His lips became tight, and he gazed, thunderstruck, at the gentleman whose whim meant wealth or poverty for him out here. Merriwether kindly bowed once more, the tar and dirt of his seaman's labors streaking his chubby face and hands.

At last Ross was able to croak a weak apology, trying bravely to grin and shake off the profound distress that nearly made his knees knock.

"Mr. . . . Mr. Merriwether, sir! How could I . . . I mean, you must realize . . . That is to say, I'm sure *you're* not a rebel— I mean— If I'd only known— Oh, woe! If I'd only known!"

Compounding his misery at being driven westward and then sunk, this ill-starred beginning to his new life on the frontier overwhelmed Cole Ross. He put his head in his hands, nearly succumbing to unhappiness. But then he stiffened. He took a deep breath and, throwing back his shoulders, once more addressed Merriwether.

"Sir, I offer my sincere apologies to you. But I can do no more than that, sir, no matter what you think of me. I've been through too much to grovel. I'm sure you'll agree, any man that's suffered as I have is entitled to get hot at the mention of Whig or rebel!"

Merriwether nodded, then offered his hand, which was taken and pumped vigorously.

"Entitled to anger you are, my good Mr. Ross!" Merriwether said, helping haul the fellow up onto the deck. This was an unusual familiarity from a gentleman, which surprised Ross, who was used to a sharp division between his class and the merchant nobility. "If you'll be kind enough to forgive us for nearly killing you, I can easily excuse a king's man's anger toward those he suspects are rebels."

From up in the swaying rigging, Jeremy watched with amusement. Already he had taken a liking to the blustering Ross and the two bold women with him. He was sure Ross and Merriwether would get along well after this near-disaster. Folk with the courage and strength that the new-comers displayed would make a success out here before very long.

Relieved, the shivering women were returning to the door of the cabin. Ross spoke in low tones with Merriwether, and Jeremy went on unfurling and shaking out the topsail. Then he saw Gwen Hardy staring up at him. He looked back, startling her. She ducked immediately into the cabin after her cousin and closed the door. Gwen was a pretty one, he thought. Both women were. They would have the favor of many a man at Fort Detroit. Then the rolling laughter of Dawson Merriwether took his attention. Jeremy noticed the Virginia merchant was also looking up at him, while Cole Ross stood nearby in confusion, shifting from one foot to the other.

Merriwether cried up, "Mr. Ross can't understand why I'm traveling with Frontier Company Whigs, my lad! He fears my reputation will be irrevocably tarnished!"

Turning to Ross, Merriwether said, "This vessel's crew and the Frontier Company partners at Detroit wish to remain aloof from the struggle, and I respect their decision."

Ross pressed, "But if ye ain't with 'em rebels, ye got to be against 'em! Won't be long afore ye all see that. Just wait till a ragtag rebel army comes a-marchin' out to Fort

Detroit! Then ye'll sing a different tune, Dr. Bently—ye and yer *neutral* friends!" Touching his forelock to Merriwether, Ross said, "Forgive my temper, sir, but no man can stay aloof in this trouble. I'm one as has chosen King George, and I'll live and die by that choice!" His right hand was raised high, and as he brought it down, he looked sharply at Jeremy, who made no reply.

Under a radiant blue sky, the *Trader* soon heeled eastward around a wide bend in the river. The wind was strong, billowing the white sails full and fat, and the vessel skimmed upriver. At the helm, Simon Clancy sang the tune Gwen and Annie had been singing just before the canoe was rammed. When the women came on deck, they joined him, to everyone's enjoyment.

Annie was dressed in a light green cloak, with a warm, dark-green woolen skirt and bodice beneath. Gwen wore a pretty beige and brown riding habit with a matching wide-brimmed hat that lent her the image of sophisticated good taste. Jeremy, now clean-shaven, was emerging from the forecastle hatchway when he saw them go up the steps to the quarterdeck. He caught himself, vaguely uneasy. It had been his idea to offer them Penelope's clothes to replace their own, but still the sight of strangers dressed in her garments was jarring. He tried not to think at all.

The wind and water and low shoreline were all fresh and beautiful in the sunlight, as Clancy and the women sang away. Cole Ross and Dawson Merriwether were sorting through the goods from the canoe, which lay on deck. Most of the cargo, wrapped watertight in oilskins, was undamaged, so Ross was recovering from his distress. When Jeremy approached, the man said the amount owed him would not be over twenty pounds.

There came a cry from high above in the rigging, where Little Hawk stood, pointing upriver. "The fort!" he yelled in English. "Fort Detroit ahead!"

The stockade was a smudge of brown across the crown of a gentle slope on the left bank of the river. The red of the fluttering Union Jack could be glimpsed from here, and the gray wisps of smoke from the eighty or so dwellings within the walls rose high into the clear air. On the same bank, just below the fort and even with the *Trader*, were dingy clusters of bark-and-skin lodges of a Potawatomie village. More to the left was the mouth of Rivière Rouge, a swampy, placid stream where Jeremy had often raced pony carts on the ice. On the right were the first small, white-washed *habitant* cabins, built of stone, with steep, thatched roofs and gaggles of geese and children running about in the yards.

The first canoeloads of French settlers, returning home from the Christmas service at Sainte Anne's, waved to the *Trader* as it sped past. Like Jeremy, the men all wore the scarlet stocking cap that was traditional among these folk. Those few who made their living as *voyageurs*—canoeists who transported pelts and trade goods—also wore a scarlet sash about their waist. Every man smoked a white clay pipe. Every woman wore her best churchgoing clothes, with hair curled or pinned up and adorned with anything from feathers and sequins to lace patches and bright ribbons.

For *habitants* it was a happy time, and they sang gaily as they paddled by. The singers on the ship stopped to listen and then join in. Standing in the bow of the *Trader*, Jeremy felt his heart leap as Fort Detroit drew nearer, its palisade walls growing larger. At Simon Clancy's direction, a small cannon on the ship's port side was run in, and Merriwether, Ross, and Tamano readied it to fire a salute.

In the bow, Jeremy was observing the many changes ashore—new log cabins that obviously belonged to Americans from the British colonies, and the enlarged shipyard below the fort, where several vessels were being built. There also seemed to be more Indians—tribes he did not recognize—inhabiting clearings near the water.

"Dr. Bently!" Clancy called. "Will ye give the command, sorr, to let go a bang?"

At first Jeremy was surprised that he was being asked to order the salute, but then realized quickly that his place in the Frontier Company required him to assume such responsibilities. Nodding to Clancy, Jeremy said to fire when ready.

Clancy held the smoldering linstock close to the touch-hole. Then he hesitated and, with a wink, gave the match to Gwen Hardy, who was standing nearby with Annie.

Startled, excited, Gwen looked to Jeremy, a gleam in her eye. "With your permission, Dr. Bently?"

Jeremy nodded again and smiled. Gwen bit her lip, giggled, and turned to Annie, who put hands to her ears. Clancy stood proudly, broad chest puffed out, for all the world like a gallant gentleman.

Gwen touched the hole with the linstock. There was a hiss, followed by a deafening boom. The gun jumped back, restrained by ropes and pulleys, and blue smoke swept over the cheering group on board. Jeremy was pleased to see Gwen's joy.

The echo of the salute rolled back from the wooden stockade, followed promptly by a blue spurt of smoke from a corner blockhouse and the dull clap of the cannon that had been waiting to reply. Soon, all around the ship crowded boatloads of French and Americans, Indians and half-breeds, most asking for news from the East, some looking for work unloading the *Trader*.

Cole Ross leaned over the railing, angrily yelling that the rebels had fortified Montreal and were probably already in Quebec. His bad news was met with loud groans; the fur trade with Britain would be cut off and soldiers would be without pay and supplies until the British recaptured those two key gateways to the northwest.

"Poxy rebels're everywhere!" Ross shouted as the *Trader* neared the wooden landing, where a squad of Redcoats were lined up, several officers standing near them. "Detroit's in for it next if we ain't careful! They slaughtered a hundred king's militia at Longueuil last month, and they've took forts Saint John and Chambly on the Richelieu River! Ain't but a company of soldiers down at Fort Niagara to stop 'em invading this country and wiping out the rest of us loyal folk!"

Ross kept on as Mawak tossed a line to a small boat that had rowed out to haul the vessel in to the landing. There, the *Trader* would unload what little cargo it carried. All the other local merchant ships—five of them—were already out of the water and up on stocks, safe from the ice that soon would choke the straits and crush any hulls left afloat. All along the shoreline people were gathering to view the *Trader,* wondering why the ship had come back so late in the season. It should have been in dry dock back at the eastern end of Lake Erie. Was there even more bad news?

Up in the rigging, Little Hawk and Tamano furled the topsail as the ship was towed slowly in. The rowboat was manned by eight sturdy Frenchmen hired by the post commissary, a civilian official who oversaw trade relations and commercial affairs at the post.

Jeremy was joined at the rail by Gwen and Annie, both excited to be in this strange, faraway place. They had long heard of Fort Detroit, emporium of the romantic American wilderness.

Eyes shining, Gwen spoke first. "The stockade is immense! Look how it goes on and on along the shore!"

"Six hundred yards," Jeremy replied, looking among the soldiers on shore for some sign of Ensign Richard Weston of the Seventh Welsh Fusiliers, his best friend from England and Penelope's cousin.

Annie spoke. "So many Indians—more than whites! And they look so impoverished. Some are almost naked under their blankets!"

Jeremy replied softly, "They like to dress that way. They're a proud race, and they're wearing the clothes they prefer."

Annie almost whimpered, "It's not at all what I imagined. So rough and uncivilized...Oh, Gwen...Gwen, I'm not sure I'll be happy here. I wish we'd never left Montreal."

Jeremy stepped back as the two women embraced, Gwen consoling Annie. Again Jeremy could not help take note of their clothing—Penelope's clothing. How he wished it was she standing beside him, seeing Fort Detroit for the first time.

The *Trader* was tied up, and Little Hawk and Merriwether lowered the wooden gangway.

An excited din rose from the shore, and the mob thickened. Dressed in Christmas finery, the people of the straits gathered on the slope between the shore and the log walls of the fort. Feathers, furs, garlands, trade shirts of many colors, beads, sequins, glittering buckles, buckskin shirts, and flowing serge capes glowed in the sunlight.

The line of twelve soldiers stood stiff and formal, a slash of scarlet and white in the midst of the gaudy civilian mob. Jeremy peered again for Richard Weston, who would have to be told of Penelope's death.

Gwen spoke to Jeremy. "Our thanks for the loan of such lovely clothing, Dr. Bently."

Jeremy nodded, hardly hearing.

Annie said, "You have wonderful taste in ladies' clothing, sir, and we'd be happy to have the first opportunity to buy them before you offer them for sale."

"What's that?" Jeremy said gruffly. "They're not for sale."

"Oh?" Annie answered, her eyes dropping momentarily before she went on. "Then the sweetheart you have waiting here is fortunate—"

Annie was startled by the sudden harsh look Jeremy gave her before abruptly turning back to the landing.

Gwen spoke up. "Dr. Bently, my cousin meant no offense—"

"Please don't mention any such things again," Jeremy snapped. "Just . . . just don't talk about—The clothes are yours for the moment, and when you've the leisure to change into your own garb, kindly have them returned to me at the Frontier Company warehouse."

"As you wish," Gwen replied and looked down at the landing, as the moored *Trader* bumped ard creaked gently against it. "Forgive our indiscretion, if indiscretion it was, sir."

Jeremy was troubled. He was anxious to find Weston and get the worst over quickly, but he realized the two women could not be blamed for their innocent comments. "It is I who should ask forgiveness. I'm sorry, ladies. I'm at your service."

Bowing slightly, he excused himself and headed for the gangway amidships. Then he thought better of it and offered his arms to the women to escort them properly to shore.

"Dr. Bently," Annie said, pausing a moment, "there is nothing for us to forgive. Whatever I have done to distress you, if there's any way—"

There came a shout from the gangway: "Jeremy! Penny! At last!"

A smart British officer came running, very unsoldierly, up the gangway and across the deck, waving and grinning, making right for Jeremy and the women. Annie Ross had her back to Richard Weston, who sprang toward her and spun her around in a sudden embrace. Jeremy caught his breath, and a pained expression crossed his face. There came a rush of dismay and exclamations as Annie stepped back, flushed, and the surprised Weston declared his apologies. With a warm smile he bowed, obviously taken by these two beauties.

"Forgive me, mistress," he said, his beaming, boyish face aglow with mischief as he looked at Annie Ross. "I mistook you for another most exquisite young lady." To Jeremy he said, "Your ship's laden with precious cargo, my man!"

Shaking hands vigorously with Jeremy, the newly promoted Lieutenant Weston was a striking figure in his immaculate scarlet tunic, white breeches, and black tricorne. Hanging at his neck was the symbol of rank, a silver crescent called a gorget, engraved with the insignia of the Seventh Welsh Fusiliers. Weston was the same age as Jeremy, fair, slender, and erect, a few inches shorter than his friend. Splendid in his uniform, with its gleaming buttons and sword hilt and polished black knee boots, he exuded confidence and gallantry.

Before Jeremy could speak, Weston bowed to Gwendolyn Hardy, warmly welcoming her to the northwest and hoping her journey had not been too taxing. Then he remarked on Gwen's clothes, and Annie's, too.

"I see my cousin Penelope has been sharing her finest raiment with you ladies. My own mother presented her with these pretty things last Christmas. Oh, yes, a welcome and a happy Christmas to you all! May I assist you with your baggage, ladies? I'll have some dependable laborers unload for you. Where are you staying? And, Jeremy, my good fellow, where's my Penelope? Seasick, below deck? Tell her if she doesn't come up immediately I'll be forced to postpone my welcome in order to escort these two lovely ladies!"

The women were flattered by Weston's compliments. His attention caused them to laugh, and they replied in kind to his friendliness; but Jeremy was stiff, and it took some time before the others noticed. Gwen Hardy was the first to recognize that something was amiss. She looked closely at Jeremy, who had turned away and was staring at the deck while Weston bantered with Annie.

"Dr. Bently," Gwen said softly. "Are you ill?"

Jeremy turned to see her gazing at him, her blue eyes searching.

He shook his head and cleared his throat. "No . . . not ill, mistress." His voice was hoarse. "I'll have to ask that you and Mistress Ross permit Lieutenant Weston and me to be alone for the moment."

Weston and Annie heard, and looked around. Concern and curiosity came into the officer's face. Gwen and Annie glanced at each other as Jeremy asked Dawson Merriwether, hovering nearby, to see them to the fort. Merriwether knew what Jeremy would have to reveal to Weston; he led the ladies to the gangway, but before leaving the ship, asked them to pause a moment.

Glancing back at Jeremy and Weston standing at the bow, Merriwether took a deep breath. Before he could speak to the women, he saw Weston stagger backward as Jeremy caught the fellow by the shoulders. Breaking free, Weston went to the side of the ship opposite the dock and hurled his black tricorne to the deck. He covered his face with his hands as Jeremy came to him and put an arm about his shoulders, which rose and fell convulsively.

Then Merriwether spoke to the women, almost in a whisper. "Penelope Graves was Dr. Bently's young wife, my children; she died a few days ago, slain by pirates."

Both women went pale. Gwen looked down at her borrowed clothes, gaped in horror at Annie, and then at Merriwether, who nodded once to confirm her guess as to whom they belonged.

"Oh . . ." Gwen murmured. "That poor, poor man! Oh, I'm so terribly sorry!"

Annie, whose eyes, like Gwen's, filled with tears, gazed at Jeremy, who was standing with the sobbing soldier. Softly, almost to herself, she said, "These times are so sad for us. Dr. Bently is alone in the world. He needs a woman who can care for him . . . A woman good enough for such a man."

Though she did not speak, Gwendolyn Hardy fully agreed.

## chapter 3

## MANOTH

In the dim interior of a small cabin, typical of a junior officer's spartan quarters in crowded Fort Detroit, Jeremy Bently and Richard Weston drank hard cider. They had come directly from the ship to drown their sorrows, hurrying through the fort, past cabins, whitewashed clapboard residences, and log trading houses that lined the narrow, rutted streets. Jeremy had seen little change within the fort, though there were more *Anglais,* as the French called British and Americans; most looked like they came from New York or New England.

Jeremy also had noticed that the outer defenses were being rebuilt. New palisades were replacing old, rotting timbers that had not been fired upon since Pontiac's failed uprising twelve years previous. Weston said that Lieutenant Governor Henry Hamilton, the fort's new commander, was industriously fortifying in case the rebels invaded next spring.

Weston had thrown his hat onto a narrow bunk in the corner and unbuttoned his scarlet tunic so that the white cotton undershirt showed, stained with sweat and cider. Through a single small, glazed window, daylight fell upon the wooden table where the two men sat. An iron stove stood crackling against one wall, overheating the room, but the men were too drunk to care. Near the door hung a painting of Weston's family seat in Derbyshire, England, where Jeremy had met Penelope last year. The white stone mansion and perfectly manicured gardens were a far cry from the rugged, rudely constructed homes of Fort Detroit. Not even Valenya, Jeremy's family home across the river, was a match for the smallest English manor house. With a mingling of nostalgia and rising anger Jeremy looked upon the painting; he could almost see Penelope and himself strolling over that green lawn, spending joyful moments by the ponds, feeding ducks and swans.

Jeremy told Weston how Owen Sutherland had killed the pirate leader, Hugh Meeks, who had caused Penelope's death. Jeremy wondered whether someone else was behind the murderer's expedition, and bitterly he said as much. How could Meeks have outfitted himself? There must have been money somewhere. How else could he have paid his men? They would not have seen enough booty to keep them alive through a fierce northwest winter. Questions plagued him. Drink fuzzed his mind. Both fired his rage, frustration, and instilled a hunger for revenge.

He and Weston also exchanged news of events abroad, in the colonies to the east, and here in the northwest. Weston said Lieutenant Governor Hamilton had arrived at Detroit soon after Montreal fell, and planned to defend the entire northwest against rebel attacks.

"We need a surgeon major if we're to carry the war to the enemy at Fort Pitt or Montreal," Weston said. "Hamilton will give you a commission, I'm sure. You'll do great work for your king and country, and—"

Jeremy was already shaking his head. Weston's eyes, dull from the cider, grew even duller with disappointment.

"I'm staying out of this conflict altogether," Jeremy said. "The best thing I can do for my country—and by that I mean America, not just England—is to set up practice out here as a physician and surgeon."

Weston grumbled moodily and poured each of them more cider from an earthenware jug.

Jeremy took a drink. "Besides, what good would I be traipsing through the wilderness with a handful of loyalists?

There're a thousand people living at the straits nowadays, and they'll need a doctor more than a few men off on a scout."

"On a scout?" Weston exclaimed, voice rising. "You think we'll do no more than scout the woods with a handful of regulars and civilians? You think we mean to sit out here, trembling like chickens about to have their necks wrung by Dr. Franklin's henchmen? You think the British army won't destroy this rabble who've turned against us like dogs biting their master's hand?" Weston jumped up and stamped about the small cabin.

Deep in thought, Jeremy finished his cider. From outside came the noise of passing carts and horses, adults and children. Christmas carols could be heard as a Protestant choir sang out in a barracks converted to a chapel.

Jeremy set down his glass. "What can you and your Henry Hamilton do, then, Richard? Retake Montreal by yourselves? Lift the siege of Boston? Don't underestimate the rebels—as I've warned you before. Don't think you can march into Philadelphia with a few regulars and demand—"

"I'm not speaking of regulars!" Weston whirled, his face red. "There are more fighters loyal to the king out here than simply the garrison at Detroit. And I don't mean just the few hundred loyalists!"

Jeremy paled. "Indians?"

Momentarily, Weston's eyes lowered, as though he was ashamed at the idea of unleashing Indian war parties on border settlements that supported Congress.

"Precisely," he said, under his breath. Then he recovered and spoke sharply. "Indians—but under the control of responsible British commanders. British commanders, not French ones—God knows what those Frenchmen would do if allowed to command war parties as they did during the French and Indian War . . ."

Jeremy was incredulous, shocked. "Do you truly believe white officers could control Indians who have tasted blood? Have you seen them in raids? They are terrible! Nothing will stop them if they're winning! Surely you can't—"

"Goddamn it all, Bently!" Weston leaned on the table,

eyes aflame. "Come to your senses, man! This is war, not a family quarrel! The American empire is at stake! A thousand of my brother soldiers fell on Bunker's Hill! Hundreds of loyal civilians fell at Montreal! In nine short months British blood has flowed like water. Perhaps you've been in Scotland too damn long. This is no war of words, no mere economic—"

Jeremy slammed his fist on the table, knocking over his glass, and sprang to his feet, face close to Weston's.

"And you, Richard, don't know shit about Indian fighting! You've got your shiny brass and your pretty uniform, and you think these redskins will file along nice and smart like your privates, obeying every command, sportingly taking prisoners instead of roasting little children for the fun of it!"

"There will be British officers—"

"British officers will be useless! Not unless the Indians respect them and fear them, and they will only respect the officer who is as ruthless and bloodthirsty as they, one who'll let them have their bloody way with prisoners, satisfying their lust for killing! They drink blood! They eat hearts! They're cannibals on the warpath! Did they teach you that at the university? Or were young officers told only how to please an Asian pasha or how to seduce a Chinese mandarin's concubine?"

"Enough! Hold your insolent American tongue, Bently, before I wrap it around your neck."

"You talk like a lobsterback who's never seen an Indian! But there are plenty of soldiers who've fought them, and beaten them at their own game! They can tell you how they'll fight! And I can teach you how. Right now!"

Jeremy towered over his friend, but Weston was fearless in anger. Quivering, on the verge of coming to grips, they stood face to face. One false move would set them off. They were so upset with the death of Penelope, so enraged by the bloody events of the past months, and so very drunk, that they might have fought it out had not the cabin door flown open and daylight poured into the room.

There stood Tamano, a large shadow looming against

the light. Jeremy and Weston blinked and squinted, their eyes unused to the brightness.

Tamano ignored their condition and said rapidly in English, "You must come, Jeremy. Valenya is in peril! The Seneca Manoth has heard of your return, and he is going across the river to destroy the house."

Reeling, Jeremy grabbed his coat and Weston's sword from a peg behind the door. Manoth was the Seneca warrior who had forced Jeremy's mother, Ella Sutherland, to flee Valenya. Before the fight with the pirates, Manoth had attacked her on the island in Lake Erie, and only a desperate hand-to-hand struggle with Jeremy and Owen Sutherland had defeated the Indian. Manoth had escaped, however, by leaping into the lake from a high crag. Now he had returned to Detroit, and he had friends among the British officers. If Manoth were not stopped, the house at Valenya would be ashes before the sun set that evening.

Without a word to Weston, Jeremy darted from the cabin, his head clearing. He and Tamano raced through the busy fort, where a lighthearted knot of officers' wives drifted out of the chapel barracks, singing carols. The festive holiday mood was all around, but Jeremy did not see it as he dashed for the shore. Most people were startled and annoyed to be shouldered aside by these two burly men. Then a Frenchman in a stocking cap, driving a two-wheeled pony cart called a calèche, came whirling by, shouting, "Jump on! Jump on! I'm with you, *mes amis!*"

It was the *voyageur* and former soldier of New France, Jacques Levesque, who yanked Jeremy aboard the speeding cart. Jeremy helped Tamano leap on, and away they went through the crowded streets, collecting insults and angry shouts all the way.

"Jacques!" Jeremy slammed the powerfully built, black-bearded Frenchman on the shoulder. "There's no one I'd rather have along! How did you know about Manoth?"

Levesque was in his late thirties, and like most northwest *voyageurs* he was short and stocky. Showing perfect white teeth in a fierce grin, he said, "I'm the one who warned Tamano. I have been watching that Seneca monster ever since he came back a couple of days ago. The Indians said he had been beaten by you and Donoway, and he wants to take revenge!"

Levesque hurried the horse with a crack of his whip. They skimmed out the fort's water gate, nearly running into a squad of half-drunk soldiers marching languidly to change the guard.

Levesque shouted, "Manoth has called on some of his Seneca cronies, and they have the favor of their British friend, Lieutenant Davies, an enemy of your step-father—"

"I know of Davies!" Jeremy cried as the cart came to a lurching stop near two canoes, where Little Hawk and Mawak were ready to push off. "Owen told me how he cowed him at Stanwix, shaming him in front of his men." Owen Sutherland, Jeremy knew, had dared Davies to arrest him as a rebel during their confrontation at the remote British post of Fort Stanwix, just east of Lake Ontario. Davies had backed off, for the New York provincial troops under his command were restless and might have mutinied rather than fight such a respected colonial as Sutherland.

Davies, Jeremy also knew, was an ally of the savage Manoth. Just after the Stanwix trouble, Manoth and some warriors had tried to take Sutherland prisoner at Davies's direction. Sutherland had been traveling through Iroquois country in western New York Province, and Manoth had planned to fall upon the Scotsman's party.

But Sutherland instead had drugged the Indians with opium-laced rum, and Manoth had been so humiliated that now he could not rest until revenge was taken. That was why he had tried to kidnap Ella Bently Sutherland—and why at that very moment he might already be disembarking, about to torch the house at Valenya, just a few miles upstream.

The two birch boats with Jeremy's party thrust out into the straits, everyone paddling furiously. Time was short; for Tamano the situation was even more serious, because his wife Lela and their two children lived in a lodge near Valenya. There was no doubt in Tamano's mind that his wife would stand up against Manoth, even if she risked her life.

Tamano shouted, "Onward!" and his Chippewa paddling song resounded across the straits. Then it became a song of war, rhythmic and rapid, and the five friends stroked in time, until the canoes flew across the water.

After ten minutes, Valenya came in sight by a peaceful cove, a two-story white building of clapboard and cedar shingles. It thrilled Jeremy to see his home, which he had helped build just before leaving Detroit.

From half a mile off he searched for signs of the marauders. Even though he feared for Valenya, expecting to see smoke and flame billow from its roof, Jeremy could not help but notice the many changes at the homestead. Up behind the house stood hundreds of bare apple saplings. There was a fine new barn to the right, and the grounds had been landscaped, with gravel paths and shrubs. It looked like a good place, just what Ella Sutherland would have wished. In the many flowerbeds and evergreen shrubs he could see the hand of his mother.

Also to the right was the bark-and-skin lodge Tamano had built to be close to the house for as long as the Sutherlands were away. As yet, though, there was no sign of Tamano's family, nor of the Senecas.

As the canoes drew closer, Jeremy's heart jumped as he saw a torch being lit near the barn. There was another, and another, each preceded by flares like powder flashing in a rifle's pan. The Senecas were beginning their work; the new barn would be first.

Four large canoes were drawn up by the wooden landing at the water's edge, sixty yards from the house. Apparently the Indians were approaching cautiously, perhaps thinking an armed defender might be inside. Indians were not given to risking their lives in a rash frontal attack. They preferred to triumph by deception, without losing a man. Honor went to the warrior who slew his enemy without endangering his own neck; white man's standards of reckless, disciplined bravery and sacrifice in war were stupidity as far as Indians were concerned. And Senecas, because of their stealth and ability to kill from ambush or from behind, were the most feared warriors in the northwest. These were being very cautious before they struck at the house.

Suddenly the barn bloomed like a scarlet and yellow flower, then darkened into a surging pall of black smoke that drifted toward the water. With a cry Jeremy urged his friends on, but then realized with dismay that in his haste he had brought no firearms—only Weston's sword in its scabbard. He saw that Little Hawk and Tamano had rifles and sidearms consisting of knives and tomahawks, but Levesque and Mawak had neither rifles nor pistols.

The Senecas were probably armed with muskets, he knew. When they saw his canoes coming in, would they fire from shore? He did not want any of his friends killed. If he could, he meant to take on Manoth one-to-one.

The canoes shot toward shore. The fire raged, and here and there appeared a feathered Seneca or two, capering in glee. They wore the small round cap of the Iroquois warrior class, with stout armor of wooden shafts formed into a breastplate. Jeremy still could not tell why more Senecas were not in sight, and why they had not yet attacked the house.

Then there came a single musket shot from a lower window, next to the front door. A prancing Indian leaped high into the air, like a wounded jackrabbit. When he hit the ground, he skittered away into the woods. The other dancing Indians also took cover.

"Lela!" cried Tamano, who was wildly stroking in the stern. "She guards the house! Hurry, brothers!"

At that, Jeremy's Indian friends sent up their battle shouts—Chippewa, Sioux, and Ottawa. From within the house came an ululating wail of welcome from Lela, accompanied by the defiant, high-pitched cries of Tamano's two children.

Then, in answer, a dozen gruff Seneca voices took up a fierce war song, challenging their enemies.

Jeremy did not want this. The quarrel was between him and Manoth alone. He stood up in the canoe, cupped his hands, and yelled in pidgin French, which all Senecas knew well, having been France's closest Indian allies in a hundred years of wars against the English:

"Dog of a Seneca! Manoth, lowest crawling beast of the

slime! Show your miserable self! Come out and meet the man who will cut out your heart and feed it to the swine! Come out, Manoth, devourer of squaws and children! Face the man who chased you from the cliff, and who would finish the dishonorable task of taking your worthless life!"

On that high bluff on the island in Lake Erie, Jeremy had barely saved his mother's life by knocking Manoth back, compelling him to leap from the cliff. It was astonishing that he had survived, but the man was at least six foot six, tremendously strong, and brave enough to jump eighty feet with all his senses and body under control.

There was silence from the shore, now just seconds away. The crackle of flame and the lapping of river water were loud in that moment. Jeremy hoped the Senecas would not answer with a volley of rifle fire. He shouted again as the canoe neared the shallows:

"Come out, Manoth, and meet the one who will prove you the coward you are! Come out and fight me without firesticks, and show us how Seneca dogs die!"

With that, Jeremy leaped ashore and drew Weston's sword, which glittered in the sunlight. At the same moment, the Senecas appeared, a dozen of them, from the trees beside the flaming barn. In the fore was Manoth, just thirty yards away.

The Senecas were all armed with rifles, but at Manoth's orders they laid aside their firearms and drew out their hideous Iroquois war clubs. These were heavy rounded balls of ironwood at the end of a carved stick. Some clubs had nails and spikes fitted to the ball, and all were feathered and adorned with tufts of dried scalps.

Though heavily outnumbered, Jeremy's party did not waver. On his right hand Tamano advanced, with a Chippewa ax that also served as a pipe; next was Jacques Levesque, tomahawk drawn in one hand, skinning knife in the other. To Jeremy's left was Little Hawk, carrying a Sioux spear and the coup stick that had belonged to his father. It resembled a shepherd's crook, and it, too, was adorned with human scalps. Mawak, glorying in this moment, when he might die a hero, strode next to Little Hawk, a polished

English hatchet ready for action. Jeremy's group had little chance of winning, but they would make the Senecas pay a price.

"Manoth!" Jeremy motioned for his friends to pause. He paced forward three steps and pointed his sword at the Seneca war chief, who came on slowly, methodically, his men behind him.

In the hush, the sound of silver bells tinkled strangely. The bells of Morris folk dancers hung at Manoth's ankles; some Indians prized them and wore them even on the warpath. It was then Jeremy realized all was not well with the Seneca. The big warrior visibly dragged his left leg. Also, the scarlet ostrich feather he usually wore on his round cap had been snapped off; only a small piece remained. No doubt it was a visible reminder of the Indian's encounter with Jeremy and Owen, a warning to all who saw it that Manoth was determined to avenge himself. Afterward, he would replace the feather with a new one—a symbol of triumph.

"English dog," Manoth hissed through dirty front teeth; he had thick, scarred features, his nose having been broken by the hilt of Owen Sutherland's claymore. He had a large mouth and glittering black eyes, quick and keen. His head was shaven, save for the long scalp lock that hung down his back. He was almost a head taller than Jeremy, and much broader. His thighs, covered by buckskin leggins beaded and adorned with quillwork, were as wide as an average man's waist. His arms were long and muscled, naked, as was his torso, except for the wooden armor of his chest plate.

Manoth kept coming, his men ready to strike. In French the Seneca snarled, like a wolf on the prowl. "I have sworn to slay all of your family, English dog. I begin with you, tit-licking whelp! Come to me, and I'll devour your heart—if you have one."

Jeremy threw back his head and laughed. He was just ten yards from Manoth, who stopped momentarily, a black look crossing his face. The other Senecas also paused, startled by Jeremy's scorn of their chieftain.

"The Senecas are a people of the past," Jeremy replied

smoothly. "They have no power in this country, though once they were masters of it and its folk. Go back to your dunghill, you spawn of the lowest dregs of the Six Nations. Go back or face me, Manoth, single-handed, if you dare!"

Manoth's eyes grew wide, and his men were uneasy to hear this Englishman curse so well in a bastardized tongue abundant with curses and insults. No one had ever addressed the dreadful Manoth in this way. The Senecas were interested in seeing how all this would end—perhaps more interested in watching a fight than in fighting themselves. At least for the moment. When Manoth was through destroying this madman, they would finish off the others. If they killed these men, it would mean they must flee eastward to their own country near Fort Niagara, lest Ottawas, Chippewas, Sioux, and Frenchmen come after them. But they would have slain some of the toughest men in the northwest and would be greatly honored at home.

Manoth's vast arms spread wide, gesturing casually for his warriors to hold off. He held a beautiful Pennsylvania rifle, engraved and decorated with scalp locks, human teeth, and bear's claws. Handing it to a young, handsome Seneca who had a haughty, cruel expression, he slipped the war club from its throng at his waist. It was the largest club Jeremy had ever seen, but Manoth held it in one hand, lightly whirled it about once or twice, and advanced.

The gravelly beach was forty feet wide and about a hundred long. Jeremy's four friends faced away from the water, and Jeremy stood before them, ten feet away. Manoth slowly approached, club in hand, silver bells tinkling with each dragging step. The dozen Senecas, all painted and wearing wooden armor, had their backs to the house, where the door suddenly opened. Out came Lela, a middle-aged squaw whose former beauty had mellowed into warm and friendly features. But Lela's gentleness was masked this day by stern resolution, and she held a rifle at the ready. Beside her were the boy and girl. They, too, held rifles.

The tinkle of bells was all Jeremy heard just then. He crouched, eyes locked on his enemy, whose massive club swayed slowly from side to side, at knee height. Manoth, he noticed, also carried a scalping knife at his side—but

Jeremy had a thin-bladed dirk secreted Scottish fashion in his own stocking. He suddenly realized he still wore his best British-made clothes; for a fight, he would have preferred buckskin and linsey.

Manoth came straight in, grinning, eager for blood. He had a longer reach than Jeremy, but the sword darting before him had to be dealt with before he could get in a killing blow with his club. He chuckled and poked with the club. Jeremy parried sideways with the sword, but his weapon rang off the ironwood, unable to deflect it. Manoth lunged the club at Jeremy's head, but immediately grunted and stepped back quickly, his forearm slashed almost to the bone, blood spilling onto the ground.

Jeremy said, "This isn't like killing women and children, scum."

Viciously Manoth swung the club, as if it were weightless. Jeremy stepped aside, and it came down where he had stood. Manoth was so quick that Jeremy hardly had a chance to take advantage of the opening; though he tried to stab Manoth's left side, the club sped up in a backhand arc, clanging against the sword, nearly knocking it out of his hand. Suddenly the club came straight down again, alive in the Indian's hand. Jeremy felt its spike cut his cheek. The force was so sudden that Jeremy had to duck; he found himself reeling backward, the club grazing his thigh, then flying past his bobbing head.

Jeremy had caught a glancing whack on the side of his face. Almost stunned, feeling his thigh wet with blood, he kept moving, sensing Manoth come in. He feinted a retreat, about to counter with a well-aimed thrust of the sword, but in the next instant he saw the terrible stroke of the club descending. Thrusting fiercely, into thin air, he ducked at the same moment, then cut downward. He spun away, hearing a muffled grunt of pain.

Regaining his balance, head ringing crazily, Jeremy saw Manoth gaping with surprise at his left hand. The tips of his last three fingers were gone, scattered on the pebbles. Jeremy shook off the blow he had taken and flicked two of the fingertips away with the point of his sword. That achieved the desired result: Manoth bellowed, charging wildly, club raised.

Jeremy should have fallen back to avoid the brunt of the assault—at least that was the normal tactic. Instead, he met it full force, ramming his sword at Manoth's club. So skilled was Jeremy that he caught the tough club with the sword-point, but the force of Manoth's attack caused both weapons to fly from their hands and fall to the ground. The two fighters broke apart, chests heaving.

Manoth would settle for this. Bare-handed, Jeremy was done for. The Seneca straightened, and a black humor came into his eyes. He noticed how his enemy longed to dive for the sword, which lay on the stones a little to the Indian's right. The Senecas shook their clubs and laughed. Jeremy's men were uneasy. There was no way to save Jeremy but to fight them all.

In English Little Hawk said, "Now we join you, brother."

But Jeremy waved them off. He felt a sudden surge of confidence just then. A feeling came over him that he could master even this mighty fighter in wrestling. Jeremy crouched, hands out, ready to grapple. His mouth was parched; sweat poured from his face. Manoth's hand and arm bled, but he showed no pain, no concern. He did not even take a wrestling stance, but stepped forward fully erect, willing to deal with whatever Jeremy attempted. Then he would casually break his back.

Manoth had not counted on Jeremy's leap, legs first. In the next instant, to Little Hawk's howl of joy, Jeremy had Manoth's head locked between his knees, and in the same fluid movement of his spring, he wrenched the Seneca to the ground, like a beast caught in a snare. The jarring fall would have snapped a normal man's neck. Though it hurt Manoth considerably, he tried to scramble to his knees and almost got free of the brutal leg lock.

Just as the Indian found a grip on Jeremy's thighs, the white man flipped backward, releasing him. Jeremy continued to move away, acrobatically landing on his feet. On hands and knees, Manoth rushed forward with an agility remarkable for such a giant. But he was too used to having his enemies flee. Once again Jeremy tricked him by countering with an attack of his own.

Jeremy lashed out with his right foot, his hard English shoe thudding Manoth between the eyes, and the Indian went down, half stunned. It was a wicked stroke, so hard that Jeremy himself was sent sprawling. Falling forward over the Indian, he rolled, feeling intense pain in his foot. He had lost the shoe, and guessed toes had been broken. Springing to his feet, he kicked off the other shoe, realizing he should have removed them both earlier. He would have been faster and might have made a finish by skilled swordplay. He had forgotten too much in his peaceful years in civilization. Though his foot ached and his thigh still bled, Jeremy was readier than ever to wrestle the big man, who was trying to get up. Confident, full of fire, Jeremy forgot caution and charged, crashing chest-to-chest against Manoth, intending to drive him down, get a grip on his throat, and finish him off. But as groggy as the Seneca was, he was still too powerful.

Manoth had absorbed the battering force of Jeremy's charge. Great arms went about Jeremy, squeezing the breath and the life from him. Through a haze of agony and blood, he heard his friends shout for him to break out, but the guttural cheering of the Senecas rose above it all. The pain was awful. Manoth, greasy and sweaty, stinking of bear oil and rum, grunted and squeezed. He slowly crushed Jeremy, trying to break his back. Suddenly Jeremy was lifted off his feet—the prelude to Manoth's killing him. Arms pinned at his side, Jeremy could do little but writhe and kick as the Indian worked his own hands together, trying to lock them behind Jeremy's spine.

Manoth bawled like an animal, his face close to Jeremy's, eyes aflame with the passion of killing. Jeremy felt himself ebbing, the strength and breath going out of him. Next would be the snapping of bones, and when his spine cracked, he would not hear or feel it. In desperation he gave cruel blows with his forehead, smashing Manoth's already battered nose to a bloody pulp. The Seneca yielded slightly but held on. Staggering back and forth on the beach as Jeremy butted him again and again, Manoth finally joined his hands together. He would wrench Jeremy hard, once or twice, and it would be over.

Jeremy's right leg bent at the knee as he brought it up behind him. He stretched painfully down to his stocking. The dirk was there. He had to pull it free. . . .

It was in his fingers. Then Manoth gave a tremendous lurch and squeezed Jeremy even harder against his chest. Jeremy gasped in agony, losing the dirk, which remained partly in his stocking. Feeling himself failing, he used all his strength to butt viciously at the Indian's face. Manoth reeled, momentarily releasing his awful, crushing squeeze.

He must have that dirk! Manoth was recovering his balance, recovering from the dizziness inflicted by Jeremy's blows. Regaining mastery, Manoth began to spin, about to throw himself forward and land flat on his victim. Jeremy was like a rag doll in the Indian's arms. He tried to butt Manoth again. To avoid it, the Seneca bit Jeremy's shoulder, digging in his teeth to keep Jeremy from getting a solid whack with his forehead. The Senecas were howling with delight. Jeremy heard them through it all, through the pain and nausea, and he fought to get the dirk—his only chance.

Manoth spun once, twice, three times.

Then the dirk was in Jeremy's hand, and he raked Manoth's belly, under the wooden armor. Manoth howled, released Jeremy, and staggered back. Jeremy collapsed to the ground. Managing to rise to all fours, he somehow scrambled away, then got up, feeling limp and badly hurt. Manoth was standing in amazement, cut across the stomach.

Jeremy panted, unable to catch his breath. "I could . . . have finished you with that, Seneca . . . but you are only scratched. Next time, you die. Now use your own blade!"

Manoth swayed on his feet. Indeed, the gash Jeremy had inflicted was not deep, considering that he could have ripped the man's belly open, spilling out the Indian's life in one swift stroke. Now Jeremy was in a crouch, his face blue from lack of air. He brandished his dirk, ready for the final combat.

Manoth grunted, and laughed. To his friends, he said, "The white fool would have been wiser to cut deeply." To Jeremy he said, "I will use my knife, little one."

Manoth took the scalping knife from his belt. Blood, dirt, and sweat covered him, and the glint of steel against his bronzed and filthy torso focused Jeremy's attention. Dazed and battered, in severe pain, Jeremy paid too much attention to the sunlight gleaming on the Seneca's blade.

Suddenly, the light was gone, though Manoth had barely moved. A terrific force thudded into Jeremy's chest and knocked him backward three steps. He looked down and saw the scalping knife sticking in his breastbone. Astonished, dizzy, and nauseated from exhaustion, Jeremy nearly swooned. He heard Manoth's voice ringing loudly inside his head. There was shouting, then the ripple of musketry. Manoth approached. Jeremy fought to remain conscious, and with a fierce cry hurled his own knife at the Indian, whose surprised face disappeared from sight. Then Jeremy went black. He could still feel and hear, but knew, without doubt, he was dying.

## chapter 4

# MONTREAL

Ella Sutherland felt the pain, like a knife in her heart. She staggered, hand to her breast, and leaned against the counter in the small pantry, where she had been preparing morning tea. Head whirling, hands tingling, she became faint. She heard her husband's voice and the happy chatter of their two children as though they were a hundred yards off instead of just beyond the door. There was a ringing in her ears that would not relent, and it was all she could do to keep from falling to the floor.

Ella did not know what had come upon her so, but she could not stop worrying about her eldest son, Jeremy. He would be back in Detroit by now, just as she and her party had reached Montreal after a swift journey. They had taken little-used trails across Redcoat-occupied territory near Niagara, then sailed by whaleboat. Yesterday, Ella, Owen, and the two children had arrived at Montreal, where they would spend the winter. Thanks to the elderly Michel and Marie Devalier, longtime business associates, they had found comfortable lodgings on rue Saint Paul. The back of the two-story stone house overlooked the broad Saint Lawrence River.

The ten other friends in their party were also moving into

new homes in the occupied city. Most, like the Sutherlands, had rented former residences of loyalists who had fled down to Quebec or up to Fort Detroit, both places still in the hands of king's supporters. Though Montreal was burdened with hundreds of ragged, impoverished rebel troops crammed into barracks and stables, many apartments were left empty, because rebel leaders had been careful not to alienate the French proprietors by billeting troops in private homes.

The ringing in Ella's ears subsided, and her hands no longer tingled, but she felt weak and kept from collapsing only by leaning on the counter. Taking several deep breaths to regain her equilibrium, she focused on the stack of dirty dishes, which would be washed in water now heating on the sitting-room stove.

She picked up a knife to cut the raisin bread, but her hands still shook. A tray of clean cups and saucers was on the counter at her right, and next to them, on a grate warmed by a candle, sat the teapot. Ella had already made the apartment homey, even though it was not her beloved Valenya. She sliced slowly, thinking they would make this place do until they could finally go back to the straits. She prayed that this exile would not last long and that they would not have to flee Montreal. Yet they all knew that if British troops at Quebec were reinforced and came up the Saint Lawrence, they would have to go again. But where?

Sunlight broke through the clouds over the river and poured in the pantry window. Ella was grateful for the warmth and comfort. Pausing in her work, she wiped sweat away with a hand towel, then finished placing the raisin bread on a pewter plate. Though Jeremy was on her mind, she was able to clear away the startling sensation of weakness that had nearly overcome her. Adjusting her yellow brocaded gown and absently touching her blond hair, she readied herself to return to the sitting room. On a slender chain around her neck was a cylindrical silver pendant that gleamed in the sunlight, but she wore no other jewelry, nor any makeup. Ella's beauty was natural in every way, and she was as lovely as she had ever been, even though she was past forty.

"Ella?" The door opened, and Owen came in from the

sitting room. He was tall and dark, a few years older than his wife, and looked aristocratic in dark blue clothes of fine linen and wool. He was handsome and ruggedly built, and far too big for that small pantry, but he came all the way in anyway, a worried look in his gray eyes.

"Ella, what is it, lass?" His voice had a Scottish burr, for he was a native of that land, having come to America twenty years earlier as a fur trader in the northwest. He took his wife's hands and looked closely at her, seeing something was wrong. "Are you ill? You're feverish."

Ella shook her head and collected herself, breathing a sigh. "I . . . I don't know, darling. I . . . just had a strange feeling, a feeling about Jeremy—"

"Jeremy?" Owen lifted her chin to look into her hazel eyes. They were glazed, troubled. "What feeling, then? A mother's intuition?"

When she nodded he tried to smile, saying she should not think that slight fainting spells meant something serious was happening to her loved ones. But Sutherland was a Scot and knew something about the second sight. He fully trusted his own uncanny intuition.

Squeezing Ella's hands, he kissed her lightly. "The lad's full-grown now," he said. "He can take care of himself better than we can."

"I know." Ella picked up the tray, which Owen took from her. "It's just that so much has happened to us, and I'm so worried for him." Looking at her husband, she said, "Will he ever join us, Owen? Will he ever, ever see the rightness of our cause? Or . . . or will we be forced, one day, to . . ."

She could not say it, and neither could Sutherland. Neither could speak the words, "fight him," because they knew only too well that such a tragedy might lie ahead. They were not sure how stubbornly Jeremy Bently would support the unbending rule of Parliament, but they themselves would oppose any attempt to overthrow the rebel government, which controlled most of the fourteen colonies, including Canada.

If Jeremy joined the British to counterattack the rebels, he might find himself battling his own family, as others

were doing at that very moment. The nine-month-old conflict could erupt into full-scale civil war if Parliament did
not soon compromise with Congress and make peace.

Owen set down the tray and put an arm around Ella's
waist. They stood close together, looking out the pantry
door to the sitting room, where their two children, Benjamin, eleven, and Susannah, nine, were playing chess on
the floor near the stove. The Sutherlands were celebrating
a quiet Christmas, as were their other friends in Montreal.
In a few days they would all gather to decide how to proceed
now that the Frontier Company was being broken up by the
revolution. The partners on the rebel side of the conflict
intended to reorganize, enlarging their operations here in
Montreal, a major trading center for northwestern pelts.

For now, though, the Sutherlands were determined to
have a good Christmas. They had been singing carols, Ella
playing an old spinet that was in the apartment. The spinet
stood in the sitting room, near a beautiful evergreen shrub
that Owen had somehow procured yesterday, despite the
bustle of their finding a place to stay. The Sutherlands liked
having an evergreen in the house at Christmas, a custom
learned from German immigrants in Pennsylvania.

Owen saw that Ella was better, but the luster had left
her eyes, as though she suffered an inner ache or had some
secret knowledge too hurtful either to speak of or to forget.
He closed the pantry door partway. "Ella, lass, why don't
you get some rest? The past weeks have all been too much
for you—the journey from Erie, the danger, the cold . . ."

Ella put the teapot on the tray and tried to smile. "I'll
be fine, dearest. Our lives have changed so very much,
though. I'll just have to accept it."

She stood staring at the tea tray. He again asked what
was on her mind. She closed her eyes momentarily before
replying in a soft, hoarse voice.

"Jeremy's dying . . ." She swayed and caught herself on
his shoulder. "Owen, I'm afraid for him. I can almost see
him. I can feel the pain!"

The door opened quickly and in came Susannah, looking
frightened. She was so much like Ella. Both were blond,
with delicate features and fair, sensitive skin tanned by sun

and wind. The girl went to her mother's side, as though she, too, had sensed something. Indeed, Susannah and Ella had a remarkable unspoken bond—an understanding so close that they often knew each other's thoughts before they were put in words.

From the sitting room Benjamin yelled in his changing voice, which rose to a squeak, "Susannah, come on back! You can't quit now, when I've got you in check! Susannah?"

Susannah seemed not to hear. To her mother she said, "It's Jeremy, isn't it? I've been thinking of him, too." Trembling, she embraced her mother.

Sutherland stood back and rubbed his sore left shoulder, wounded in the recent battle on Lake Erie. It was healing well but still distracted him as he wondered what was happening to Ella. Then there came a pounding at the door. Heera, the husky, barked loudly in the sitting room, and Sutherland went to quiet him. Heera lay down by the stove and stared at the door, which Benjamin was about to open. The boy, almost as tall as an average man, was already filling out. Though dark like his father, he had his mother's features, and it seemed he would not be as broad and robust as Sutherland. He wore a drab linen smock over soft leather breeches and had no shoes on his stockinged feet.

Throwing back the door before the visitor pounded it through, Benjamin stepped away to let an enormous, blond fellow come shouldering in, shouting "Happy Christmas!" to them all. Peter Defries, an Albany native of Dutch descent, was a rebel like the Sutherlands. Though in his early thirties and possessing the constitution of an ox, Defries had kept his boyish good looks. He had battled the lake pirates with the Sutherlands and had shared many adventures in his twelve years as a partner in the Frontier Company. His own wife and daughter were in rebel Albany, where he would go soon; but he had lived in Montreal for years and knew its people well.

"Happy Christmas, laddie!" Sutherland shook hands with his friend, then, nodding at the duffel bag Defries carried over his shoulder, he asked, "On your way to Albany already?"

Defries shook his head. His florid face became drawn

and tense, almost angry as he set down the bag and threw off his heavy brown frock coat, which Benjamin took to hang up.

"Ain't goin' to Albany!" Defries growled, and began to pace. "Ah, Christmas! Havin' a happy Christmas ain't gonna be easy—not when I tell you what's what down at Quebec!"

Defries stopped pacing, stared at Sutherland and at Ella, then went to the window to glare outside. After a moment he swung round and took something out of his pocket. "This is for you, Owen. I near forgot it in my itch to complain about things."

He handed Sutherland a letter tied with blue ribbon and fixed with the official blue seal of a rebel military dispatch. Sutherland took the letter, but before opening it, he asked why Defries was so agitated.

"I'll tell you!" Defries poured himself a brandy from the decanter on the dinner table, drank swiftly, and made a face as the stuff burned down his throat. "I'm makin' for Quebec! Right now!"

Ella gasped. There must be trouble with the invasion.

"Them Tories stopped our army!" Defries gulped down another brandy and paced to the window. Light glinted on a pistol butt and knife handle visible under his short jacket. "General Montgomery's bogged down at the gates of the citadel, and Colonel Arnold's men're like so many scarecrows—starved, naked, and half-dead from a march through the wilderness."

Sutherland knew that if several hundred Tories and a few companies of Redcoats were resolute enough, they could easily hold Quebec. Richard Montgomery and Benedict Arnold together had fewer than a thousand fighting rebels, and Arnold's incredible forced march through Maine had greatly weakened his men.

Sutherland sat down on a settee, the unopened letter in his hands. It was a personal dispatch from General Montgomery himself. A brave and experienced officer, Montgomery was overall rebel field commander of the northern theater of war. Sutherland knew what the letter would say.

Defries went on: "If our boys don't take the city afore winter really hits, Owen, it won't no way fall afterward!

Ain't no time to lose!" He nodded once at the dispatch. "Friend of mine brought it here from Montgomery, and he'd been told to memorize what it's about. . . . Don't mean to pry, Owen, but I reckon since my name's mentioned, I got some right to know about it. Leastways my friend thought so."

Ella sat down next to her husband. Now her worry for Jeremy was joined by another fear. The room was silent save for the ticking of a clock as Sutherland methodically undid the ribbon and opened the letter. Montgomery asked Sutherland and Defries to come north to Quebec City immediately. Supplies were desperately needed, and whatever hard cash Sutherland could collect would be essential to pay for food and clothing, as well as ammunition and arms for what might be a prolonged siege. Further, there was a critical need for experienced officers to lead the raw rebel troops.

Susannah and Ella glanced anxiously at each other, knowing this meant Owen would be leaving right away. Benjamin excitedly blurted out that he wanted to go along.

Sutherland looked up from the letter, a shadow crossing his face. "You'll get your chance in due time, son. For the moment, you're needed here with your mother and sister."

The boy was disappointed, but knew better than to object.

"How long will you be gone?" Ella asked softly. "Do you really have to go right now?"

Sutherland looked at Defries, then said, "If Peter's going now, then he's got a good reason, and that's enough for me."

Defries cleared his throat. "Ella, if I could, I'd traipse off to Albany and see my Mary and Jeanette, you know that. But things're getting pretty desperate with our boys at Quebec. They been serving for months without letup, and the enlistments of half the men in Montgomery's army run out in January. If he means to storm the citadel, he'll have to do it quick, before his troops go home to look after their families and farms."

Ella could have said that both of these men had families, too, but she knew they were not the kind to let the cause down. Besides, they were not farmers, with the many seasonal chores that must be done to prevent economic ruin, or simply to keep from starving.

Sutherland said to her, "And they need artillery to take Quebec, so I mean to get what I can and send it on the way as soon as possible, before it's too late."

Ella nodded, but there were tears in her eyes; she knew she would be parted from Owen and that his life would be in danger.

To give them privacy, Defries rose and went to the pantry to feed himself. Sutherland took Ella's hand and said, "Until Quebec falls."

Benjamin blurted, "But it's the strongest fortress in America! As strong as Gibraltar itself! How can Montgomery take it?"

"Don't be so quick to judge men," Sutherland demanded. "The question is not how, but when the city will fall. That's not a trained regular army behind those walls. Soon enough they'll be as hungry and cold as our lads. They're just civilians like us; they can't hold on if we throw enough iron at them. . . ."

Sutherland caught himself as he realized he was talking of slaughter. He pursed his lips, saying to Ella, "It doesn't matter how we get it accomplished. Forgive my talk of such things on Christmas, before the children."

"I'm no child, Papa! Younger men than I are with the troops before Quebec! Won't you—"

"No," Sutherland said and stood up. "If what we have won't take Quebec, one more hungry and overbusy mouth won't change things down there! Silence, now, and restrain yourself if you want to prove yourself a fighting man!"

Seldom had Ella seen her husband so severe with the children. She touched his arm, and he stared out the window. Benjamin was downcast, and Susannah had tears in her eyes.

"So I go again, my darling," Sutherland said, looking at Ella. "If you are pressed here before I return, you must make for Albany and join Peter's family. You'll have funds enough, and I'll come for you as soon as I can."

"I want to wait for you here!" she declared.

"I hope, my darling, that you can," he said quietly. "But

if the Redcoats come and I can't get to you, then make your own way straight to Albany."

"And thence?"

He shook his head once. "There will be no retreat from there. If we lose Albany, it will soon be finished with our cause. The Hudson Valley will be next, cutting New England off from the other colonies; the rest will fall one by one."

Normally, Sutherland would not have talked of such matters in front of the children. But time was precious now, and already the youngsters knew about war and danger. He turned, put his hands on their shoulders, and made them promise to stand by their mother, no matter what happened.

"Benjamin," he said, "you're the man here now. Do nothing rash, and do not seek honor in reckless bravery. There's much I would teach you before you have to fight, but if I cannot be there, then go slowly and carefully, and trust to your heart for what is right." He hugged his son, feeling the strength in the lad's young, lithe body. "Forgive my harsh words, but understand me well."

"Depend upon me, sir," Benjamin said, voice cracking, lower lip atremble. "I'll not fail us."

To Susannah, Sutherland said, "It's the women who keep life going when men go off to destroy it. Be the woman your mother is, and you'll do our family and our cause a greater service than you would carrying a rifle, my girl."

Susannah threw herself at her father, head against his chest. She refused to break down weeping, though she shook with the effort. "We'll be looking for you every day, Papa!" she said. "But if war seeks us out, don't expect me to sit home and knit stockings for soldiers!"

He gazed into Susannah's lovely face and smiled. "I don't expect you to flinch from anything, my lass, not even stockings." He kissed her cheek. "It's simpler being a man in this world, but it's women who are the bravest."

Owen turned to Ella. Standing with hands clasped, they sought the right parting words. Then Ella exclaimed, "Stockings, indeed, husband! Susannah, Benjamin, pack your father's campaign gear! Cold-weather underthings! Extra stockings! Blankets!"

The children scurried off, searching through bags yet
unpacked. They found a small box of medicines and bandages, salves and purgatives. There were tools and utensils
to be packed in their father's well-worn knapsack, and his
weapons and their accouterments to be assembled.

Sutherland embraced Ella, then said, "If you can't make
Albany, then trust to the Oneidas to aid you in the Mohawk
Valley."

The Oneidas were the only tribe of the Iroquois Six
Nations that supported the rebels. The other five, including
Manoth's warlike Senecas, were allies of the king and might
endanger fugitives fleeing eastward through the Mohawk.
The Sutherlands had friends among the Oneidas, including
a white man who had married a woman from that tribe and
lived now in Montreal.

Ella said, "Must we talk of war before you depart?"

Sutherland kissed her. "Would that we could talk of love,
lass, but the sooner I'm gone——"

"The sooner you'll come back! Yes, I've heard that often
of late. And I weary of it, Owen! Would that you never
leave me again."

"I cannot make that promise . . . not yet." They kissed
once more, and the children came back into the room. A
pile of outdoor gear, a heavy Scottish sword—a claymore—
and a Pennsylvania rifle in a protective bag were all prepared
for their father.

Defries shouted from behind the door, "Can I come out
yet? You done sentimentalizin'? I've ate all this raisin bread,
and I run outa tea! If I got to stay in here, send me some
brandy!"

Ten minutes later Owen had changed into his winter gear.
The Sutherlands kept their farewells brief. Owen left his
family standing at the door of the apartment, and he had to
send Heera, the great husky, back inside. The dog had long
been his faithful companion and more than once had saved
his life. He would not take Heera to Quebec, however, for
the animal was needed here. And if a siege was necessary
at Quebec, there would surely be hunger, and dogs were
first to be eaten, even before horses. Going down the narrow
stairs, Sutherland could hear Benjamin holding the dog back.

Ella had agreed not to come down to the street. Her heart was sore for Owen and for Jeremy, and it was best not to prolong the farewell. Besides, Owen had a great deal to do before leaving Montreal, arranging for supplies to be sent to Montgomery. At the foot of the stairs, letting Defries go out first, Sutherland turned to call a last good-bye. He felt his words catch in his throat as he listened to his family bid him a safe journey. Then he stepped into a cold wind that blew in from the northeast, bringing clouds to blot out the sun and spreading a chilly gloom over Montreal. He and Defries set off down the narrow street, silent and lost in thought.

On Sutherland's head was a flat, brown felt hat, on his back a knapsack. The long Pennsylvania rifle was slung over his shoulder, and the basket-hilted sword hung at his side. For the rest, he looked like a well-to-do frontiersman going off on a long hunt.

Over his buckskin shirt he had a thick flannel coat, and his legs were covered with soft doeskin leggins wrapped over wool garments to keep off the damp and cold. On his feet were stout moccasins, which he often wore stuffed with straw in winter. Hanging over the knapsack was a pair of webbed *racquets*, or snowshoes. Save for linsey and wool instead of buckskins, Defries was dressed about the same, and he also had snowshoes over his shoulder; in winter, *racquets* were essential gear.

The two friends strode rapidly through the streets of Montreal, between gray stone houses with steep slate roofs and small windows. The streets were almost deserted, for everyone was resting or feasting on Christmas Day. Church-bells tolled noon, echoing in the empty city.

Rounding a corner, Sutherland and Defries had not gone ten paces down a windy side street when they saw a group of people hurrying toward them, shouting and waving.

It was their friends from Fort Detroit, all bundled up against the cold and carrying pots and jugs and bags of what could only be Christmas delicacies. Sutherland and Defries glanced at each other, and the Dutchman burped softly, saying he was glad he had eaten already, or it would be difficult to turn down what was about to be offered. In the forefront of the group was the stout, red-faced Lettie Grey, followed by her huge husband, Jeb, both in their late fifties.

Lettie cried out in her north-of-England accent, "Where be thee off to, then, lads?" Smiling cheerfully, she held up a picnic basket. "We've come to surprise you. Dumplings and gravy, ready to eat! Owen, drag thy friend back home, and let's get on with the celebration!"

Lettie grabbed Sutherland by the arm, and for the first time noticed he was carrying his long rifle and heavy knapsack. A look of concern came into her eyes as the others gathered round.

Sally Cooper Morely, newly wed to Lettie's son Tom, embraced Sutherland and said cheerfully, "You can't both be thinking of going hunting on Christmas Day, surely?" Sally was a tall, beautiful woman in her early twenties, with dark hair and eyes and a fair complexion. Like Lettie and the two other women in the group, she wore a flowing cape and mantle, as well as boots and a long dress.

Sally was like a daughter to Owen, for he had raised her as a foster child after she had been rescued by Jacques Levesque from Indian captivity. Reluctant to answer her question, Owen looked about and found her husband standing at the back of the group. Tom Morely's head was still swathed in bandages from a tomahawk wound taken in the fight on Lake Erie a few weeks previous, and his stern expression as he met Owen's eyes showed he was aware that something was up—something more than a winter hunt.

Sutherland began to reply to Sally and Lettie but was interrupted as the others pressed in with more questions. They included Matilda and the Reverend Angus Lee, a distinguished middle-aged couple who had left Detroit with the Sutherlands, as had all the others, save two: Mel and Hickory Webster. The Lees, Greys, and Morelys had all been accused of being rebel sympathizers at Detroit and had been forced to flee, lest they be attacked or imprisoned. But the Websters were essentially neutral; he was something of a philosopher, tinker, scientist, and adventurer, all in one, while she was the daughter of an Oneida medicine man. Like the others, however, the lank, slender Mel and the stocky Hickory had been caught up in the Lake Erie battle and had come to Montreal to reorganize their lives in these troubled times.

"Sorry, my friends," Sutherland said, shaking his head. "Peter and I have no time to dally."

But Defries, sniffing at Lettie's basket of food, muttered, "Maybe I am just a mite hungry, Owen. And it is Christmas Day."

The others sent up a chorus of agreement, and Lettie again said Owen should not leave his family alone on this holiday. "Thee can do thy hunting after the New Year, when the snow'll be on the ground for sure and tracking will be easier!"

"Besides," Jeb rumbled, smiling, "we ate enough venison on the trip from Erie to last us till next Christmas! I tell you, lads, Lettie's outdone herself with these dumplings, and"—he cocked a thumb back at Matilda, a chubby, kindly woman with soft brown eyes—"Mrs. Lee's been cooking a turkey ever since she set foot in her new house!"

Reverend Lee, his glasses fogged, smiled and attempted to lift high the large covered tray he carried. But it was too heavy for the frail minister, and the strapping Tom Morely offered a hand.

Tom closed his eyes and took a long sniff. "Smells awful good, Owen. Peter, it wouldn't be like you to go off without doing justice to Matilda's turkey. And my Sal's been baking, too."

Reverend Lee said in his high, New York Town voice, "You see, all of us were determined to surprise the Sutherlands and our friend Peter today, whose own loved ones are down in Albany. Well?" He had the most genial, friendly smile, anticipating a wonderful celebration. "Shall we hie ourselves to Owen's for the earthly commemoration of God's precious gift to mankind? Eh?"

They all began to push and laugh and joke, trying to bustle Peter and Owen back to the house, but the two men were not to be moved. Sutherland smiled bleakly and said, "Have a wonderful party, and think about us. But we must head for Quebec. A letter came from Montgomery today.

But I think it would do Ella good to have you barge in and lift her spirits. If you want to honor me with any favor, that would mean the most to me."

They fell silent a moment, and then Lettie took a deep breath and nodded. "Owen, my lad, thee be a hard man to pin down, that's a fact." With a glance at the others, she handed her basket to Jeb, took a carrying bag from her elbow, and began to collect food. In a moment it was stuffed with something from each dish and was slung over Peter's shoulder. Sutherland and Defries each had a turkey leg in one hand, and were kissed and given handshakes by the whole group.

As the pair turned away, Lettie struck up a holiday song, and the others joined in:

> Wassail, wassail, all over the town!
> Our toast it is white, and our ale it is brown;
> Our bowl it is made of the white maple tree;
> With the wassailing bowl we'll drink to thee.

It was a joyous song, one of Owen's favorites, and it lent a swing to his step as he and Defries rounded another corner. It was good to hear their friends still singing in the distance. After all, it was for folk like these that he was heading to Quebec. They deserved whatever he could do to protect their freedom.

Sutherland, however, was not yet ready to leave the city. He quickly explained his plan to Defries as they walked southward along windy, rutted rue Notre Dame. They made for the rebel headquarters at the corner of rue Saint Jean.

"Before we set out I'll arrange to ship food, equipment, and clothing to Montgomery and Arnold," Sutherland said. "We'll buy horses and ride on ahead; the supplies can follow us. But what Montgomery really needs at Quebec are cannon, and that's what we'll have to fetch him!"

"Cannon!" Defries exclaimed. "How'll you get cannon to Quebec before snow flies? The British still patrol the river; are you goin' to haul 'em overland? And who's goin' to pay for that? And who'll give you the cannon, anyway?"

Sutherland said Montgomery's letter authorized him to take whatever was needed from Montreal to support the campaign against Quebec. As for paying the freight and the manpower, he tapped a wallet underneath his buckskin shirt.

"Two thousand pounds sterling will get us whatever we need in the way of ox-sleds, supplies, and strong backs." He nodded to the stone building across the street, where the red flag of revolution snapped in the breeze—the Americans still had no other symbol for their cause. "We'll get the city commandant to give us at least ten guns, and within the hour I'll have a hundred able Frenchmen with oxen and harnesses. They'll set off tomorrow, and we'll scout the road ahead, making sure they get through."

Entering the Congress army headquarters, they were brought to the city's commander, a stolid, slow-witted colonel from Connecticut. Seated in an armchair in a disheveled office, the man looked to have been roused from a nap. Without giving much weight to the letter of authorization from General Montgomery, the colonel said that he could not turn over the cannon. They were required to protect the city and to intimidate the French inhabitants, lest they rise against their occupiers.

Sutherland immediately became angry, saying the man was disobeying the orders of his commander-in-chief. But the colonel replied that a Connecticut officer was not absolutely subordinate to a York officer, and since Montgomery was a Yorker, he had little authority unless he was actually stationed in this city. Montgomery was not directly in charge of the garrison, which was mainly Connecticut militia.

"Furthermore," said the man, a reedy fellow, pompous, and slow in speech, "I answer only to the city's commissary general when it comes to the disposition of ordnance. If you desire to carry this matter further, you'll have to speak with Mr. Bradford Cullen—after the holidays, of course."

Sutherland flushed at the mention of Bradford Cullen, but said nothing.

Defries muttered, "Ah, there's a name what chills this poor rebel's weary bones. So the old dog's got hisself made commissary general, has he?"

The colonel leaped to his feet, furious. "How dare you speak disrespectfully of such a patriot as Mr. Bradford Cullen? You're not fit to shine his boots!"

"But I'll wager you're fit to lick them, Colonel," Sutherland said, touching off a storm as the officer threatened to arrest them.

"Hold your water, Colonel," Defries said. "We ain't in the army yet, but we got a request from the general hisself to get our tails up to Quebec directly. So don't get in over your head by clappin' us in irons."

The colonel knew Defries was right, and grumbled sourly. He ruled in the city as long as General Montgomery was away, but once he returned, he would hold even Connecticut commanders liable for interfering with Sutherland's orders to come north. The colonel sat down, face set in anger.

"I want those cannon," Sutherland said, staring the officer down. "If Cullen's the one to authorize my getting them, then I'll see him immediately."

"Impossible. Mr. Cullen at this moment is conducting a formal dinner in honor of the wealthiest French families in Montreal."

"We ain't gonna eat his Frenchy dinner," Defries declared, waving the gnawed turkey leg from his pack. "We don't like snails anyway!"

They strode out to find Cullen. Sutherland knew the man had a house around the corner on rue Saint François, and no doubt he was busily shaping himself a role as a leading Whig in Canada. For twelve years Sutherland and Cullen had been competitors in the peltry trade, and no one was more unscrupulous, more underhanded than Bradford Cullen.

An uneasy truce existed between them, now that both were supporters of the rebellion, but Sutherland was certain that the man would still do whatever he could to prevent the Frontier Company from ever again rising to prominence in the northwest. As commissary general, Cullen was in charge of all military stores, including the disposition of the city's cannon. Sutherland suspected that Bradford Cullen might one day turn his coat and support the Tory cause again. At the moment, however, no other northern Whig could match Cullen's immense wealth, and Congress had accepted him as a valuable ally against Parliament.

The rebel army had little financial support from Congress, which was impossibly poor. Military goods were procured largely through the pocketbooks of men such as Bradford Cullen and Owen Sutherland, who would be repaid after Congress found some way to finance the rebellion. Sutherland had spent more than five thousand pounds already, but had accepted no political benefit in return. That was obviously not the case with Cullen, who was consolidating and expanding his own power at every opportunity.

Sutherland and Cullen both had much influence with the rebels, but Sutherland's sway was over fighting men, not gentry. Sutherland had trained in the famous Black Watch regiment and knew much about warfare. It was for him to march and fight, while the elderly Bradford Cullen stayed in Montreal, gathering power to himself by exchanging favors and patronage with influential people in the city.

These people, Sutherland knew, largely controlled the northwest peltry trade. When the war was over and trade resumed, Bradford Cullen would have created a network of support that could make him the most powerful merchant prince in all America. At the very least, Cullen could hope to be named Congress's governor of Canada once that colony formally joined the thirteen that had already rebelled against Parliament.

Sutherland meant to confront Cullen and be given the cannon Montgomery needed. Dinner or no dinner, French nabobs or no, Sutherland and Defries marched right up to the polished mahogany door of Cullen's opulent residence on rue Saint François.

*chapter* 5

# BRADFORD CULLEN

It had begun to sleet when Sutherland and Defries reached Cullen's rented residence. The house was one of the handsomest in the city, built of granite brought from distant quarries at tremendous cost. Cullen had moved in a week previous, renting from a French Canadian named Meloche, who owned a seigneury—a baronial estate left over from the French rule—a few leagues downriver from Montreal.

Meloche had no apparent reason to favor Bradford Cullen by renting him the granite residence. It was known the French Canadian had turned down several spectacular offers from American loyalists before the rebellion had forced them to flee. Sutherland wondered what common interest Meloche and Cullen had, but as he and Defries stood in the icy rain at the door, he put aside suspicions and concentrated on matters at hand. Most important was getting those cannon to Quebec as quickly as possible. There was no doubt in Sutherland's mind that Cullen would release the guns—after all, how else would Quebec be taken? The real problem was how to manhandle them over winter roads in time to aid in an assault on Quebec.

Wet and cold, Sutherland and Defries grew annoyed and

impatient as they waited at the top of a short flight of broad stone stairs. From within the heavily curtained windows came the sweet sound of violins. Dignified laughter made Defries grumble and slam the knocker harder, sending a raucous booming through the house. He and Sutherland muttered about greedy wolves in a city that would have trouble finding enough food for the winter.

Then the mahogany door swung slowly open, revealing a very tall, thin butler in a powdered bob wig. Looking down his long nose, as from a great distance, the man addressed them in impeccable Parisian French: "You have no business here on this holiday."

Defries touched his hat and with a winning smile said in English they were looking for a whorehouse, and this sounded like a cheery one.

The butler's face reddened, though he declined to admit he understood English, particularly English spoken by an American.

"Be off," he hissed indignantly in French, "before I call the city watch!"

About to slam the door, the fellow became purple when he realized Sutherland had slipped the blade of his dirk into a hinge, stopping the door from shutting.

"Ruffians!" the butler growled, turning to call for assistance. Sutherland addressed him crisply, in French that was as perfect and haughty as his own.

"Your master will box your provincial ears should he learn you've turned away a message such as the one I bear for him."

The butler turned back. Now he was joined by three burly men, all bewigged and garbed in matching silks and lace. The sound of the party could be heard through the open door—the clink of glasses and the coquettish giggling of women.

"Give me the message," declared the butler, "and it will be delivered to Monsieur Cullen." His pole of an arm thrust forward, palm flat to receive Sutherland's delivery.

The Scotsman simply smiled, leaned forward, and said in English, "It's a secret, and must be transferred to your master in person."

The butler shuddered with annoyance, and one of the footmen moved forward, ready to get rid of the intruders.

Sutherland removed his dirk from the hinge and calmly wiped the blade on his buckskins, as if the weapon had been dirtied by contact with Cullen's door. "Tell Cullen that Owen Sutherland wants to give him word about his captain, Hugh Meeks—the late Hugh Meeks."

The door was immediately closed, and from within the butler snapped, "Wait there!"

Once more the two men were standing alone outside, cold rain spattering on their hats and shoulders. Defries was containing his anger—a good thing, because when he lost his temper he was a demon, a veritable bull that would not stop until the object of his hatred was pulverized.

Defries asked, "Think we'll ever find out if Cullen sent Meeks after us out on Erie?"

Sutherland shrugged. Cullen had declared Meeks no longer in his service some time before the battle on the lake, but Sutherland still suspected that Meeks and his pirates had been in the pay of Cullen and Company. The matter was confused because Cullen, trying to win the rebels' trust, had been the one who warned Sutherland that Meeks was out prowling the lake.

The Scotsman guessed, however, that the pirate's name would get Cullen's attention. He was right. A moment later, the indignant butler let them in. Aloof and fiercely formal, the man showed them along a corridor fragrant with the scents of food and perfume, to a small, windowless room in the back of the house. They were far from the gay party behind the double glass doors of the front chambers.

This tiny room, heated by a corner open hearth, seemed to be an office for Cullen. Sutherland and Defries sat down in elegant upholstered armchairs and looked about. There were two whale-oil lamps on the desk before them, and another lamp stood on an elegantly carved secretary filled with books and ledgers behind locked glass doors.

Eyeing the ledgers, Defries muttered, "There be something revealing of Cullen's shenanigans amidst them tomes, I'll wager."

Sutherland looked at the ledgers. "Nothing in there would

likely prove any illegal dealings. Cullen's too crafty to write down how he really made his fortune."

The door opened abruptly, and Bradford Cullen was framed in the doorway. Hunched over a walking stick like some fat toad, Cullen wore an old-fashioned gray cassock, buttoned down the front, with large, upturned cuffs and gold buttons. His head was covered with a vast periwig that fell in curls over his sunken chest. Though out of date, his garments were of the richest silk and lace, and even the buckles on his shoes were pure gold.

The two men did not stand up as Cullen shuffled in and closed the door. He made no acknowledgment of their presence, but hobbled across the room to the desk. A repulsive bulk of a man, he was close to eighty, with round, bloodshot eyes that flitted here and there, seldom directly at his visitors.

Sighing ponderously, Cullen sat down in his armchair and laid aside his cane. Lamplight flooded his face, throwing the sallow, flabby cheeks into stark relief, forming shadows on his double chin. Adjusting himself in his chair with difficulty, he wheezed with every breath; a kind of malevolence issued from him, an invisible poison that almost stank.

When he was at last comfortable, he looked across at Sutherland with those piggish, burrowing eyes.

"So you did for old Hugh, eh, Sutherland?" Cullen rasped, and suddenly smiled. It was amazing how he was transformed from an ogre into the image of a kindly, prosperous gentleman.

Cullen chuckled, leaned back in his chair, and gazed at the ceiling. He would have been more pleased if Sutherland's bones had also gone to the bottom of Lake Erie, but he was glad enough to be rid of the troublesome Meeks.

Even though the ex-pirate Meeks had been a valuable asset to Cullen and Company, he had foolishly tried to woo Linda, Cullen's middle-aged daughter and only child. Having sworn Hugh Meeks would never become the heir to his mercantile empire, Cullen had sent him out to kill Jeremy Bently, who was crossing Lake Erie on his way to Detroit— and then had betrayed him. By warning Sutherland about

Meeks, Cullen had ensured that the two would fight, and that at least one would die. Now Meeks was gone. Sutherland would be next.

Cullen lowered his gaze to Sutherland. "Congratulations! That must've been a match! The great Donoway and the dastardly Meeks, hand-to-hand on a deck running with blood!" He stared at Sutherland, mirth in his glittering eyes. "How did you kill him? Must've had to hold his head to the mouth of a cannon...that's what it would take! Considered having it done to him myself, more than once." He laughed, a wheezing, shallow guffaw that made Sutherland furious.

"I came for cannon, Cullen," he said, cutting off the laughter. "General Montgomery has sent for me, and he has instructed me to commandeer whatever supplies are necessary to take the Quebec citadel."

Sutherland passed Montgomery's letter across the polished desk, but Cullen did not pick it up. Instead, thrumming his fat fingers on the desk top, he smacked his lips and considered something.

The Scotsman said, "I'll need ten pieces in all; field guns: one eighteen-pounder, three six-pounders, four howitzers, and two heavy mortars, along with their ammunition and equipment. We can send their officers ahead on horseback, and at Quebec we'll train the additional men necessary to man them. I want them on the road tomorrow morning."

"My, my, Sutherland," Cullen declared, beginning to laugh again. "You don't mean to tell me you'll transport an entire grand battery overland all the way to Quebec with winter already overdue! Hah! You're more of a dreamer than even I thought! Come, come, we haven't the time to gamble our few precious guns on such a scheme. They'll be left and lost to rust, bogged down or snowed under before you've gone fifty miles. Neither Quebec nor our gallant Richard Montgomery will ever benefit from them, nor will Montreal."

"I'll worry about getting them there," Sutherland said quietly. "Just authorize me to take the guns from the city's defenses, and you can get back to your party. I'll be personally responsible for whatever happens."

Cullen became angry, his jowls sucking in as he leaned forward. "You will be responsible? Hardly. It will not be your neck if we lose those guns. Congress will come to me and accuse me of irresponsible behavior if—"

"If Quebec does not fall, there may be no Congress by summer!" Sutherland could not understand why Cullen would balk at supplying such essential weapons.

Cullen shook his head, as though sorry for Sutherland's folly. "Where will you find the men and oxen to take the cannon? How will you pay for them?"

"I'll find them! I'll pay. Just give the authorization."

Cullen darkened. "I cannot do so."

"Montgomery must have them!"

"Then let him order that they be sent! Does your dispatch from him directly order ten guns to Quebec?"

"Montgomery doesn't even realize it can be done! He was a British captain and hasn't seen Americans at war yet. He would not think it possible to make such a march."

"Nor would I."

"It must be done, Cullen, and done now, before the roads are drifted with snow! Before Montgomery's army is too weak to fight, too hungry to besiege the place!"

Cullen's eyes narrowed. "Get Montgomery's direct order, and I'll authorize the cannon. I cannot take the responsibility otherwise."

"I'll take the responsibility!" Sutherland was on his feet now. "Sign the order! In the name of the cause!"

"In the name of the cause I'll not approve such a fool's errand! Go, if you wish, to Quebec, Sutherland, but I'll not strip Montreal of its defenses when so much depends on this city remaining in our hands! Go!"

Sutherland knew that in another month the guns could not be shipped to Quebec until spring, for the snow would be too deep on the river road. Cullen would know this. Even if Sutherland could get a specific written order from Montgomery and return in three weeks, the chances were small that the guns could be transported until the Saint Lawrence thawed and ships could be employed.

As bright music played in the other rooms and laughter drifted into this small, dark chamber, Sutherland stared at Bradford Cullen.

"Why are you doing this, Cullen?" Sutherland whispered. "What will *you* gain?"

Cullen took a slow, shaking breath and jutted out his weak chin. "I told you. It's for the cause." He hissed, "The *glorious* cause!"

Sutherland straightened, and Defries stood up. There was no moving Bradford Cullen. The guns would not be made available without a written order from Montgomery.

Sutherland said, "I don't count you as a true supporter of the cause, Cullen. And when I find out what you're really about, I'll make you pay, just the way you're making our poor lads at Quebec pay!"

Sutherland and Defries swung out of the room, barging past the three big footmen, who were tossed aside, crashing into walls as though they were weaklings. One of them swore and grabbed Sutherland from behind, and in the next instant was heaved bodily through double glass doors. He crashed feet first onto a banquet table set with punch and delicacies that most Montrealers would never in their lives even think about, let alone taste. The crowd shrieked in fright as the other footmen set upon Defries, who, with a shout of joy, cracked their heads together and threw them into the same room. The coiffured, spangled, powdered guests were horrified, the sprawling footmen stunned and cowed.

Sutherland and Defries stood in the doorway, waiting for other takers. Men blustered and complained, but not a sword was drawn. Women gaped and some tittered behind fans to see these two fighters defy a roomful of the most influential gentlemen in French Canada. Sutherland moved back into the hallway, and Defries wished the guests all a happy Christmas.

At the outer door, with his back pressed against the wall and anguish on his rubbery face, was the butler. As Sutherland passed, he ignored the terrified fellow, but Defries could not help himself. He tweaked the man's long nose, and a most satisfying yelp was evoked. The visit had not been such a total failure after all.

Jeremy Bently sojourned with death. In the border regions of dream and reality, he saw his life rush by like a river that he could not stop nor ever again journey upon. His mother and stepfather, his long-dead father back in Massachusetts, all came and went in his consciousness. He saw his father, John Jeremy Bently, slowly dying of war wounds. He saw the whaleboat that took him as an eight-year-old boy out to Detroit in 1763.

There was a handsome man in an immaculate scarlet and white uniform—his uncle, Major Henry Gladwin, brave commander of Fort Detroit, besieged by two thousand Indians under the Ottawa chieftain Pontiac. Long and hungry days, lonely and dark. Months of uncertainty, stalked by danger and death. Jeremy's life passed without his being able to change it, to help fight the enemy, to touch his loved ones, or to speak to them.

There were scenes of captivity, when renegade whites had kidnapped him as a boy, intending to kill him because Owen Sutherland had inflicted defeat upon them. Then Owen rescued him. Owen! The man he admired most and wished to be like. His own father, who had once meant so much, was now only a vague memory, a blood link to the distant past.

There was a woman. Penelope? So beautiful. Auburn hair, with eyes that spoke, that said they loved him. Was it Penelope? Those eyes loved someone, something, but was it he they loved? Sometimes he thought they gazed right past him, to an idea, a shadow, an image that was not real, not him at all. *Penelope? Penelope?* My beloved wife? Was that his own voice shouting her name? Could he hear after all? Was he dead? *Penelope!*

If he was dead, then he wanted to join her, never to lose her again. Penelope? *Penelope!* He could see her!

The lovely face materialized before him, and he steadied himself, afraid he might drive it away. He whispered, *Penelope. Is it you?*

"Jeremy."

*Penelope?*

"Hush now, Dr. Bently," the face said, over and over again. Those loving eyes, those kind and beautiful eyes that spoke to him but seemed unable to see him, that looked at someone, something else.

"Hush now. Rest now, Jeremy. Rest, Dr. Bently. You'll be all right. Rest."

Pain, throbbing, merciless, and insistent came over him. But he knew not from where. He could not stop it. Every inch was aflame.

He had sensation.

He could hear.

He was alive! The knife had struck him in the chest, but he was alive! He hurt too much to be dead.

But where was Penelope?

He called her name and tried to sit up, but was pushed back down by soft, strong hands. There was another face, this one also beautiful, with blond hair and soft, blue eyes.

"Dr. Bently. Dr. Bently, you're dreaming. Wake up, Dr. Bently. Come back to us."

Then there was a flood of warm sunlight. He looked up at a white ceiling. His heart was calmer now. He smelled perfume that reminded him of someone, and he tried to recall . . .

Two faces hovered above him—Annie Ross, not Penelope, and it was this woman's perfume he had recognized. The other was Gwendolyn Hardy. He remembered it all now, and weakly gazed about the room.

This was Valenya! He must be in his parents' chamber, downstairs.

"The house . . ." he murmured. "The house is safe."

Tamano was there, and so was Little Hawk, their tawny faces and dark eyes expressing concern and worry for him.

"And you are alive, brother," said Tamano, grinning. "We have been waiting three days for you to come back to us from the land of the living dead. We rejoice that you have returned at last."

On the other side of the bed, Little Hawk was also grinning. "You will hurt for some time," he said in Ottawa, "but when you heal I'll teach you a few wrestling moves—the sort of tricks meant for fighting grizzly bears and Seneca giants, my brother!" He shook his head. "I thought you knew better than to go chest-to-chest with Manoth! You've been away from here too long, too long."

Jeremy grunted, annoyed, almost forgetting his agony. In a stiff, weak voice, he said, "I'm just out of practice, Little Hawk. Give me a few months back here and I'll—" He raised his head sharply, then winced. He realized his chest was swathed in bandages, and his body was bruised and battered, head to foot. There was a question that had to be answered, though even speaking gave him pain. "Where is he? Did Manoth get away?"

Tamano clucked his tongue and chuckled. "You'll have another chance at him. Manoth lives, though he licks many wounds—even more than you. Your knife was unexpected and took his right eye. But even half blind, a beast like Manoth will not rest until he has drunk your blood."

"Where is he?" Jeremy tried to get up. Then Annie Ross was there, pressing him back down. She scolded the Indians for upsetting Jeremy, though she had not understood what they said.

Jeremy asked her, "What are you doing here? And Gwen? How—"

"We're your houseguests, Dr. Bently," Annie answered with a smile. "In exchange for keeping you alive, we're temporarily sharing your home, and so is Papa. We hope you don't object."

"Object?" Jeremy grunted. "Why, no . . . But have you both tended me through—three days? Has so much time gone by?"

In English, Tamano said, "These two women have nursed you back from the dead. I thought you'd been rubbed out on that beach, and that we'd all die there, fighting those Senecas."

Little Hawk added, in his less proficient English: "Your friend, Weston, come quick with boat of lobsterbacks, long knives and all. They stop fight before start. But I no think we die if Weston not come. Maybe we eat up 'em Seneca."

Tamano clucked again, eyeing the audacious Little Hawk,

not so sure they could have beaten so many Senecas. Then he watched as Gwen brought a tin bowl of hot water and some clean bandages to the bedside. "This squaw is sorceress, I'm thinking; no one else in the fort could have saved your life, little brother."

Gwen blushed and smiled faintly. Annie said, "Gwendolyn has always been a healer, Dr. Bently." Gwen murmured that she should not speak too much, but Annie refused to be stilled: "Gwen has been a nurse ever since I've known her, beginning with sick dogs and injured birds, then relatives, and then the sick and wounded folk at the Grey Sisters hospital down in Montreal."

Admiringly, Annie looked at her cousin. Gwen simply said Jeremy's bandages needed changing and began to pull back his blankets. Suddenly Jeremy uttered a cry of dismay and pulled the blankets back up. Gwen flushed, hand to her mouth.

"Oh, Dr. Bently, I am sorry! I'd forgotten you're conscious now! I mean . . . I am sorry! Forgive my indiscretion, but . . . but you have a wound on your thigh—"

"Woman!" Jeremy gasped. "Have you no pride? How . . . how can you brazenly—"

Tamano touched Jeremy's arm. In English, he said, "My brother, without her you would be a dead man. If it were a squaw of my people tending you, would you be so modest?"

Jeremy was angry, though feeble. "Well . . . But Indian women are accustomed to . . . to nudity, and to tending wounded men."

Gwen was trembling, now with resentment. "Dr. Bently, I was simply doing what had to be done! Yes, I do have pride. No, I am not a brazen woman. Though it may seem immodest for a woman to nurse a man, this has been, and continues to be, a dire circumstance! I do not care to watch you die!" She stormed to the door, then turned to declare, "And I've seen enough blood to know that dying men do not care whether they are covered or not!"

Gwen barged out of the room, leaving the others silent. Annie came to Jeremy's side, her lovely face wistful as she gazed at the empty doorway. Somewhat absently, she said, "My dear cousin worked for five days and nights, without rest, to save loyalist men who were wounded in the battle at Longueuil last month." She looked at Jeremy. "She saved many lives, and labored until she collapsed and was almost lost herself. Some were brought in half naked, and she helped them and was not ashamed; and she was not accused of— Gwen had men die in her arms, friends she knew well . . . very well."

Annie's voice caught. "Gwen Hardy has read as many books on medicine as any American, save perhaps for you and a few other fortunate men who have been trained abroad. Don't ever forget, Dr. Bently, that she has vast experience treating human beings! Her training comes from bloody hands, tears, and bone-weary exhaustion, not from fine colleges with musty books, high honors, and grave-robbed cadavers!"

Jeremy grumbled some sort of lame apology, but Annie would not let him finish. "Were you the healer Gwen is, you'd be a wonderful doctor, sir! But before you'll ever recover to become such, you'll have to swallow your pride and let her tend your wounds. The alternative is to ask the army surgeon, that son of an apprentice butcher, to come across and chop you up instead!"

Annie, too, angrily left the room. Then, as Jeremy and the Indians glanced at one another, she stuck her head back in and declared, "Or get a squaw to tend you, if they're so much better at it than we are!"

Annie could not keep her tears from flowing. "My cousin and I are very much relieved you're alive, Dr. Bently! But if it's your pleasure, we'll be leaving this house forthwith! Good day, sir!"

As Annie vanished, a weighty gloom descended upon the three men. Jeremy felt the awful ache of his body. Nauseated and dizzy, he regretted having treated the women so rudely. Yet female nurses for men were simply not correct, not . . . proper.

Tamano and Little Hawk looked at each other, and the Chippewa said in English, "Squaws don't talk like that to our warriors." Then he grinned and glanced at Little Hawk. "You want us to fetch the sawbones from fort? Old Doc Sennet? He'll fix you, right quick."

With his forefinger Tamano made a line across the bandage on Jeremy's chest.

"Cut here, maybe little higher...aye, that be the right place to amputate. Sawbones'll think you be better off without bottom half, anyway."

Little Hawk screwed up his face, squinting, pouting, the way he had seen the grizzled, rheumy Lieutenant Lawrence Sennet look over a patient. "You betcha, Jeremy—" He hiccupped and swayed a bit. "You feel no pain after we chop a little here...take off a little there!"

"Shut up," Jeremy croaked. He smiled, knowing that what these two wags said was all too true. According to military surgeons like Sennet, the best treatment for wounds was prompt amputation. The results were often fatal.

"I'd rather have Mawak work on me." Jeremy looked at the clean bandages, skillfully laid on and well bound. Nearby, on a table, bowls and towels, medicaments and herbal concoctions stood neatly arrayed. This woman clearly knew her business. Jeremy was astonished to see a wooden medicine chest on the floor, with mortar and pestle, iron scales, splints, sponges, an inoculating syringe, and curved needles.

Little Hawk marked Jeremy's scrutiny and again chuckled. "She's a sorceress," he said. "She stitched you up like my woman makes a moccasin! That Seneca blade stuck in you right there—" He pointed to the sternum bone. "A little lower and the knife would have pierced your heart."

"Who drew it out?" Jeremy asked, aware now of that particularly painful spot on his body.

Little Hawk said, "Lady with the blond hair." He nodded with admiration. "She's good. You're lucky. I tell her you want her to stay."

Richard Weston came that afternoon and told Jeremy what had happened. He explained that Gwen and Annie had heard from Simon Clancy of trouble brewing at Valenya and had sailed across in a whaleboat with Clancy and Dawson Merriwether. The women feared there would be injured men who would require tending. They had reached the scene on the heels of the Redcoats, he said, and Gwen had even tried to aid Manoth, who was badly cut up. The angry Senecas, however, took their wounded leader away in a canoe, paddling back to their encampment south of the fort, near the Potawatomie village.

Jeremy asked whether any legal redress would be taken against the Senecas, but Weston had no firm answer, and Jeremy was in no mood to press the point. Weston fell silent for a while. He had pulled up a chair and sat in bright sunlight next to the bed, black tricorne in his hands. Finally Weston said, "Manoth is a favorite of Lieutenant Governor Hamilton, my lad. Watch your step with that redskin, because Hamilton wants the Indians ready for a campaign if the rebels need chastising."

Once more Jeremy became enraged at the notion of using Indian raiders against Whig frontiersmen. He was too weak, however, to do more than say that Weston should not talk so lightly of such things. "You have no comprehension of the horrors that would be unleashed on settlers—loyal or rebel. Indians won't care what whites they attack when their blood is up."

Again their conversation ended on unfriendly terms, and Weston departed in a huff. Later, as Jeremy lay there in the sunshine, he heard Gwen call to him from outside the door, asking whether he would like supper. She had not been to see him since their argument.

"Please come in, Mistress Hardy," Jeremy said weakly. When she appeared, wearing a linen apron over a plain white gown that came to the floor, he looked closely at her. Gwen's hair was pinned up and covered by a small bonnet of drab linen. She seemed still troubled by his roughness earlier that day, but her eyes were full of resolve, as though she were braced for another confrontation.

Jeremy lifted a hand and said, "Forgive me for my . . . my somewhat old-fashioned ways, mistress."

Gwen focused on him, curious and surprised at what he said.

He went on, letting his hand drop and staring at the ceiling. "Yes, I know that in Britain some women nurses are assisting physicians more and more often . . . and I realize that no army could muster a complement of men if it were not for the women among the soldiers' followers who tend the ill and wounded."

He looked at her again, and she met his gaze squarely. "But I've never myself . . . been a patient of a young female nurse. You see?" He smiled wistfully, and so did she, dropping her eyes to look at her hands, which were clasped at her waist. "You've done very well for me, mistress. I . . . any physician could have done no better under these circumstances."

She told him, "An acquaintance of our family is a physician in Montreal—an elderly French gentleman named Devalier—"

Jeremy exclaimed that Dr. Michel Devalier was a close friend of his own family and was, furthermore, a minor partner in the Frontier Company.

"I know that, Dr. Bently. I've heard much about your family and the Frontier Company from the dear Devaliers; in the time I lived in Montreal—about two years—I visited them often, and I worked with the doctor to help the poor French folk who could not afford to pay an English or American physician. . . ."

Approaching the table where the medicines and bandages lay, Gwen said she was from north of New York Town. All her life she had indulged a passion for medicine and science, though she could not receive formal education in these things. She read everything she could—usually in secret—and had applied her knowledge by caring for farm animals and pets. "My mother and father were against booklearning for a woman, and since we were quite wealthy, they thought it fitting that I marry well, bear children, and so on."

"You could do worse . . . though I can understand your ambitions, because my wife had some radical notions of the same kind, and I thought those notions admirable." He said Penelope had been determined to establish a school and run it herself, even though such a profession for an upper-class woman would have been no less than scandalous. "Yet a woman nurse caring for men is perhaps even more scandalous—even if she's as good as you are."

Gwen's eyes caught fire again, though she refrained from voicing any emotion. Jeremy guessed she was disappointed that he—a doctor—would say such a thing.

Controlling herself, Gwen said plainly, "Dr. Devalier and the good French people of Montreal did not think it a scandal for a woman nurse to be something more than a midwife!" She said with some disdain, "You're correct in one thing, however: You *are* old-fashioned. Modern Edinburgh education or no!"

She began to turn away, but Jeremy used all his strength to reach out and take her wrist in a gentle grasp. She could have drawn away easily, but did not.

"You are indeed a very good nurse," he said, looking directly at her. He smiled faintly. "Forgive my stodginess and conservative ways. As I've lain here this afternoon, I've considered something at length: Perhaps we can work together to establish a real hospital for the folk out here—"

Gwen swayed and clutched his hand, excitement pouring out as she exclaimed that there was nothing in the world she would rather do.

"That's the very reason I left New York!" she gasped. "No one there ever would permit me such a thing, though heaven knows they need a hospital so desperately! I was happy in Montreal, and sad to be forced to leave, but now . . . now I'm blessed again! Oh, Dr. Bently—"

"But first, what about your parents?" he asked, calming her. "Will they come storming out here, musket in hand, to blow the head off the man who offered you such a scandalous life's calling? Or what about Cole Ross?"

"Uncle Cole respects my ambitions," Gwen said slowly, quietly. "My parents are dead. They died paupers five years ago, both succumbing to the cholera, which raged through a . . . a debtor's prison." She caught a breath and explained painfully that her father had been evicted from his estate by a powerful local patroon in the Hudson Valley. The patroon ruthlessly and skillfully ruined her father by underselling crops at a loss, by calling in a huge debt, and by bribing local judges and tax collectors to do all they could to harry and discredit the Hardy name.

"That same patroon now owns our estate, and my parents died in shame and . . . and in agony!" Jeremy held her hand to comfort her. She whispered, "I saw them both so very, very ill, but somehow I survived. Afterward I was released to the custody of Uncle Cole." She took a long, shaking breath. "Never again will I allow anyone to suffer so without helping them—even if my behavior is deemed unladylike, improper, or scandalous!"

Jeremy was impressed. With one hand Gwen awkwardly wiped away tears.

"Forgive me, Dr. Bently," she whispered, and they held hands a moment longer. "I'm a bit sleepy."

Just then the door opened and Annie Ross came in, stopping short, gazing at their hands. The couple parted self-consciously.

Looking unsurely from Gwen to Jeremy, Annie smiled and said, "There's no cure like . . . affection, and—"

"Stop that, Annie!" Gwen interrupted, smiling at her cousin's teasing. "Dr. Bently was merely, ah—"

Jeremy agonizingly turned onto his side and said, "Sealing a bargain! I've just engaged Mistress Hardy as my nurse for the hospital I mean to start in the settlement."

"Well," Annie replied, a knowing look on her face. "That's cozy, then. You can continue to seal that bargain, and I'll be about my business."

Before she could leave, Jeremy said, "Would you consider joining us, Mistress Ross? We'll have plenty to do."

Annie paused at the door and said, "Thank you, Doctor. But I'm no nurse—it's Gwen who's in command of such things." She gave Jeremy a warm, engaging smile and added, "I'll be married to a good, stalwart gentleman before too long, for that's my own life's goal. With the right husband, I'll have my hands more than full making a family. No bandages for me. No, I'm too upset by the sight of blood, Dr. Bently—unlike Gwen, who has an iron stomach."

It was agreed that the Rosses and Gwen should live at Valenya for the winter, because accommodations in the crowded fort were impossibly expensive. Valenya, Jeremy said, would be better off with a woman's hand, and while they were living there, Cole Ross could get established with Dawson Merriwether. It was the least Jeremy could do for them. Besides, he liked their company very much.

## chapter 6

## BENEDICT ARNOLD

Several days and nights of hard riding down the Saint Lawrence river road passed quickly, with few words being shared between Owen Sutherland and Peter Defries. Their failure to acquire cannon left both men moody and thoughtful, wondering how Quebec would be taken.

After having arranged for wagonloads of military provisions to follow as promptly as possible, they had left the city before dark and set out northward alone. No other rebel troops were in sight; there were too few men in Montreal for any to be spared to reinforce Montgomery. The riders got a cool reception from French *habitants* living in the endless string of whitewashed stone cottages along the frozen edge of the river. The Canadians had no love for the invaders who had disrupted their peaceful lives.

On New Year's Eve a blizzard struck. The travelers huddled in an old barn, while the wind blew and howled, whirling snow through the cracks in the walls.

Bedded down in the straw, with the smell of cows and horses strong and heady, they knew they would have to leave their mounts and continue their journey on snowshoes the next day. Montgomery might have to attack immediately, lest more snow hamper his army's movements, and

Sutherland and Defries wanted to be there when the battle began. Sutherland was acquainted with a few leading men among the civilian loyalists defending the city, and he hoped they might be persuaded to make terms and surrender rather than allow a prolonged siege.

As they lay half asleep in the straw, Sutherland wished Defries a happy New Year.

Defries returned the greeting, his blanket over his face. His voice was muffled as he said, "This here war business can be awful tedious, Owen. I think I'd be better off managin' a privateer down in the tropics, drinkin' papaya gin—what's supposed to be a cure for old age and don't thicken the thinkin' while you're countin' captured gold! We could outfit a good ship, maybe even buy a whole island down there near them Spanish colonies. We'd only work one or two days a month to pluck a ripe Indiaman or a fat supply ship . . . You listenin'?"

"Aye, laddie," Sutherland said sleepily. "After we take Quebec, you and I'll capture Havana itself if we have a day or two to spare, or maybe invade the Floridas. Make a New Year's resolution: No more campaigning in the snow. Only in sunny weather. Maybe we should take Gibraltar this summer."

Defries made a sound of agreement. "Do them Spaniard locals drink papaya gin? No, no, they couldn't, otherwise they'd never have lost the Rock to the British. I've heard papaya gin improves the senses if you drink it quick enough." He thought a moment, then yawned and turned over. "I'd rather go for a nice Caribbean island, where they're sure to have plenty of papaya gin." Almost falling asleep, he mumbled, "If I got to lie around takin' the sun between pluckin' Indiamen . . . then . . . no point not drinkin' . . . papaya gin to . . . sharpen the . . . senses." He began to snore, and outside the wind whistled, laying a deep blanket of white upon the road to Quebec.

The next day they marched onward on snowshoes, for the snow was drifted too deep for horses. They paid the owner of the barn well to feed and care for their mounts until they could pick them up again. Then they pressed ahead, now just a day from Quebec City.

Everywhere were signs of war. Broken-down carts littered the roadside, half-covered in snow, abandoned by loyalist refugees who had fled to Quebec. To Sutherland and Defries, however, the most significant proof of the war was the unwillingness of normally friendly French residents even to open their doors to them. It was apparent the *habitants* had experienced much friction with the invading rebels, who were so hungry and poor. As the two friends came to cottages, doors often were kept locked, and several times tense men and boys came to windows with muskets at the ready.

When they were only a few hours from Quebec, the sun came out, brightening the narrow, snow-covered road, which was lined by small evergreens on both sides. Soon they saw a crowd of about forty ragged men trudging toward them—Congress troops.

As they drew closer, Sutherland did not like what he saw. These were downcast, beaten men. Most of them were plodding along wearily, thigh-deep in the blowing snow. A few were crammed onto a lumbering sleigh pulled by a gaunt ox. Some of them had feet and legs swathed in rags, having worn out their shoes. Others wore blankets wrapped about their hunched shoulders, and every hat was battered and torn. Many of the marching men had nothing left of their breeches, and with every step their blankets opened to reveal bare legs.

"Is this our army?" Defries muttered, though not loud enough for the dejected men to hear him. "I know some of them! They're New Englanders, Connecticut men! There's Bill Poole hisself! Hi, Billy Poole!"

Defries ran to a short, black-bearded fellow tramping alongside the sleigh, which was filled with the worst of the ill and wounded. Bill Poole, blacksmith by trade, had lived for a time at Detroit and had been with Sutherland and Defries during the triumphant Montreal campaign. Poole's dark eyes gleamed at the welcome sight of old friends.

"What in the name of Jehovah hit you?" Defries exclaimed, looking at the threadbare blanket cast over the man's broad shoulders.

Poole stared at them through defiant but fatigued eyes, and Sutherland was dismayed to see a man who had been so burly look like a living skeleton. The blacksmith squinted, the harsh glare of sunlight off the snow dazzling him as he moved aside to let the men shuffle past.

"We got licked," Poole croaked. A few of the soldiers asked whether there was food in Montreal. "Ask the lieutenant to stop us awhile," Poole said, "and I'll tell the sorry tale; but you best give him a good yell, for he's half deaf from old age."

Sutherland shouted to the gray-haired lieutenant in charge of the miserable column, apparently all ill or wounded. The man had a dirty bandage wrapped around his head and over one eye, and he walked with the aid of a forked stick for a crutch.

"We've got grub to boil up for soup, and some rum to pass around—it won't go far, but it'll make your day's journey easier."

A few of the suffering men muttered in accord, and the wan, pitiful lieutenant mumbled a thanks. Sutherland removed his heavy knapsack and dug out dried beef, barley, and carrots. Defries passed around a large jug of rum as the men moved languidly to a grove of evergreens, where the snow was not so deep nor the wind so strong.

Sutherland and Defries sat amid the trees with Bill Poole, who seemed astonishingly helpless. Poole had a decent frock coat and good shoes, but his breeches were worn out, showing blood-encrusted bandages on one thigh. He had burns on his legs and hands, and a nasty reddish scar marked his left cheek, where lead had apparently grazed it.

Poole hardly spoke at first, giving his attention to black bread and dried beef, then biting into a half-frozen lemon. Though he tried to restrain himself, he devoured the lemon hurriedly, for he was famished.

The other soldiers sat drinking rum in bright sunshine, out of the wind. The strongest ones lit bonfires from the dismantled fence rails of some farmer's field. A man tending an ugly arm wound, washing it with snow, struck up a song of home, and a few others joined in, but most could only huddle near the fires for warmth and hungrily watch snow-melt boil in a great iron pot. Beef was broken up and tossed in, as were carrots, barley, and a handful of dried peas someone had hoarded.

Sutherland handed his friend a silver flask of Scotch whiskey and began the conversation carefully. "When's the last time you ate, Bill?"

Poole swallowed some whiskey and closed his eyes as the heat of it lit him within. "Two days, mebbe three, afore the attack. Hard to recall time. I got in the way of some iron...me and the general...but I was lucky, somehow." He sniffed and offered to return Sutherland's flask.

The Scotsman motioned for him to drink again. "The attack? On the citadel? What about General Montgomery?"

"He's dead." Poole gazed at the ground.

Defries cursed under his breath, got up and stamped away, then came back and sat down again.

Sutherland felt a tremendous hurt, and his heart was wrenched that as fine an officer and man as Richard Montgomery had been killed. He knew now that Quebec's citadel had held out, for otherwise these invalids would be housed there instead of journeying through snow to Montreal. Poole did not look up. He stared at bright white snow while his friends absorbed the disastrous news.

The three of them sat silent, listening to the crackle of the fires and to the soft, homesick song of soldiers.

Poole shivered as he began the story: "I was at Mont-gomery's side on New Year's Eve...in a whirling, blinding snow. We began to storm the lower town, advancing toward the Tory barricades. Montgomery hisself tore 'em down with his bare hands, like a common soldier! Owen, how we loved that man!" Poole set his jaw. "We was almost there, and their sentries was on the run, when somebody on their side touched off a cannon. I found out later the Tory sentries just let fly with grape shot, then quick aban-doned the gun. But that one shot was enough to blow me down and kill poor Montgomery and his best officers."

He drank again, shivering, though he was no longer cold. "I was already pretty sick. I'd had fevers for days afore the attack, and mebbe I shoulda been laid up. But a lot of the boys was the same way, and they all went in to fight!"

Poole's eyes became distant, shining with an inner light. "You shoulda seen 'em attack! Brave boys! Morgan's Virginian riflemen! Lamb's Yorkers! Massachusetts men, even some French Canadians! Our own Connecticut boys! All fightin' side by side . . . but it was a lost cause."

Slowly, calmly, Poole said they had fought a garrison of loyalist volunteers twice their number, in a citadel mounted with a hundred and fifty cannon. At the mention of cannon, Sutherland felt fury rise. Even ten of the right guns could blow a hole in the Quebec defenses; and with good officers, determined rebels could methodically reduce the city and break the spirit of the defenders—mainly French *habitants* and Indians, many unsure whom to support in this civil war.

Poole drank again, trying not to quake.

"When that gun went off, I was stunned—we were that close to it. They carried me to a house for safety, and the fight went on. But then the houses started burning, and no one could see for the smoke and confusion. The plan fell apart without Montgomery. Nobody knew what to do; even Colonel Arnold couldn't keep things straight, 'cause he got shot in the leg hisself. He's staying with the troops up there, thank God. Arnold's the man can take that city, if anyone can!"

The rebel army was cut to half, Poole said—maybe fifty dead and nearly four hundred taken prisoner. Still Colonel Benedict Arnold refused to give up and withdraw.

Defries said, "We're makin' for Quebec, Bill. Does Arnold mean to wait for reinforcements and finish the job?"

"He does that. I wanted to stay, but he ordered the invalids out—there ain't enough food or medicines to keep 'em alive. We already lost three lads since we left the city, and we won't all get down to Montreal. Even if we eat the ox, bones and all."

Poole was regaining some strength, but he swayed in his seat, in pain and exhausted.

Then he looked at Sutherland and said, "You best keep

some whiskey with you, Owen. You'll need it as long as
you're there. If you can buy or borrow grub from Frenchies
along the way, best do it now, 'cause them Frenchies what
lives around the city don't love us none, nor our Continental
currency, and won't part with a crumb unless it's took at
the point of a bayonet."

These wounded troops had not a farthing of British currency among them, so they were unable to buy food. Sutherland took a hundred pounds sterling from his wallet. Poole
was astonished and shaken by the sight of so much cash
money.

"Set yourself up in Montreal and get fit again," Sutherland said. "By the way, when is your enlistment up?"

"It's already ended. Most of these boys are in the same
fix," he said. "They want to go home but can't—unless
they walk and don't need to eat for a month or two."

Sutherland said, "With this cash, buy up as much Continental money as you can up at Montreal—it's worthless
there, as far as the merchants are concerned—and use some
of this sterling to get men medical care, walking clothes,
and food. Then give each of them a fistful of continentals
to get them through New York Province, where folk'll accept it. As for yourself—"

"I'm not going home," Poole said, hope in his eyes. "If
you're back with us again, Owen, I'll be honored to serve
with you, soon as I can get my strength up! God bless you,
Owen!"

They shook hands, and Sutherland was embarrassed
when Poole almost began to weep. After six hard months
of brutal campaigning in miserable weather, having little to
eat, wear, or shoot with, Poole was like so many other
Congress troops—weary, ill, and disillusioned. He had expected a quick victory, and at first that victory had been
achieved, step by step. Now the course of the war had
changed drastically, with the rebels' defeat at Quebec and
the loss of their best field officer.

"Forgive me," Poole said, recovering, but Sutherland
made no reply, for he had seen much of war, of suffering,
and of strong men in tears. "I'll not reenlist until you return

to Montreal, because I won't be ordered about by some fool officer. Maybe we can organize another cannon crew like we had against the forts on the Richelieu."

Sutherland recalled teaching Poole how to fire a mortar. Heavy guns had been critical in the capture of two key British forts to the south on the Richelieu River, opening the way for the fall of Montreal.

Defries told Poole, "We wanted to bring heavy guns to Quebec, but they weren't to be had in Montreal."

Sutherland added, "If we have to retreat to Montreal from Quebec, Bill, we'll need more than a cannon crew to fight off a British invasion. Our few guns would be useless; the British'll come upriver in ships with bigger guns than we'll ever have. It's a ranger company we'll organize."

Poole and Defries listened intently as Sutherland explained.

"Our army will need men who can strike the British supply lines and who can beat the loyalist Indians at their own game. Get well, Bill, and be ready for some woodsman's training. But I still hope we'll take Quebec; if we do, the British'll never get their ships upriver to Montreal. We'll blow them out of the water with the citadel's cannon!"

Already Poole was heartened, and when someone shouted that the meal was ready, he got eagerly to his feet.

"Before you go," Defries said, reaching into his knapsack, "put these on." He handed Poole a pair of woolen breeches, and the Connecticut blacksmith looked at them with amazement and longing, then shook his head and gave them back.

"I'll be down in Montreal in a few days, where I can buy a pair of warm breeches. But you'll be camped out with the army under the walls of Quebec." His face looked pinched as he murmured, "It's awful cold there, Peter. Awful cold."

It snowed again that night, and in the morning the river road lay white and silent as Sutherland and Defries approached the Quebec suburb called Saint Foy. They had met a few small rebel detachments guarding the road; each time they were stopped, challenged, and questioned at length. Thus it took an extra four hours to reach the shoreline called Wolfe's Cove and the trail leading up to the Plains of Abraham, where the main body of the rebel army was said to be lodged.

They climbed a long path up a steep bluff. Higher and higher they went, challenged twice more by scarecrows of Pennsylvania sentries. At the crest of the trail, the land rolled away into snow-covered fields dotted with farmhouses painted as white as the snow, with steep, thatched roofs. Somewhere ahead was the long fortress wall, they were told, and over in the nearest cluster of houses Benedict Arnold had his headquarters.

Sutherland and Defries trudged through the snow, and the horizon became a thin, dark line, interrupted here and there by some bulky irregularity. Before long they realized it was the citadel wall, and the irregularities were bastions made of gray blocks of stone, as grim and dreary as the steely sky overhead.

They approached a clutch of houses whose rising smoke gathered overhead in a blue cloud like a ghost. When they were sixty yards away, Defries grabbed Sutherland's arm and swung the rifle off his own shoulder.

"Britishers!" he gasped, and brought his weapon to bear on a dozen men marching toward them. These soldiers wore British army blanket coats of crisp white wool, and their hats were regular army issue. "Must be a counterattack!"

Sutherland took a step back and loaded his rifle. Biting the end off a paper cartridge, he poured the powder down the barrel, following with the bullet, wrapped in a leather patch to ensure its fit. Watching the soldiers approach, he realized they were not behaving quite right. Sutherland shook his head slowly.

"Not British troops, laddie. They're not in formation. See how they slouch . . . and look at those long rifles . . . and no bayonets."

Indeed, these men were rebels on patrol, but fitted out with captured British gear, save for their Pennsylvania rifles and worn-out breeches and shoes. To Sutherland's surprise, he recognized the officer in command.

Matthew Smith of Carlisle, Pennsylvania, was a dark,

tall, whiplike man, lean and wiry, with deep-set eyes that glittered coldly as they stared at Sutherland. Sutherland had met Smith during a tense time in 1763, when border settlers had threatened to march on Philadelphia because the city fathers were doing nothing to protect the outlying settlements against Indians. Sutherland had assisted Benjamin Franklin in facing down Smith and his tough fighting men, getting them to withdraw from Philadelphia. Now the two men greeted each other curtly, and Sutherland said he was looking for Arnold's headquarters.

Smith paused a moment and thought, while his haggard men looked on, leaning on their rifles.

"I figured you'd be fighting for the Injuns these days, Sutherland," he said. "Plenty of Injuns in them walls with Governor Carleton. Thought a fella with your sympathies for redskins might be with 'em, seein' as how you're a Britisher yourself. What's your business here?"

The Pennsylvanians were now insolently gathering around Sutherland and Defries. Though none of them made a move, they sensed Matthew Smith's suspicion. Sutherland and Defries were calm but prepared for whatever might happen.

Angry grumbles arose from Smith's men; dozens of other ragged soldiers, as if sensing a fight, appeared out of cabins and lean-tos that moments before had stood silent. A noisy crowd pressed around Sutherland and Smith. Suddenly there came a shout.

"Stand back, there! Stand back, or I'll arrest every one of you! Stand back!"

Hobbling down the road, wading through the snow with the aid of a crutch, was a swarthy, broad-shouldered man in a dark blue frock coat and hat. Behind him came four officers with swords and pistols drawn and a couple of privates carrying muskets. The leader was agile, despite a severe injury to his left leg. Sutherland immediately recognized this furious man with the enormous blue eyes and broad, large-featured face. Colonel Benedict Arnold swore quite inventively and damned them all for ignorant wastrels who should spill the blood of Britishers rather than of each other.

"Captain Smith, your orders were to patrol the cove, were they not?" Smith stiffened, obviously respectful as Arnold bellowed: "Are these men prisoners? Why, it's you, Mr. Sutherland!" He hopped to the Scotsman, whom he had met in Albany last year, and gripped his hand enthusiastically. "You got here fast! But where are the supplies General Montgomery asked for?"

"On the way, Colonel," Sutherland replied. "We didn't want to wait while the supplies were being assembled. I had hoped that what I carry on my person would help in the meantime." Sutherland touched his breast, where hundreds of pounds sterling were kept in a wallet. Arnold immediately understood, exclaiming in excitement.

Sutherland looked at Matthew Smith, who was boiling, ready to fight him even if it meant arrest. But the anger had gone out of Sutherland, for his mind was on the army and its desperate needs. It would do no good to make enemies within the rebel ranks. Soberly, he spoke to Smith.

"Captain, I for one am willing to forget our past differences. We're on the same side now." He stuck out his hand.

Defries, as raring to fight as anyone, was astonished. He was even more amazed when Smith's wrath abruptly vanished and the man grasped Sutherland's hand.

Smith said, "For the good of the cause, sir, I, too, will forget our differences, and would be honored if you forgive what was said in the heat of rage."

Arnold beamed to see these two leaders reconciled for the sake of rebellion. It was a remarkable example to the eighty or ninety soldiers—Yorkers, New Englanders, Pennsylvanians, Virginians, and even Canadians—who had collected to watch yet another brawl.

To the crowd, Arnold cried, "Look well on this, men, and see what must be done between us if we're to defeat the enemy!" To Sutherland and Smith he said quietly, "With such gestures as that handshake you'll do more to unite this army than even the capture of Governor Carleton himself."

The colonel dismissed the men, then asked Sutherland and Defries to come to headquarters before the doctor ordered him back to the hospital. Smith went on with his patrol, and as the Pennsylvanians passed, Defries nodded grudgingly at them. He could not bring himself to shake hands—not quite yet; he had to think about it for a while.

Seen from Arnold's quarters, the walls of Quebec's citadel half a mile off were so high that the tallest buildings within were hidden; not even the church spires could be seen. The wall had a deep stone trench before it and glistened with a thick sheen of ice. At intervals, the muzzles of heavy cannon stuck out through gunports.

Sutherland, Defries, and Arnold dined and talked together that afternoon, sitting at a thick plank table, eating roast beef and drinking French wine. The army was not yet completely out of food; a few cattle could still be found. The problem was that the French were steadily herding their livestock and fowl out of the district to avoid selling them for American continentals. If the British defeated the rebels, Continental dollars would be even more worthless than now—if that was possible.

Arnold sat sideways at the table, his wounded left leg bound from thigh to ankle and resting on a chair. A bullet had ricocheted, a fragment of it entering near the knee and running lengthwise down to the ankle, where it had been removed by surgery. Arnold made light of the wound and talked about the siege.

"We've eaten up most of the stock belonging to loyalists, and what we could compel the *habitants* to sell us will last another few weeks; but in April, when the campaign heats up again, we'll have the devil's own time finding food unless we have hard cash in British sterling."

Sutherland put down his mug of wine, reached inside his shirt, took out the wallet, and placed it before the colonel. "Nine hundred pounds sterling, sir. At your disposal. And there's more available in Montreal."

Arnold's face grew even more florid than usual as he stared at the fat leather wallet. "By heaven, Mr. Sutherland, you've come in the nick of time!" Calling a young officer from the next room, Arnold rapidly detailed the purchase and distribution of food, explaining which regiments should have what, where it ought to be stored, and by whom guarded.

Then he gave the man the wallet for safekeeping, and said to Sutherland, "Even a Scotch fur trader won't get a better bargain than a New Haven merchant sailor when it comes to purchasing something with hard cash!"

Arnold laughed and slapped the table loudly, causing the mugs to jump, and giving Peter Defries another good reason to like him. Any man with both Arnold's buoyant personality and his reputation for brilliance and bravery under fire was worthy of Defries's respect. A hard case like Matthew Smith might be good to have along in a fight, but a commander with Arnold's courage and genius, who was admired and obeyed by his men, was someone Defries would be happy even to get drunk with. Arnold might have read Peter's mind, for he called for some potent French cider.

While Defries set about drinking cider, Sutherland told Colonel Arnold how Cullen had refused to part with Montreal's cannon. The officer shook his head in resignation, saying that influential rebel civilians often overrode military needs for the sake of their own self-interest.

"At least Congress has promised to send us every man they can scrape up," Arnold said. "Many fellows will enlist again, and with New York, New England, New Jersey, and Pennsylvania regiments already being raised to join us, we'll squeeze Quebec like a grape by May!" He poured them all another mug of the hard cider.

The Scotsman said, "Who'll command here, sir? Down in the colonies there's a score of influential Whigs parading about in general's uniforms and hungry to take Montgomery's place."

"Hang all that!" Arnold said, clicking his mug with Defries's and swiftly downing the contents, to the Dutchman's surprise. "Whoever commands, with reinforcements and with your ability to feed and equip us, we'll take this pile of rock by spring! I'll be here, no matter who comes to take charge. If he's half the soldier Montgomery was, we'll send the British lion back home with his tail between his legs, or maybe with no tail at all!"

Defries drained his own mug and thought Arnold's remark very funny. Pouring himself and Arnold a mug of cider even deeper than before, he giggled that Mrs. British Lion would not like that at all. He hiccupped and toasted with Arnold to the arrival of a new rebel general.

Sutherland watched them guzzle, and felt it was a serious toast. He joined in, for good luck. A bad general would be a disaster, because there wouldn't be enough rebel supplies and men to permit mistakes or losses. He poured them all another mug, this time to toast with Defries to Colonel Arnold's incredible forced march across the wilderness of Maine.

Arnold poured more cider and toasted their own success in acquiring equipment and supplies at Montreal. They found a few more things to toast before Sutherland knew he had reached his limit. He got up, head full of cotton but still clear enough to stand at the window and see the ugly wall of the citadel, less than a cannon shot away. Rebels could never capture it by direct storm. But if they had to take it with only a small force, skillfully conducting a prolonged siege to starve the loyalists out, then Benedict Arnold was the man to do it.

He wished Arnold might be named overall commander of the Congress troops here, but knew that the man was too brazen, too quick to denounce fools and rascals, some of whom had influence with Whig leaders. Arnold would never be given the post, so Sutherland hoped the new man would be up to its trying demands. A British armada would surely be sent here in three months, and it would take a leader as good as Benedict Arnold to beat them back.

He turned from the window to see Arnold and Defries open another jug of cider. They were talking warmly about merchant ships, and Defries was saying thickly he wanted to be a privateer in the sunny Caribbean. Arnold thought that a fitting profession for a seafaring New Englander, but Dutch Yorkers, he said, were better at getting fat by buying up privateer prizes and selling them to landlubbers in New York Town or to wealthy Pennsylvanians.

Defries said it was not only the profit he wanted, but he longed to taste papaya gin, said to be the sweetest intoxicant since love. Arnold vowed that cider was as good as any intoxicant, and to prove it poured another mug for each of them, then another. Within the hour, Arnold won his case.

Defries was fast asleep, his head on the tabletop, and the colonel got up, limbering his arms and good leg. He joined Sutherland outside, thinking about Quebec and about his family, who would be in danger if the British still held the citadel when the war fleet arrived that spring.

"Jolly fellow," Arnold said of Defries, clearing his throat and taking deep breaths of icy air. "Stubborn, though! Wouldn't admit he could get drunk on Canadian cider. Said he'd only be able to get drunk on something called papaya gin! Wonder what that is."

Sutherland grinned, amazed that Arnold was as alert and active as ever. "He still won't admit he was drunk, even when he wakes."

Arnold chuckled. "That's the sort of men we need up here—men who don't know when they're beaten. Wars are won by men like that, and this brave little army's full of 'em!" He glared at Quebec's walls, and his cheerful visage became a scowl. "Too bad there's a few of the same sort in there. Americans can be like that—too brassy to know when they should give up. If the British fight the rebellion by using loyalist Americans, we'll have our work cut out for us, Mr. Sutherland."

Sutherland nodded absently. "The British army and the lords overseas won't employ loyalists as they should be employed—the British officers look down on us too much for that. But if they do send American loyalists against us, we would have a desperate foe."

Like the rebels, American loyalists were fighting for their homeland, and there were as many loyalists as rebels in the colonies. If Great Britain forged them into units that could fight in their home regions, the young revolution would be in deadly peril.

## chapter 7

## FRONTIER PHYSICIAN

Jeremy Bently recovered rapidly under the skilled and gentle care of Gwen Hardy and her cousin Annie Ross. Soon he was able to walk outdoors and enjoy the sunshine of cold, dry winter days. So far little snow had fallen at the straits, though the ground was frozen and pebbles along the beach were crusted with ice that steadily grew in breadth and depth from the river's edge.

New Year's had come and gone, marked by a hearty though quiet feast at Valenya. Indians and whites came to see Jeremy, many eager to sound out his political standing. Since Jeremy was still hard put to get around, he was grateful for Annie and Gwen, who not only provided welcome company, but also sheltered him from unwanted attention during his convalescence. Cole Ross, having put aside all hostility, was a hale and humorous fellow on cold nights before a crackling fire in the common room. Jeremy's family would have been glad to know their home sheltered such decent and worthy folk.

By any contemporary standards, Valenya was a large place. Its name meant "singing stones," from the sound of the wind whistling through the narrow gaps between the seven huge granite monoliths nearby. These stones were sacred to the Indians, and the fact that Owen Sutherland had been allowed to settle and build here testified to his stature among the local tribes. Sutherland and his first wife, an Ottawa named Mayla, had lived near here in a bark lodge, long before the present clapboard house had been built. She was buried nearby.

The house had the steep roof characteristic of *habitant* cottages—although covered with cedar shingles rather than thatch—and the two upstairs sleeping chambers were more than large enough for Jeremy's three guests.

Downstairs was another bedroom, which had been Owen and Ella's and now was Jeremy's. Across the hall, the common room took up half the ground floor and included, toward the rear, a kitchen with a stone sink that drained outside. The front wall of the common room, where a bookshelf extended from floor to ceiling, held one of the two sash windows made to a pattern Owen Sutherland had brought from Philadelphia. Like its counterpart in the downstairs bedroom, the window overlooked the broad expanse of the straits.

The common room always reminded Jeremy of his family. Across from the fieldstone hearth was his mother's prized spinet, an instrument similar to a harpsichord, with a chiming, crystalline sound. A magnificent grandfather's clock in the corner, polished and noble, showed Ella Sutherland's English taste. On the floor were rugs woven by Jeremy's foster sister, Sally Cooper.

Across the center hall, behind the bedroom, was a room that held a loom and spinning wheel; here Ella and Sally had spent many winter hours spinning, weaving, and sewing. Annie Ross was proving herself adept at these same skills, and like Ella, she was also accomplished on the spinet. Gwen, in contrast, was usually deep in one of the many books on medicine and science Jeremy had brought from Scotland and England. Night after night as Gwen read, Annie wove or spun or played the spinet, often singing along as Cole Ross accompanied her on his concertina. Jeremy, too, joined in with the song, and more than once they managed to coax Gwen out of her books to get her singing also. When it suited her, Gwen had a lovely voice, and Jeremy thought her more beautiful when she sang than when she studied. He did not tell her so, however.

Because he did not want to discourage her passion for medicine, Jeremy often had long conversations with Gwen about medical practices or treatments. More than once he was left puzzled as she worked out a solution to some problem, often making it seem too simple, too obvious to have been a problem at all.

On such discomforting occasions he chose to sing instead of prolonging the talks, and Annie was ever ready to encourage his decision. Night after wintry night the common room at Valenya was warm with firelight and rich with laughter and song, all potently aiding Jeremy's rapid recovery.

As soon as word went out that Dr. Bently was up and around, a steady trickle of patients began to arrive at Valenya. They came in ones and twos, sometimes in whole families, traveling through snow and across ice to tell about wounds, breaks, or maladies. At first Jeremy was not fully prepared, for he was still somewhat weak. Yet he turned no one away and did his best to treat injuries or diagnose illnesses and prescribe medicine.

Gwen was indispensable. At Jeremy's suggestion she soon transformed the weaving room into a clinic where patients could be received. The loom was dismantled, and with a spinning wheel was moved into the common room. A long table was brought in, and Cole Ross constructed shelves to hold bottles and jars of liquids, powders, herbs, roots, salves, and tinctures. Neatly arrayed in a cabinet nearby were bandages, swabs, surgical instruments, books, scales, syringes, mortars, pestles, tourniquets, needles, suture material, and a host of other necessities.

Jeremy watched with admiration as Gwen prepared that modest but well-stocked room. She knew from experience much of what was needed, and Jeremy only suggested an arrangement or requested that certain essentials be ordered from the settlement. From England he had brought scores of boxes of precious medicines and preparations that could be combined to make specific remedies: these she sorted and neatly arranged. Sometimes he explained better methods or treatments than she had learned, using modern tools and equipment, but all in all Gwen did extremely well in readying the clinic.

By the latter part of January, Gwen and Jeremy had quite an efficient workplace, and more than a hundred patients had already come to be treated. Most were *habitants* injured while cutting wood, hunting, or traveling. The rest were mainly Indians, for other than the sturdy *habitants,* most whites preferred to stay close to the fort in winter.

During this time, Jeremy instructed Gwen how to bleed a patient with the use of lancet or leeches, how to use the latest French screw tourniquet, the best way to extract a bullet or its shattered particles. He also taught her to set a dislocated hip by tying the patient's foot to a bolt in the wall and pulling on his armpits until the joint was in place. To ease the patient's suffering, Jeremy prepared *elixir paregoricum,* a soothing syrup that stupefied the individual during operations.

Gwen became especially adept at the preparation of medicines, which took a skillful hand to measure, weigh, grind in the mortar, filter, and package or bottle. Often a drug would be measured in precise doses, each folded into paper, ready to use. For *elixir paregoricum,* as with other potions and medicines, Gwen soon memorized the ingredients: in this case opium, honey, licorice, benzoic acid, camphor, oil of anise, potassium carbonate, and alcohol.

Bottles were hard to find, however, and Jeremy was grateful to Annie Ross, who one day went to Fort Detroit by dogsled and came back with several dozen bottles in all sizes and shapes. She had traveled to every storehouse, asked residents at random to sell what empty bottles they had, and even appealed to the army surgeon, old Lawrence Sennet, for whatever he would sell. Annie seemed to think nothing of doing such thoughtful and helpful deeds. Although she could not stomach the sight of blood, she would gladly clean the clinic room, play with the children of patients being treated, or prepare medicines with Gwen.

Soon everyone at the straits knew of Jeremy's practice, and only the harsh winter weather kept him from having more patients than he and Gwen could handle. They both worried about being inundated during the spring, when folk could travel. It was critical that a proper hospital be established in the fort, where they could conveniently serve the most people.

They discussed this need one afternoon as they tended an Ottawa Indian who had broken his right leg in a fall. Having been drugged to ease his pain, the man lay unconscious on the table. Jeremy had already set the bone and was applying a splint while Gwen looked on. They could hear Annie out in the common room, talking with the man's wife and three children. A wintry light fell on shelves of bottles, all full of medicine; the room almost gleamed with cleanliness, and smelled of soap and herbs. As Jeremy wrapped the leg firmly, he said, "Beds and bedding, employees to keep the place clean, equipment, food, and a dependable supply of medicines . . . all these things are expensive, yet without them we can't have a proper hospital. The Frontier Company might have an empty warehouse available, but to furnish it and to supply medicines for our apothecary shop will be difficult."

"Sell medicines!" That loud voice was gravelly and slurred. It came from the open door, where there stood a bent, glassy-eyed man, leathery and gaunt, staring through dingy bifocals, with a scowl on his face. "A doctor is not an apothecary and should never sell drugs! That's unesh— unetic—" He blinked, and pushed the glasses back on his long nose. "It ain't right!" Jeremy knew who this man had to be.

Coming into the room with a shuffling walk, Lieutenant Lawrence Sennet, surgeon of the Eighth Foot, dropped his carrying bag on the floor. He wore a soiled, disheveled wig and a scarlet coat—at least the coat must once have been scarlet, but now was a faded pink, save where it was stained and darkened by years of use.

Neither Jeremy nor Gwen had formally met Sennet, so Jeremy introduced himself and Gwen, and shook the man's gnarled hand. Sennet, Jeremy had heard, was a native of Maryland and a career military surgeon, though he had never been to university. He was new to the northwest, having come out just last year with the Eighth Regiment replacements from Montreal.

Sennet, ignoring Gwen, leaned back, peering down his nose at Jeremy, as though he was difficult to see or was blurred by some play of light.

"So this is the whippersnapper, *Doctor* Bently, eh?" Sennet swayed so that Jeremy thought he might have to catch him before he fell on the sleeping Indian. The army surgeon reeked of rum, and some of the stains on his tunic were still wet. "Philadelphia Academy, eh? Edinburgh, eh? Acquainted with the scoundrelly rascal rebel Franklin, eh?" He gravely eyed Jeremy, who finished binding the splint with strong webbing.

Sennet peered at Jeremy's handiwork, turned down his lower lip, and nodded in approval. "Neat job. But you're wasting your time."

"How so?"

Sennet pointed at the bloody bandage that covered the flesh where the bone had come through. "Bad break like that won't ever heal. Man'll get infection . . . he'll lame and have to get the limb removed sooner or later. Better sooner than later. Should've spared the poor dog the trouble and just amputated below the knee . . . no, above the knee'd be better by the looks of it."

Jeremy and Gwen carefully lifted the sleeping Indian and laid him on a nearby cot to recover. Gwen went out to reassure the man's family that all would be well.

Sennet squinted and said, "Why the hell's he sleeping? Pass out from pain?" He chuckled and shook his head. "Injuns ain't all they're cracked up to be when it comes to taking pain. Just because—"

"I put him to sleep," Jeremy said, washing his hands in a bowl. *"Spongia somnifera."*

Sennet would not try—did not deign—to repeat that phrase, which he had never before heard. Jeremy explained it meant "sleep-bringing sponge," and was a method used by the ancients to sedate patients before an operation. A mixture of opium and dried herbs was dispersed in warm water, then taken up by the sponge and applied to the patient's nostrils. Sennet muttered that it seemed a waste to foul up valuable opium with all those other costly ingredients.

Gwen came back in and replied, "We can be sure of a safe sleep for him, and he won't get sick afterward——"

"We?" Sennet squeaked at her. "We? Why, lad, you're a mite young to be referring to yourself in the same breath with an Edinburgh-trained physician and surgeon! We?" He laughed, but not with insult or scorn, for Sennet was not a bad fellow, simply worn out and drifting far back in the wake of modern medical advances. "You're an ambitious boy. No mistake about it!"

Gwen said curtly, "I'm a woman, sir."

Sennet stopped his cackling and squinted at her. Again he leaned back and peered down his nose, scratching his scalp under the shabby wig and muttering, "So you be." He slowly nodded his head. "And a comely one, no mistake about it! Times are changing, ain't they? Maybe I ought to get an Edinburgh education, too. You come with it?"

Gwen rolled up extra webbing and ignored the man. As Jeremy put away unused leg splints, he changed the subject, asking why Sennet thought a physician who sold medications was unethical.

"Why? Because there's too much room for improper gain! It's too tempting to prescribe medication that ain't right, or ain't needed, but costs the patient plenty! The apothecary should make the money for mixing and bottling, not the doctor! That's why!" He abruptly changed his tone and snorted, chuckling as he said slyly, "But then I suppose a doctor out here needs to earn what he can, however he can. No mistake about it!"

Sniffing with disdain at the sleeping Indian, Sennet said Jeremy would not be paid by the likes of him except in chickens, beads, and fish. Out on the frontier, folk did not have money and were even unwilling to pay in furs.

He continued, rocking back and forth on his feet, "But if they want to take their medicine, they'll have to pay you for it, won't they? They might not count your examination time or your Edinburgh training worth paying for, but they'll pay for something in their hands, something they can drink or swallow, and they'll believe any medicine that tastes bad must be worth paying for, that's sure." He again shook his head and cackled as he strolled along the shelves of bottles, saying, "No, it ain't right for a doctor to profit from the apothecary's work, but it's a neat idea, I'll admit, neat and tidy, and no mistake!"

He began to examine every bottle and jar, one after the other, reading all the labels: Peruvian bark, cantharides, Fowler's solution, Hoffmann's anodyne, potassium chlorate, phosphoric acid, angostura bark, Canada balsam, Gregory's powder, Prussian blue, senega root—"Ah, Seneca rattlesnake oil," Sennet exclaimed, at last coming on a name he recognized. "Hear it's good for pleurisy." He read on: clematis, pulsatilla, foxglove—this last the most important of them all, Jeremy said, called the opium of the heart, for its ability to slow the rate of the heartbeat. Soon Sennet stopped looking over every one, for there were simply too many, the names too strange and undecipherable.

When he came to several shelves of medical books, his face puckered as he stared at them, and he muttered, "Hmmm, Priestly's *History of Electricity*. Fuller . . . *Exan—the—matologia*. Hale, *Statical Essays* . . . Newton, Socrates, Pringle . . . yes, interesting . . . Mesmer, Wesley, Berkeley . . . yes, quite a lot of reading. Must have cost a small fortune."

He moved back toward the medicines, casually asking whether Jeremy had really read all those tomes. He was told they were mostly Gwen's books and that Jeremy's collection was in another room. At this, Sennet stopped short. Recovering, he merely cleared his throat as he peered up at a bottle of tartar emetic on a shelf. He took the bottle down, his nose close to the label, and made a sound of approval.

"I ain't one for purgatives; not as effective as bleeding, and no mistake. Get out the bad blood! Stimulate the body to heal itself, and don't waste good money buying purgatives." He grinned broadly, showing that his mouth had few teeth left. "But then, I ain't an apothecary and a doctor all wrapped in one, who makes a copper at both ends of the treatment. I ain't so educated as that, and ain't so neat and tidy about making my fortune. Otherwise I wouldn't be wearing the king's scarlet tunic, a surgeon for a trifling four shillings a day, would I? I'd be an apothecary and medical doctor, neat and tidy, and no mistake about it."

Jeremy simply smiled at the fellow, but Gwen was angry. She would have told him off for his rudeness had she not caught a warning glance from Jeremy. Moving away in a huff, she took a kettle from an iron stove, poured water into two bowls, then began washing her hands in one.

"Would you like to stay and watch?" Jeremy asked Sennet, washing his own hands thoroughly. "I've got a patient coming in with a severe popliteal aneurysm that needs to have the vein ligated; I think you'll be interested to see the technique I use."

Sennet squinted again, not at all sure of Jeremy's terms, but nodded. "Just happens that I brought my surgery apron along just in case you needed help." He fumbled through his bag and displayed his operating gown with considerable pride. Gwen gasped and held her nose, for the gown stank and was crusted with dried pus and blood. Jeremy knew that many surgeons gloried in how foul their aprons were, for the stains proved them experienced, if not learned, in practical medicine.

Before Sennet could put it on, however, Jeremy offered him a fresh one. "We must take heed of cleanliness whenever there are patients with open wounds, sir, so I'll ask that you use this one."

Sennet grew almost sober. "My surgery apron's seen more work than your neat and tidy university instructors ever have or ever will see, my lad." But at Jeremy's firm insistence, Sennet grudgingly accepted the clean gown and put his own away.

Soon the Indian revived and left with his family, and a white settler was brought in by friends. They had to carry him to the table, for his right leg was so painful he could not walk. Jeremy rolled up the fellow's breeches and revealed the aneurysm in the form of a black swelling behind the knee. Sennet was immediately at the man's side, poking and probing with a dirty forefinger. The poor patient—a friendly, middle-aged baker, polite and ruddy-faced—tried his best not to wince.

Before Jeremy could say anything, Sennet harrumphed

decisively and shook his head in sympathy. To the baker he said plainly, "Have to take it off, my man! That's right! Not too much of an operation, really. Quite routine, you'll see! Done in a trice!"

The shocked fellow's eyes went very wide, and the blood drained from his face. Sennet whispered behind his hand to Jeremy that they'd better tie him down before he fled. Gwen watched with a pained expression.

At that, Jeremy spoke kindly to the trembling baker.

"Steady, there, my friend; we don't intend to take off your leg, not unless it's a matter of life or death."

The fellow sighed with relief, smiled, and closed his eyes. Sennet, on the other hand, stiffened, his lower lip angrily protruding.

"It *is* a matter of life or death, young man!" Sennet waved his arms at Jeremy, who was at a side cabinet, preparing surgical tools. "This poor wretch'll die of poison from whatever it is that's started this swelling!"

The baker, terrified again, gaped at Sennet, who nodded once, pointed emphatically, and cried out, "You will die, and make no mistake about it! That leg has to come off, and quick, or your wife'll be a widow, or remarried, in a month's time! Got any children? Well, think how they'll be if you're dead and can't work to feed them!"

Gwen came to the fellow's side and said firmly, "We intend to ligate—bind—the vein that's having trouble, and within a month it should have healed, and you'll be up and about again."

Sennet's eyes were popping from his head. "Why, you . . . you child!" He sprang up and down on his toes as he blustered, all the while trying to think of a cutting remark to put Gwen in her place. "I've seen dozens of these cases," he blurted at last, quaking with anger. "I've cut off thousands of limbs! Thousands! It's the only way, the safest way, and the most uncomplicated way! You dare toy with this poor creature's life! And you, a mere woman!"

Gwen would not be cowed by Sennet's abuse; she said, "Ligating the vein is the correct procedure, sir; there is no need to take off the man's leg." She nodded curtly to the medical library as she laid out Jeremy's scalpels, sutures, needles, bandages, and wash bowl. "Please take a moment to refer to an article by Dr. John Hunter of Saint George's Hospital, explaining that when the passage of blood through the main trunk is arrested, collateral veins are capable of continuing the circulation, and if the seat of the disease is in the fettered part, the result will be complete healing of the tumor."

Sennet was squinting hard again, looking down his long nose at Gwen, and all the while the miserable patient was swallowing, over and over, and glancing from the woman to the surgeon, back and forth. Jeremy stepped toward the baker and said:

"I can take off your leg—"

"Right!" Sennet cried and whirled toward the surgical instruments, but stopped short while poking along the wall where bulkier implements were hanging, for he could not find a large saw.

Jeremy continued speaking to the baker, "But if I were you, I'd have the binding of the vein and let nature take its course. You'll be well enough to walk by springtime."

The man seemed reassured and agreed to the ligature. Sennet clucked his tongue dismally, shook his head, and sat down in a chair, full of pity. He still had not found the amputation equipment, because Jeremy had put such gory tools in a separate cabinet, not to be used unless absolutely necessary.

Sennet's annoyance turned into absorbed interest as he watched the preparations for the operation. The "sleep-bringing sponge" was applied to the man's nostrils, and soon he was fast asleep.

Jeremy and Gwen acted swiftly and skillfully to open the man's infected leg at the thigh. Sennet muttered that it was a scandal that Gwen should even be in the same room while this was being done; but once he saw how deftly she applied clamps to the vein being treated and kept the wound free of blood, he forgot she was a woman and observed the delicate operation with unguarded fascination.

At one point Sennet came close and pointed at the vein, his finger nearly touching the wound. "Take care," Jeremy said firmly, "for you've not washed your hands, and you might put foreign matter into the wound. That would cause suppuration that could work against the healing."

That was more than the dismayed Sennet could accept. He stepped back and with a sigh of exasperation said, "Is that wound any cleaner than my hand? Look! It's got blood in it—but my hand's not bleeding, so what's the difference if I touch the wound? And what do you mean that suppuration will interfere with healing? It's essential that pus be formed in the wound! Everyone knows pus is laudable! To heal properly a wound must have pus, for heaven's sake! Anyone knows that!"

He ranted on like this for a few minutes as Jeremy finished binding off the vein, then Gwen proceeded to stitch the incision.

Jeremy said to the surgeon, "In my library are tracts by Place and Pringle, both concerning the need for antisepsis, Lieutenant; as you surely know, Dr. Pringle is recognized as *the* authority on military sanitation."

"Sanitation!" Sennet croaked. "Suppuration of the wound is more important than sanitation! Suppuration promotes healing! What good is sanitation if one cannot heal?" He sniffed and made a waving motion of his hand. "This room is more like a laundry than a surgery! I miss the good old surgical stink! Surgery and pus go hand in hand! Blood and gore are surgery, but in the end the patient is healed!"

Gwen began to bandage the leg, and as she worked she said, "There's another tract by Henri de Mondeville, the great French surgeon, whom you no doubt have heard of."

Sennet looked grumpy but made no reply.

"De Mondeville says many more physicians know how to cause suppuration than how to heal a wound; he insists that the wound must be washed thoroughly, kept clear of foreign matter, and that the formation of pus should be avoided, because it doesn't promote healing, but rather is a complication."

She was direct and unemotional as she said this, and after hearing it, Sennet shook his head and asked, "What upstart young quack is this De Mondeville? When did he write these radical new ideas? Last week?"

"Five hundred years ago," Gwen answered.

Sennet's eyes half-shut, and his lower lip stuck out once more. "I have no time for such prattle, child! I'm an army surgeon! Theory and fanciful experimentation are no answer to life-and-death tribulation upon the battlefield! A battlefield is a teacher that no amount of booklearning and scholarship can ever replace. But you would not know about that!"

Jeremy, washing the blood from his hands, said quite calmly, "Mistress Hardy is credited with personally saving forty-two loyalist lives after the Battle of Longueuil last November—in three days."

Sennet's pointed chin dropped open. He had, it seemed, become quite sober. Gwen looked briefly at Jeremy and with a faint smile said Annie was forever talking too much about matters that were not her affair. Then she blushed as Jeremy smiled back at her in a way that spoke of affection and pride. Meanwhile, Sennet was sniffing about the wound Gwen was bandaging, and he gave some grudging approval that it was done well enough.

"In a month," he grumbled, "we'll see who was right, but by then it'll be too late to save this wretch, never mind his leg." He shook his head as Jeremy and Gwen lugged the man to the cot the Indian had used earlier. "I could've taken off that leg in a trice, in one-hundredth the time you took; and with a bit of hot oil to sear the wound, he'd be nearly good as new in two weeks, never mind a month."

Just then there was a knock, and in strode old Mawak, looking as regal and proud as ever in his bright array of feathers and beads, wearing several colorful trade shirts, one on top of the other. He knew Sennet as a capable fellow medicine man. Sennet in turn was aware that Mawak was looked upon as a wise and knowledgeable dispenser of Indian cures and herbal treatments, not to mention being a practitioner of preventive medicine by the use of charms and amulets.

Mawak stuck his chest out and grinned as they all greeted one another with the usual "How." The Ottawa said to Jeremy, "Bad gut, Doc." He pointed to his stomach. "Feel sick; no can hold down grub."

Jeremy told him to sit on a chair and raise his shirts—

it would have taken too long to remove them all. Though Sennet once again was annoyed that Gwen should be in the same room with a man's bared chest, the surgeon kept quiet. Jeremy sat on a chair before Mawak and began to strike the Indian's breast with his fingertips. Mawak's face screwed up as he tried to grasp what was going on. Jeremy put an ear to the Indian's chest, listened, and tapped some more. After a while, Sennet leaned over and asked Jeremy what he was doing.

"Ascultation and percussion," Jeremy replied. "Come, put your ear to Mawak's chest." Sennet took Jeremy's seat and with great intensity listened to the puzzled Indian's thorax.

"This is a new method of diagnosing internal ailments, heart problems, or lung difficulties," Jeremy said, and explained the various sounds of the chest, tapping occasionally to indicate how the body responded. It was possible to hear the condition of heart valves, breathing passages, and clearness of the chest cavity, he told the officer.

"Amazing, no mistake," Sennet murmured in awe when Jeremy interpreted what was being heard, saying the physician could tell what to prescribe for certain conditions once an ailment was pinpointed by ascultation and percussion.

Finally, Jeremy said to Mawak as the Indian put his shirts down, "Perfect health, my friend; you'll live to be a hundred if—"

"Oh, ho!" Mawak declared, slapping his knee and laughing loudly. "Me no got problems! New wife got problems! She sick, not Mawak!" With that he gave a call, and in came the beautiful young squaw named Fawn Eyes—Mawak's fourth wife. "Squaw got troubles, Doc, not Mawak. But she afraid of white doctors." He winked at Sennet, who was staring at the seductive Fawn Eyes and breathing harder. "She afraid you chop her up in little pieces like you do the soldiers."

Beckoning to Fawn Eyes, Mawak said he had been examined first to show it was safe. Sennet licked his lips and said, "We better try ascultation and percussion, I think, Dr. Bently."

Jeremy smiled and glanced at Gwen, who motioned for Fawn Eyes to sit down in another chair. Sennet was hovering near as Jeremy sat next to the squaw, who seemed uneasy, her dark eyes flashing from one person to the next.

The military surgeon was rubbing his hands in anticipation; but Gwen handed Jeremy a tube of stiff paper, which he placed delicately against the woman's clothed chest, to Sennet's disappointment. Jeremy listened and used a small hammer to lightly strike the squaw's chest. He could not tell anything, however, for she, too, sounded normal. After asking a few questions about her general health, he was told she was often nauseated lately, had a kind of fever at the most unexpected times, and was hard put to eat or keep food down.

Jeremy thought about that and decided that a purgative, cold baths, and a change of diet were in order, but he had no idea what was making Fawn Eyes so sick. Sennet harrumphed and declared importantly that the best thing for her was an old family recipe of his, which never failed to do the trick.

"After a good bleeding, say seven or eight ounces, thus voiding the corrupted humors, prepare a decoction from the urine of a billy goat, and mix well with pounded carrot tips, dried and powdered real fine, and add crushed eggshells that are mixed with garden snails taken in the month of May.... But it's too soon for May snails, so forget them; I've always found that snails don't really matter...."

Mawak listened intently, nodding and ruminating, for he knew well the magic potency of the right ingredients if a gifted medicine man understood the more subtle aspects of nature. He was quite impressed with Sennet's family recipe and promised faithfully to see that his new wife took a good dose.

"It is this Injun's honor," Mawak said, standing up and thumping his chest, "to hear great secret of white healer! And it be this Injun's honor to share own secret." He half closed his eyes, as though listening to some inner voice, and folded his arms. "In old hours of night, bad spirits are weak when medicine man come at 'em with loud turtle rattle, if medicine man wear medicine bundle that has powers of ancestors."

Mawak passed to Sennet a small leather sack that had hung from his neck, and the surgeon opened it, grimacing at its smell. At Mawak's suggestion, Sennet reached in and drew out a polished black charm stone, a bone whistle, a thong with one bear claw, and a crooked bird's leg. He knew Indian manners well enough not to comment unfavorably on any of these items, though he was convinced old Mawak was mad to think they had magical or medicinal properties. The last things he took from the medicine bundle were the source of the stench—three round objects wrapped in leather.

"Strong medicine!" he said, wrinkling his long nose.

Mawak nodded gravely. "Strong! Bear's eyes in grease! Pretty fresh! Strong medicine."

It was then that Mawak noticed something dangling around Sennet's neck. He pointed at it with interest, until the surgeon displayed it—a four-century-old gold coin of England, stamped with Saint George in a ship on one side and the cross of Saint George on the other.

Sennet was pleased at Mawak's interest and said proudly, "It's been in the Sennet family for hundreds of years—ah, thousands of moons, my dusky friend."

"Aiee," Mawak said softly, nodding in admiration.

While this conversation was going on, Gwen was softly speaking with Fawn Eyes.

Sennet said this gold coin, called a noble, was minted in the reign of King Edward the Third.

"It has . . . certain powers, which I cannot deny, in spite of my training and modern understanding of natural science." Sennet glanced at Jeremy, who was at his medicine shelves, trying to decide whether to give Fawn Eyes a jalap concoction or the dependable Glauber's purging salts. "It guards against dropsy and accidents in riding . . . and has some effect against epilepsy, my old granny told me."

"Aiee . . ."

"Make no mistake, I'm not one to pay mind to wives' tales or drivel, but all these years I've never fallen off a horse—'course I never get up on one—but make no mistake, I've never been laid low by fits or watery pockets."

Mawak was excited, and drew from within his shirts his own medal, this one of silver and bearing the image of King George the Second. Identical medallions had been given as a gift to thousands of Indians after the defeat of the French, as a token of their new allegiance to the British king. Many venerated the medallion; British officers had said it bore the sacred magic of divine kings, and having seen the might of Redcoat armies, some Indians believed it.

Mawak said, "Great medicine! Good against firewater. Never get drunk. Drink kegs and kegs! Never get drunk!" He laughed and slapped Sennet on the shoulder, as though they were brethren in the bond of sorcery.

Sennet did not believe any such thing about the Peace Medal, but when Mawak declared he had an especially effective elixir for rejuvenation and for attracting pretty young squaws, the surgeon paid close attention. Mawak was of untold age but had several wives, others almost as appealing as Fawn Eyes. Jeremy bottled some Glauber's salts as Sennet and Mawak left the room to talk in private, the old Indian speaking softly, a hand on the Redcoat's shoulder.

"... seven hairs from black cat, seven scales from rattlesnake, seven bits of feather from owl..."

As they went out the door, Sennet loudly declared, "Good heavens! I know that potion, for it's an old English charm! You say it really works?" He glanced back into the room and gazed longingly at Fawn Eyes. Mawak might have something, after all.

Jeremy came toward the seated squaw and Gwen, who stood near her. He held up the bottle of salts and was about to explain the dosage when Gwen smiled and said, "She needs no purging salts or bleeding or billy goat urine."

"No?"

Smiling, Gwen said to Fawn Eyes, "You're with child."

The girl brightened, caught her breath, and then comprehended with amazement and joy what Gwen had said. She jumped up, embraced the white woman, shook hands with Jeremy, and dashed from the room, calling Mawak's name. Jeremy and Gwen laughed to hear Mawak, outside, whooping for joy. Gwen sat down to rest, while Jeremy replaced the unneeded salts on a shelf.

"Lucky her," Gwen said contentedly.

"Lucky not to be bled or dosed?"

"That also."

"You mean to have Mawak as her child's father?"

"If it pleases her. Yes, if she loves Mawak, then lucky she is, indeed."

Jeremy observed Gwen a moment, once more struck by her beauty—a subtle loveliness that shone from within, but also was reflected in her face and figure. It amazed him that she should be so pretty, and yet so brilliant at medicine. In his experience, only men had been doctors, although midwifery was generally left to women. Gwen was different from anyone he had ever met, and, yes, she was very attractive.

A little later, while Jeremy was bidding Sennet farewell, Annie Ross found Gwen strolling near the river. The wind was fresh and invigorating, tinged with the scent of wood smoke. The afternoon sun was low in the sky as the two cousins walked slowly along the beach, both bundled in capes.

Gwen told all that had happened that day, and Annie laughed to hear about Sennet and Mawak, especially about the old Ottawa's love potion. It had been a long day, and Gwen was weary, but she felt content, for the work had gone well. Jeremy had been impressed with her—she had sensed that—and together they had done well for those who had come for help. This was the opening of a whole new world for her, an exciting, challenging world in which she could be of great worth to people in need.

She could not deny it was exciting to work side by side with Jeremy Bently. What a wonderful healer he was, and so learned—even though he was not especially trained in pregnancy, which was a woman's realm. An hour working with him was like a month studying a medical book. The fact that even the slight touch of his hand gave her a chill was something else that absorbed Gwen's thoughts. She could not quite grasp what it all meant, for no man had ever made her feel so—

"A penny for your thoughts," Annie interrupted, and Gwen blushed slightly, for she could not tell even her dear cousin what she was thinking about Jeremy.

Annie smiled as though she suspected something, and bent to pick up a stone and skim it across the glistening ice, which glowed in the sunset.

"You're thinking about a man, aren't you?" Annie asked, her smile becoming a giggle as Gwen blushed even more. "He's a fine and charming man, who cares for you very much!"

Gwen turned sharply and said, "That's not true.... I mean he's fine and charming, but he doesn't care for me— not very much, anyway."

Annie took her cousin's hand and squeezed it. "Yes, he does, and I'm glad for you. You see, he told me that he thinks you— How did he put it? Yes, he said you were the fairest damsel ever to grace this enchanted wilderness, which in all its glorious beauty was not a worthy setting for such an exquisite jewel!" Again Annie giggled. "Quite poetic, eh?"

"Did he really say that?" Gwen had stopped walking, her heart pounding away. "That doesn't sound like him at all!" She gazed at the western horizon. "Would he really—"

"He did!" Annie said, again squeezing Gwen's hand. "Those very words, and his nice brown eyes were soft with love."

"Brown? His eyes are hazel!"

"Brown, cousin! Haven't you taken a close look at your suitor's handsome face? Wait... whom do you mean?"

"Whom do you mean?"

"Why, dear Simon Clancy, of course! Who else?"

But Gwen simply said they had best get back to the house, for dinner had to be made. "And don't go telling Simon that I'm dreaming about him! Don't dare, or I'll tell Mawak you want to be his next wife!"

With that, they both laughed and set off running along the beach, past the magnificent standing stones. As Gwen ran, she looked at those monoliths, so austere and grand,

and saw before them the lone granite headstone marking the grave of Mayla, Owen Sutherland's first wife. She slowed to a respectful walk, feeling herself such a stranger out here, a newcomer to an old and enduring land. As she passed the grave, Gwen thought of the dead wife of Jeremy Bently, and knew there was no easy way for him to rise above the deep pain of that loss.

Gwen longed to help him through this difficult time, but sought not to charm him or entice him. Rather she would be glad just to see him truly happy. Whomever he chose to spend his life with, what really mattered was that he was content.

Annie came alongside her and said, "That grave makes me think of Jeremy's loss. Isn't it a shame?" They walked a few more paces, both slightly breathless. Annie glanced back at the granite marker. "But he can't go on mourning forever. He mustn't!" She touched Gwen's arm and they stopped. "Cousin, do you think he'll ever get over losing his wife?"

Gwen did not know.

Annie said, "I have a secret. If you'll tell me whom you were thinking about, I'll tell you my secret."

Gwen shook her head. "I wasn't really thinking of anyone in the way you suggest." She almost knew what Annie was about to say, and it made her restless.

Annie could contain herself no longer. "I have to tell someone who'll understand, but someone I can trust not to breathe a word. Gwendolyn, I'm in love with Jeremy Bently!"

Gwen smiled wanly and nodded once.

"Can you believe it?" Annie went on, her eyes dreamy. "After all these years of being courted by officers and gentlemen in Montreal and New York Town, I find the perfect man for me all the way out here! I tell you, it's fate! It's the act of a divine hand! Isn't it wonderful?"

Gwen drew her cape about her shoulders. Annie was so excited, so relieved to be able to talk that she did not notice Gwen's uneasiness. For her part, Gwen tried to be kind and changed the subject gently, saying Jeremy had worked very hard that day and was no doubt more than ready for a hearty meal.

Annie grasped Gwen's hand, and off they went, running toward Valenya, which took on a rosy hue in the light of sundown. How Gwen loved this place! She knew they would have to leave in the spring, however, and begin another life somewhere in the settlement. Perhaps, she thought, she would stay in the northwest after the hostilities were over. This was a glorious land. Already it felt so much like home—particularly Valenya.

*chapter* **8**

## REBELS

As Bill Poole had said, it was awfully cold at Quebec. The days dragged by, and that long gray citadel wall seemed to loom higher, and the icy stone trench before it looked deeper.

There was little the Army of the United Colonies could do, save stay alive. Occasional cannon fire from the citadel worried troop movements and annoyed rebel sentries, but there were no counterattacks from the defenders. Arnold, from his bed, sent a stream of orders that kept the rebels alert. He had been promoted to brigadier general, but was too badly wounded to get around. Yet his fiery spirit was not subdued by pain, nor was his bravery tempered by the fact that his army was so small and feeble. Few reinforcements came from Montreal, though it was hoped more would arrive come spring.

One afternoon, Sutherland paid a visit to the general's cottage. Arnold began the conversation by discussing General David Wooster of Connecticut, who had come to Montreal to take overall command.

"I'd hoped Wooster would come up here, but I'm told he'll stay in Montreal. That's no wonder, I suppose, for the gentleman's well over sixty, and such a winter journey would be too hard on him. Yet, still, we must try to go on. . . ."

Arnold painfully limped about the room, then with a curse he threw his cane into the corner, swinging to face Sutherland.

"But what good would one more general do?" he cried out, glaring through the window at Quebec. "We need five thousand men! We need cannon, supplies, and money— real money, not worthless Continental paper!"

He stared at Sutherland after saying that last, because insulting Continental dollars was little short of treason. Yet Arnold was right.

The Scotsman then told why he had come, saying he had received a special package from Ella. Taking a bound leather packet from inside his shirt, he handed it over. "It came in good time, General."

Once again Owen Sutherland provided a thousand pounds in British currency to buy food for the suffering American army. Arnold's eyes lit, and with a bound he leaped to the window, as though he were not injured at all.

He shook the satchel at the citadel and cried, "We'll get you yet! If you won't come out and fight like men, we'll come in! We'll come in, I say!"

"I've been scouting upstream, General. At Three Rivers I visited a French blacksmith and ironmonger I used to know upcountry. He's no lover of the British, and if we can get him enough hard cash, he'll furnish us two thousand round shot and five hundred shells by March . . . and forty barrels of black powder within a week."

Arnold laughed with glee. His excited capering caused his leg wound to bleed, but he ignored it.

The Scotsman was not finished yet. "If you were wondering where else I've been these days—"

Arnold raised a hand. "Not inside Quebec?" Sutherland smiled slightly, and Arnold chuckled, limping to the table and sitting down, looking very pleased as Sutherland went on.

"When we take the place, we'll capture upward of three thousand barrels of powder; ten thousand stand of arms— seven thousand brand new and just arrived last summer—

seven thousand uniforms that could be dyed a nice Connecticut shade of dark blue; a large quantity of artillery stores—not to mention the hundred and fifty guns—and two frigates and other vessels in the harbor."

"Enough to equip an army to hold the river against the British this spring!" Arnold whooped for joy. "We'll get in! We've got to!"

Sutherland sat across from Arnold, answering his questions. The Scotsman had hidden in a wagonload of hay brought into the city late one night. The rebels were spread too thin to stop all these clandestine deliveries, and Sutherland had made the most of the one he had discovered.

On his return he had drawn a map of the fort, showing positions of cannon, quarters for troops, places vulnerable to fire, and portions of the wall that might give way to heavy cannon fire.

"Pity that we have so few cannon," Arnold said under his breath. "They captured most of ours when they drove us back on New Year's Eve."

Once again Sutherland rankled to recall how Bradford Cullen had thwarted his efforts to get guns from Montreal. The roads had been mostly free of snow back in December, and Sutherland would have got the cannon through. Now they were impassable, and the rebels would have to wait until spring, when guns could be shipped downriver. Arnold would hang on, however, determined to maintain the siege.

Suddenly there came a tremendous roar of cannon from the citadel walls. Men shouted, and shells burst all around. Arnold and Sutherland dashed out of the cottage, soon joined by Peter Defries, who cried that the enemy was attempting to capture two rebel fieldpieces. Redcoats were coming out of the Palace Gate.

Sutherland looked to Arnold, whose expression showed intense frustration and pain, for the man's leg wound was bleeding profusely. He could not ride.

"Stay!" Sutherland shouted, and began to rally frightened soldiers who were fleeing. Arnold yelled for the Scotsman to take his magnificent black horse, saddled and waiting near the door.

Sutherland was no great rider, but would do his best.

"This is a hell of a way for a Scot to fight! We're infantry!" He grabbed the reins, leaped astride, and drew out his claymore.

"Just don't look down!" Arnold yelled, and with Defries's help began to stop men and form them up.

Sutherland went galloping along the road, calling to the men to turn and fight, to reorganize, and to stand their ground. They were pouring down the snowy track in groups of ten and twenty, some half dressed because they had been resting in cottages or lean-tos. Shells were exploding on every side, cannonballs bouncing past, crashing into buildings, rebounding off tree trunks.

"Owen! It's mostly loyalists. They're following two companies of Redcoats out of the Palace Gate!" Peter Defries shouted as he ran alongside Sutherland. Sutherland howled the Highland yell, and men began to turn and gather behind him. Here and there officers were trying to assemble a defense, and from them Sutherland learned that the enemy numbered about five hundred, almost as many as in the entire force of rebels spread out before Quebec. But the rebels were hardened, trained militia, and most of the loyalists were inexperienced civilians.

Sutherland shouted and waved his sword, calling men around him. He saw over the white fields that the enemy were coming on slowly, in a long column led by Redcoats whose bayonets glittered in the sunlight. The rebel guns stood abandoned behind an earthworks, just fifty yards from the British troops. Already parties of loyalists were marching captured rebels back to the Palace Gate. But now Sutherland had two hundred determined men gathered around him, with several junior officers assembling them into companies. Defries was bellowing at every straggler and fugitive in sight, calling for them to come on the double.

Sutherland reined in his excited mount and shouted, "They expect us to run, men! Let's show them how we run! Right at them! Have you brought those borrowed Redcoat bayonets with you?"

"Yes!" they roared, holding up bayonets captured earlier.

"Fix bayonets, then!" Sutherland stood up in the stirrups and swung the claymore. "Let them taste rebel steel! Drive at their left flank. Make them think they'll never get back into the gate alive! Advance at a trot!"

Sutherland led that little force in a swift run down the frozen road. They shouted and cheered as loudly as they could, and when they came to a gap in the left-hand treeline, they swung onto the field, the better to be visible to the loyalists. With Sutherland riding at their head, directing the advance straight for the open city gate, the rebels howled and sang like wild men, their bayonets glittering as brightly as those of the approaching Redcoats, who were now at the guns in the middle of the field.

Seeing the rebels, the force of loyalists far across the field halted, crowding up and bunching in uncertainty. The sixty or so regulars, however, moved forward, past the rebel cannon, as though intending to outflank Sutherland's left. Sutherland positioned a company of Pennsylvania riflemen under Matthew Smith on that side and told them to fire away as long as they could hold their ground.

"If the lobsters come at us without the support of volunteers, Captain Smith, they'll be cut off when we turn back from the gate!" he shouted. "But keep them from getting behind us!" Then he saw how the inexperienced civilians who made up the bulk of the enemy force were wavering, letting the regular troops go on alone. "Now, lads," Sutherland cried to the rest of his men, "Let's race 'em for the gate!"

It was a bold and reckless gamble, for the rebels were greatly outnumbered. If the loyalist volunteers made a stand, Sutherland's men could be cut to bits.

"Charge!" Sutherland roared over and over, heedless of sharp cannon fire from the citadel. Shells whined and burst, covering the field with a black pall that stank of gunpowder. His horse whinnied and reared, eager to run, but the Scotsman had no wish to ride right into the heart of the enemy force. This was a calculated trick he was playing—a trick that must work to perfection.

The loyalists saw his rebels dashing for the gate. Fearing they would be cut off, they hastily retreated, firing sporadically and without effect as they went. By now the Redcoats were completely on their own. They had taken the guns and were hauling them to the citadel, half a mile off, but they were in danger. Sutherland's ferocious troops were closing on the volunteers, who were scampering for home, falling and bumping, like a panicked herd of cattle.

Belatedly the Redcoats realized what was happening, and when a deadly fusillade from the Pennsylvania marksmen cut several of them down, they, too, began a rapid retreat.

It looked like Sutherland's men and the loyalists would reach the gate at the same moment. The rebels were fearless now, despite losses to cannon fire. They charged on, full of battle madness—but when Sutherland surprised them all by calling an abrupt halt to their attack, they obeyed like veterans. He shouted for them to take cover behind a thick hedgerow—and it was good that they did, for massed cannon fire thundered even more destructively from the citadel walls.

In the meantime, the Redcoats were making an orderly though hasty retreat, stopping to fire volleys as they went, keeping the rebels at arm's length. The two fieldpieces were abandoned. Sutherland stood in his stirrups and shouted at the British, waving his sword. His men began to hoot in mockery at the fleeing enemy, raising hats on bayonets, and shaking muskets.

The besieged Quebeckers had learned that the rebel Americans were still strong and bold enough to blunt their sallies. Also, Sutherland now knew that the defenders, mainly raw civilians, would surrender if matters got too hot. If only the rebels could get more artillery, Quebec would never hold—not with several hundred cold, angry, and determined rebel troops banging relentlessly at the gates.

Late in January the Reverend Angus Lee and his wife, Matilda, decided to go down to Albany. The minister had no means of support in Montreal, where most people were devout Catholics, and the wealthy Protestant fur traders were mostly unsympathetic to rebels. Since Lee enthusiastically backed the rebellion, the city's Protestants spurned him, and the rebel soldiers who came to his makeshift church in an empty warehouse near the waterfront were destitute. So the reverend thought it best to go to Albany, and from there petition the Presbyterian commissioners, headquartered just outside Boston, for a new position.

This departure seemed a defeat to Angus Lee, who had come to the frontier twelve years earlier hoping to carry the word of God to the Indians, perhaps even to the French. A close friend of the Sutherlands, Lee had shared their dream of building a thriving community at Detroit, but his plans for establishing a Presbyterian church there had never reached fruition.

On this Sunday evening, Lee and Matilda were at Ella's apartment, where their closest friends had come to bid them farewell. The wind blew stinging ice against the windows, but within the brightly lighted apartment the company shut out the cold, even the dreariness of war. They celebrated as they might have if the Lees were a pair of *voyageurs* on their way to distant fur grounds.

Nearly everyone was there: Jeb and Lettie Grey, James Morely, Mel and Hickory Webster, and the Sutherland children. The Lees were delighted with the warmth and loyalty they found that night, and the minister forgot his sorrows. The high-strung Lee was very thin, and his modest, dark clothes and single-curl bob wig seemed overlarge. The coming journey would be difficult, especially for Matilda, the daughter and only child of the widowed Dawson Merriwether of Detroit. Yet she was as determined as he to make the winter trip. To see her laughing lightly and pretending nonchalance in the face of danger, one might have thought Matilda used to the trail. But she was a fragile young woman, prim and chubby, with perfectly curled dark, glossy hair. Her expression was innocent, and in speaking gaily of the uncertain future, Matilda showed great courage.

Matilda, however, needed security and a home. Not aggressive or strong, she was seldom given to taking radical political stands, as was her husband. It had been painful for her to part with her loving father back in Detroit, but Merriwether had wished them well, praying they would soon meet again, in a time of peace. Matilda fervently believed peace would come soon, and no one in that room had the heart to say otherwise.

The friends all worried for the Lees, who were not accustomed to the strain of winter travel. The couple had already arranged passage, however, and would leave in two days with a convoy of sleighs that was expected to reach Albany three weeks later.

The Lees' friends resolved to make the most of this last celebration together. Ella's apartment was quite crowded, and for those first few hours she hardly had a moment away from the spinet, because Lee had drunk too much ale and wanted to sing and sing. Ella played the minister's favorites, one after the other, with not a single hymn in the repertoire.

Even Matilda imbibed more peach cordial than she was used to, and joined Lee and Ella at the spinet. They were vigorously accompanied by Mel Webster, who played the violin even better than Ella played her instrument. Mel was in his thirties, with yellow hair and a fuzzy, unkempt beard. Dressed in a faded red linen smock and breeches, he looked disheveled, but his blue eyes were alert and intelligent. As he played, his reedy frame seemed part of the violin, and he swayed to and fro with the music, singing cheerfully at the same time. Beside Mel was his husky Indian wife, who was twenty and had long, stringy brown hair and a square, pleasant face. She wore European clothes embroidered with many bright colors, but her dark complexion, large features, and the way she sang harmony with Mel in a hoarse, almost coughing voice left no doubt she was Indian. Her muscular forearms explained why her native Oneida name meant "hickory splitter who is stronger than a white lumberjack." They called her Hickory.

The daughter of a leading Oneida medicine man, Hickory had married Mel Webster about a year ago, having met him during his travels through the northwest. She adored her husband's eccentric ways and took great pride in his ability to teach Indians about modern science, technology, farm methods, and fundamental crafts such as ironworking and carpentry.

Mel was known as Singing Bow wherever he played his violin among the tribes of western New York, Pennsylvania, and the Ohio country. He had wandered this border region of the northwest for several years as a patient and brilliant teacher, beloved by the many young Indians eager to learn all they could about white man's civilization. He had met Hickory during a visit to the Oneidas at the headwaters of the Mohawk River. The Oneidas were one of the smallest of the six Iroquois tribes, and the only one that now supported the rebel cause.

Also thoroughly enjoying themselves were Lettie and Jeb Grey, both lusty and boisterous. He was her second husband, a fair-haired Jerseyman, tall and wide, once a British soldier. Lettie, in high spirits as usual, seemed more like a young country girl than the graying mother of two grown sons, Tom and James Morely. Her first husband, a fur trader, had been killed a decade ago by renegade whites, and Jeb's family had been wiped out by Indians. Both tragedies were long enough ago to have healed over, and the couple were well suited for each other, Lettie being just the woman to keep the big, bearlike Jeb manageable.

As Mel and Ella played and the others sang, Lettie and Jeb danced merrily around the cleared floor. There was hardly enough room for the burly couple, who were determined to master the new dance known as the German waltz. They nearly trampled the white husky, Heera, lying on the floor before the stove; with a yelp he jumped up and slunk into a corner.

There Benjamin was playing with a loud buzzing toy made from a worn-out copper coin with two holes bored in it and a string passed through. Beside him Susannah plunked on a jew's harp between her teeth, although whatever she was playing could not be heard over the music, singing, and stamping. Her long hair was braided over her shoulder, and she was dressed prettily in a cream-colored brocaded gown. Though looking elegant, she did not care for formality and sat shoeless on the floor, cross-legged, busy with the twanging harp. Heera lay down at her side; these two had always been closest of friends, and although Heera was past his prime as a lead sled dog, he was a fierce protector of Ella and the children.

The only couple missing were the newlyweds Tom and Sally Morely. For some reason Sally was often feeling ill these days, and she and Tom had already bade farewell to the Lees.

Tom's younger brother, James, sat in an armchair behind the children, reading old copies of *The Gentleman's Magazine,* which was published in London and recognized by men of education and standing as a worthy periodical. James was a long-legged, slender young man of twenty-one, with black curly hair that he kept quite short despite the fashion of the day, which called for queues or clubbing the hair if a wig was not worn. Those who did not know James thought him overly serious, but to certain girls, his dark brown eyes, always thoughtful and dreamy, were wonderfully attractive. He was quiet, almost shy, and had a good-natured way that had served him well as the manager of one of the Frontier Company warehouses at Detroit. James often wished he had the formal education of his close friend Jeremy Bently, but his family had not been able to send either son to school beyond Reverend Lee's elementary classes at Fort Detroit. James had turned his genius to trading, managing the store brilliantly and keeping the ledgers of the company.

Now he sat near a pile of Owen Sutherland's favorite books and periodicals, which Ella had brought from Detroit. She could not carry many, but these few had been lugged in a knapsack all the way to Montreal. Owen's many essays published under the pseudonym Quill were in a leather satchel beside the books, still not unpacked. With a glass of cider on the table next to him and his feet up on the chair, James had settled in to read, so oblivious of the others that he might have been at the Oxford library instead of in the eye of a stormy send-off.

After considerable singing and dancing, Susannah, Lettie, and Ella fetched trayloads of food from the pantry. This was a precious hoard that had been saved for weeks, and it amounted to far more than was really prudent to consume at one time. These were uncertain days, when hunger haunted Montreal, but out it all came anyway: whitefish, puddings, roast deer meat, shellfish, spruce beer, tarts, fresh rolls, wild turkey, boiled corn kernels with maple sugar, omelette soufflé, pears, apples, jams, fresh cream, and Ella's famous raisin bread. All this was followed by strong coffee—somehow procured on the black market—and delicious sweet biscuits baked by Hickory according to an Oneida recipe.

Everyone quickly surrounded the laden table. The food was so inviting that James Morely even forsook his magazine right in the middle of Benjamin Franklin's satire, "The Speech of Polly Baker," in which a woman accused of begetting a bastard child persuades her judges to release her, then marries one of those judges the next day.

Candles and lamps blazed extravagantly away; nothing was spared for a hearty send-off. Who knew when the Lees would again have such a feast, friendship, or warmth?

All through dinner the talk was lively and animated. When the food was nearly finished and coffee was served, Mel Webster rose with a smile and raised his glass of brandy to toast their departing friends.

"...and I pray their journey will be full of warm cottages and lodges, will be memorable for long feasts with Mohawk Valley farmers, and will have as its high point a refreshing visit to Oriska, the finest Oneida village in the northwestern Indian country, where my wife's genial family will make them welcome!"

There was a chorus of approval, but Reverend Lee looked slightly embarrassed, pushing back his spectacles and saying he was sorry, but they had no plans to visit Hickory's people, who lived near the wagon road through the valley.

"I'm sure they're the fine God-fearing Christians I've heard tell they are," Lee said, with a slight stammer of self-consciousness. "But we'll not have the time to dally there; we must keep up with the rest of the convoy."

In response, Mel glanced at Hickory, and both smiled. Mel toasted again, and declared, "To the Lees, honored winter guests of the Oneidas at the village of Oriska, home of the most Calvinist Indians on the frontier! Yes, Reverend Lee, they're not exactly Presbyterians with a Scotch-Irish twist, like you are, but they're Calvinists like you, and will welcome you...especially when you come there in company with Hickory and me!"

The group applauded at what seemed to be good fortune for the Lees, who would have the aid of Mel and Hickory on the journey. By the time they reached Mohawk country, they would be grateful for a warm bed and a roof over their heads. The Websters planned to go with the same sleigh

convoy as thé Lees, which would travel up the Saint Lawrence and along the shore of Lake Ontario, thus keeping to
lowlands all the way, and from there follow frozen rivers
toward the Mohawk Valley. The Oneida lived in several
villages near Fort Stanwix, a rebel-held bastion being re-
stored at the head of the Mohawk River.

Lee was openly enthusiastic and leaned over to his wife,
who was not so sure. "It's said the Oneida cabins are finer
than many white residences, my love." He smiled and patted
her hand to reassure her, but the delicate, meticulous Matilda
could only paste a polite grin on her pudgy face.

"It will be an arduous journey," she said in a sweet voice
with a Virginia lilt. "We'll be grateful for . . . for any succor,
my friends, and of course we'll be honored to be guests at
the village, if it's friendly to our kind."

Mel's expression became unusually serious, and he looked
directly at Lee. "You might like Oriska so well, friends,
that you'll want to stay there permanently."

Angus Lee was startled and gaped at Mel. Amazed at
such a thought, he adjusted his frayed and worn-out wig
and exclaimed, "No! No, the commissioners of the church'll
not grant such a thing! How——"

Hickory struck the table with her fist. "Yes, they will,
Rev'nd! Yes! Oneidas got some money saved. Got money.
And if we get minister to shepherd us, elders back in Bos-
ton'll be happy to pay for the man! Happy to pay!"

Lee was confused, and with brows puckered, he glanced
from the surprised Matilda to Mel and then back at Hickory.

Jeb Grey declared that there were more than good reli-
gious reasons for the Boston commissioners to send a minister to the only tribe of Iroquois that supported the rebellion.
He said in his deep, gravelly voice, "Sure, Reverend, they'll
likely set you up real handsome in Oriska, and Congress
itself'll probably kick in some cash—Continental dollars
only, I'm afraid, but better than nothing. They'll all want
a minister who'll hold the Oneidas to the cause, not one
who'll lead them to the Tory side."

"Dratted Anglicans!" Hickory murmured to herself, then
added, "All the Iroquois but us be dratted Anglicans! Mo-

hawks, Onandaga, Cayuga, most Tuscarora, and even Seneca who are not Catholic—all bad dogs of Tories!" She then gazed at Lee with eyes so admiring and pleading that it disconcerted him.

"We need the word of God, Rev'nd! We need the god of the Congress party to protect us from Tory enemies in these times." She became extremely agitated and left the table, entering the small pantry. Hickory closed the door, but the sound of her weeping could be heard.

Ella asked Mel what was wrong, and he said the Oneidas were deathly afraid of the powerful Senecas and other warlike Iroquois, who might wipe them out for allying with the rebels.

"There've been serious threats lately; it seems the Iroquois League is breaking up after two hundred years of cooperation." Grave, he sat down. "Never before have the Iroquois let their sacred council fire go out, but now, they've done just that. If the Oneidas don't return soon to the loyalist fold, the league will be no more, and their tribe will be in deadly danger."

Jeb asked, "What's Congress doing to protect 'em? Ain't they rebuilding Fort Stanwix? Ain't there enough rebels in Albany to protect 'em?"

Mel shook his head. "Congress and New York troops are stretched to the limit, and they can't justify sending troops or even military supplies to a couple of hundred Oneidas so far away."

It was Ella who said what they all were thinking. "But if they have a Protestant minister to plead their case and get white support, then the Oneidas won't be forced to turn Tory."

"Right," said Mel, looking at Lee. "They need a minister who cares about Indians."

Lee was unsure how to take this, and sat perplexed and silent. Seeing his distress, Lettie Grey clapped him on his bony knee, saying in her North-of-England accent, "It be a godsend for thee, I be thinking, Angus! Thee'd be the only rebel minister serving Injuns in all the northwest territory! Why, thee'll become famous through all the colonies, and they'll be hailing thy mission as an inspired testimony to the power of God." She winked. "And the Congress will wisely pay to spread the word of peace amongst Injuns."

Both Lees were dumbfounded. Had this offer to serve as missionaries come years ago, they would have been ecstatic. Preaching to Indians and converting them had been the minister's dream. But times had changed, and a minister living with outnumbered Oneidas would be in a very precarious, even dangerous, position.

Lee said precisely this, and asked, "Don't all of you see that? What you're asking of me is to be a rebel agent and a minister of God at the same time! Would the Lord approve of that?"

"Ask him."

This last was said in unison by seven voices, including Hickory's; she had poked her tear-streaked face out the door. Even Matilda had spoken, and Ella thought the woman showed a real stirring of inspiration.

Lee glanced about, like a bird, his glasses again sliding down to the tip of his nose. He smiled wanly, looked at Matilda, who seemed uncommonly intense, then cleared his throat.

"I shall!" Lee declared, then became resolute. "I'll pray for guidance this very evening! This very moment!"

Jeb was startled; he cleared his throat awkwardly until Lettie discreetly kicked him on the shin. Lee solemnly took his wife's hand and bowed his head. Hickory fell to her knees by the pantry door, hands in prayer, like a little child. The room was silent.

Lee did not speak aloud, but prayed in his own heart for some sign, some divine guidance. After a while, he sighed and raised his head. The others also looked up. Lee's eyes were vacant. He was lost in thought, and his companions waited for him to say something profound.

But it was Hickory who spoke first. She was praying aloud, eyes tightly shut, hands in supplication.

". . . that we might have a noble shepherd to show us the way to heaven, and feed our souls with spiritual food. And that he should accept the call of the Harvard Corporation, the corporation, who have offered their support for ministration to my people—" At this Hickory opened one eye to take a look at her husband. ". . . and the commissioners in Boston, who have granted permission and means to erect a grand new meetinghouse..." Again she opened one eye, this time to look at Lee, who had lifted his head slightly at her last words. "...meetinghouse with steeple...so the Oneidas, and perhaps Tuscaroras, too, can be instructed, and souls saved on path of regeneration, repentance, and faith! This we ask, Lord, that we may go with one heart, one mind, and with Thy blessing, as Presbyterians of the new light." Before saying the "Amen," Hickory quickly added, "Or Anglicans come with money and rum to force us down evil path, along with the king and his damned ministers."

Again there was silence, this time a dramatic moment that ended when Lee again sighed and looked at Matilda. She was as moved as he—particularly at the news about the meetinghouse.

Lee licked his lips, swallowed, and spoke to Hickory, who was yet on her knees. "The steeple might not be necessary, my child, for religion loves simplicity, and God would dwell in the meanest cottage if it had but a single humble and penitent inhabitant."

Lee cleared his throat and nodded to Mel, who was observing him closely. "If my beloved Matilda will consent, I'll consider the offer of the Oneida, and will do whatever the good Lord permits me, his unworthy instrument, to do for the salvation of these humble folk."

Hickory was aglow, and Mel grinned broadly, saying, "They like real long sermons, Reverend, and they think that since Mohawks have steeples, they should have one, too."

Matilda said immediately, "I have a fondness for steeples myself, I must confess, though they should be modest. It's nice," she said, her eyes a little distant, her expression whimsical, "to see a steeple, like a signpost to the Lord, rising out of a grove of lofty trees..." Her hands described the steeple, the branches, and ended upon her husband's right hand, giving it a squeeze.

Mel lifted his glass. "To Oriska!"

• • •

A few days later, the Lees said their final good-byes at dawn in the Place des Armées, a large square fronting the imposing Church of Notre Dame. The sky was bleak and cloudy, and piles of dirty snow lined the footpaths.

In the square were twenty sleighs drawn by small, sturdy horses, stamping and frisky, eager to go. Since the track southward was fairly well used, it was expected to be clear all the way to Albany. If roads were drifted or blocked, however, the convoy would follow a succession of frozen streams, most of which were wide enough to accommodate these light, fast sleighs.

The Lees, with a short Canadian driver up on the dashboard seat, were bundled under furs in one of the sleighs, its hood pulled closed against the wind. Their possessions were piled on the opposite seat, and they rode facing forward lest Matilda become nauseated. Both were cheerful, though nervous, and when their friends arrived to wish them farewell, everyone became nostalgic. In the following sleigh rode the Websters, excited to be returning to Oriska. They would take care of the Lees, Mel declared with a wink as he discreetly showed Ella a satchel of six black grenades amid his luggage. That was some comfort to Ella, and she tried to be cheerful as she kissed first the Websters, then the Lees, good-bye.

Filling the square now were several hundred other well-wishers who had risen early to bid farewell to friends. The travelers included merchants, Whig dignitaries coming and going between the lower colonies and Canada, and folk like the Lees who could no longer remain in Montreal. There were plenty of tears, bits of songs, and shouts of encouragement.

The horses snorted and blew clouds of breath into the frosty cold. Their stocky drivers, mainly aging Canadians, all seemed to be related. Each had a stubby pipe, stocking cap, cleanshaven face, and keen eyes. At the head of the convoy two sleighs of rebel soldiers rode as escort, and another followed as a rearguard. It had cost Mel Webster and Angus Lee dearly to pay for this journey, but many in Montreal thought them fortunate to be able to get away at all.

With the blare of a horn, the crack of whips, and the shouts of drivers, the convoy set off. The crowd in the square moved back, waving handkerchiefs and hats, calling out best wishes, and drying their eyes. It was over in a flash as the sleighs whisked one by one through the square and down rue Saint Jacques toward the frozen river.

Ella was standing with her two children, and beside them were Lettie and Jeb Grey and James Morely. The friends were four fewer now; already the city seemed a bit less hospitable, the wind colder. As the crowd dispersed, church bells tolled heavily, filling the square with an echoing din. It was time to go home, but Benjamin gave a cry and darted toward a snow-covered bush near a corner of the church. The boy hunched over, and was joined by Susannah and Heera. Susannah kept the dog back, and Benjamin picked up something, putting it in his felt hat before returning to Ella and the others.

It was a young blue jay with an injured wing. As Benjamin showed it to Ella, Heera stood on his hind legs, one paw on Susannah's arm, to take a sniff—and received a sharp peck on the nose. Heera yelped, sniffed indignantly, then sat down.

"I suppose you want to tend it," Ella said. Benjamin said he did, and Susannah was in full agreement.

"We'll keep it in the cellar for now, until it can fly again, then we'll let it go," Benjamin exclaimed, hoping his mother would agree. She did, and rubbed his tousled head.

James took a look into the hat and jumped back when the jay tried to peck him as it had Heera. "Well, you've got no grateful patient there," he said. "Jays are rude and mean. You'll have a goodly share of holes in you before you're done, children."

"Please don't call me a child," Susannah said in an exasperated voice, glaring at James, who bowed. Susannah was satisfied, and said, "Jay won't peck me; we'll make friends." She reached very gently into the hat, and amazed them all by taking the bird in her palm.

Benjamin said that if she held the bird, he would splint the wing when they got home. James agreed to be a consultant to the operation, and off they all went to rue Saint

Jacques. The blue jay gave a loud squawk whenever some-one passed them on the street. More than one passerby thought Benjamin was making fun of them, and there were annoyed looks and wagging heads all the way down rue Notre Dame.

*chapter* **9**

# LIEUTENANT GOVERNOR HAMILTON

The small wooden ball skittered across the ice until it was trapped and controlled by a long stick in the hands of Benjamin Sutherland. With the speed and grace of a wildcat, Benjamin hunched low, skating through two defenders, steering the ball in a blur of fakes and deft touches with the curved end of his stick.

Few shinty players were better than he, and he was sure of himself, sensing a goal at hand. First he would shake off the big lad crowding him from behind; then he would be open for a shot to tie the game. The goal was just yards ahead, with only the crouching keeper to defend against him.

He swerved to his left, making a full spin; the boy behind him was still going, outwitted. All in the same movement, Benjamin whirled for the goal, the ball seemingly glued to his stick. He cut in behind the beaten opponent. The goal was there, its keeper already throwing himself down to block the shot. Benjamin cocked his stick for a hard backhand shot, knowing it must go in.

But as the stick met the ball, the defender rammed him from behind. Benjamin went down hard. The shot flew wide.

With a groan of dismay, Benjamin got up and skated back slowly, head down, stick dragging. He was angry that he had given the defender a chance to hit him. He was even more angry that he was too small to have kept his balance.

"Too small," he mumbled, skating sluggishly toward his dejected teammates. "I'll never be big enough. . . ."

The bells of Notre Dame began to toll five o'clock, signaling the end of the game. Benjamin skated off the ice, past cheering opponents, who said he had played well and wished him better luck next time. Susannah was waiting on the bank with Heera, having come to this cove on the Saint Peter's River to fetch her brother for Sunday supper. Sensing his dismay, she kept silent as he sat down heavily and unstrapped the skates from his shoes.

Then a voice behind said in a French accent, "My young man, you have to learn to lean . . . to use your weight better!"

It came from a hooded sleigh standing at the roadside, and the children looked up to see the round face of Dr. Michel Devalier smiling out from within. They waved to him, for he was a close friend of the family. He was also an avid sportsman who loved to watch shinty, a game brought to America by British soldiers. Benjamin knew Dr. Devalier had been quite a lacrosse player in his youth, so he listened when the elderly gentleman explained how to anticipate a shoulder charge and to keep low so it would not bowl him over, no matter how big the other man was. Devalier was eighty by now, with a pure-white goatee and eyebrows that gave him a spritely appearance.

As the doctor talked, he stiffly got out of the sleigh and came down the slope to them. Susannah took his arm, for the bank was slippery. His lively eyes glittered with enthusiasm as he gave Benjamin a few valuable pointers.

"I'm just too small," Benjamin complained, gazing at the ice.

"Look, you," he said, poking the lad's arm, "you're as tall as I already, so you're not too small to play well." He winked. "Win or lose, I never needed an excuse at lacrosse! Ask the old-timers! A few still rub places where I hit them— it was good I knew medicine, for their sake." He chuckled, and Benjamin's gloom vanished.

The sun was setting, turning the sky deep blue and purple. The cove grew quiet, the only sound being Dr. Devalier's frail voice, instructing Benjamin how to use whatever strength he had to best advantage. Heera lay down to watch, while Susannah became party to the good doctor's demonstrations—sometimes acting as opponent, sometimes a teammate; and while lights twinkled on inside the city, the friends in the cove forgot everything except shinty.

There came a slow clopping along the road above the cove, and a heavily laden sleigh making for the city drew into sight. The sleigh was pulled by an old nag, and sitting on the dashboard was a skinny, toothless Frenchman. He stopped the horse to hail Devalier and light a pipe, and the doctor waved to him, then told the children this was Félix Joffre, who worked as a teamster for Bradford Cullen.

Eyeing the burden of crates on the sled, Susannah said softly, "He's got a lazy man's load tonight! But he can't be lazy if he's even working on the Sabbath."

Devalier nodded, watching as the Frenchman urged his poor horse slowly onward.

"Bradford Cullen makes his people labor when he demands it, and there is nothing to be done for poor Félix. He has no pride, I'm afraid, and will even work for the likes of Cullen. Yet, in these times, if I had eleven children . . ."

Dr. Devalier then said he should be getting on to the hospital, and the children ought to go home before their mother blamed him for delaying them. They escorted the kindly doctor to his sleigh and bade him good night, then trudged along the road, following the sleigh of Félix Joffre. Benjamin was in better spirits now, chattering to his sister as Heera loped ahead, sniffing trees and casting about from side to side.

Then they heard a grumbling and complaining, and in the dimness made out Joffre's sleigh. It was canted to one side, a runner in the ditch. The horse stamped, alarmed, and the lanky Joffre was swearing loudly as he fussed about, trying to figure a way to get the sled out.

"Too dark for anyone to drive on this road," Benjamin said. "Maybe we can help him get—"

There was a loud noise behind them, and they sprang aside as another sleigh drawn by two magnificent gray horses came thundering past. The children were surprised that neither this sleigh nor Joffre's had running lamps lit. The second sleigh pulled up close to Joffre, and someone stuck his head out of the hooded interior.

"You imbecile of a useless French fool!" he wheezed. "I can't depend on you, Joffre! I told you everything must go perfectly according to plan."

Joffre shook his fist at his whickering horse. "It is all the fault of this miserable beast, Monsieur Cullen!"

At the mention of Cullen's name, the children became frightened and hung back. They were near enough to watch, however, and called Heera to their side. Then Susannah noticed several crates that had spilled from the sleigh when it had toppled. One crate was shattered.

"See," she whispered, hand to her mouth. "See there, brother! Those are muskets in the Frenchman's crates."

Benjamin was astonished, for he knew the rebel army closely controlled the shipment of arms in occupied Quebec Province, yet there were no soldiers in sight. Arms shipments were few and far between, because Congress was too poor to afford much military equipment. Yet here were twenty or more crates, probably five hundred precious muskets in all—enough to arm a regiment. But why were they being moved on a Sunday night, and without an escort?

Susannah asked the same question, but he reminded her that Cullen was the army's commissary and could ship muskets however he pleased.

They spoke in a whisper and were distracted when they heard Joffre cry out, "You did not tell me these were weapons, *monsieur!* You lied to me! I will not—"

Just then two men leaped from Cullen's sleigh, and Joffre stopped speaking. In the gathering dimness, the children could see only shadows moving back and forth, but Heera growled ominously. They held the dog steady and hoped they would not be seen. By now it was dark enough that they were safe, as long as Heera did not give them away.

There was some commotion near the sleigh; then a man—

not Joffre—called out to the horses. Cullen's own sleigh had been linked by a rope to the one in the ditch, and it moved forward. In a moment, Joffre's sleigh was free. After the spilled crates had been reloaded, Joffre's sleigh went on, following slowly behind Cullen, who drove rapidly ahead and out of sight.

"Strange," Susannah said, "but I don't think Monsieur Joffre was driving his sleigh anymore."

Benjamin thought the same, but this was really none of their business, hardly worth mentioning to their mother. They set off once more for home, Heera loping ahead. As they passed the place where Joffre's sleigh had been stuck, the dog whined and hurried by. Benjamin glanced down at a darker patch on the ground, which in the shadows of early evening looked almost like blood.

From the downstairs bedroom at Valenya there was a view of the apple orchard on the rising slope. Jeremy Bently slept in this airy chamber, with its large window, four-poster bed, chair, and writing table. Here Owen Sutherland had composed many of his essays on political conditions in America, and each time Jeremy looked at the well-worn desk, he thought of his stepfather.

Sutherland's famous essays had been published in every major periodical in America, as well as in England. They had never failed to stir strong response with their novel and sometimes radical ideas.

Sutherland used the voice of an imaginary Indian sage named Quill, who observed the tumultuous modern world through wise and witty eyes. Quill's pointed comments often scorched Whig and Tory alike; always they defended the cause of the American Indian. Parliament, Congress, politicians, philosophers, businessmen, and soldiers were poked fun at, and Sutherland's remarkable ability to unearth pomposity, ignorance, and tyranny—Whig or Tory—had made him quite a name. Even the French were translating Quill's ruminations, and it was said the Prussian court had taken great interest in American affairs because of Quill's witty narrations.

Now, however, Sutherland had thrown in his lot with the rebels against Parliament, and his name and Quill's were despised by most American Tories—as Jeremy had quickly discovered.

But Quill was not to blame for the fear and hatred Jeremy's stepfather's name aroused—for not only was Sutherland a skilled essayist, but he was a seasoned soldier, and old-timers here at the straits never forgot that. In fact, no one knew the Five Lakes of Canada and its inhabitants better than Owen Sutherland, and few rebel commanders were more of a threat to loyalists at Fort Detroit. Though Jeremy was resolved to remain neutral in a war he considered foolish and cruel, he hoped Sutherland would never come armed to the gates of Detroit. But the loyalists might lose the fort even without an armed rebel invasion.

With Montreal in rebel hands and Quebec under attack, the supply line to Detroit had been cut. Unless the British army broke the siege at Quebec, retook Montreal, and established firm control of the Five Lakes, the few hundred Redcoats stationed out here were doomed. What, Jeremy wondered, would rebel government of the northwest mean for the Indians and the French?

Gazing out the window late one afternoon in January, Jeremy considered the future, but saw no way to get through it without bloodshed. He leaned on the sill and stared at the brilliant red and purple sunset. Beyond that horizon all was peaceful, but for how long? Behind him, to the east, were his family and many of his friends. Beyond were the embattled colonies. He was far from that war, but for how much longer?

There came a knock at the door, and Gwen entered, saying Lieutenant Weston had come across the ice in a dogsled driven by Mawak, who had gone to see Tamano. Jeremy was eager to talk with Weston again and hurried into the hallway as Gwen excused herself and went upstairs.

In the common room, Weston was chatting with Annie Ross. Both sat in polished, hoop-backed chairs before the massive fieldstone hearth, where a fire warmed the cozy room. Although there were two Pennsylvania cast-iron stoves in the house, the common-room fireplace was always kept burning in winter, making all who called at Valenya feel welcome and at home.

Weston rose with a friendly smile and offered his hand. As usual, he was resplendent in his immaculate scarlet tunic and white breeches. Every piece of brass shone, as did his black shoes. Jeremy was pale, but vigorous enough, and he looked well in a brown vest and breeches, with a blouse of the best linen, and matching brown silk stockings. After Weston remarked on how improved Jeremy seemed, they sat down to business. Annie excused herself, but before leaving poured each a glass of port from a crystal decanter.

Jeremy thought Annie lingered overlong, and he looked up to find her gazing at him.

"Forgive me," she said softly, and smiled in that disarming, lovely way she had. "I just wanted to see how you were. You've been so much with Gwen these days, discussing that notion of a hospital, that I haven't had the opportunity to take a good look at you." She smiled again, curtsied to both of them, and departed in a rustle of blue gown and white petticoats.

"What a beauty!" Weston murmured. "Ah, what I'd give to live in the same house with her—and with an excuse to lie abed much of the time, too!"

He winked at Jeremy, who offered an unspoken toast and sipped some wine.

Weston drank, eyes twinkling as he looked at the door through which Annie had gone. "Were I you, lad, I'd stay abed through the winter, and then I'd find a way to get cut up again so these two damsels could indulge themselves soothing my hurts!"

Jeremy put down his glass and stiffly sat back in his chair. "I ache too much to think of anything but getting well again. It seems like only days since I faced Manoth—by the way, where is he now?"

Weston became serious, and with a swift swig finished the port. "Don't you have anything stronger?" He rose and went to a wall cabinet, where a bottle of the best Scotch whiskey was always to be found. "Now, this is more like it," he said, pouring himself a liberal dose. "Not as civilized as port, but better than the cider these Frenchies cook up.

At least it's not the rotgut our traders sell the Indians and call high wine for lack of honesty and imagination. High wine, indeed!"

"What would you call it then, Richard? Liquid chains? King George's holy communion with the redskins? Parliament's elixir? Guaranteed to sway the hearts and minds of the meanest savage—"

"Come, come," Weston said, returning to his seat; he was slim and lithe, fluid of motion, and with clear blue eyes that were intelligent and penetrating. "We don't depend on firewater to hold the Indians to us. Look at Manoth. He won't touch a drink ever since Owen Sutherland made such sport of him with a mixture of laudanum and tobacco juice!" He cackled at the thought of that and sipped the whiskey with relish.

Jeremy pressed. "Where is Manoth now?"

Smacking his lips, Weston said, "In the service of the king. That's all I'm at liberty to say, because the fiend's away on a secret mission. Yes, he's recovered from your waltz with him, and he's been warned by Lieutenant Governor Hamilton to refrain from abusing loyalist physicians ever again."

A black anger welled up in Jeremy. "You mean he's been let off even after he came here with his henchmen to burn me out?"

Weston nodded, contemplating a moment. "Lieutenant Mark Davies is a favorite with Hamilton, and Manoth is the right hand of Davies. The lieutenant himself interceded with Hamilton, though I did my best to have the Indian arrested and made an example of." Sighing, he said, "The army is unsure how to treat leading Indians these days, for fear they'll turn against us and support the rebels."

Jeremy got up and went to the window. He stood there, staring out. "So we scrape to Indians, do we? If Hamilton ever asks me about that—"

"That's why I'm here, my friend," Weston said. Jeremy turned as Weston helped himself to another Scotch. "Hamilton sent me over with his compliments, asking that you appear in his presence tomorrow morning, at nine sharp."

Weston shrugged. "Don't ask me what he wants; Hamilton has no secrets to share with a lowly lieutenant."

Jeremy thought a moment. "Perhaps he wants to make an example of me for fighting his darling Seneca allies! Anyway, he'll have something to think about when I'm done with him."

"Hmmm. He will, no doubt," Weston mused. "No doubt you'll both have something to consider before your interview is done."

Weston stayed overnight. The next morning, a winter storm threatened over the straits as he and Jeremy set off across the ice in two sleds, each hauled by six dogs. It was Mawak who had introduced to Detroit the use of several sled dogs to carry passengers, instead of the usual one animal per sled, transporting only goods. The old Ottawa drove Weston, and Jeremy drove his own sled, having purchased a team of dogs from Mawak a few days earlier. For winter travel most French used small, shaggy ponies pulling sleighs, but dogsleds were the safest way to cross the river ice.

Jeremy brought the women's shopping list; while he met with Hamilton, the list would be filled at the Frontier Company store, now run by French partners. This would be the first time Jeremy had been to the fort since his arrival. He wanted to learn what military arrangements Hamilton was making, particularly with respect to the Indians.

They mushed across the gray, icy straits, dogs yelping, Mawak and Jeremy whistling and crying out commands. The animals obeyed as if they, too, spoke Ottawa. Jeremy's dogs followed Mawak's sled, so he needed to pay little attention as he drove, letting the animals have their head. The gloomy sky was lowering, almost black in places, but the sheen of ice and the snow-covered far bank reflected what little sunlight there was, giving a crisp, clean look to the straits.

As his sled skimmed up to the fort's water gate, Jeremy again felt that familiar sense of being home. The place was quite busy, for it was Saturday, when hundreds of Indians and *habitants* made special shopping trips to the trading houses. Many carried beaver pelts stretched on hoops or in forty-pound bales. The fort hummed with activity, and the bright scarlet of *voyageur* caps and sashes stood out against the plain leathers and furs of the Indians. People hurried through the gate, some pushing handcarts, others stamping in from the river road, trying to finish up their business and get home before the snow fell.

Leaving Mawak to see to the dogs and the shopping, the other men approached the fort's gate. A sentry of the Eighth Regiment, dressed warmly in a duffel coat, snapped his Brown Bess musket sharply to attention. Weston touched his hat in reply, and he and Jeremy entered. The narrow rue Saint Pierre was before them, and Jeremy paused a moment to take in the sights. The fort was jammed, streets lined with carts of wares and food for sale. Many more people lived here now than five years ago.

"How will these colonials ever make a living out here, Richard?" he asked, seeing a number of Americans standing beside handcarts, with trinkets, tools, and homemade food-stuffs displayed for sale to Indian and French trappers.

Weston shook his head as they pushed through the crowd and made for rue Sainte Anne. To the right it led toward the parade ground, where the lieutenant governor's quarters stood. "Prices are so low that folk are willing to go into debt just to pick up some skins. They hope that pelts will be more valuable next year if the rebels hold Montreal and stop the trade long enough."

They walked past off-duty soldiers in uniform, tasting a trader's keg of local cider. Then they came upon a young corporal seated on a stool, playing a lively concertina and singing while a tethered monkey gamboled and leaped about to the delight of watching children.

Jeremy could see this talented corporal was very poor, taking note of the patched and stitched uniform, which was otherwise neat. Even the concertina's bellows had been repaired more than once. Nevertheless, for the moment the man was a noble troubadour whose onlookers took pleasure in both his music and monkey. The fellow sang in a rich Welsh voice; as Jeremy passed, another man in the crowd joined in.

It was Simon Clancy, happily full of ale and in love with the world. Clancy stood beside the corporal, and he no longer wore the bandage about his head. He had a buxom half-breed girl on his brawny arm, and she smiled pleasantly as his voice rang out.

Jeremy and Weston pushed on to the parade ground, where a cannon stood near the flagpole. A Union Jack fluttered in the breeze, and Jeremy wondered how long it would fly over this vulnerable frontier post. Near the flagstaff a tall, slim man in a black cape sat before an easel, sketching with charcoals. His subject apparently was the square, massive Church of Sainte Anne at the far side of the parade ground.

To Jeremy's right was the lieutenant governor's house, whitewashed, well maintained, and trim as ever. A smaller British flag hung over the doorway to the two-story stone building. In this house Jeremy had spent his first years on the frontier after coming out with his mother in 1763. His uncle, Major Henry Gladwin, had been Detroit's commander in those perilous days, when Pontiac had nearly captured the fort by trickery. His uncle's courage and audacity had prevented that, and Sutherland's timely leadership of British troops had decisively defeated the Indians at Bushy Run in Pennsylvania. For ten years now, the tribes of the straits and the surrounding region had been quiet.

As he and Weston walked across the parade ground, Jeremy recalled what he had learned from Weston about Hamilton. The man was a professional who in twenty-one years of service had fought courageously everywhere from Quebec to Martinique. Of noble Scottish parentage, but born on an Irish estate, he had been appointed lieutenant governor partly because he had been through the French and Indian War and knew Britain's former Canadian enemies quite well. Indeed, Hamilton of all men had good reason to refrain from employing Indians against the rebels on the frontier: He had been a prisoner of war and had seen what Indians did to captives.

Pausing near the artist by the flagstaff, Jeremy glanced at the drawing and saw it was very well done. He was surprised to see such a dignified gentleman seated on a folding chair, powdered wig perfectly arranged, damask cape thrown dashingly over his shoulders.

Jeremy was even more startled when Weston stopped short next to the man, came to attention, and removed his tricorne, which was held out to the side in salute.

Lieutenant Governor Henry Hamilton turned and looked closely at Jeremy, who sensed that this artist was no ordinary man. Hamilton rose to his full height—as tall as Jeremy—and threw back the cape so that his splendid scarlet and white uniform showed, with all its gold braid. He was an imposing figure, refined and proud, at forty-two in the prime of life.

Jeremy bowed as he was introduced, and Hamilton did the same. The man was slender, with long legs, and seemed active and vigorous. His face was also long, with a high forehead and a slightly hooked nose. His chin was narrow, his lower lip full. Hamilton's blue eyes were keen and observant, full of good humor as he said cordially that he had heard much about Dr. Jeremy Bently and was honored to meet him at last.

"It is my honor, Your Excellency," Jeremy replied. He felt no stiffness or haughtiness about this man. Immediately they took a liking to each other, and Jeremy showed such admiration for the sketch of Sainte Anne's that Hamilton offered it as a gift. Leaving an orderly to pack up the drawing materials, the three went to the commandant's quarters. With a damp cloth Hamilton wiped charcoal from his fingers as they walked, and remarked that it would be strange for Jeremy to be a guest in a house that had once been his home. Jeremy agreed, glad to see that the man in command of thousands of Indian warriors was so sensitive to others. Hamilton surely would not spill blood simply for ambition, honor, or reward. That was some relief.

Inside the house, Jeremy stood in the main sitting room. He had spent many a night here as a boy, playing chess with Owen Sutherland or with his uncle Henry, but the place had changed considerably. The low ceiling beams, previously exposed, had been boxed in, plastered, and painted white, giving the room a more open, airy feeling.

The blazing fieldstone hearth was to the right, and on

the wall to his left was a new bookcase filled to bursting. Jeremy gave his cloak to another orderly, then went to see this treasure. In all the northwest, only Owen Sutherland's library at Valenya could match it. As Weston and Hamilton spoke quietly, Jeremy browsed along the bookcase. Hamilton had wasted no time collecting all the volumes to fill these shelves. Since he had come to Detroit by whaleboat, two months ago without much baggage, he surely had scoured the settlement to buy up books.

Jeremy remarked on this, and Hamilton joined him, looking pleased, hands behind his back.

"Yes, Dr. Bently, my home would not be complete without a good library. Unfortunately I was compelled to slip out of Montreal in secret, and could take nothing much with me, save for these few—"

He gestured with slim, graceful fingers at a shelf of a dozen books. Jeremy liked what he saw: Shakespeare, Swift, Addison, Steele, even Rousseau and Voltaire, those arch-enemies of British imperialism. Hamilton evidently was widely read. There was also a family Bible, obviously an heirloom, along with some manuals of military organization, including Bland's *A Treatise of Military Discipline*, and the innovative 1764 British army manual, known as "The Sixty-fourth."

Two of the most-thumbed books interested Jeremy: the explorer Jonathan Carver's journal, which concerned the country and peoples of the northwest; and Daniel Defoe's *Robinson Crusoe*.

As Jeremy touched the spine of *Crusoe,* Hamilton said it was his favorite, "an inspiration to me when I feel as though I've been cast upon a lonely isle amidst a sea of trees."

Jeremy replied, "As a child, I, too, owned that it was my favorite." Then he looked directly at Hamilton. "But now I find it unreal, fanciful. It should not cause a man to believe the wilderness is his, easy to shape and change, for that is impossible, and would cause much pain and disappointment."

Hamilton caught Jeremy's meaning. "I assure you, I have no such illusions, Dr. Bently. I do not see myself as some

Crusoe who can civilize this wilderness. Even I, a lieutenant governor, could not presume to have such powers."

Jeremy nodded once. "That, sir, is a comfort to me, for in these dangerous times, ambitious idealists are to be feared most of all."

"In every time." Hamilton looked closely at his guest, then smiled and went to attend to some business with the orderly, who waited near the dining-room door. Jeremy noticed that the old French map of the northwest, which once had hung on the wall opposite the hearth, had been replaced by a modern, tinted chart lettered in English. The new one showed fewer military posts in the region, from the far north at Michilimackinac, to Kaskaskia, just above the confluence of the Ohio and Mississippi.

Once there had been thirteen government forts west of Niagara, but now there were only two—Detroit and Michilimackinac. The lesser posts had been destroyed in Pontiac's War, or, for lack of funds, had been abandoned to local militias. But there were some new names as well, including Saint Louis and New Madrid, possessions of Spain, which had received the country west of the Mississippi in a treaty with France. To the east, Fort Pitt had been renamed Pittsburgh, and there were a number of inked-in notations along the Ohio and Kanawha rivers, indicating recent white settlements. Hamilton must have studied the exact location and size of each community—Bryan's Station, Draper's Meadows, Boonesborough. All were rebel-held.

At the door, Hamilton finished speaking to the orderly, who bowed and vanished into the kitchen. Richard Weston and his superior stood near three chairs; Jeremy was still examining the map. Hamilton spoke first:

"It's not the same country you left five years ago, Dr. Bently." He strolled to Jeremy's side and gazed at the chart, rocking on his heels. "The army's had to turn over forts like Kaskaskia, Vincennes, Cahokia, and Pitt to the militia. More's the pity for Pitt, because the rebels now hold it. The British army in the northwest is understaffed, undermanned, underfinanced—and undermined by every government that rises to power at home. We're considered a lamentable drain on their resources and a source of irritation to whoever longs to rid the empire of the frontier lands altogether. And there are many at home who would do so in a trice!"

Jeremy said, "If it wasn't for the fur interests in Britain, there might be no Fort Detroit, no northwestern territory, and no unfortunate soldiers garrisoned so far from the glory and the promotions of war available in other parts of the British empire."

Hamilton smiled. "There are not so very many unfortunate soldiers out here, Doctor—no more than two hundred under my command. Two hundred men to guard all this . . ." He swept his hand across the map, from the Ohio to the Wees-konsan country west of Lake Michigan. "It would be an impossible assignment for even three thousand soldiers, let alone two hundred."

Jeremy looked the man over and said, "Do you mean to try? Do you mean to keep the rebel frontiersmen from advancing westward? They hold a forward base at Pitt, and I doubt you'll drive them from there with only two hundred Redcoats."

Just then the orderly brought a silver tray with brandy. Hamilton politely thanked the man, who filled glasses on a low table before the hearth. Jeremy poked the fire up into a warm blaze.

Hamilton said, "Our intentions cannot be discussed with . . . merely anyone." He eyed Jeremy.

Jeremy picked up his brandy and toasted, "God save the king!"

The other two also stood at attention and drank their sovereign's health. As they sat down, Hamilton asked whether Jeremy would offer his surgical services to the military. Jeremy agreed that he would do so, at no charge, save for medicines and any cost involved. Then Hamilton said he could arrange for Jeremy to have access to the best available drugs and medical equipment, which were in storage at the fort. He added that Sennet, the military surgeon, was too ill-trained to attempt to use them.

Excited at this unexpected offer, Jeremy thanked Hamilton for such generosity. But the greatest surprise came when Hamilton said he wanted to establish a hospital in the fort. Jeremy glanced in delight at Weston, who discreetly kept out of the conversation.

Jeremy said he also was preparing to start a hospital. Then he waited as Hamilton mulled over his response. The officer said slowly, "I am prepared to offer you the hospital facilities in an empty barracks to accommodate at least a hundred patients, along with the necessary equipment, beds, linen, food, and even servants to maintain the place. Why, Dr. Bently, there won't be another hospital as fine between here and Philadelphia. I daresay it will be amply used before long."

Jeremy sensed the officer was leading up to something and reined in his joy. "And in return, what do you expect of me, sir?"

Hamilton was about to sip some brandy, but he put down the glass, and said, almost in a whisper, "Lead my Indians against the rebels."

chapter **10**

## A KING'S MAN

Jeremy's expression did not change, but inside he seethed at Hamilton's assumption that he would be willing to go on the warpath.

Hamilton may have sensed Jeremy's turmoil but did not remark on it. Enthusiastically he explained his plan to commission Jeremy as a surgeon major, which would make him one of the most important regular officers in the northwest. Though such a commission was subject to approval by the War Office in London, the army, desperate for qualified officers, would surely approve the rank as permanent.

"You'll come and go as you choose, and after the unpleasantries are over, you may either resign or sell the commission, or stay in the army and eventually receive the full pension and all the honors due you."

Jeremy remained unmoving. He had anticipated some such offer; but the high rank was a surprise.

"Dr. Bently, I want you to help me organize a force of Indians for a major campaign against Fort Pitt. And I'll be honored to count on you as special counsel on Indian affairs. I need someone I can trust, someone the Indians respect, who can hold them in check."

Hamilton intended to coordinate Indian raids up and down

the frontier, combining the warriors with a fast-moving force of loyalists and regulars. Eventually they would capture Fort Pitt for the crown, denying many small settlements the protection that key post now offered.

Abruptly Hamilton stopped talking and stared at Jeremy, who was gazing at the fire. There was a moment of heavy silence. Weston cleared his throat and set his glass on the tray with an unintentionally loud clink.

Jeremy said, "The hospital would do a great service to all, and I'm even prepared to help finance it, Your Excellency; but I'll accept no commission, nor will I be a partisan fighter for you." He looked at Hamilton, who governed his own emotion. "There's no white man alive who can hold back Indians who've tasted blood. I need no more reason than that to refuse. You, who have fought with and against Indians, surely know that to be true."

Hamilton lost some composure. "Dash it all, man!" He strode to the map and shook his fist at the rebel communities to the eastward. "I have my orders! I wish no unnecessary bloodshed, and that's precisely why I want reliable white, British officers with the war parties! If I chose to I could unleash five thousand howling savages under French leadership and burn out every hovel and stockade from Montreal to Savannah! But I'll not do that! Can't you see I want to conduct a humane war, a war which will achieve limited objectives? After the first raids, those frightened rebels will flee back to the colonies. We will control the frontier, and the traitorous Congress in Philadelphia will have to spread troops up and down the borders to fend off the Indians! Then the British army can strike from the sea, and the rebels will be too weak to prolong the war."

Hamilton came to Jeremy and asked, "Are you not a loyal king's man? Or was that toast a lie?"

"A king's man I am, sir! But this trouble was caused by wrongs on both sides, and I'll stand neutral until you all come to your senses! Sending Indians on the warpath, with King George's name as their war cry, is madness, treacherous, and—"

"Jeremy!" Weston cautioned, lifting a hand.

Hamilton stepped back again and went to the hearth to

stare glumly at the fire. Jeremy's accusation was not new to him, and it was obvious that he was tormented by what he had to do. But he most certainly would do his duty.

Above the hearth was an exquisite sketch of the sun-dappled harbor in Martinique, where Hamilton had won glory and promotion. Now this cultured, intelligent officer looked deeply troubled.

Sighing, he turned to Jeremy. "If I do not employ Indian partisans, I might as well surrender this post," he said quietly. "I will not sit here and wait to be struck by a swarm of Virginians or Pennsylvanians or Carolinians who decide to win the northwest for their colony. That's what it will come to before long if I do not keep the colonies, their frontier settlements, and their backwoods fighting men off-balance."

He went to the map again. Indeed, it seemed very large, with Detroit merely a pinpoint at its upper center. Gravely, Hamilton said, "I am charged with the responsibility to hold this country for our king. Dr. Bently, I mean to do that, with whatever resources fate and my government have given me. By taking Montreal the rebels have cut off our communication with London and New York Town, so obviously nothing but Indian allies can stop the rebels from fighting their way to my very doorstep!"

He strode to the window and indicated the people milling about on the parade ground. "Those, too, are my responsibility, and if rebels take them, they'll suffer."

Jeremy knew that many loyalists had been persecuted, imprisoned, and even executed by rebels. Some who had taken refuge at Detroit were wanted by rebel courts back in the colonies. As for the Indians, their future under the rule of Congress was precarious at best. He knew the Indians would be happy to fight rebels, especially those who had settled illegally in Indian country.

Hamilton said, "There will be difficult and tragic times, I'm sure, and it will lie heavy upon me if innocents suffer in this war. That is why I intend to assure that only armed fighting men are attacked, and that women and chil-dren—"

"You cannot do a thing about it!"

"Do not interrupt me, sir!" Hamilton's military bearing and strict discipline brooked no such insolence. "I brought you here to assist and advise me in this endeavor! If you truly wish to save lives, then join my staff forthwith, and—"

"Neither can I do a thing about it when Indians go battle-mad! Don't expect me to be able—"

Hamilton threw his glass into the fire, shouting, "I told you not to interrupt me, Dr. Bently!"

Jeremy was on his feet, his own temper boiling. "Speak common sense, sir, and I'll listen to what you say, not before!"

"Jeremy!" Weston cried and leaped between them. "Do not address my superior in this way! You do us all an injustice!"

Weston had grabbed Jeremy by the arm, but was shaken off as Jeremy declared to the furious Hamilton: "Prove you can manage the likes of the Seneca Manoth and I'll believe there's sense in what you say! Keep that murderous dog at heel even among us loyal folk, if you can! Should you bring him back to Detroit I'll go for him again, and you'll have to decide whether or not to hang me when I'm done with him!"

"Leave off, man!" Weston gave Jeremy a slight shove, nearly causing him to retaliate, but Jeremy contained himself. "The lieutenant governor has ordered Manoth away from the straits. I told you that!" Turning to Hamilton, Weston pleaded, "Forgive him, sir. He's still suffering from his run-in with Manoth, and from . . ."

Hamilton straightened his tunic, obviously aware of what Weston had left unsaid—that Jeremy's wife had just been killed. Jeremy drew back, quivering with anger, for he knew he could not change Hamilton's military plan—no doubt directed from London, by ministers who had no understanding of the brutality of frontier warfare.

Hamilton stood erect, his voice trembling with indignation. "This is your final warning, Dr. Bently, and hear it well: Men have been put in irons for less than you have said today. We are at war, and any man who presumes to remain neutral is liable to severe punishment. Assail me in public as you have done just now, and you will rot in prison! Am I understood, sir?"

Jeremy glared at him, and Hamilton bristled. Then Jeremy realized there was no use in pushing this any further, not if he wanted to be at liberty to work here.

Composing himself again, he bowed correctly to Hamilton. "Your offer of a commission to help save lives by going to war is a well-meaning one, Your Excellency, but I have more fruitful means of saving lives." He simply could not help but add, "I'll not be a party to a bloody slaughter. Nor should you. Good day, sir."

Jeremy spun on his heel and stepped to the door. Hamilton's face was red, and Weston was aghast at such blatant disrespect toward the most powerful dignitary for a thousand miles. If only Jeremy had simply declined and departed with common courtesy!

Jeremy opened the door, aware he had pushed the officer too hard. When Hamilton called his name, he turned, expecting this time to be arrested.

Hamilton's face had fallen, and his mouth worked slightly at the corners. He stared at Jeremy through dull, listless eyes.

For an instant Hamilton's voice nearly broke with emotion. "As for . . . the . . . hospital." He cleared his throat. "I cannot offer the use of an army barracks to a doctor who is not also an officer."

They regarded each other for the briefest moment, and Jeremy nodded, beginning to leave.

"Dr. Bently . . ." Hamilton made a small conciliatory gesture with his right hand. "Establish a hospital elsewhere in Detroit and I'll supply you with whatever His Majesty's government can spare."

"I am grateful, Your Excellency, for any help you can give." Jeremy once again saw through the uniform, the rank, witnessing the man who wore them—a complex man whose duty was an awesome and heavy burden. He had no idea how Hamilton would respond to this requirement: "But the hospital must accept everyone in need, white or red."

Hamilton nodded once. "Tory or Whig."

Jeremy's dream would become reality! They held each

other's gaze while Jeremy thanked him again. He went out and closed the door, thinking how duty and unbending discipline sometimes made villains out of decent men. He hoped it would not happen to Henry Hamilton.

Jeremy was thrilled about the hospital, but deeply worried about what might befall his country. He made his way through the teeming fort, hardly seeing anyone. Then, hearing a shout, he turned to see Weston hurrying after him.

"Don't be disheartened," Weston said when he caught up.

Jeremy kept walking toward the Frontier Company warehouse with Weston at his side. For a while neither spoke. By now Jeremy had guessed that Weston must have told Hamilton he wanted to build a hospital, and must have known the man would ask Jeremy to lead Indians.

Weston finally said, "You know, he's a good man, and an honorable officer."

Jeremy agreed it was so.

Weston grimaced, saying, "I mean he's earnest about merely frightening the rebel settlers away, and not killing the pack of them!"

Nothing was offered in answer.

"He goes a bit too much by the book, but he knows his business, and he does have a great responsibility to the people—"

"So have I." Jeremy stopped and turned to his friend. "Richard, will you be one of the officers to keep the Indians under control?"

Weston stiffly said he had volunteered for the coming campaign, even though he admitted knowing little about managing Indians. "Everything'll be agreed with their chiefs beforehand," Weston blurted. "They'll be paid well for bringing in live rebel prisoners—much more than just for taking scalps, and—"

"Scalps!" Jeremy grasped Weston by the front of his tunic and nearly lifted him off the ground. Soldiers and civilians nearby turned and fell silent, scenting a brawl. "You mean to tell me Hamilton's paying for scalps?"

Weston shook himself free, anger rising at such an insult. "Do that again, my lad, and I'll ask you to draw sword!"

He adjusted his tunic and said, "Paid for victories, yes, and enemy scalps are symbols of victory—victory over rebel fighting men!"

Jeremy was repelled at the thought of a scalp bounty being offered for white settlers, and he said: "There will be wholesale slaughter if money is offered for scalps, for who can tell whether a scalp came from a rebel or a Tory, or a male or female, or even a child? We have nothing more to say to each other, Richard." Jeremy strode away down rue Sainte Anne. Weston sadly watched him walk away into the crowd.

Seldom did war favor the kindly and the just, Weston thought. Jeremy might be right about the Indians, but Hamilton had a sacred duty to save the northwest for the crown, even at the risk of being labeled a bloodthirsty scoundrel.

Weston understood the reasoning quite well. His own proud regiment had shamefully lost its standard in Canada last year, so he had that humiliation and the deaths of many brother Redcoats to avenge. Weston wanted no innocent blood on his hands, but he was determined to fight rebels to the death for the sake of a British victory.

Returning to Valenya by sled, Jeremy mused bitterly over what had happened. He would indeed have his hospital, but nothing could outweigh the horror that would erupt when the British army sent Indians on the warpath.

The wind died as he crossed the ice, sled dogs trotting easily, runners gliding through a thin layer of blown snow. The sun was setting behind him, and the black standing stones took on a soft tint of purple, their bulk shining against the dark blue sky in the east.

Valenya looked homey, its windows glinting the color of sunset, smoke drifting straight up from its stone chimney. To the right, between the house and the standing stones, were the charred ruins of the barn destroyed by Manoth. Strong emotion rose in Jeremy as he thought of that Seneca, who one day would pay for all he had done.

Approaching the shore, he mushed the dogs up from the ice, and it was a pleasure to see the door of the house thrown open in welcome. Annie Ross stood in the entrance, her father, in shirtsleeves, beside her. As Jeremy ran the sled around the right side of the house, Annie came scampering toward him, skirts flying, and leaped lightly aboard, excitement and admiration in her eyes.

In spite of his dour mood, Jeremy could not help but smile. As he stepped on the foot brake, crying for the dogs to halt, Annie was nearly thrown forward, and with a squeal she kept from falling by throwing her arms around Jeremy's neck.

He laughed and stepped away from the sled, carrying her, feeling how supple and light she was. His injuries hardly hurt at all. Annie laughed, too, and made no effort to stand. For the moment, she and Jeremy were alone at the side of the house, and she gazed intently into his eyes.

Annie said, "It's nice to see you laugh."

"You just cheered me up, Annie." Jeremy gave her a little toss so she had to land on her feet. "It's good to be welcomed home."

"A special dinner is almost ready," she said, rubbing her arms against the chill.

As Jeremy set about unhitching the harnesses, preparing to lead the dogs to their kennels, Annie stood shivering and bit her lip, as though expecting to hear something. Jeremy hardly spoke as he worked, but felt her watching him. He knew she was attracted to him, but he was not interested in anyone at all. His mind was on the hospital and the war. When he thought of a woman, he thought of Penelope—a thought that hurt too much.

Then he realized that Cole Ross was at the corner of the house, pipe in his mouth, also staring expectantly. Jeremy, harnesses in hand, nodded to Ross, who waved back, smiling. Jeremy led the dogs to the kennel shed and Annie walked alongside, eyes on the ground, arms crossed.

"A special dinner?" he asked.

"Gwen prepared everything—a special meal for the occasion."

"What occasion?" He unhitched a dog and directed it into its compartment, which had a door that slid up and down.

"Your new commission, of course! We're all so proud!"

Jeremy stopped short, dropping the sliding door of the kennel too soon, startling the dog, which backed up and became restive until Jeremy sharply told it to be still. Then he peered at Annie and saw how she was full of excitement, barely containing her joy.

Making no reply, Jeremy put the dogs away, and Annie quickly helped him water them. As she worked, she said that Jacques Levesque had come over and was waiting at the house. Jacques had heard that Hamilton would appoint Jeremy surgeon major, and Annie wanted to be the first to congratulate him.

Jeremy stood listening at the end of the row of kennels, not sure how to reply. He did not feel good. Annie approached deliberately, taking his hands and saying how wonderful it was that he would be a king's officer. Jeremy noticed Cole Ross slipping away. At the same time, Annie came very close, face tilted slightly back, lovely lips parted. Whispering his name, she closed her eyes and kissed his cheek, then his lips, a lingering but careful kiss.

Jeremy had been confused and annoyed at first. Annie's kiss, however, had changed those emotions, setting him ablaze as her body pressed against him. It would have been so easy to put his arms about her lovely body....

He held her off, and her eyes opened wide as he stared at her before saying coolly, "Your felicitations are... appreciated, Annie. But they are not warranted. I've turned down Hamilton's commission."

Startled, Annie caught herself, swallowed, and came to her senses. "How could you—how could you do that, Jeremy? Do you know what it will mean for you? For your future? Why, one day a man in your position, with your ability, might be governor of this territory, of all Canada! A man like you—"

He took Annie's soft hands and said firmly, "Hold on, girl. Let me worry about what it means for my future. A man in my position has enough to do already, without sniffing around for political advancement."

Annie gripped his hand in both of hers, which suddenly were quite cold. "But His Excellency would depend so much on you! On you, above all, to save us from the rebels! You would surely be his successor, and after the rebels are defeated, you'll be honored for having helped hold Detroit! Oh, won't you reconsider? Won't you—"

Jeremy touched her lips with the back of a finger and looked into those large, shining eyes that told so much about Annie Ross's feelings for him—as well as about her own ambition.

"I've made the decision, my pretty one. I'm a physician, and my place is to save human lives, not counsel Hamilton on how to destroy them."

Annie suddenly looked away. He saw the glint of tears.

"Of course, Jeremy." She tried to smile. "I understand you have to be true to your oath. But I only pray that being denied your service will not cause us to lose the straits to the enemy. And I pray that one day Lieutenant Governor Hamilton will offer you another place of prominence."

Jeremy smiled. "Perhaps. But no matter. At least he's offered to support our hospital, with beds, linen, supplies— all the help in his power—"

At that there came a shriek of delight, and both Jeremy and Annie turned quickly to see Gwen a few yards away, arms laden with firewood. She was wide-eyed, ecstatic to hear that the hospital was finally becoming a reality.

"Forgive me, both of you, but I could not help over- hearing...such wonderful news!" She quickly curtsied, looked at Annie's hands resting intimately on Jeremy's fore- arms, then forced a little smile before hurrying toward the house.

Annie's look said she thought Gwen sweet but naive. "I fear she's somewhat jealous to find me...here in your arms."

Jeremy smiled at Annie and answered, "She has no rea- son to." At that Annie masked whatever she felt, but stared at him. Jeremy went to the nearby woodpile and gathered an armful, saying cheerfully, "Take a few sticks, Annie; don't stand out in the cold without doing something pro- ductive."

Annie lifted her chin slightly. She turned with a whirl of her skirts and gathered a goodly pile of wood. Without another word, she went to the house, walking with head back proudly. He smiled. He liked her—he liked both women, very much.

For just an instant he thought he saw Gwen standing in the window, watching him. Then the image was gone, and he could not be sure. Lamps began to be lit in the house. Yes, it felt good to be home, and it would be fine to meet with Jacques Levesque again. There was much to discuss about war and politics, and Jeremy wanted to find out where the French and half-breeds stood, and what Jacques intended to do.

That evening, after a delightful dinner, the three men retired to the fireside while Gwen and Annie cleaned up. The war was temporarily put from their minds. Cole Ross had played down any disappointment he had felt when Jeremy explained why he had refused Hamilton's offer. Jacques had not said a word about it.

The cozy fire and Jeremy's satisfaction with a good meal combined to give him a sense of relief. He avoided spoiling the evening by discussing the touchy subject of British plans to use Indians against rebel settlers.

Smoking pipes, they listened to Ross tell about his past in Montreal and New York. He had been a soldier in the York militia during the French war and had seen some of the most savage fighting at Ticonderoga, Oswego, and Niagara. Like many other men who had settled on the frontier after seeing it while in the army, Ross had great hopes for the region's future.

"Naturally, New York Province should govern the northwest," he said between puffs on his white clay pipe, "York currency being the most common money, and all the military supplies and such coming up from New York Town. The British army's American headquarters have always been in New York Town. Our region's administration might already be called a York administration. We just ought to make it official and annex the whole country as a county of New York."

Jeremy chuckled and said Virginians, Pennsylvanians, and Carolinians felt the same way as New Yorkers did about possession of the northwest. "Not to mention Connecticutters, Massachusetts folk, and even Marylanders! They all want the Indian country, and they're willing to come out and take it over, maybe even fight one another to do it—after they're done fighting Parliament."

In his strong French accent, Levesque grumbled at that. "Your colonials want this country, that is true. After this uprising has been quelled, they will still clamor for control of the northwest, and land speculators will be just as active as ever. Pah! Damned *anglais* thieves! This is not their country at all!"

Ross and Jeremy were startled at the sudden change coming over Levesque, who had drunk amply that evening. Now a latent, buried anger was beginning to rise, like a volcano expelling lava.

"They all want this country, and it does not matter who has power—Parliament or Congress! It is only a matter of time before they come and take it from the Indians—yes, and from us French, too! They don't love us any more than they love the red man!"

There was a silence. Even the two women at the stone sink had paused in their work, listening to this sudden tirade. They all felt included in the category of *anglais* invaders greedy for the land that for two centuries had given Jacques's people a bountiful living.

Levesque sighed heavily and knocked out his pipe on the hearth. "Maybe I say too much. I am sorry, *mes amis*. It is not fair of me to speak so in your home." He stood, saying he would retire; a cot had been set up for him in the clinic. Then he hesitated and looked at Jeremy. "It is time to tell you, my friend, that I have also chosen a path in this trouble—the path that will best serve my own people, keep my country free of *anglais* settlers for as long as possible. I am joining the loyal forces."

This clutched at Jeremy's heart. Jacques did not have to say he would be a partisan leader of war parties. He would be one of the best men in Canada for this, having served New France in this role, and having been a renegade with Pontiac against the British army.

Jacques and Jeremy both were pale. Only Cole Ross was excited, and he leaped to his feet, pumping the Frenchman's hand. Levesque seemed embarrassed, and he politely released the Yorker's grip.

"I take no great pride in this, Monsieur Ross." It was apparent Jacques had considered the step at length before committing himself to it. "Nor does my family. It is a dirty war. It will get no better before the rebels are beaten and overthrown." He looked down at his hands, opening and closing them, then rubbed them absently on his velvet breeches, as though they were covered with something that repelled him. Quietly, he said, "As they must be, lest they devour my beloved wilderness..."

To Jeremy he said, "I will do my best to follow Hamilton's orders and to keep the warriors in check, *mon ami*. I wish that you, too, would join me in this, for the sake of all our people. It will not be easy, and we need good officers."

Jeremy and Levesque stared at each other in silence. The stillness was broken as Gwen suddenly dropped the pewter dish she was drying and dashed from the room in tears. Annie, however, came resolutely forward and said with a voice full of emotion, "Our prayers go with you, *monsieur*. We all know the painful decisions loyal folk must make in these times, and we are grateful to you for your sacrifice in the name of the king!"

Levesque gave a helpless, curt laugh. "Not in the name of the king, *chérie;* but in the name of *les Canadiens,* my people. My people who have a homeland, but no rulers they can call their rightful government. My people are free, like the Indians, and we will fight to preserve that freedom."

He looked at Ross, then back at Annie. "For the moment, the rebels in Philadelphia are my worst enemy, because if they have their way, their settlers will populate my land. Parliament at least will keep this country wild, as I want it to remain, even though Parliament will do so only to save the fur trade, to profit the wealthy lords oversea."

They were quiet as Levesque considered what he would say next. Perhaps he wanted Jeremy to respond, but Jeremy was too saddened that such a good man as Levesque might soon be responsible for many deaths.

The *voyageur* pursed his lips. "This choice we will all

have to make, sooner or later. The sooner the loyal forces rub out the rebellion, the sooner the killing will be over, and we will have peace again."

Again there was embarrassed silence; outside the wind had picked up, rattling the shutters. Jeremy knew the might of the king would eventually win. No puny colonial volunteer militia could withstand the greatest sea and land forces in the world. Levesque was right to want it over soon. Jeremy understood the feelings of Canadian French and respected them. A rebel triumph would surely launch wholesale settlement of the northwest, especially if the Indians were allied with the British. The vengeance of rebels against loyal tribes would cause bitter, full-scale war in the northwest, and Indians could not possibly win against the colonies.

Jacques left the room, saying a quiet good-night. He would be a valuable ally to the British and Indians. The warriors respected and trusted him, and he knew how to fight their way. He would lead the Indians well against their toughest, most formidable enemy: the bold frontier folk who dared penetrate Indian country—every man, woman, and child of them.

*chapter* **11**

# SHADOWS OF WAR

Winter deepened around Montreal, and with it came hunger and disease. Every morning saw funeral processions, with mournful bells, priests, and black-clad bereaved. Rebel militiamen and French children began dying from smallpox and malnutrition.

Ella Sutherland's family was never hungry; but buying food—even finding someone selling it—became steadily more difficult. When bread was available, it cost ten times the usual price; any produce or meat was almost invariably half spoiled or short-weighted. Still it always sold out, to those who could buy. Nowadays, the sellers were seldom the usual French shopkeepers or farmers, but more often mysterious men, surly rogues of a low sort, who seemed to be in someone else's employ.

Each Saturday market morning there were fewer French vendors at the square, and fewer stalls. Prices went up steadily, and decent merchandise became ever more scarce. Merchants were required by martial law to accept Continental currency at a fixed rate of exchange, but if a buyer showed British sterling, the best merchandise would magically appear. Poor rebel soldiers with their worthless Continental dollars stood before vendors and shopkeepers, staring at moldy, weevily bread, rotten meat, and wilted cabbage. Yet such things were all they could buy. Even sour local wine or diluted cider was exorbitantly expensive for rebel troops, who these days were seldom paid at all. Congress simply did not have the cash—even in continentals—to meet paydays. One shipment of dollars from Philadelphia was stolen, its guards killed. Though it seemed as if someone who knew of the shipment had conspired with the robbers, there was no evidence. But even when troops were paid, their money did not go far to alleviate suffering.

French residents helped one another, sharing the burden. But few French were willing or able to help the occupying troops, who so desperately needed food and medical care. There were five thousand French inhabitants in the small city and vicinity, and nearly four hundred ragged, sickly rebel soldiers. These crowded quarters caused friction, brawls, knifings, and thefts. As winter waned, there was no chance of winning Montrealers over to the rebel side. The troops, who had to fend for themselves, were hated by the citizens for their insatiable hunger and uncanny ability to steal anything left unguarded.

Ella did what she could to help both soldier and citizen, but her funds could go only so far without bankrupting herself. Owen needed much of their hard cash at Quebec, and no money was coming in, because the fur trade was stopped. In any case, foodstuffs were so expensive that even an impossibly large sum would not solve the problem of feeding hungry people through the harsh winter.

Ella knew someone was profiting from the sale of food, and suspected it was Bradford Cullen. Whenever a herd of cattle or a load of produce neared the city, men met the shipment on the road, miles from Montreal, and bought up everything on the spot. Then the food was carted the rest of the way to the city and sold at great profit. The common merchant had no chance to get into this arrangement. Unable to earn a living, he, too, was thrown out of business, to starve like everyone else.

Ella and her friends combined their efforts to open public kitchens, where the poor could have a meal of bread and soup for almost nothing—indeed often for nothing. She also saw to it that Dr. Devalier and his associates were well supplied with whatever medicines were available. When the smallpox terrorized the city in February, a sustained effort by the elderly Devalier managed to quarantine the victims. With proper nourishment and cleanliness, the epidemic was curtailed five weeks after it broke out.

Often Ella and her two children dined with friends. Good company kept spirits high, and that was important, for it was seldom that letters came from Quebec, and she heard from Owen only two or three times between January and early March.

The Sutherlands made the best of a difficult winter. The children took much interest in the blue jay, which Benjamin trained to answer whistled commands. Among the family's closest companions were Sally and Tom Morely, who lived near the Greys, a few streets away.

Dark and tall, with long hair and a lovely face, Sally had been admired by the young bachelors of Fort Detroit. But last December, in the aftermath of the battle on Lake Erie, she had wed a young man who for years had been her suitor. Tom Morely was a big, strong fellow, lean and good-look-ing, with black, curly hair and a ready smile. He was an ardent rebel, but having been wounded severely in the head at the Lake Erie fight, he was forced to recover in Montreal before joining the troops facing Quebec. The couple were a perfect match, both optimistic, hearty, and good-humored. They would surely have beautiful children, they often were told, and it seemed everyone urged them to do so quickly.

Ella was reading the sonnets of Shakespeare before the stove one March afternoon when someone knocked at the door. Sally entered, a strange, anxious look in her eyes. The Sutherland children were away with Heera, and Ella was glad to see Sally, always a welcome companion.

Sally closed the door softly, and Ella laid down the book beside her on the settee. Her feet were up, and she wore a green housecoat and an extra pair of warm socks. Missing Owen so, she found comfort in books, and Shakespeare's poetry always made her feel content. These poems were Owen's favorites, too, and she heard his voice when she read them.

Sally paused, as if uncertain of what to do next. Her fingers nervously touched the buttons at the breast of her dress and she stood gazing at Ella, making no move to take off her dark woolen bonnet.

"Just in time for tea, dear," Ella said, sitting up. Her own blond hair hung in loose curls over her shoulders, and the unruly wisp at her forehead was, as usual, not to be managed. She was aware that Sally was staring hard at her. "Or something stronger?"

Sally looked disturbed but tried to be casual as she sat down in an armchair. When Ella suggested she take off her hat and cloak, she seemed startled at that idea. She did so, letting them lie on the back of the chair, then busied herself with her new wedding ring.

Ella said, "September's always a good month to give birth."

Sally's mouth dropped open. "Do I show so much already?" She felt at her middle, which told nothing at all. "It's only just come clear to me that . . . that I'm really to be a mother!" She became dreamy. "Is it possible?"

Ella smiled. "Of course summer is a hot time to carry, so you'll have to get plenty of rest and good food, and try not to do too much in the garden. We'll rent a vegetable plot just outside the walls, and you and Tom can share it with us. Susannah and Benjamin will be happy to do your part of the work." She stopped abruptly, her own attempt to be casual falling apart as she felt her eyes fill with tears of joy. "Bless you, child!"

Sally moved quickly to Ella's side, and they embraced, tears flowing freely. They laughed, held each other back, and Sally bit her lip as Ella looked her over.

"You're fine and strong! Ah, Sally, this is like my own first grandchild! Be prepared for me to spoil—him? Her?"

"Oh, Ella! I never knew what it meant to be happy until now! Tom doesn't know yet, but when he does, he'll . . . he'll— What do men do when they learn they're to be fathers?"

Ella laughed. "He'll be more nervous than you, and at first you'll have to keep him from worrying too much about you. He'll get in your way trying to help you with everything, but after that he'll almost forget you're pregnant, and you'll be expected to work as hard as ever! Ah, my Sally dear, it's so wonderful!"

Again they hugged each other. Ella pushed her away and said, "You must fetch Tom from the cabinet shop and tell him now! Go there immediately, for there's only an hour left to the workday! Give him the joy of boasting to his friends right on the spot!"

Sally hurriedly put on her cloak and bonnet, fumbling in excitement. Her husband and two Frenchmen had set up as cabinetmakers a few weeks earlier.

At the door, Sally said, "It is your grandchild!" She kissed Ella's cheek. "Write to Owen and tell him that if it's a boy, we'll give him his name."

"First talk that matter over with Tom, dear. Don't be too hasty about anything right now. Why don't you both come for dinner tomorrow? We'll make plans for the birth. Dr. Devalier will be at hand, if necessary, and Lettie makes a wonderful midwife."

Upon closing the door Ella leaned against it, a pleased smile on her face. She, a grandmother! She must be getting old! But it was not so bad, not when Sally and Tom were happy, and the other children were growing as fine as she could ever want. She knew not why, but she no longer feared for Jeremy. There had been no mail from Detroit, what with war and winter, but she knew he was alive. How she longed to hear something from him, though!

If only the war would stop and Owen would return, they could go back to Valenya. Dear Valenya! She was sure Jeremy was keeping it in order, but hoped he had the spinet tuned now and again. The apple orchard would need tending in the spring, and the new barn. . . .

Ella missed her home, but Sally's news made her incredibly jubilant. She would write Owen immediately. Whatever he was enduring out there, this news would instill new hope and would remind him of what he was fighting for.

Since the Frontier Company had been broken up and the partners scattered, its two warehouses at Fort Detroit were

one too many. The one that had once belonged to Lettie
and Jeb Grey was closed, its stock and furnishings transferred to the store of Jean Martine, an aging Frenchman
who had been a founding partner of the company in 1764.

Jean, the father of Jacques Levesque's wife, Angélique,
was looked upon as a worthy merchant who supported the
loyalist cause. He still traded under the name Frontier Company, but was freely patronized by everyone in Detroit.

Along with Jeremy Bently, Jean Martine and his daughter, Angélique, were the only chance the Frontier Company
in the northwest had of surviving the war. If, as everyone
hoped, peace was soon made and some reconciliation
achieved, then perhaps the trading firm would again be
reunited, and the Sutherlands and their friends could resume
their careers out here in the wilderness. For now, the company at Detroit was small, its future uncertain.

Martine actually did fairly well that winter, considering
there was scarcely any fur trading to speak of. Lieutenant
Governor Henry Hamilton was the reason. He had put in
an enormous order for thousands of pounds sterling worth
of trade goods, including vermilion paints, beads for wampum belts, hand mirrors, blankets, trinkets, essential tools,
hats, colorful shirts, and ammunition. The army bought out
nearly the entire stock of the Frontier Company and the
other traders in the fort. Hamilton had announced a great
Indian council at which he would shower the tribes with
gifts and honors.

Already at least two thousand Indians from twenty nations of the northwest were camped in bark and skin lodges
around the fort. They anticipated generous quantities of
goods—gifts were always generous during times of war.
The Indians knew only too well that the loyalists wanted
them as allies. In the past they had shifted between French
and British in the struggle for domination in America, always careful not to let either side permanently control them.
With France defeated, however, they had not been able to
play one side off the other for twenty years; perhaps now
was their chance to resume that ancient role.

But only the British offered gifts now, and only the
British could prevent white settlers from taking Indian lands.

Thus most chose the side of the king—a giver of presents bountiful enough to content an Indian's heart.

In fact, Hamilton bought so much merchandise that little was left for merchants to trade to Indian trappers for pelts. New shipments of trade goods were not to be had that spring—not as long as the rebels controlled Montreal—so Indians who wanted the manufactured necessities of life would have to be in good standing with Hamilton. In the name of King George the Third, the great white father across the sea, Hamilton would present these indispensable articles in order to win the Indians' support in the war against the rebels.

And, as everyone knew, it was not the tools and clothing that mattered most among the army's store of presents. Above all, the Indians needed muskets, lead for bullets, kegs of gunpowder, hatchets, and the services of the fort's gunsmith to repair their firearms. In the fur trade, sales of powder and ball were strictly limited, but Hamilton now was generous with such dangerous goods. Indians also liked the short-bladed knives known casually as "scalping knives." The once-ominous name had lost its significance; but with spring opening paths in the forest for Indian runners to carry British war belts of red and black beads, Hamilton's gifts of scalping knives renewed the old, dreaded meaning.

One day in late March, Jeremy Bently stood in the empty warehouse with Jean Martine, discussing how to convert it into a hospital. The portly, merry Martine wore a leather apron over his drab linen and woolen clothing; whenever he spoke, he took the clay pipe from his mouth and stabbed the air with it for emphasis. Jeremy was at the back, examining a window that needed repairing, when Angélique Levesque entered and hurried to her father's side.

Jeremy waved to her, but she did not seem to notice. She was wearing a short skirt, Indian-style, revealing her ankles, and her auburn hair was pinned up in back. About thirty years old, Angélique was a dusky beauty, slim and strong. The dark tone of her Huron mother mixed with her Norman father's ruddiness to make her, in Jeremy's opinion, the most beautiful married woman in Detroit. She and Jacques had three young children, but even these births had not dimmed her looks. She was as lovely as she had been at eighteen.

Now, however, as she turned slightly, Jeremy noticed that she seemed agitated and wan. Perhaps she was worried about her husband, who had been away for nearly two months. Jeremy shouted a cheerful greeting, but she hardly glanced up, then continued to murmur to her father quickly and softly. Martine glanced at Jeremy, and he grasped that whatever distressed Angélique somehow involved him.

Jeremy heard Angélique hiss, "Keep him here! Please, Papa, keep him here!"

Martine was grave as he patted his daughter's hand. Jeremy came toward them, saying that if this was none of his business, he would leave them alone.

"No, *mon ami,*" Martine said. "This concerns you." He stroked Angélique's hair, and now Jeremy could see that she was so upset she could not look at him.

"Angélique," Jeremy said quietly, "since when did you have to keep anything from me? Since when did you have to tell your father—"

"Jeremy, *chéri!*" she blurted, "Manoth has come back!"

Immediately Jeremy made to leave the warehouse, and she ran to him. "In the name of the Holy Virgin, do not go! Please, do not go! He is with Hamilton, and with the evil officer Davies! Please, do not go!"

"I must," Jeremy said, easing her away, his resolve making him grim and tense.

Then Martine was in his way, hand up to stop him from going through the door. "Not yet. For the love I bear your mother and stepfather, I will not let you go to Manoth."

"Step aside, Jean."

Angélique wailed. "They will destroy you! Hamilton will throw you in jail even if you kill Manoth! Jeremy!"

"Out of my way—" He was angry enough to use force.

But Martine blocked the door. The Frenchman was squat and sturdy, hard to budge.

"Jean—"

"I will not move!" Determination was fixed on Martine's face like a weapon. "I will fight you if you lay a hand on me!"

"And I!" cried Angélique, who leaped to her father's side.

Jeremy's fury was surging, but not at them. He felt caged, and did not want to drag them into this. They meant only the best for him, and he must avoid hurting them. There were other doors in the warehouse, but all were locked and barred. He gritted his teeth and demanded they let him through.

Martine said in a hoarse voice, "Not until you swear you'll not go after Manoth—not today at least!"

"I cannot!"

"You must! Or you fight me!" Martine was deadly serious. Angélique, too, would not let him go without a struggle.

Jeremy leaned forward, planning to throw them aside, hopefully without injury, but then he saw that Martine had picked up a thick length of stove wood. The Frenchman meant business.

"This is not your affair, Jean!"

"I make it my affair! You do not leave, except over my body. Unless you promise you will let your temper cool one day—until the sunrise."

Jeremy exploded, "He might be gone by then!"

"So be it," Martine said in a low voice. "Then I will be glad for having resisted you and having tempted your wrath. I'll not let you throw your life away! You will not pass me without a fight."

When Jeremy realized Angélique, too, had picked up a stick, he felt a sudden pain, a deep sorrow at being pitted against two of his oldest and closest friends. They, too, must have felt anguish, for Jean swallowed loudly, and tears ran down Angélique's cheeks. But they did not waver, nor did they yield the doorway.

Jeremy slowly shook his head and looked down at the floor. Fury flooded through him, tempered only by an intense love for these two people. It was no use.

"Ah, you crazy *habitants!* How I'd like to . . ." He gave a brief, helpless chuckle of exasperation and shook his head. "I will do as you ask. I give my word to wait one day."

Angélique flew into his arms and hugged him, murmuring in French that it was better not to act rashly against Manoth, who was highly regarded by Hamilton for his ability to lead Iroquois. Jean Martine put a meaty hand to Jeremy's shoulder, saying the young man had more restraint than Sutherland, who might have needed a few solid French blows to his Scottish head before he would have seen the light.

"Where is Manoth?" Jeremy asked Angélique.

"I am not sure. . . . The woman friend of yours, the one called Gwendolyn, is watching him."

"Gwen? What in blazes is she doing watching Manoth?" Abruptly he made to leave, but Martine reminded him of his promise.

Angélique said quickly, "She is clever for an English girl, and seems to know something about spying." Grinning, she added, "Gwen told me to stop you from going after Manoth, for it was she who saw him return; he and Lieutenant Davies came in with rebel prisoners from the Susquehanna country. Gwen has gone to see to their health, for many are ill and weak from the long journey."

Jeremy said, "As a physician, I must go, too!"

But Angélique stopped him. "Gwen said she will come for you when she knows what those poor people need. I've heard they are to be housed in some old, unused cabins. She insists that you wait until she summons you."

Jeremy was angry that Gwen dared to be so haughty. "Who is she to tell me when to come and go?"

Angélique took his arm and smiled. "She is a nurse, Jeremy, and she hopes to serve you, rather than bury you before your time."

Martine nodded. "We need a doctor who is at liberty, not a jailed killer. Now, keep your word to us and wait until Gwen sends for you, *mon ami.*"

A short while later, leaving the warehouse with his two friends, Jeremy stepped into the bright sunshine and a street muddy from the spring thaw. The mud slowed the crowd streaming through the fort on the way to view the rebel captives.

Jeremy had to keep his promise to leave Manoth alone for at least one day, but he longed to go immediately to the prisoners, who he knew would need medical help, food, and probably clothes. Yet if he went, he might be unable to avoid challenging Manoth on the spot, thus breaking his word. The residents of the fort were hurrying to the parade ground, off to Jeremy's left. They were all chattering excitedly. Jeremy gazed down the mobbed street. Off in the distance, near the middle of the parade ground, he could make out feathered headdresses and the bobbing heads of leaping Senecas. A drum was thudding rapidly.

"Come," Angélique said, tugging him in the opposite direction, toward the Martine residence. "Do not think about it."

Someone shouted Jeremy's name, and he looked around to see Richard Weston shoving through the crowd. The lieutenant sloshed up and said Hamilton wanted Jeremy to come immediately to the parade.

"There are sick and wounded folk there who need tending, and Hamilton's too much a gentleman to let your friend Gwen Hardy care for them all without having a physician on hand."

"What about Sennet?" Martine asked. "Why can't he care for them?"

Weston gave a helpless shrug. "Sennet's dead drunk. Anyway, he's a soldier's sawbones, and these are women and children—"

That was all Jeremy needed to hear. Taking Angélique's arm from his, he swore to keep away from Manoth, and in the next moment was striding swiftly down the muddy street, with Weston a step or two ahead. Angélique and her father followed, very worried.

At the parade ground, Weston called for people to make way for the physician. By now most whites had become very downcast. The Indian spectators, however, were shouting and laughing, making jokes that Jeremy understood were scornful of rebel fighting ability. There were many people in the way as he followed Weston toward Hamilton, who was seated at a table beneath the Union Jack, which snapped in the spring breeze. Jeremy could not yet see the captives, nor the Seneca raiders, nor Gwen. His heart beat faster, because he dreaded to see the prisoners, hedged tightly in by the circle of onlookers.

"Step aside!" Weston cried. "Make way for the physician! *Allez! S'il vous plaît! Allez!*"

All around Jeremy, whites were staring with a strange, uncertain fascination, as though seeing something both unreal and horrifying. The Indian spectators were not so spellbound; most of them had a gleam in their eyes, a proud look of triumph.

Then Weston was through the encircling crowd, and so was Jeremy, who immediately stopped short. He was face to face with Manoth. The Seneca stared at Jeremy, but not with hatred or anger. Rather, smug, deliberate humor was in his expression. The entire mob abruptly fell silent, even the drummer, an old Chippewa in a dirty gray trade blanket. Jeremy glared at Manoth. Only the snapping of the flag and the whimpering of a frightened child broke the stillness. Manoth folded his arms and stood squarely before Jeremy, who planted his own feet wide apart, braced for battle.

*chapter* **12**

# PATH TO WAR

It was then Jeremy realized Manoth's right eye was injured. Though the eye was still in its socket, Jeremy's dirk had given it a bad wound, and it now seemed dim.

Not sure what Manoth would do, Jeremy readied himself for anything, but remembered his oath to Martine and Angélique. If Manoth attacked, however, the oath was void.

The Indian grinned broadly, showing his teeth. Then he thrust out his chest and turned away to walk slowly toward Hamilton. The officer sat tensely behind a table near the flagstaff. The crowd was still silent. It was then Jeremy realized Manoth carried eight hoops, each about a foot in diameter, letting them swing casually in his right hand. Each hoop held a human scalp, dried and stretched like a beaver skin.

As though Manoth had given a signal by turning his back on Jeremy, the old Chippewa drummer cackled and began to thump with a stick on a hide-covered drum. The Indians chortled, and the whites whispered uneasily. Everyone had expected a fight, for the emnity between these two men was well known. But Hamilton had to be respected inside the stockade, and he would have stopped any conflict.

Holding up the hoops, Manoth stood before Hamilton

and proceeded to make a speech. The crowd grew quiet again.

Jeremy saw a movement to his right. It was Gwen, kneeling beside the captives. These were huddled on the ground, some on tarpaulins, others sitting dejectedly on chairs brought by sympathetic residents.

The prisoners numbered twenty, all of them women and children, dingy and ragged. There was no male over the age of six, yet these women must have come from at least five families, with husbands, sons, and uncles as well. There were several other hoops in the hands of Manoth's followers, who sat on chairs in the center of the parade ground, heads held high.

The women captives were downcast and haggard, with hollow eyes and tear-streaked faces. They sat with head in hands, or hugging children; one young mother tried to hush a crying baby swaddled in a torn buckskin shirt.

The parade ground was thick with mud, and as Jeremy went quickly to Gwen, his feet made a loud sucking noise. Manoth whirled to glare at this interruption, the Morris bells on his leggins ringing sharply. When Jeremy spoke quite audibly to the miserable captives, the Seneca nearly lost composure. Jeremy behaved as though the Indian were not there at all, the triumphal speech of no importance.

None of the women met Jeremy's eyes as he went from one to the other, speaking kindly, trying to assure them they would be safe. Gwen was treating the cut hand of a child of four, and several other children already had been bandaged. Jeremy sensed Manoth was still staring angrily at him, demanding that he should be quiet and listen to the boasts of victory, according to wilderness etiquette. But the physician paid no attention, even when other Indians became restive, eager to hear the Seneca's tale.

Loudly, Jeremy spoke to Gwen. "Take them to our company warehouse, and I'll arrange for beds to be sent; then we'll find clothing for them and see to it they have enough food. Ask the mothers what they need to care for . . . what's left of their families."

Jeremy felt someone behind him, and Gwen looked up, startled. Jeremy turned. The handsome young Seneca warrior who was Manoth's closest friend stood glaring, hands on hips, his face twisted into a vicious scowl.

"Move on," Jeremy said in the pidgin French understood by Senecas, "before I put my shoe in your pretty face."

The Seneca's eyes widened and his mouth curved downward, but he was unsure of himself and glanced at Manoth, who was barely restraining his rage. Then the young warrior burst into a flurry of speech, telling Jeremy to leave the prisoners alone, for they belonged to the Senecas until handed over to Hamilton.

Jeremy made a sound of exasperation and turned away to look at a frightened girl whose legs had been cut by the strokes of a lash. He knew these Senecas were incensed, but he did not care. His promise to Martine and Angélique did not cover other Senecas, and if this whelp pushed too hard . . .

"Move on, puppy-face," Jeremy said, without bothering to look at him.

There was an hysterical shriek from the Seneca, and with a cry Gwen jumped up swiftly. Jeremy sprang around to see that she had placed herself between him and the warrior, who had pulled a knife.

Instantly Jeremy grabbed Gwen's shoulder, but she struggled free and blocked the way so that Jeremy could not come to grips with the Indian. At the lieutenant governor's command, several Redcoats unshouldered their muskets. The crowd grumbled, some shouting for a duel. Manoth looked on, enjoying this confrontation, as Hamilton turned beet-red and shouted for order. Manoth obviously knew the British commander would have to accept these insults against whites now and again. But everyone was wondering how much Hamilton might permit in order to humor his touchy Indian allies.

Then a British officer called loudly to the young Seneca: "Otchaka!" In the Indian's own tongue, the man said, "Do not strike! Obey me, and trust me!"

The officer was a lanky, pockmarked fellow of thirty, with a thin, ruddy face, bony shoulders, and extremely long legs. He was dressed in the perfectly creased uniform of a lieutenant in the Eighth Foot, his bob wig freshly powdered and brass buttons gleaming. His eyes were strangely pale, almost white, and glittered with a predatory coldness, though he wore a polite smile. This, Jeremy guessed, must be the notorious Mark Davies, who despised Owen Sutherland and was an ally of Manoth's. Striding casually toward Jeremy and Gwen, the officer let one hand rest on his sword hilt, while the other absently pulled on his slender nose.

"Dr. Bently," said Davies, introducing himself with a slight bow. "Have you not been a resident of the frontier long enough to know Indian formalities? This wench of yours may be new to our—"

"Shut your trap, Davies," Jeremy put Gwen behind him. "Shut it or we'll go at each other, too."

Davies was cool, but had no reply at hand.

Henry Hamilton was on his feet now and shouted, "Silence! Both of you! All of you! Lieutenant Davies, hold that warrior in check! Pull him off at once!"

Davies bridled, surprised at Hamilton's severity. He did not know this new commander well, and perhaps expected that Hamilton would defer to the whim of such important Indians. Hamilton, still behind his table forty feet away, demanded that Davies call the Seneca raiders together, away from the captives. In a high voice the lieutenant protested that it was against all protocol.

Hamilton stepped quickly away from his chair, fists clenched. "There is no protocol for dealing with British subjects who are captives of Indians in a British fort! I'm making protocol! Now, obey immediately, Lieutenant!"

With a curt bow, Davies did so. Just then there came a croaking shout from beyond the crowd, followed by a hub-bub, as someone tried to break through to the open parade ground. Lieutenant Lawrence Sennet reeled out of the mass of people. Drunk and red-faced, Sennet wore dirty gray breeches, and his disheveled wig was askew, showing cropped gray hair. He squinted through glasses that had slid down his nose to his flaring nostrils, then cried out to Hamilton that he had come to do his duty and see to the patients. He staggered once, twice, reached to remove his hat in salute, then discovered he was not wearing one.

Hamilton stared blankly at the elderly man. Nearly everyone at Detroit knew that Sennet should have been forced to retire long ago because of his drinking, but was being kept on so he could draw a pension for twenty-five years of service. With admirable self-control, Hamilton quietly said, "Return to your room, please, Mr. Sennet. Arrangements have been made, and your . . . expertise is not at the moment required, thank you."

Sennet again reached for his absent hat, saying thickly, "As you wish, Your Excellency!" He was content to return to his room and get even drunker. Jeremy realized the man had been brought by someone else. But who? Then, as Sennet turned, wobbling, to reenter the crowd, Cole Ross appeared and began to help.

Jeremy immediately guessed that Ross had been part of the effort to aid the prisoners while keeping Jeremy away from Manoth. Jeremy caught his eye, and the trader gave a little shrug that said he had tried to keep matters in hand.

From his table, Hamilton spoke sharply. "Dr. Bently, kindly wait until I accept these captives—according to protocol—and then you can take them to your new hospital. But in the name of heaven, stand easy for a few moments, and let's arrange this unsavory affair with some sense of decorum. Next time the Indians might not bring their captives in at all, and simply settle for . . . for—"

"For selling you just the scalps?"

"Bently!" Hamilton roared, nearly upsetting the table in his anger. "I buy no scalps, sir! There is no bounty on rebel scalps!" To the people he cried, "Hear me well! There is no official bounty on scalps! I reward the Indians who have done their duty, as these Senecas have! There is one less illegal nest of rebels squatting in Pennsylvania, and one less base for rebels to use if they mean to strike at Fort Niagara!"

As if suddenly aware that he was fuming in a very ungentlemanly manner in public, Hamilton looked about at the sea of amazed faces. Then he shook his fist, evidently not caring what anyone thought of his bearing.

"Let it be known to all," Hamilton cried, "that the British army does not pay for scalps! The British army does pay for its allies to conduct war, and for prisoners brought in unharmed—but no scalps are ever to be purchased!"

Jeremy shouted, "Then what do the Seneca have hooped like so much peltry? Those tell the full tale of precisely what has been paid for!"

"Enough!" Hamilton roared and stepped forward. "Dr. Bently, I'll not debate this further. Continue to defy me and you'll find yourself in irons."

Then there came a third voice, loud but calm. "If you please, Your Excellency—" Davies was erectly at attention, a smug look on his face. "The rightful trophies of war are not to be denied His Majesty's loyal Indian fighters. Now, as is the custom, the great Manoth stands before His Excellency, Lieutenant Governor Hamilton, to relate his heroic exploits as a faithful subject of the king, at war with a cruel and treacherous enemy!"

Hamilton calmed himself; loyalists shouted in agreement. Gwen shuddered and returned to the captives, most of whom were sobbing now, embracing one another and stroking the dirty hair of their exhausted, terrified children.

In a strained voice, Hamilton said, "Dr. Bently, I requested your presence to attend to these prisoners; the cost will be paid by the British army. They will be lodged in appropriate housing until peace is declared. They may all come and go as they please, although they will not be allowed to leave the fort without a written pass. Now, sir, I officially accept these captives, and I would be grateful if you and your nurse would see to them before I am compelled to arrest you for disrespectful behavior!"

There was as much sadness in Hamilton's eyes as there was anger. Jeremy could see the turbulence within this British gentleman, whose duty required him to do what he did, yet who obviously ached to see the wretched widows and orphans.

Jeremy made himself cool down. Immediately Mark Davies stepped forward, again begging his commander's pardon, and asking whether he might consult with Manoth. Hamilton agreed, and the officer and the Seneca spoke in hushed tones in the Indian tongue. An expression of annoyance crossed the war chief's face, but Davies seemed to be insisting. After a moment Manoth reluctantly agreed.

Then Davies stepped back and, standing ramrod straight,

said with much pride, "The noble Manoth naturally wishes His Excellency to care for the captives as soon as His Excellency so desires; the noble Manoth will waive his right to have the captives present while he relates the trials and dangers of his conquest on behalf of His Excellency and the king."

"God save him king!" Manoth bellowed and grinned.

Since an Indian speech was melodramatic and lengthy, full of anecdotes, supplications to ancestors, thanks to nature spirits, and detailed explanations, everyone knew it would be best if the miserable prisoners were not required to wait through it before receiving treatment.

Gwen and Jeremy led away the dazed women and children. Then Annie Ross appeared and came to the side of one of the captives, joining in the long, silent walk through muddy streets toward the empty Frontier Company warehouse.

Few gave a kind word to the mournful prisoners, though many watched them pass. Even decent people living at Detroit were unsure what to say or think, or how to behave to their new enemies. Though the war was over for these women and children—indeed, might never have existed for them until the moment the Senecas killed their men—loyalists and French at Detroit held strong grudges against all suspected rebels.

These were the first captives to be brought in, but Jeremy knew there would be more—many more—before the killing was done. As he walked, carrying a sleeping two-year-old boy, he heard Manoth shouting. The drum beat in time with his fierce narrative. Savage yells rose from the throats of a hundred Indians as Manoth told of his exploits in Pennsylvania—but the white folk of Fort Detroit listened in silence.

In that makeshift hospital, Jeremy and Gwen worked without pause to treat and comfort the captives, but there was little they could do to console those whose loved ones had been murdered. The warehouse was dim, the sun having swung around to the west. On that side there were no windows, because just beyond the warehouse was the outer promenade, which followed the wall all the way around the fort; then came the eight-foot pointed palisade itself.

Mawak had come to the warehouse to help, and Jeremy sent him to fetch the medical bags from Valenya. Tamano, Lela, and their two children soon appeared, and before long the captives had a sympathetic and kindly group to care for them, including Annie and Cole Ross, Angélique, and Jean. Simon Clancy also arrived and spent the afternoon coming and going with something or other for the hospital. Others brought food, herbal medicines, cooking and eating utensils, and what blankets they could spare.

Jean Martine, on behalf of some anonymous French residents, brought bedding, towels, children's undergarments and dresses, wooden shoes, and all sorts of minor essentials that only families would have on hand. The baby in the old buckskin shirt received a beautiful lamb's-wool blanket. Through Richard Weston, Hamilton promised to send cots and food as well as chairs and more medicine.

Few of the victims were seriously hurt, but all had nasty lash-marks on their backs and legs, where the Senecas had whipped them to make them run faster on the grueling trail to Detroit. All were reluctant to talk—although this was a usual habit of frontier women, who were not given to chat with strangers until their husbands had examined and accepted them. These women had lived with strong men who seldom talked, and when they did it was about crops, hunting, the cabin, or imminent danger. Unlike many new settlers on the frontier who were well educated and who came to the wilderness to fulfill a dream or build a utopia, these were simple folk. Their kind had been in the frontier valleys for two generations.

Jeremy watched Gwen work on the wounds of the women, who were uneasy whenever he came close to them. None had been treated by a real doctor before. They had stringy hair and callused hands, but there was something fine and noble about their faces, which were open and almost childlike, though they knew great pain and sorrow. Jeremy walked slowly along the row of straw mattresses laid on the floor and contemplated these shy folk.

The children all had blue eyes, and each woman had light

brown hair and blue eyes. They were fair in complexion, though tanned by sun and wind, and all glowed with a vigorous good health that made them seem almost beautiful, despite their emotional desolation. These settlers might all be related—sisters, or at least cousins.

At an opportune moment he called Gwen to him and asked quietly whether she knew if it was so. A rush of tears filled her eyes, and her lower lip trembled as she opened her mouth to speak. Instead, she took a deep breath, wiping her face with a hand that shook slightly.

Jeremy said, "You're exhausted, girl. It's been enough for one day, I think. Why don't you go to Angélique's and get some sleep?"

She shook her head and swallowed, then said, "They're all so very afraid of us." Gwen seemed about to fall into Jeremy's arms, as though she needed someone to hold on to. Then she fought back her weariness and sorrow and said, "They hate us! They think we're such terrible people... think we're all murderers."

Jeremy felt deeply what Gwen was saying. He gazed at a middle-aged woman with three toddlers lying at her side. The woman noticed him and quickly looked away. She stroked a child's blond, curly head, then laid her own head on a pillow.

Annie, who had just finished passing out soup, joined them. She and Gwen looked at each other, then both averted their gaze for fear of breaking down.

"Three are sisters," Gwen said, clearing her throat, "but they're all sisters-in-law."

"What?" gasped Simon Clancy, who was nearby. "All five of them?"

Gwen nodded once and put her hand to her mouth, this time unable to stop the weeping. Annie moved away; she could stay in the room no longer. With a sob, she pulled open the door and was gone. Gwen said, in a hoarse voice, that their married name was Moriarty, and their husbands' grandfather had come from Baltimore forty years earlier.

"All the brothers were killed..." Gwen sobbed, and then leaned against Jeremy's chest. He took her arms and tried to say something, but could not.

Clancy moved away and knelt beside the woman with the three toddlers. He spoke softly to her. She glanced sidelong at him, eyes wide and afraid. He smiled as he spoke. Then she became more intent on what he was saying. Nodding, she looked away, and then back at him. One of the children—a boy with curly blond hair—came to Clancy, who had said something to him. Clancy sat on the floor, knees up, hands locked over them. He was talking in low tones, but everyone else in the dim building was aware of what he was saying, especially the mothers.

Jeremy whispered to Gwen, "They're all Irish, like Simon."

Gwen, hands resting on Jeremy's arms, watched the sailor get on the good side of the child, joking lightly with him. The boy smiled weakly and shook his head. Another child stood up, watching. Others drifted near as Clancy's friendly laugh reverberated gently through the room. The mothers watched, but did not object. A few began to clean up the empty wooden bowls and the spoons. One asked Lela softly where was the latrine for their youngsters, and was told it was out back. Lela assured the dubious woman it was safe to go out there, and Cole Ross offered to go along as escort.

The atmosphere seemed to lighten, and Mawak, who had returned, brought Gwen and Jeremy chairs to have their own soup at a table near the front door. Clancy soon had the blond curly-head bouncing cheerfully on his knee, and he began a song that comforted the folk in that large room. The soothing ballad was one by the famous blind Irish harper, Turlough O'Carolan, and was well known to these country folk, whose elders had sung it before their firesides.

The children tentatively sang along with Clancy, and soon even some mothers joined in, for it was like a lullaby. The youngest ones were laid upon fur pelts that in their poor homes would have been reckoned as priceless treasures, but which out here were as common as wool. Clancy's child soon was fast asleep in his arms, as he went on to sing another sweet Irish song. For the captives, the horror, dread, and exhaustion of the past weeks melted away, at least for the moment. Mothers and children lay down in the light of lamps that Lela and Tamano had lit.

Gwen, too, sat listening to Clancy sing, her soup un-touched. When Clancy laid the child by its mother and came back to Jeremy and Gwen, she took his hand, saying he had done a fine thing. The brawny sailor, whose own eyes were soft with sentiment, offered to stand guard that night, along with Jeremy and Tamano.

"First," he said, clearing his throat, "I think I'll take some air. Would you do me the honor of joining me in a walk by the river, Mistress Hardy?"

Gwen rose, and Jeremy saw a smile cross her face for the first time that day. He was glad for that, and considered Simon Clancy a lucky man. As Gwen and Clancy went out the door, Annie Ross returned and joined Jeremy. She said her father was waiting outside to take her home to Valenya, and asked what she could do the next day, when they would come back to the fort.

Jeremy spoke of a few essential things, and then saw how Annie was sadly observing the survivors, who were all asleep. The fort's night watch went past, swinging lan-terns and calling out seven o'clock. Sitting in the light of candles and oil lamps, Annie gazed at the captives as though her heart would burst.

"Why do we do it?" she asked. "Why must it come to this?" She looked at Jeremy, but he had no answer. She said, "It was people like these who began this terrible war, but I . . . I don't want them to suffer so! How can it be stopped, Jeremy?"

He took her hand, and her other hand covered his. He could think of nothing to say to Annie, who radiated such goodness and such beauty.

Again she spoke. "I wish, Jeremy, that you and I might have met in a happier time."

He smiled. "This is the only time we have, Annie. We had better make it as happy as we can, as long as it lasts."

She looked hard at him and squeezed his hand. "You may think me wrong to say this, Jeremy, but isn't it true that if you . . . if you would serve as a leader of the Indians, that this sort of tragedy would not happen?"

Jeremy stiffened, tired as he was, and became grim. He tried to be calm. "I could not stop five thousand Indians scattered across the frontier in hundreds of war parties, each group capable of causing such misery wherever it went! Annie, don't you see, if the British army can't win this war without sending Indian marauders against settlers, how can we justify what we're fighting for? If our American empire can stand only by the suffering of these innocents, perhaps the rebels are in the right! Perhaps they deserve to be respected as people who are willing to defend their liberty, and die for it! People who deserve to be allowed to live in peace."

Annie shuddered, eyes pleading. "Jeremy! Have a care what you say, my dear! This is disloyal—"

"Disloyal? Is it? Then let us not speak of it tonight." He released her hands. "Annie, what is happening to our land can never reunite Americans."

Annie sat back in her chair and sighed shakily. Outside, Cole Ross called softly for her to come home. She was distressed and clutched fiercely at Jeremy's hand. She stared at him as if trying to discover who he really was. He wondered whether she knew him at all.

At last, Annie rose and said, "Sometimes I think I understand why we have to fight the rebels . . . and then, at times like this, I don't understand anything anymore. You're right, it's best not to speak of it at all. It's best only to live for the moment, for whatever good we can do, and whatever pleasure we can find in life—even if we're so far away, out here."

"When you live out here," he said, "it's other places that are so far away. This is my home."

Seeming not to comprehend, Annie released Jeremy's hand and rose to go. But first she whispered, "How I wish I had met you in time of peace. It would have all been so much simpler. So much happier."

A baby cried, startling Annie, and her attention flitted through the room. Jeremy saw she was worn out, her nerves frayed. He stood up and took her soft hands to kiss them. "Get some rest. Perhaps you'd best not come back for a few days."

She nodded. "Perhaps not. But be assured I'll do what I can. I'll arrange food, mend and sew . . . whatever." She glanced at the people, but the crying of the baby again disturbed her. "I don't think I can come back here at all." She moved away a little and breathed in a whisper: "All of them sisters-in-law . . ."

Then she turned abruptly and went out the door. Jeremy closed it behind her. He stood there, eyes closed, forehead resting on the door. The baby was quieter now, and someone was singing a lullaby, tranquil and serene. The child whimpered once or twice and then was silent.

The lullaby ended, and Jeremy opened his eyes. Then he realized, with a tingle, that it had been Lela singing. An Indian lullaby had quieted the infant, and eased it lovingly to sleep.

For the next few days Fort Detroit throbbed with council drums, and the smoke of three hundred campfires outside the walls hung in a dark pall over the straits. Indians were coming in by the score for councils with Hamilton, who was tirelessly meeting with them, making speeches, and sending out presents by the wagonload to the encampments around the fort.

One Saturday morning, Martine and Jeremy stood at the fort's western gate, watching a dozen handcarts being hauled by soldiers toward the camp of the Iroquois, who had built several large longhouses near the river's edge. Around the two men crowded feathered, painted warriors and squaws in blankets, striding proudly through the fort, as though they all were honored dignitaries—as indeed many were.

The weather was clear, but unseasonably hot and dry. The sun had baked the mud, and the handcarts and crowds stirred up a cloud of dust that mingled with cooking fires and council fires to make the atmosphere foul and stifling.

"Never," said Martine, taking the pipe from his mouth, "never have I seen such wealth distributed by a commandant to the redskins! If Hamilton keeps this up, they'll be richer than we, and too contented to fight for King George."

"I suspect they'll be glad to take to the warpath if they can acquire all this and more," Jeremy said. "I only hope the fur trade will open up again, so the Indians will work for a living instead of going to war for it."

"Then you had better write your family in Montreal and suggest that Owen and his rebels give up the town so we can get back to doing business with Indian trappers."

They headed for the warehouse, where the women and children captured by Manoth were living. As they walked along rutted rue Saint Joseph, Jeremy found himself unconsciously keeping step with the beat of a war drum. He was about to comment wryly on this to Martine when he was distracted by a loud shriek. The people in the street all turned to look toward the warehouse, and Jeremy rushed ahead, afraid something was wrong.

But he pulled up immediately and laughed to see Little Hawk in the middle of the street, standing on his hands upon the back of a frisky pony. As the animal pranced back and forth, obeying the Indian's commands, Jeremy saw that the audience was the captive children. Dressed in clean clothes, they stood on the porch of the trading house, gazing in awe at Little Hawk, all laughing with rapt delight. Even the mothers were watching, though somewhat grudgingly, from the warehouse windows.

Jeremy and Martine stopped to watch as Little Hawk sprang lightly from his mount and caught up a seven-year-old boy, who giggled without fear when he was put on the back of the pony. Little Hawk jumped up behind the lad, and with a few words of encouragement, had him try the same difficult trick. As the boy's sisters and relations looked on in amazement, he soon had his short legs stuck up in the air, fairly wobbly, but held there by Little Hawk, who once more screeched in enthusiasm.

Then Little Hawk righted the lad, danced his horse on its rear legs, and trotted toward the child's mother, who actually smiled as her son was let gently down to her arms. Immediately, there was another commotion as Tamano and Lela called from the door of the warehouse that there was a gift of maple sugar candy waiting for the youngsters. They added that Mawak was within, ready with another colorful tale about manitous and the times before even the Indian owned the northwest.

With yelps of excitement, the dozen children rushed into

the warehouse for their treats and story. Martine and Jeremy chuckled, feeling as though their world was not so dreary after all. Just then Gwen and Simon Clancy came up, arm in arm. Jeremy had never seen her so radiantly lovely, and without thinking, he said, "Why, you look beautiful this morning!"

He caught himself, not meaning to be overly forward in the presence of Clancy, who clearly was courting her. "Of course, you always look beautiful, Gwen, but today . . . you look especially well."

She smiled at him, pleased, and said she had a new dress. Jeremy stepped back and remarked that the yellow gown, pinned up in front to show full white petticoats, was very fetching. Clancy winked at Jeremy, saying Gwen was the prettiest woman in Fort Detroit.

Gwen replied, "You'll make me blush, Simon! But what makes me feel so good today is the way our patients are recovering at last! Isn't it wonderful?"

"Indeed," Jeremy said. "We'll soon have to get permanent homes for them, where they can find work, raise a garden, and fend for themselves." He smiled at Gwen and added, "Thanks to you, they're going to be all right."

Gwen's gaze dropped briefly, until she said, "Thanks to you, Jeremy, it was possible to care for them properly."

As she looked at him, it seemed that the noise of drums, voices, and carts was shut out. He was not aware of it at first, regarding her without self-consciousness; but then he blushed slightly, sensing that Gwen's eyes had touched his very soul. And how very lovely she was!

"All right!" Clancy cleared his throat and grinned, a bit forcedly, breaking the spell. "There's a day of leisure to be spent, my friends, and if Gwen'll honor me with her companionship on a row downriver, she'll be even more beautiful for the enjoyment of it!"

Gwen agreed she would join him. "Would you like to come along, Jeremy?"

Clancy abruptly raised a hand. "Only a small boat, my lady!" He winked again at Jeremy, but Gwen noticed. "No room for anyone but us and a hearty picnic basket."

Clancy touched his hat to Jeremy and Martine and was about to draw Gwen away, but she paused and asked what Jeremy would do that day.

"You really should rest now," she said with feeling.

Jeremy smiled. "I mean to. There's a pretty spot I know at an old gristmill, where I have..." He might have said "fond memories," but did not. "...I have a special liking for the atmosphere." He glanced about at the smoky skies and said, "No council fires, no war dances, and no noise."

Gwen smiled at Jeremy and went with the Irishman, who took her on his elbow and strode off, singing a lively tune. Jeremy parted with Martine and went to the company stable. Soon he rode out the western gate and left the dirty, crowded fort and its raucous din far behind.

As he rode that beautiful spring morning, his spirits rapidly soared. He cantered over open meadows, where the grass was sprouting in pale green shoots. He tucked his hat inside his waistcoat and pressed on faster over the open fields, hallooing to French farmers at their plows, stirring up bevies of quail from thickets, and enjoying the fresh breeze in his face. He journeyed away from the blue waters, enjoying the sunshine, which was strong and bright. When he was several miles from the fort, at the edge of the dark forest, he turned southward in a long arc back to the straits.

Here and there groves of aspen were coming into leaf, and pines stood proudly against the light green buds in the maple stands. It was so good to be here again, good to breathe deeply of the air of the northwest wilderness, and Jeremy shouted to his horse, urging it into a headlong gallop.

The broad, blue straits came into view beyond a knoll, and Jeremy leaned forward on his hands and brought his feet up high above his head, just as Little Hawk had taught him years ago. The horse thundered on, the wind blew, and the colors and smells of spring were so wonderful that all else was forgotten. Only sensation. Only excitement. Only heady, intoxicating power and speed as he shot over that blurred meadow.

Jeremy Bently galloped on that way for a hundred yards. Finally, he let down his legs, stood in the stirrups, and let out a Highland battle yell, releasing his exulting spirit in a ringing shout of freedom.

Some time later, Jeremy rode leisurely to the old mill. It stood beside a pond that fed a stream running to the river's edge, and was gray and weathered, with a rickety, warped waterwheel. Nearly collapsed against the roof were the remains of broken, crossed sails that had powered the grinding stones when the brook was frozen. The mill had been out of use for ten years, ever since better gristmills had been built closer to the fort and settlement.

Dismounting, Jeremy let the horse graze alongside the broad, quiet pond, which reflected blue sky, clouds, and large green willows leaning over the water. It was here Jeremy had said his last good-byes before leaving Detroit five years ago. He sat down on the soft grass and idly tossed pebbles into the water, watching ripples drift in rings to the far side. There was much to remember, much to think about, but he did neither. Instead, he sat peacefully in this lovely glade, determined to make the most of the present, and of the future.

After a little while he heard his name called, and saw Gwen Hardy in a rowboat beyond the dam where the pond spilled into the stream. She waved to him, and he was pleasantly surprised to see her here. But where was Clancy? Jeremy waved back, got up, and strolled along the edge of the pond to help Gwen haul the boat ashore. Clancy was there, fast asleep in the stern, snoring contentedly. Jeremy and Gwen both chuckled at how childlike Clancy appeared, and they left the boat in the shade of a willow, while they walked together beside the pond.

Gwen bent to touch the bud of a tulip growing near the mill, and Jeremy stood back, observing how golden her hair shone in the sunlight.

"What brought you here?" he asked, crouching beside her to look at the flower. "How did you know I was here?"

"I didn't really know," Gwen said, looking briefly at him and then at other tulip buds nearby. "But I happened on this place a few days ago, and I like it, too." She turned to him again and smiled. "I suppose I did think I might encounter you here."

Gwen had a sunburn that made her eyes all the more blue. Once again he and Gwen regarded each other closely, forgetful of themselves, lost together in a timeless moment.

After a while Jeremy stood up, and she did the same. They were both silent, walking back around to the mill and its dam, near where Clancy slumbered in the rowboat. They sat on the dam's huge boulders, next to the cool, rushing water, and enjoyed the shade of the willows that lorded over the millpond. Gwen asked about this place, and Jeremy said it had been a favorite of his family's for quiet picnics.

"A very good spot for that," she said. "I'd offer you some of our own picnic, but I'm afraid dear Simon's gobbled it up, along with the wine and some of his own brandy!" She looked fondly at the curly-headed Irishman in the rowboat.

"You make a handsome couple," Jeremy said, and Gwen looked up at that, surprised.

"He's a handsome man," she said softly.

"And you're—"

She gazed at him, waiting. Once again they found themselves in that same, absorbed silence that seemed to speak for itself, though Jeremy was unsure exactly what it meant.

"And you're a beautiful woman." He took a breath and held it, tossing a pebble carelessly into the water. "I don't mean to sound . . . that is, I'm not trying to charm you; do you understand?"

Gwen gave a little laugh and plucked a blade of grass, which she took between her teeth and tasted absently. "I know, and yet I am pleased you find me—" She looked closely at him. "Just how do you find me, then? Besides being the beautiful part of a handsome couple?"

Jeremy was surprised that his heart was beating quite rapidly. Yet he was stubbornly determined to remain unattached, and he would not let his heart take command. Meeting Gwen's gaze, he said, with a twinkle in his eye, "I find you an excellent nurse."

At that her head moved ever so slightly, but she kept staring at him. He stared back, and this time saw a searching, penetrating look that challenged him to say more. He did.

"And of all the folk I know here at the straits, you're the one I'd most prefer to sit with me right here now . . . to share a place that means very much to me."

They both smiled wistfully at that, and Gwen put the grass between her thumbs, blowing through it and making a squeak loud enough to cause Simon Clancy to stir and smack his lips. Just then there came another sound. Someone was shouting and riding on horseback along the path from the fort. Through the trees, Richard Weston came into sight, posting rhythmically on his mount, every inch a noble, splendid British officer.

"Jeremy Bently? Are you here?"

At that, Jeremy darted into bushes at the side of the road. In the next moment, as Weston rode toward the mill, the officer was suddenly pounced on from the trees and yanked from his horse. Jeremy knew what he was doing, however, and broke his friend's fall, hardly smudging the beautiful uniform. The two friends soon were sparring and laughing.

Then Weston slapped an arm over Jeremy's shoulder, and they made their way to Gwen. The lieutenant ignored Jeremy's teasing comments that British Redcoats were woefully inept in the woods now that the experienced wilderness-fighting regiments such as the 60th and 80th foot had been sent to the Floridas.

"I'll learn soon enough!" Weston declared, acknowledging Gwen, who waved in welcome. "I'll be gone in the morning."

Jeremy stopped short. He had expected this day would come, but felt a chill to realize it was actually upon them.

"I'm to join Lieutenant Davies's command for a thrust eastward, toward Montreal." Gwen, listening at a distance, sobered as Weston said four hundred Indians, a hundred Canadian volunteers, and fifty picked Redcoats would be marching before dawn.

Thinking about his family in Montreal, Jeremy said, almost inaudibly, "So the spring campaign has begun?"

"It has," Weston replied with enthusiasm. "We'll drive those damned rebels out of Montreal, while Quebec is relieved by an armada from Europe! Jeremy, thirteen thousand trained troops are about to strike up the Saint Lawrence past Quebec! We'll meet them in Montreal!"

He was too excited to sit down next to Gwen, who was nervously pitching stones one after the other into the water, her eyes blank. He said, "The rebellion's end's in sight! The rebels haven't a chance. Your uncle Henry Gladwin has written me a letter saying another thirty-five thousand troops will invade New York and the middle colonies at the end of the summer! Thirty-five thousand! Have you ever imagined such a force? The greatest army ever assembled by the British empire! Combine them with our advance from the north and northwest, and we'll crush the bloody rebellion like—"

Weston grabbed a tulip bud and squeezed it savagely, causing Gwen to cry out in dismay. Weston suddenly realized what he had done and apologized, but his fierce excitement was scarcely tamed.

"By autumn we'll have Albany and New York, possibly even Philadelphia and Savannah! The colonies soon will be garrisoned by fifty thousand troops, and insolent, traitorous American rebels will never again rise against the king."

"Don't be so sure of that," Gwen snapped, her harshness surprising both men. "It'll take more than fifty thousand soldiers to quiet our people now that they've tasted liberty, and even a hundred thousand won't keep them down forever."

She stood up suddenly, glaring at Weston. Then she began to shake, and tears wet her cheeks. Breaking down, she fell into Jeremy's arms, sobbing.

Weston was hurt by Gwen's anger, for they had become close friends. His hand went to her shoulder, and he said, "I did not mean to glory or take joy in whatever unfortunate hardships befall your America, my dear. . . ."

Gwen turned to him, her eyes soft and moist, then embraced him, saying, "I know, Richard, I know. Forgive me, but my anger was not intended for you. It was for the cruel lords and ministers who pit you soldiers against my folk! I'm angry at lords who are too heartless, too stupid, and too stubborn to see that the rebellion cannot be defeated by soldiers, not if we fight for a hundred years! We must have reason, compromise, mutual respect. Can't you at least see that?"

"Gwen!" Weston exclaimed. "You speak as though you favor the rebel cause!"

"I'm an American!" she cried out. "I care about Americans! Do you understand that? Can't you see how British colonial policy has torn my people apart? How it has put us at one another's throats? Call me a rebel or a traitor or whatever you will, I don't care! I just want peace, and I want...I want you, and all my friends, not to kill one another, Richard!"

Again she embraced him, and he sighed as she wept on his shoulder. "Have no fear, Gwen," he said kindly. "This war won't take long. It'll be all over mercifully soon."

Jeremy watched with a mixture of surprise and concern. He understood what Gwen had said and knew she was right that a stubborn, haughty Parliament had forced open fighting to start. But there was no way the frail rebel Congress could send its meager troops up against forty or fifty thousand British soldiers and the entire royal navy and expect to win.

He said so, and Gwen stepped back, wiping her eyes with a handkerchief he gave her. "Richard knows what he's saying, Gwen. The sooner government troops march, the sooner the rebels will surrender and the killing will stop."

Nodding, Weston said, "But defeat them permanently we shall, Gwen; do not delude yourself. And do not fear that there will be many unnecessary deaths, for no one wants wholesale slaughter. We must see justice done, however, and the guilty punished. The misguided followers of Congress must be shown the path back to productive, loyal lives as true British subjects."

Gwen sighed, her shoulders rising and falling. Her tears had stopped, and she apologized for having lost control. Trying to smile, she said a curt good-day and went down to the rowboat. As she climbed in and clattered the oars, Simon stirred and yawned, waking up and asking where they were.

"Go back to sleep," Gwen said gently. "I'll have us home soon."

Clancy yawned once more, folded his arms, and snuggled

down. Gwen looked up at Jeremy, and then pulled on the oars. The boat moved away down the stream, but before Gwen was out of sight, she again looked back at Jeremy. He felt his heart skip. Then she was around a bend and gone.

"Quite a woman," Weston mused, and walked with Jeremy to their horses. "Talks like Ben Franklin, though. She'd best not let too many of our loyal folk hear that sort of chatter—bad for her reputation. Keep an eye on her, will you, Jeremy?"

Jeremy took the reins of his horse, which stopped grazing to be mounted. "I'll watch out for her, Richard."

Weston got his own animal, glanced back over his shoulder, and smiled impishly. "I didn't think you'd find that too taxing a chore, my friend." He swung up into the saddle. "Either she or Annie! They'd make a fellow like you a very happy man!"

Jeremy shrugged that off. "I've been a happy man already! And you know I'll never forget Penny." Weston pursed his lips in thought, but was interrupted as his friend yelled, "Come on, Lieutenant, show me whether Redcoats can ride!"

With a yell they spurred their horses onto the narrow path and raced away side by side under the arched boughs of maple and willow. It was a good match, for both were fearless horsemen, and very proud.

**PART TWO**

# Retreat
# From Canada

## chapter 13

# THE SCOUT

On April Fool's Day, General David Wooster took command of the sorry, impoverished rebel army facing Quebec. The sixty-five-year-old Wooster had brought reinforcements, swelling the army to three thousand; but he had no heavy guns, and he had no plans. Though American spies had told of a great armada ready to depart England for the Saint Lawrence that spring, Wooster was unable to handle so many men, and he accomplished little.

Sutherland and Defries were revolted to see hundreds of fresh troops come down with smallpox just days after they arrived in camp. Hospitals were set up in barns and tents, for frightened men were inoculating themselves from the sores of the mildly sick, in the hopes of having only mild cases themselves. As a result, the American army soon had fewer than five hundred able to stand and hold muskets. Doctors worked to near collapse, and men died by the score.

As bad as all this was, another disaster soon came to pass. From the start, Wooster and Arnold were at loggerheads. The elderly Wooster was cautious and slow to move, and too often drunk on rum flip. By contrast, his subordinate Arnold was a storm of activity, even with his injured leg, which had healed well enough for him to ride around camp, always planning some trouble for the loyalists. In three dangerous months, Arnold had employed no more than eight-hundred men—half usually ill with fever—to fool and harry the garrison of fifteen hundred holding the citadel. At any time the enemy could have swept outside the walls and driven the weak Americans like dry leaves before a wind, but Arnold's reckless brilliance had kept the enemy off-balance.

Then Arnold and his horse had taken a spill, and the injured leg had been crushed beneath the animal. This incapacitating injury, and the growing conflict with Wooster, compelled Arnold to request transfer to Montreal, where he would be garrison commander.

At Arnold's urging, Sutherland agreed to remain before Quebec, although he would have preferred to go to Montreal and be with his family. In the bleak days preceding Arnold's departure, Sutherland found his spirits the lowest they had been since he arrived at Quebec. The only thing that cheered him was a long letter from Ella.

She had much to do, reorganizing the Frontier Company affairs in Montreal. Although there was no communication with the partners in Detroit or Michilimackinac, a whole new trade network was being woven from Montreal. Ella said the Greys, James Morely, and even the Devaliers were actively trading for peltry now being brought into the city by Indian and French trappers.

> We are fortunate to have sterling with which to purchase these furs, because the price is astonishingly low nowadays—low in sterling, but high in York money or continentals. My husband, do not think it vanity if I express the belief that we'll see a tidy fortune this spring, if only we can get the furs down to Albany.

Ella did not need to write that the main obstacle to shipping the pelts was the war; if Iroquois raiders became active on the route from Montreal to Albany, only a powerful armed force would get shipments through.

There is an association being formed in the city,
called the North West Company; most of the important
English traders here are involved, including the Frob-
isher brothers, James McGill, Alexander Henry—you
know them all. It is as we guessed last year. They are
forming on the same lines as the Frontier Company,
all of them partners, and they've asked us to join them.

Ella had declined; she was sure Owen would not break
the partnership with the Frontier Company members for the
sake of this new association. But she added that once the
Northwesters—as they called themselves—were organized, they would be formidable competitors.

Sutherland knew that these Northwesters were staunch
loyalists. They were tough, wise, and experienced, and once
they reopened commerce with Britain they would indeed
challenge the Frontier Company for domination of the northwest trade.

The most welcome news was that Sally was expecting,
and this made Owen all the more impatient to return. Also,
he was amused to read that Benjamin and Susannah had
nursed a blue jay back to health and made it a pet. He knew
jays could be troublesome, even nasty creatures who would
attack humans who got on their wrong side. It was good
that the children had something to divert their thoughts from
the war and the danger that intensified with every day Quebec held out.

Sutherland immediately wrote a long reply; Arnold would
be leaving tomorrow and had offered to deliver it. At the
general's request, Sutherland asked Ella if she had heard
any rumors of a shipment of muskets that had gone missing
near Montreal. Otherwise the letter was lighthearted, newsy,
and full of hope now that more reinforcements were reported
coming, including some of Washington's regiments, which
had just forced the British to evacuate Boston. He wrote
little about the pathetic shape of most of the troops in camp,
and nothing about the British fleet just over the eastern
horizon.

* * *

The cold weather passed, each day bringing the British armada that much closer. News of the British army's departure from Boston in March had lifted everyone's spirits, giving the rebels stronger resolve to take the citadel before the fleet arrived. As long as the ice held in the river—as it did well into April—the fleet would be unable to sail upriver, and the garrison in the Quebec citadel would remain captive. Still, the loyalists showed no sign of surrendering.

Late in April, Defries and Sutherland left camp to scout downriver to a headland on the north shore thirty-five miles below Quebec. They were part of a daily stream of scouts sent out to learn what they could about the armada.

Leaving the siege camp on foot, the two friends moved slowly along the muddy, rutted track that skirted the river's rocky shore. Their duty was to search out signs of enemy scouts or supply wagons and to learn what they could from the inhabitants.

The weather was mild, and all along the river road the French were busy around their cottages, repairing fishing nets and readying the ground for spring planting. Crowds of children played in the warm sunlight—until the rebels were spotted; then they would flee, full of fear and suspicion.

Occasionally there was a wayside inn, where the travelers would stop to eat and ask pointed questions. They were answered only with vague hints and sarcastic suggestions that the British were already in the mouth of the Saint Lawrence. Yet in this stretch of river the ice was drifting in such hazardous floes that Sutherland guessed no ships could come up to Quebec until the end of May. Thus a full month of siege was possible before British reinforcements arrived to challenge the rebels. Daily, scores of fresh American troops were arriving from the lower colonies; marching companies were strung out on the roads and waterways leading northward to Montreal, where they were to assemble for the final march to Quebec. If only the rebels and the Saint Lawrence ice could hold out, there would be enough men to take Quebec before the British armada even began to ascend the river.

Two days after leaving camp, Sutherland and Defries

had traveled more than twenty-five miles along the northern shore, through some of the most beautiful country the Scotsman had ever seen. To the left, frowning gray cliffs rose to plateaus of spruce that ran back to bleak precipices, sheer, forbidding walls of stone. The few *habitant* residences in this country each had its fishing boat, canoes, and racks for drying nets. Turned upside down in the bright sunlight, nearly every boat was being painted or varnished by clean-shaven, wiry men smoking pipes.

Occasionally great flocks of crows would emerge from groves of fir and pine, cawing and wheeling across the sky in a black cloud that obscured the sun. Then they would settle again, sometimes near the briny edge of the river, where the tide had withdrawn and left a glittering band of wet stones. There gull and crow fought over stranded water creatures.

It seemed that every few yards a spring issued from the rocks, or a stream clattered over gravelly beds, bursting down from a ravine cut into the hillside. The road was washed out in many places but passable for two determined men on foot.

As Sutherland and Defries pressed onward, cottages were scarcer, clinging to the base of the cliffs, which pressed ever closer to the water's edge. It was a wild and grand country, full of geese and caribou, bursting with the fragrance and feel of springtime.

From high ground, the two friends could see for miles up and down the broad, icy Saint Lawrence. More than once they spotted porpoises in herds of six or eight, leaping and frolicking near the shore, darting up between ice floes, then submerging again, to appear in another crack, swimming playfully.

Surrounded by beauty, Sutherland almost forgot the war. This land was so tranquil it seemed new-made, with only the occasional fisherman's cottage. Indeed, much of the region was new, he had read somewhere, because a century earlier the earth had shaken in an earthquake for six long and frightful months.

Leaving the high ground, they walked on awhile, and Sutherland told Defries about earthquakes. He explained that along a hundred miles of shoreline, lakes had suddenly been formed, hills lowered, and falls leveled. Islands had come out of the water near the shore, and entire forests had been swallowed up, drifting right into the river.

"The quaking earth is said to be caused by internal thermal energy that is so mighty that it can actually create continents," Sutherland said, adding that there had been several more quakes here in the past century.

The Albany Dutchman stopped walking and rubbed his square jaw, which, like Sutherland's, needed a shave. He squinted as he thought hard about quaking earth and thermal energy. As though testing the massive rock shelf he stood upon, he jumped up once and came down heavily.

"Feels safe enough to me—"

Then there came a distant boom, and Defries nearly dropped his rifle. Sutherland listened as the sound reverberated and echoed. It was neither earthquake nor thunder. There came several answering booms in succession, rolling across the river and echoing off the cliffs.

"I thought I liked this country," Defries said uneasily, "but it feels like it might get up and turn over any time now."

"No," Sutherland said sharply, his expression grave. "Those were naval guns. They've come!"

Neither man spoke as they tramped onward, moving along lower ground with less of a view. The broad Saint Lawrence opened wider and wider to the right, where ice floes were moving slowly toward the sea, three hundred miles away. As the afternoon passed, they wished they were riding swift horses, but the steep ravines and waterfalls of this land did not permit their taking mounts.

After a while, they became conscious of a change in the attitude of the Canadians they occasionally passed. Earlier the *habitants* had at least been grudgingly courteous; now they completely ignored the scouts, or disappeared inside their houses.

It was late in the afternoon and the sun had clouded over when Sutherland and Defries saw a man in a scarlet stocking cap thatching his steep roof. He was sitting high on the peak, and Sutherland called in French, asking if a meal could be purchased. He and Defries paused at the picket fence, but the man looked away from them and silently went about his business.

Hungry, Defries was angered at this rude rebuff. "Why that frog eater, I'll—" Sutherland grabbed his arm to keep him from challenging the man to a fight.

"His family's inside," Sutherland said. "See, there— they're watching us like they already know who we are and why we've come."

Behind the half-closed shutters small faces peered out. In the past hour the men had seen no one on the road, coming or going, so it was not clear how these people could have known rebels were about to pass. Yet in the farmyard were sticks and hoops, a skipping rope, and even a doll, apparently thrown aside by children fleeing to the house. A woman's spinning wheel sat abandoned near the door, yarn still dangling and unwound.

"Who's tellin' 'em we're on the road?" asked Defries, rubbing his growling stomach. "Ain't been an American scout along here in months, accordin' to Arnold. But they sure enough know us, and want no part of us."

"I would guess we're being watched by someone who doesn't want us to learn anything from the people along here. And he's got the influence to tell them to ignore rebels. He might be French. Let's see if we can catch him."

The path narrowed, climbing steeply to another vantage point. Far back upriver to their right, islands, heavily wooded with cedar and spruce, lay in the channel, which was more than ten miles across here. High cliffs of a headland blocked their view downriver. A northwest wind scudded down from the slopes, buffeting Sutherland and Defries as they stood on the rocky promontory and gazed over the river. Then sun broke through and lit the river valley with bright patches of light.

Below them a little settlement of white houses was clustered among tall pines, with the needle spire of a church in the center. Here they would learn something, if there was anything to learn. The track ran down a steep grade to the village, crossing streams of groundwater and snowmelt that sparkled in the sunlight.

The two men went toward the houses, slipping and sliding in places where the track was washed out. It was here Sutherland took note of footprints in the mud and examined them closely. These were the only human markings on the ground, and they were less than an hour old.

Kneeling beside the print, Sutherland said, "Moccasins. Locals wear boots, even the Indians." A little farther he knelt to examine where the tracks entered underbrush to bypass an exposed section of road. "He's moving fast." Sutherland peered up at the stony outcrop where he and Defries had stood. "Must have been watching us." He stood up. "Likely watching us now. Unless I miss my guess, this fellow knows his business and is aware we've spotted his sign."

Defries showed no emotion, but let his eyes rove casually about at groves of spruce, dark and mysterious, on the hillside. Trees grew between massive rocks large enough to conceal a squad of king's troops. Sutherland took a look at the roofs of the village.

"Maybe our friend's down there."

Defries said, "Should we expect trouble from these Frenchies?"

Sutherland shrugged. "I suspect this fellow's a stranger to them, too. They might not join him in an attack, not unless he can convince them to prove their allegiance to the king. If the fleet's close at hand, they'll easily be convinced."

"Let's go down and see what's in store for us," Sutherland said. "We may have to make a run for it, but I want to go farther downriver and get an eyeful of whatever's there."

Defries slipped a flask of brandy from his knapsack, and they shared some. Eating black bread and dried beef, and drinking from a cold rivulet, they made certain they would not be overly hungry if they were forced to keep moving quickly. Then they loaded and primed their rifles, and slinging the weapons back on their shoulders, they set off down the rocky trail.

Five minutes later they came to the first cottage, on the left side of the road. It was deserted. A fishing boat was half painted, still wet, and the brush lay on a bench nearby. Whoever had left the brush had even neglected to put its bristles in a tin of turpentine that stood close at hand. The street grew muddy here, where carts and horses had been moving very recently. A warm early-evening sun glowed on the walls of empty cottages built in a row on the left side of the road. To the right, narrow, newly turned fields led toward the water. The village was in a cove, backed by high bluffs in a semicircle, cutting off a full view of the river. For just a moment, Sutherland felt the strong urge to get back on high ground, to look downriver as far as he could.

As they walked through the village, not a soul was to be seen. A stray dog barked, came running over, sniffed once or twice, then trotted away toward a little white church with its burying ground. A public tavern on the right was closed and locked, with its sign, *Fleur-de-lis,* swaying in the fresh breeze.

Defries said softly, "I'm thinkin' we're expected but ain't welcome." With that he unslung his rifle and primed the pan. Sutherland did the same, and they moved along the street. By now it was too late to head back up the slope. They had to go on, through the village and out the other side; if they showed fear and began to retreat, villagers who otherwise would be reluctant to attack might take heart and strike.

Though at least twenty families must live here, the men would think twice about trying to capture American rebel scouts, because the village might be burned out in retribution. But should the scouts suddenly flee, there was no telling what some headstrong *habitants* might do if the man in the moccasins urged them to fight. The village was silent, with only an occasional cat slinking between a house and a woodshed. Swallows twittered and dived overhead, and the breeze whipped into the cove over the ice, strong and cold.

When the two men came to the other side of the village, Sutherland paused and touched Defries's arm, telling him to listen. Defries glanced around for some sign of an ambush. But there was none. Only the muffled sound of wood, like oars thudding and creaking on a gunwale. Then there came the distant shouts of men, and a whacking sound, as of hammers or axes striking some hard substance—many such tools at work. The noise was borne on the wind off the water, and Sutherland tensed as he listened. He was staring out the mouth of the cove, jaw set, eyes narrowing. It was as though the sound came from some invisible ship passing before them. Defries leaned forward, scanning the vast white surface that spread outward from the cove. There was nothing but ice in sight on the river.

"They're here," the Scotsman said.

Puzzled and troubled, Defries again strained his eyes at nothing. "How can it be? The river's frozen!"

"Hurry!" Suddenly Sutherland dashed away up the narrow trail to the bluffs bordering the left-hand end of the cove. With Defries puffing and grunting behind, they shoved their way past broken branches and under thick spruce boughs that hung low over the track.

Sutherland soon pulled away, disappearing around a bend in the trail, and Defries stumbled on, nearly losing his hat to a branch. The path became steeper and more stony, and the Albany Dutchman gamely struggled upward, though he had no idea why Sutherland was in such a hurry. He paused at a bend in the trail, breathing heavily, and listened. There was a definite sound of oars and axes and men shouting or singing, but with trees blocking his view he could see nothing. Then he heard rustling, as if someone was following, and he whipped his rifle around at the ready. The sound stopped at that same instant, and Defries moved slowly toward it, as silently as a former teamster could creep. He cocked his weapon and moved in a crouch under the cover of a dense spruce, to wait there for whoever it was following them.

After a few moments, he could still hear no one. Perhaps he had been imagining it all. Perhaps it was Owen's footfalls he had heard. Defries was the first to admit he was no woodsman. He listened a little longer. The sounds of voices, oars, and tools were louder now. He decided to move to the edge of the bluff and take a look at the river before going on. As he moved to get up, he sensed someone behind him.

"Do not turn, Peter," said a familiar voice, with a French accent. "Slowly lay down your rifle; slowly and carefully, please."

Defries did not do so immediately, but the touch of a gun barrel on his shoulder convinced him. He uncocked the weapon and laid it at his feet.

"Put your hands on your head, *mon ami,* and then turn to greet me."

"Jacques Levesque!" Defries was astonished and dismayed to see this Frontier Company partner at the other end of the rifle. "What in the name of—"

Levesque was grim, and deadly earnest. The rifle was aimed at Defries's left leg—no danger to his life, but a pointed enough hint that Defries would go down, badly hurt, if he tried anything rash.

"So it was you spying on us," Defries said, putting up his hands. "You! With the Britishers!"

Levesque whispered, "No more talking, Peter. Turn around and put your hands behind your back. I have to tie you up, but that's better than having to hurt you. Turn!"

Unsure what to do, but certain Levesque meant business, Defries again obeyed, grumbling and cursing to himself. He had to think this through in the seconds he had before being trussed. He had to comprehend that Jacques Levesque was his enemy. At last Defries realized that the sounds he and Owen had heard were boats being worked through the ice. They must be the vanguard of the British fleet on its way to Quebec, three weeks earlier than expected.

Defries's hands were behind his back, and he felt the rifle barrel again touch his right shoulder as Levesque used one hand to slip a noose over the Dutchman's wrists and tighten it. This was the moment to fight, but that gun was there, and Levesque was a man who could use it. Still, Defries was fuddled and could not bring himself to kill a man whom he had befriended for years, a man he had fought alongside and shared mess with.

Suddenly Levesque's rifle muzzle was clicked aside by

something metal, and the Frenchman snarled. Defries threw himself sideways, wrenching at the knot about his wrists. He stumbled to his knees, and heard the sound of grunting and blows being dealt. Defries turned and saw Sutherland and Levesque rolling on the ground, kicking and punching. Sutherland had tossed his claymore aside, and it lay at Defries's knees.

The Dutchman got his hands free and picked up the sword. But he caught himself, swore violently, and tossed it aside. He leaped into the fray, and together he and Sutherland pinned Levesque to the ground. Levesque kicked and struggled a few more seconds, until at last he knew he was beaten. Sutherland and Defries were angry from their bruises and from the shock of discovering that Jacques was a spy for the British.

Breathless, Sutherland demanded, "Give your word you'll not try to escape, and we'll let you up!"

Levesque was dark in fury, and he clenched his jaw, his body still shaking from the useless effort to break loose. He was well aware, however, that these two could have killed him on the spot—just as he could have silently killed Defries. He looked away, and said through bloodied lips, "You have it."

Sutherland and Defries released him, the Dutchman putting his forehead in his hands and cursing fate to have brought them to this. Sutherland was on his knees, chest heaving, and Jacques sat up, taking a glance at his old friend.

"You all right?" Sutherland panted, and the Frenchman gave a curt nod.

"You?"

Sutherland's jaw felt cracked, but he did not acknowledge the hurt. Like Levesque, he was bruised and scraped, with a fat lip and a welt under his left eye.

Defries grumbled, "Well, good thing you two pals be all right, but I ain't!" He glared at Levesque. "I'm damned pissed off, that's what! I ain't been this pissed off since . . . I don't know when!" He swore and got up to stamp around a bit, recovering his rifle and pack, Sutherland's sword and rifle. Then he tossed Levesque's rifle to him, realizing too late what he had done. The Frenchman caught it, startled, and held it in front of him, as though at any moment it could be brought to bear.

Then Levesque smiled and laid the weapon aside. "What difference would it make if I fought you? Your cause is lost. Listen to your doom."

There was quite a commotion beyond the cove, many British voices crying out orders through trumpets, now loud enough to be heard distinctly.

"There is nothing you can do to stop them; your friends at Quebec are finished, even if you get back to warn them. You two chose the wrong side, I am sorry to say."

Sutherland and Defries could not wait any longer to see what was happening on the river. With Levesque between them, they filed up the trail to the headland. The white river swept wide open for miles, and as they came to the crest of a windy bluff, Sutherland and Defries gaped in astonishment.

For as far as they could see downstream, British warships, transports, and merchant ships were strung out along a narrow channel in the ice. The river was visible for at least eight or nine miles, and the invasion fleet had no end in that entire distance, which melted into the dimness of the eastern horizon. Holding his hat from blowing away, Sutherland counted—fifteen before the ships were too distant to distinguish. The fleet must have crossed the ocean under perilous, icy conditions to get here so early.

Sutherland took a long look at the lead vessel—an old merchant ship fitted out with extra hull planking and a metal bow; it served as a stout icebreaker, with sails full of wind. Slowly cutting the path through the floes, this vessel pounded ahead of the other ships, which were hauled by longboats filled with men who rowed or used poles, sledgehammers, and axes to fend off ice. Sutherland well understood why the British army and navy were recognized as the best in the world. This was awesome proof of it, and proof as well that the government leaders could transfer their regiments wherever they wished. He wondered whether the American rebels could ever match this military strength and ingenuity.

There was no way for the rebellion to succeed but to find a means to fight on equal terms.

Levesque said, "In another few days they'll be at Quebec and it will be over; you had better save yourselves and get away from the province before retreat is impossible."

With dismay Sutherland realized there was no chance to take the city now, even if Washington's troops arrived as Arnold had hoped. The most active American force in the field was in grave danger, and those thousands of reinforcements hurrying to its aid would be in jeopardy, too, once these Redcoats landed.

Sutherland said to Defries, "We have to get to Quebec with the warning!" He looked at Levesque, wondering what to do with him.

The Frenchman said, "If you are to flee, then go now." He nodded at the near headland of the cove, where Sutherland saw dozens of *habitant* families gathered to watch the naval spectacle. "I suggested that they go there to avoid you, but I did not tell them exactly when you were coming. You see, if I had, some would have counted themselves fortunate to capture or kill rebel scouts and thus prove their loyalty to the king. Instead, I hoped to catch you both myself and hold you for a few days until the danger was past."

"Then you would have let us go back to Montreal?"

Levesque said it was so, because he wanted them to escape the British counterattack. Defries again declared he was angrier than he had ever been in his life. Just then the people at the end of the cove started home. If they came upon the two rebels, there would be a fight, and the only way Sutherland and Defries could escape would be to shed blood.

The villagers were just minutes away. Jacques stood staring fiercely at the British fleet, as though imagining what it could do to liberate Canada from the troops of Congress. Sutherland was watching him when the Frenchman turned and said time was running out.

"I cannot help you if these *habitants* decide to become heroes."

Sutherland thought of taking Levesque as their prisoner to Quebec, but that might mean death for the man.

"Give us two hours' head start, and then you are at liberty, Jacques."

The Frenchman nodded. "It matters not to me that the rebels know they are about to be destroyed. I will not try to stop you now that I have seen the immense size of this armada and know how puny the rebel army is."

Then Jacques held out his hand to Sutherland, who gripped it tightly and said, "Godspeed, Frenchman. May we meet again in a better world."

*"Bonne chance,"* Levesque said. "Before you go—Jeremy is in Detroit, and the British commandant has asked him to be their surgeon major."

Defries blurted, "You mean he backs 'em, too?"

Sutherland was shocked.

"Not yet," Levesque said. "The British want to organize the Indians, but Jeremy will not support that, so he has not accepted the commission. Not yet. Otherwise, he is well, although he fought Manoth to a draw." In a few words, Levesque told what had happened to Jeremy at Detroit. "He is brave and independent of mind, but I fear he cannot long remain neutral . . . nor can any of us."

They all wanted to say more but had no time. Defries brusquely shook the Frenchman's hand, and with a nod they parted. Levesque stayed to slow the villagers and give his former friends a chance to get well away. Sutherland and Defries hurried on without looking back, meaning to reach Quebec as quickly as possible. The rebels' only hope now was escaping to bolster the defense of Montreal, preventing a quick British thrust into New York, toward exposed Albany.

As he trotted through the empty village and up the road beyond, Sutherland thought of all he and Levesque had shared over the years. But it was too painful to dwell on, too much to try to understand. War was war. They were enemies. Perhaps one day, if the British were not too strong, and the rebels won their freedom, he and Levesque might again be reconciled; but for now their friendship was over.

As he hurried up that hill, knapsack bouncing on his back, rifle slung over his shoulder, Sutherland glanced back at the Saint Lawrence, which was a sprawling panorama of ice from here. The line of ships had cleared the headland and came on steadily, irresistibly. In all America nothing the rebels could assemble could match even this one British army in firepower, equipment, supplies, and training. Nothing at all.

And it was only one army.

## chapter 14

## STOLEN MUSKETS

May in Montreal was beautiful, with the city taking on the gentle color of trees in new leaf. People made the most of a warm spell that brought spring early to the city, and every garden and flowerbed was tended with care.

Benjamin and Susannah Sutherland were caught up by the enthusiasm that had smitten everyone in those first warm days. Often the two of them went to watch the Indian trappers arrive in canoes for the annual trade fair near the waterfront. Though Dr. Devalier said this year's gathering was much smaller than those in peacetime, the children were impressed by all they saw.

City squares were filled daily with brightly dressed Indians from the high country, mostly peaceable Algonquins who lived up the Ottawa River, far from rebels or loyalists. There was a fairly good fur harvest that season, and Ella Sutherland joined with James Morely and the Greys to make large purchases of furs, which could be had cheaply. Since few other folk in Montreal were as wealthy as the Frontier Company partners, there would be an excellent profit that year after all, once the pelts were sold at Albany.

Although the spring brought hope of better times, the Sutherlands still felt the hostility of the French. Late one sunny afternoon at the fur fair, three tough French boys began to pick on Susannah, and when her brother sprang to her defense, a lively scuffle broke out. Since Heera was not along on this trip, the Sutherland children were over-matched, and they were forced into an alley between ware-houses. Fists and feet began to fly, and eventually the battlers fought to a standstill. Benjamin and Susannah, their clothes torn, found themselves trapped in the alley, while the gasp-ing, bruised city boys stood blocking their escape, ready to attack again.

No sticks had yet been used, but the French youths were so furious at Susannah and her brother for standing them off that now they took up boards, and one even hefted a brick. Benjamin and Susannah, ready for a serious struggle, also armed themselves with sticks. It would have been better to escape, but there was no way to get around their enemies, and nobody out in the noisy square seemed to notice what was going on in the alley.

The biggest of the city boys came forward, his eyes hard, board raised. He was joined by another at his side, both intending to take Benjamin on while the third boy kept Susannah back.

Brother and sister prepared themselves, neither showing fear, though they knew they were in for a real beating unless they were lucky.

That luck came in the form of Punch. The jay had been off on his own earlier, and now he returned, flying into the alley. With a loud screech, he sped down and landed a solid peck on the back of the first French boy's head, drawing blood. The other boys turned and swung at the bird as it dived and squawked recklessly, just missing wicked swings with the clubs. That was all the chance the Sutherland chil-dren needed, and they laid into their opponents with their own boards, getting in some stinging blows that knocked the leader down and sent the other two reeling.

With Punch shrieking overhead, the Sutherlands sprang out of the alley and into the square, both of them laughing in their relief to have escaped. Soon the two were striding on home, proud and confident, the warlike Punch flying overhead.

When they got to their apartment door, the jay whipped up to a birdhouse James Morely had built and hung outside a window. The children set about wiping off dirt and straightening their clothing so their mother would not know they had been fighting. Upstairs, Ella heard them and called excitedly that there was a letter from their father. With a whoop of joy, the children raced upward. They found Ella in the living room, on the settee, the rosy light of sunset pouring through the window.

It was a wonderful letter from Owen, full of encouragement for the children, telling them to study hard and to keep up their spirits. As usual, Ella kept her part of the letter to herself, not reading it aloud.

"The letter came from General Arnold's staff here in Montreal," she told the children, who were impressed that such an important rebel commander would trouble to carry their father's letter home from Quebec. "Your father says the general himself asked a favor of us, wanting to know if we had heard rumors about certain muskets— Well, that's not anything for you children to think about."

Ella put the letter aside, and a distant look came into her eyes as she thought fondly of her husband. She was interrupted by Benjamin, who had stood up, and now looked very serious.

"As the man of the family, Ma, I ought to know what General Arnold had to ask of us."

Ella did not smile as she regarded the boy, who was so close to being a young man. He was waiting solemnly for her reply.

"Yes," Ella said softly, after a pause. "Well, my son, it seems we have hundreds of troops in Quebec who do not have muskets or else must borrow muskets from men who are ill. Our army is lacking at least five hundred, and perhaps a thousand muskets that Congress sent here over the winter, but somehow became lost."

Benjamin and his sister vividly recalled the evening at the cove on Saint Peter's River, when they had seen Bradford Cullen escorting a shipment of muskets. As their mother explained that General Arnold desperately needed them for the troops, the children gaped at each other in surprise.

They knew enough about Cullen to guess that the unscrupulous merchant might very well have diverted the muskets for secret resale later on.

Quickly Benjamin and Susannah told what they had seen during the winter. Ella, too, realized there might be a connection between the merchant and the missing weapons.

"But why would Cullen work against our cause that way?" she asked. "If we lose, then so does he."

Susannah said, "He's turned his coat before, Mother, and now that Quebec has held out against us—"

"It'll fall!" Benjamin cried. "Pa's there! It'll fall! It can't hold out! It can't!"

Ella said, "What matters most is finding those muskets. How can we discover what happened to them? Or how can we find others to replace them?" It would cost at least ten thousand pounds sterling to purchase five hundred muskets new, but even if that kind of money was available, enough muskets could not be located down in the colonies and shipped north in time. "Too late," she murmured to herself, then said aloud, "We have to find replacements here, and soon."

"Monsieur Joffre!" Benjamin cried out. "He was the one carting them that night! He'll know—"

"Benjamin," Ella interrupted. "Do you mean Félix Joffre? He's dead. Dear Lord! Someone murdered him about the time you saw Cullen and the muskets! He was found in the woods near the cove where you played."

There was no question now that Cullen and those missing muskets were part of the same conspiracy. Resold to Indians, the weapons would be worth a fortune in pelts, perhaps as much as fifty thousand pounds sterling. But if the British recovered Lower Canada, only a loyalist would be able to carry through a deal like that. Clearly, Bradford Cullen meant to blow with the political wind. Selling those muskets was a strong incentive for him. A British military success was another. Everything hinged on the campaign at Quebec. If the British and loyalists began to win, Cullen likely would declare himself on their side.

Benjamin cried, "I have an idea!" He jumped up and grabbed a small candle and a tinderbox in the shape of a pistol. In answer to his mother's rapid questions, he said she soon would see what he had in mind. Running to the door, he declared, "I know where the muskets have to be, and we can tell General Arnold! But first I want to be sure." He yanked open the door as his mother protested. "No, don't follow me! I'll be back soon!"

"Benjamin!" Ella grabbed at his arm, but he bounded down the stairs and was gone. Afraid for him, Ella grabbed her mantle, and Susannah got her own. Soon they were standing in the busy, darkening street, looking up and down, past carts and pedestrians, but the boy was nowhere in sight.

Susannah called to Heera, who was nearby, "Find him, Heera! Find Benjamin! Go!"

Off they went, behind the husky, who loped ahead, sniffing at Benjamin's trail. They headed toward the waterfront, and Ella searched frantically for some sign of the boy. But the light was failing, and he had too much of a start. She did not notice the blue jay whisking through the air. Punch flew around a corner and darted straight for a one-story warehouse owned by Celoron Meloche, the wealthy French nobleman who was such a generous landlord to Bradford Cullen.

By now the sun had gone down behind Mount Royal, and the city lay in long shadows. Benjamin was a shadow himself as he flitted down the narrow alleyway beside Meloche's warehouse. The fieldstone walls had several small windows, high up, under the eaves. They were unbarred, but too small for an average man to fit through. Benjamin found one that was open, however, and by climbing on a rain barrel, he got close enough to jump up and grab the sill.

Grunting and kicking, scraping knees and elbows, he managed to hook one ankle over the sill, then pull himself through the narrow opening. It was dark in the warehouse, but the boy did not hesitate. He lowered himself inside, dangling by his fingertips before dropping with a thump to the floor.

He listened, his heart pounding. The warehouse was like an enormous cave, cool and silent and spooky, with no light at all. There seemed to be no watchman to interrupt his search. The boy drew out the candle and the pistol tinderbox from the pocket of his frock coat. He cocked the hammer and pulled the lighter's trigger several times to get a spark, and soon had a little blaze going in the tinder with which to light the candle.

Still panting from the dash to the warehouse and the struggle through the window, Benjamin moved slowly along rows of boxes, bales, and crates, kegs, barrels, jars on shelves, and stacks of everything from tools to fabrics to foodstuffs. He searched out crates that would be large enough for muskets, and pressed close to read labels by the flickering candlelight. He had no sense of time passing, because all he thought about were those muskets and finding proof that Cullen and Meloche had stolen them. He was sure Cullen had caused the murder of poor Félix Joffre, and that the dark patch he had seen on the snow had indeed been blood.

So intent was Benjamin in his hunt that he did not notice Punch come fluttering to the open window and perch there, staring down into the darkness. Then, at the deepest corner of the warehouse, Benjamin found what he was looking for—the same musket crates Joffre had been carting. He examined them closely and even found that one was splintered, obviously the box that had fallen from the sled and burst open. Poking his finger through the split in the wood, he felt the muskets inside. The labels on the boxes seemed to have been burned on after another brand had been chiseled off, but the evidence of an original label was clear. The new labels said the muskets belonged to Celoron Meloche.

This was all Benjamin needed to know. He had to tell his mother what he had found, and she would go to General Arnold's headquarters. Whether Bradford Cullen could be proved guilty was another matter, but at least the rebel troops at Quebec would have arms.

He made his way through the warehouse, along an aisle of boxes toward the open window. Candle wax dripped down his fingers, scalding him, but he dared not cry out for fear of being heard.

Just as he was about to stack some smaller boxes near the window so he could climb up, there came the sound of the front door, forty feet away, being unlocked. He quickly snuffed out the candle and hurried to stack another box, but in the darkness he stumbled over something and fell hard. The door creaked open, and there were hushed voices. Light came into the warehouse.

It appeared he hadn't been heard. If he were quick enough, no one would see him get up to the window; but there was no time to stack more crates. He took a little run and sprang up to the windowsill, missed his hold, and fell back. The door was opening wide, letting in the glare of several lanterns. The voices were louder now, one a rasping, wheezing sound that the boy immediately recognized: Bradford Cullen himself.

Benjamin leaped up again, his fingers just snagging the sill. He dug his toes into the stone wall and grasped for a better handhold. The light of the lanterns touched him, seeming bright after the blackness of the warehouse. Cullen would see him at any moment. He had to escape right now, had to pull himself to the window.

But then one of his feet slipped. In desperation he kicked and tried to heave himself upward, but his fingers began to slide off the sill.

Cullen was speaking to two other men. "The muskets're in the back corner. I want them moved tonight onto my sloop in the harbor. . . ."

Benjamin almost cried out in his strain to hold on to the window. The men were coming toward him. He gasped and pulled, but his feet kicked helplessly, and he knew he would soon fall. How could they not yet see him?

At last he could hold no longer and slid down the wall, landing heavily. Everyone stopped moving. Staying low to the ground, Benjamin huddled, listening. He could not escape through the window now.

The three men were listening, too. Benjamin remained very still, hardly breathing. The light of lanterns cast shadows on the sides of bales and boxes near him. He dared not move. In a moment of sudden fear he recalled Félix Joffre's fate. The same would happen to him. His heart thudded so loudly he thought they must hear it.

There was hushed talking beyond the piles of boxes and

bales. Benjamin knew the men were looking for him. Lantern light drifted to his right. Then another beam moved to his left. They were coming at him from both sides. He wanted to hide, to crawl under something, to hunch down as small as a mouse. But there was no way to hide. They were coming closer.

Then he heard the front door creak closed. He was utterly trapped. Both lanterns were coming nearer. He had to do something, and quickly. The man approaching from the left would at any moment come around the bales of cotton fabric. The man at the right was moving slowly, as though searching through nooks and crannies. On that side were heavy crates of iron tools.

Benjamin glanced at the window and knew that if only he could knock the cotton bales against it, he might bound up and somehow get out. But the man on that side was so close . . . just beyond those bales.

He had no other choice. The man was coming around the cotton, his lantern blazing. Benjamin leaped up, charging the bales with his shoulder, ramming them over with all his might. They slid down, and there came a shout of surprise. The bales landed on the man with a ponderous crash, and the lantern was knocked to the ground.

"Fire!" the man shrieked, and as Benjamin sprang up the bales and dived for the small window, he saw the fellow slapping at flames, trying to stamp out a blaze that had caught on the fabric.

At the window now, Benjamin spotted Punch strutting back and forth. As the lad's head stuck through the opening, there came a grunting and shouting behind, along with a wheezing bellow: "There! At the window! Get him! Kill him!"

Benjamin heaved forward, but someone clutched hard at his legs and yanked, jerking him back into the warehouse. Barely managing to hold on to the window, he kicked and squirmed, catching the fellow's head with his heel, but the cursing man held fast.

All the while he heard the hoarse commands of Cullen near the door and the frantic yelps of the man fighting the fire. Then Benjamin felt his jacket grabbed tightly. His pursuer had him well in hand, and with a roar, dragged him back inside. The boy went down suddenly, landing on the cotton bales, with the tough clutching at him.

"Get him!" Cullen wheezed. "Cut his throat! Throttle him!"

The strong, shadowy figure grasped Benjamin by the shirt and pinned him down. The boy kicked, and the man staggered away, letting out a cry of rage, for he had been struck hard on the face. The man came in again, and Benjamin scrambled backward, crashing into the wall. The fellow grappled for him and grunted, "Got ye!"

Suddenly there was an inhuman shriek. Punch skimmed past Benjamin's ear, striking the ruffian's face as though the bird were a bolt fired from a crossbow. The man yelped in pain and swung savagely, but was hit again, right in the eye. This was Benjamin's only chance. Kicking at the hunched fellow with all his might, he caught him right between the legs. Hearing the scream, the boy scrambled madly up the bales, through smoke from the smoldering fire, and dived headlong at the window. Benjamin heard Cullen howl in fury, but the next moment he was through the window, tumbling headfirst to the ground. Picking himself up, he suddenly remembered Punch, who had not followed him through the window. He had to save the bird.

Then he heard the front door of the building thrown open, and a figure came bounding around the corner into the alleyway. Benjamin had hesitated an instant too long. The man was on him in a few swift strides. Benjamin leaped aside, trying to get away, but he had no second chance. The ruffian had a blade, which glinted dully in the faint light.

Suddenly Heera was there, growling and snapping. So were Ella and Susannah, all of them attacking. Heera drove the screaming man down, and Ella swung a wooden club at him, knocking the knife from his hand as Susannah helped her brother to his feet. The man yelled for mercy and covered his head with hands and arms. It was all over in an instant, and the three Sutherlands ran out of the alleyway, Heera close behind. By now smoke poured from the warehouse windows, and there came a cry of fire from somewhere in the neighborhood. Then Benjamin shouted and pointed at a carriage driving rapidly away.

"That's Cullen!" he declared. "I'm sure of it! I heard his voice in the warehouse!"

People were running through the streets toward the Meloche storehouse, and the Sutherlands paused, breathless, to watch from the shadows of houses across the street.

Smoke billowed out of the front doorway. Cullen's men were crying for help to put out the fire before it was beyond control.

"Punch!" Benjamin cried in terror. "He's still in there!"

Ella grabbed the boy, stopping his dash across the street. Susannah could not be held, though, and she ran toward the warehouse, shouting the blue jay's name.

"No!" Ella shouted. "Don't go in there! Susannah!"

Susannah made for the door, covering her face with her cloth cap, about to enter the smoky pall. Then something fluttered about her head, and she stopped in her tracks as Punch squawked triumphantly and lit upon her shoulder.

With a squeal of delight, Susannah whirled and ran with the bird back to her family, through a mob of people rushing to contain the fire. Ella embraced her daughter in relief, and Punch hopped onto Benjamin's finger. They stood in the darkness, with Heera at their side, as soldiers and firemen arrived with a double-handled pumper wagon.

Before long, the blaze was under control, and the Sutherlands hurried home, Ella intending to tell Benedict Arnold right away what Benjamin had found. At least the Frenchman named Meloche would be held responsible for stealing the muskets, and the troops would be properly armed. As for Bradford Cullen, there was no proof other than what two children had seen, and that was not enough to accuse him. Once again this ruthless man might elude punishment, but he had come closer than ever to being caught.

General Arnold was not at his headquarters that night, however, and would not be back until morning. Ella made an appointment for as early as possible, and the next day went with her son to the rebel headquarters on the corner of rue

Saint Jean and rue Notre Dame. She and Benjamin were asked to wait, because General Arnold had another guest. The weary Sutherlands sat quietly in the warm light of the sun rising over the river.

They had discussed what they would say to Arnold. It was important that they not seem driven or obsessed by the long-standing feud between them and Cullen. Rather, it must become apparent to Arnold that their suspicions were well founded.

There was too much enmity between colonials as it was, and Arnold would frown on unproved accusations against the wealthiest rebel in Montreal. Although Arnold had the highest regard for Owen, he would undoubtedly be upset if a major scandal that had no foundation further disrupted the fragile unity existing among the forces occupying Canada. In any case, what was most important was to have Arnold order the Meloche warehouse immediately searched for the muskets.

Ella thought of these things as she and Benjamin waited. Fifteen minutes passed before Arnold's orderly returned to show them in. Just as Ella and Benjamin stepped out the door of the waiting room, they came face to face with Bradford Cullen.

They were all startled, but Cullen was smooth, smiling genially and bowing to Ella. He wore a gray broadcloth frock coat and carried his tricorne in one hand, while leaning on a cane with the other.

"What a coincidence, eh?" Cullen rasped. "But then I had a premonition that you would be here this morning." He nodded and chuckled, his eyes like small points of cold light.

Ella did not step back, though the man repelled her. Benjamin was at her side, as though to protect her from this obese, wheezing creature who blocked the narrow hallway.

"We know all about you," Ella said, "and soon General Arnold will know as well!"

Cullen tilted his head back slightly and cackled. Then he regarded Benjamin, and the boy felt a shiver as those piggish eyes bored into him. "Growing up, are you? Just like your father." He nodded and stuck the hat on his be-wigged head. "Indeed. We'll have to deal with you, too, before long, won't we?"

Cullen pushed roughly forward. Standing his ground as Cullen shouldered past, Benjamin was sturdy enough not to be moved. Then Cullen was out the door, and the orderly was waiting at the entrance to Arnold's office. Inside they found the general beaming, rubbing his hands as he welcomed them and offered seats.

As Ella sat down, she guessed what had just happened, and hardly heard Arnold welcome them warmly and say he was honored to finally meet the family of Owen Sutherland. In fact, she almost interrupted him as she said, "What do you intend to do with the five hundred muskets Cullen discovered, General?"

Arnold stopped short, jaw slack.

Ella said, "I'm sure it's now a well-kept secret that Bradford Cullen has found them to the great benefit of the cause; but you see, the Sutherlands have ways of knowing such things."

Arnold said not a word. He listened closely as Ella explained all Benjamin had discovered. The general sat with fingers tented to his lips, elbows on his desk, contemplating what he heard. When Ella was finished, he leaned back in his chair, a weary and doleful look coming over him.

After a moment, he sighed. "What you say has the ring of truth, Mistress Sutherland, although it may all be circumstantial evidence that points unfairly to Mr. Cullen. Perhaps there's far more to know in this case. But as it stands, Celoron Meloche clearly is guilty and will be arrested within the hour."

Arnold said Bradford Cullen had come in that morning to reveal the Frenchman's smuggling operation, which Cullen and his agents had uncovered last night. He said Cullen had been to the Meloche warehouse to seize the muskets, and the run-in with young Benjamin had been an unfortunate accident caused by misunderstanding.

"Mr. Cullen told me the entire story, you see, and said his men thought your son was a watchman for Meloche." Arnold said all this with an impassive expression, but something seemed to haunt his eyes, which were quick and nervous as he spoke. "Mistress, you must understand my position and realize that what really matters most at the moment is that the muskets have been recovered and will be sent to our troops at Quebec before the day is out. Give me time to get to the bottom of all this—but do not expect me immediately to pursue an investigation or make accusations, when it's all I can do to prepare for a defense of Montreal."

Ella understood. She glanced at Benjamin, who was downcast. They stood up to take leave of Arnold, knowing that for the moment Cullen had again triumphed.

Now, however, there was no doubt in Ella's mind about Cullen's true loyalties. At the door, she turned and said to Arnold that even though other rebel leaders regarded the merchant highly, the Sutherlands would be watching him carefully. When he tried to turn his coat again, they would stop him, no matter how.

Arnold had no reply to make.

*chapter* **15**

# COUNTERATTACK

Fog settled in as Sutherland and Defries raced back up the Saint Lawrence. They hoped General Wooster would have time to withdraw his little army before it was caught and destroyed by a counterattack from the city. Once British troops disembarked, they would waste no time before striking at the Americans besieging Quebec. The loss of the two or three thousand men in the rebel army would be a terrible blow to the cause.

Hour after hour, through the night, the scouts trudged, ran, climbed, and scrambled across that rugged terrain, and all the while the British fleet pushed relentlessly upriver, the warmer weather melting the ice and speeding their progress. Whenever Sutherland and Defries snatched a few minutes of rest, they could make out the distant sound of oars and men shouting, or see the far-off flicker of lanterns on boats and ships. The British rotated crews regularly and continued their advance without pause. The two scouts were utterly exhausted after a night of almost constant movement. Still they seemed to keep hardly more than a mile or two ahead of the fleet.

By now Sutherland guessed that the British knew of their presence. Levesque must have told them to press on without delay. It crossed Sutherland's mind that he should have secured his old friend better, either tying him up or taking him prisoner. But he had done the most he could do in good conscience, and anything ruthless enough to silence his friend would have gone against the very ideals he was fighting for.

He ran on, through a narrow track that cut away from the main road and took them along cliffs above the river. It was just after dawn, cold and blowing, with a dusting of snow whirling hard enough to blind the two friends as they pressed onward. Their clothing was soaked with sweat and frozen stiff, but on they ran until their limbs and minds grew numb. From here the fleet was no longer in sight. At last their torture had achieved something, Sutherland thought numbly. Sometime near dusk they would reach advance rebel positions.

Their weapons became a terrible burden; their legs seemed no longer part of their bodies. Indeed, their very bodies seemed detached, and physical pain was almost like the pain of someone else—observed from afar. Step after weary step, on and on and on.

When night fell, the two men collapsed in exhaustion on high ground, knowing they were not far from an American outpost where they could get horses. The sky was clear, the air cold, and stars glittered like crystal in the black sky. There, far to the east, other lights twinkled on the horizon, like a yellow constellation that formed a snake.

Defries gasped, "It's them!"

Chest heaving, every breath a burning agony, Sutherland watched the distant lights. "Even the wind is with them. Come on!"

Away they went, scuffing down a long, rocky trail, Sutherland in front. Grueling and hurtful, and seemingly endless, the next few hours brought them finally to the outpost by the falls at Montmorency. There they acquired mounts to ride on to Quebec.

It rained until morning, and they were wet and dreary as they galloped across the fields and into Saint John's, the little headquarters village west of the citadel. The soggy American camp was listless, for it was Sunday, and men were drifting back from the church tents. Sutherland and Defries trotted through muddy streets between tents newly pitched by reinforcements from New Jersey and Pennsylvania. Sutherland saw hundreds of newcomers, but realized that scores were already lying sick in their tents.

They reined in before the cottage Arnold had used, which had been taken over by Wooster. There were fewer Connecticut officers here than when Wooster first arrived. Now they were mostly Massachusetts men, and one said that Wooster had been replaced by General John Thomas, a veteran regimental commander from the French wars. Sutherland's spirits rose, for General Thomas was highly respected. One of the eight brigadiers first appointed by Congress, he had led a brigade in the Boston siege, and now had brought fresh battalions, some of the best fighting men in the colonies.

Thomas was away studying the citadel wall, but as soon as Sutherland said the fleet was coming, word was dispatched to the commander. The officers to whom Sutherland spoke did no more than whisper this grim news to one another, for fear of creating panic among the sickly, despondent troops. So many men from those fine new battalions of Washington's army were already laid low. Fewer than a thousand were fit for guard duty; two thousand were on their backs, shivering in fevered misery wherever they could find shelter.

Sutherland and Defries needed a bed as much as anyone. Since both had had the pox years ago, they would not fall ill, so they did not care where they rested until Thomas arrived to interview them. After giving a full report, they slogged to a nearby regimental mess. It belonged to Pennsylvanians, among whom was Captain Matthew Smith. Thanks to Smith, the exhausted scouts were well fed and given straw bedding. They immediately fell asleep.

They awoke at dark, and Smith said Thomas knew of their report, but there was some disagreement among the commanders about whether to withdraw the army. Sutherland exploded in anger and stamped off to tell the general that the force coming upriver was too immense to withstand. But at Thomas's quarters he was told the general was still away, planning a defense of the river approach below Quebec. Besides, large quantities of arms were due shortly, and the general's staff was busy planning their distribution. Several fresh regiments would strengthen the rebel army within a week; surely, he was told, the British could not disembark, form up in battle order, and make an assault in less time than that.

Sutherland was at a loss. Angry and astonished at how the confused colonial officers debated and argued before making major decisions, he rejoined Defries and Smith and tried to rest. Their scouting trip might turn out to have been wasted effort unless the rebels acted decisively and withdrew to consolidate their forces. He went to sleep that night to the sound of Peter Defries learning how to plunk a jew's harp. He twanged away, often clattering the metal against his teeth, but he liked the sound so much that he went on trying. Defries managed to master the melody of "Revolutionary Tea," and even improved as he and Smith shared a great deal of sourmash whiskey.

Sutherland thought he had just laid down his head when there came a tremendous din of cannonading and musketry. He and Defries leaped out of a deep sleep and clambered from the tent into a mob of running, shouting men, half of them without uniforms, many others without weapons. It was just after dawn.

"Attack! Attack!" came the alarm. "They're coming out! The fleet's landed troops! We're being attacked!"

Sutherland and Defries shook off sleep and caught up their rifles and packs. Struggling against the mass of men streaming away from the citadel wall, they called out for Matthew Smith. The enemy infantry could not yet be seen, for they were beyond a rise in the land. Rebel soldiers by the hundreds were swarming toward the rear. Cannon from the citadel thundered steadily, battering the rebel forward lines.

Soon Sutherland and Defries found Smith rallying troops, and they joined the few score men who were determined to stand and fight. Defries was angrily tucking in his shirt, grumbling that he had been having a fine dream about papaya gin and captured treasure ships. Over the pandemonium, Smith shouted to his men to form a firing line and wait until the enemy came over the ridge. The Pennsylvanians were joined by several Virginia riflemen, some Jersey troops, and a collection of others from New England and New York.

Sutherland asked Smith, "Why weren't we interviewed by the general staff? Why didn't the army pull back right away when they knew the Redcoats had come?"

Smith growled, "Congress doesn't want us to pull back without a fight! If the Britishers make us run without a fight, they'll think they can chase us all the way to Philadelphia and round us up there, like a herd of stray sheep! We've got to make them pay for attacking us, so the general was thinking we'd make a defense right here. So here we be. But we weren't ready for this! Nobody expected an attack, not yet!"

Nearby stood a Jerseyman armed with only a wooden club. "Just got five hundred muskets shipped to us today!" he commented sourly, pointing at a stack of wooden crates across the campground. "But we ain't even had time to open 'em and clean off the grease they're packed in!"

Defries suddenly cried, "And there! Look at that store of powder kegs! Must be two hundred of 'em!"

Off to the right, near a stone farmhouse, stood kegs of black powder just brought from Montreal. They and the muskets represented all the rebel army had in reserve.

The clamor of retreating soldiers faded as the last men ran past the thin line, which, with Sutherland, Defries, and Smith, stood its ground, waiting. The rest of the camp was empty, wind flapping deserted tents, and wisps of cooking-fire smoke drifting slowly into the air. The hundred or so determined soldiers arrayed themselves in two lines, one rank kneeling. In the distance they heard the rattle of drums. The cannonading from the citadel had stopped; the British and loyalists had swept everything before them and now held the rebel works beyond the ridge, less than four hundred yards away.

"Ready on the firing line!" Smith shouted as the crash of many snare drums sounded from beyond the grassy rise.

"They're signaling the charge, so expect 'em to come over that knoll on the run! Hold your fire until the command!"

Smith was right. Suddenly there came a fierce roar of a thousand men shouting, as if a great tidal wave were sweeping against the other side of the knoll. Sutherland cocked his rifle, and Defries did the same. Nearby a man prayed softly.

Just then the enemy surged over the hill. Nearly every one wore the scarlet coat of the regulars. The frail rebel line wavered just an instant, and men gasped at the sight of so many Redcoats charging, bayonets flashing in the sunlight.

Defries, who was kneeling, said in amazement, "They landed reinforcements and put 'em out against us all in the same hour, somebody told me!" He slowly shook his head. "I'd rather be a privateer." Bringing up his rifle, he waited for Smith's order to fire. Sutherland was in the second rank, and after the first volleyed, he would step forward with the men in his line and deliver another volley.

The horde of Redcoats came swarming over the knoll and down toward the empty rebel camp. There were at least nine hundred men charging, and as if by magic they formed three dense attack columns eight men wide. This was no Bunker Hill suicide, with soldiers charging in open rank. These were massive battering rams coming on, one to the right, one to the left, and another in the center.

The British and loyalist troops and their Indian allies had split in a smooth maneuver, just out of good firing range. They sent the two outer columns wide, to outflank the camp. The center force, of at least four hundred, came pounding ahead, confident and shouting, voices ringing out in a raging tumult.

Sutherland and Smith eyed each other, both knowing that in minutes they would be lost. It galled Sutherland that there was no chance to save the new muskets or powder.

Suddenly, as though reading each other's minds, they unshouldered their rifles, handing them to a sergeant standing nearby. Smith ordered him to take command, then sprang with Sutherland from the firing line, both men dashing for the powder kegs. Defries whooped, threw down his rifle, and came on behind. The other troops opened up with a roar of covering fire. A swath of enemy in the right wing went down, slowing the column's advance, but the king's troops brought their own muskets to bear.

Running in a crouching sprint through the smoke of battle, Sutherland and his two friends picked up flaming brands from campfires. The British and loyalists in the center force saw them and knew what they were up to. Bullets came whizzing at the three rebels, but British-issue Brown Bess firearms were inaccurate at any range. The men on the rebel firing line, however, were armed mainly with rifles and were firing as individuals. Their targets were British officers, whose silver and gold made them obvious marks. The attackers suddenly found themselves with many dead or wounded officers, and for a moment they bunched up indecisively.

That gave Sutherland enough time to throw down his flaming sticks, whip out a hatchet, and burst apart a wooden powder keg. Smith and Defries did the same, and soon three long black trails of gunpowder ran across the ground toward the rebel defenders. British gunfire became more concentrated as other officers took over. The enemy began to charge.

Sutherland lugged four barrels of powder to the sealed crates of muskets. He could hear the cries of warning from his firing line, not far off. The enemy was moments away as he tomahawked a keg, poured out a trail, and glanced around to see Defries and Smith toss torches on their own fuses. Hissing smoke and flame sped toward the barrels of powder.

"Get the hell out!" Smith screamed to his men, and dashed with them back through the camp. Defries lumbered behind, calling for Sutherland to run.

As the last rebel soldiers fired final rounds and spun to fly before the powder went up, Sutherland lit his fuse and ran, quickly catching up with the sergeant who had his rifle. The shouts of loyalists and Redcoats had grown louder as they desperately crowded away from the gunpowder.

When the kegs went up, the tremendous blast blew the

camp apart, sending smoking, burning debris and splintered muskets in every direction. Sutherland and his companions were clear of the camp, however, and soon they regrouped, loading as they trotted, skillfully manipulating weapons, powder horns, and ramrods. Eventually Smith ordered a halt, and they fired a volley at the nearest pursuers, once more causing casualties and making the British think again about trying to outflank this determined party.

This slight delay in the Redcoat advance gave the rebel rearguard a chance to escape, firing often as they did so. If it accomplished nothing else, their show of discipline proved to the British that American rebels would not all run without a fight. At such a dismal hour in the rebellion, that was something.

The British counterattack drove the rebels from Quebec for good, but General Thomas rallied his men, and the first British advance came to a halt without further serious fighting. The rebel camp and all the precious stores, munitions, and artillery were lost; there was no other choice but to retreat quickly upriver. Even without the additional twelve thousand men still in the naval transports, the British had broken the siege, and the rebels were in full retreat. Where that retreat would end no one knew.

Thomas appointed Sutherland and Defries to take dispatches down to Arnold at Montreal, and they set out immediately on horseback, on a grueling one-week journey, also with little rest. They had endured so much in their rush back to Quebec that this second fatiguing trip nearly broke them. If it had not been for the desperate urgency of the moment, neither would have been able to continue after the third day. Yet they hastened on.

Sutherland was driven by the longing to rejoin his family in Montreal and to send them to safety in Albany. He knew there was no holding the Saint Lawrence now, and that Arnold had been right to want to withdraw the army a month ago to avoid this serious defeat. Still, under General Thomas the rebels had recovered well and moved upriver in good order. Sutherland hoped the withdrawal would continue smoothly down into New York, to stop at Fort Ticonderoga and the strongpoints in the Mohawk Valley. From there a solid defense could be formed to await the onset of winter, when most military activity would stop. Time was what Congress needed now—time and the support of those British political leaders who would demand that Parliament call off its soldiers and end the civil war.

On the way to Montreal, they passed fresh regiments marching to join Thomas. These new troops were Pennsylvanians, Massachusetts men, Connecticutters, and Yorkers; well-fed, provisioned, and equipped, they would give a good account of themselves if managed properly. By the time Sutherland and Defries galloped through the northeastern gate of Montreal, their hopes had risen once again. Congress had sent enough men and equipment to slow the British force, and that was proof of a concerted effort by all the colonies to blunt this critical British thrust.

Yet Montreal was soon in an uproar. Sutherland and Defries delivered their dispatches to Arnold, and within a few hours word had spread through the city that the rebel army was in retreat and the British were on the move. Loyalists exulted, the French were pleased, while rebel civilians grimly prepared for withdrawal. Even Indians became abruptly surly and rude to Americans. Some of the French residents grew so boisterous that several companies of rebel troops had to be dispatched to maintain order.

Owen was impatient to get to Ella and his family, but he had much to report, and the general kept him there a full hour. Arnold's leg was fully mended, and he was as active as ever. He seemed very tired, however, no doubt from the strain of organizing the city's defense and policing Montreal with too few soldiers.

"I have no more than a thousand men in the whole district," Arnold said as he paced the room. "And four hundred of those are forty-five miles west of here, at a fort near the rapids called the Cedars. Most of the others are sick but doing duty anyway."

Arnold swung on Sutherland and Defries; they were haggard and drooping, covered with sweat and the dust of the road. Arnold said all rebels in the city were in danger now.

Sutherland replied, "I mean to get my family to Albany as soon as you are finished with me, General."

Arnold paced again. "Yes. Yes. I believe your enlistments are up, gentlemen. I don't blame you for leaving."

Without thinking, Sutherland and Defries said in unison, "We're staying on." They glanced at each other, a glint of amusement in their weary eyes.

Arnold was observing them intently. "As I expected." He became grave then. "I can give you leave of twelve hours . . ."

Sutherland and Defries both looked up sharply at that. Arnold pursed his lips and said with a sigh, "Forgive my insensitivity to your needs, gentlemen. Twenty-four hours."

Though he said nothing, it pained Sutherland to know he would have so little time with his family. But when Arnold explained their next mission, he understood the urgency.

"We face a new danger. The enemy is advancing in force from Detroit, and we must have scouts west of the Cedars to warn of their approach; you may pick the men you want along." He sat down quickly and wrote out a requisition for equipment and food. "Be on the road westward by this time tomorrow." Arnold sanded the letter and shoved it across the table to Sutherland. "Report to the garrison commander at the Cedars, Colonel Bedel of New Hampshire. Lieutenant Governor Hamilton has raised the western Indians against us, and if they hit us in the rear by surprise, we'll never get out of Montreal, or out of Canada."

Their spirits dampened by the deteriorating military situation, Sutherland and Defries stood up, bones and muscles stiff. Arnold rose and shook their hands, thanking them for their sacrifice.

"By the way, Mr. Sutherland, I have the honor of conveying the greetings of Dr. Benjamin Franklin, who arrived in this city a fortnight ago."

Sutherland was startled. "Franklin made the journey from Philadelphia?"

Arnold nodded slowly and smiled. "All the way, though he's old and fragile; so you see there are others giving completely of themselves for the cause, though I fear the good doctor's attempts to win over the French in Canada are doomed to failure now that the British fleet has arrived."

Sutherland had been with Franklin a year earlier, when the elderly statesman had first returned from England to Philadelphia. Franklin had been instrumental in guiding the Second Continental Congress, and no one symbolized the highest ideals of the rebellion better than he. Sutherland deemed him a close friend and had to see him for part of the precious twenty-four hours of leave.

Mind whirling, near physical collapse, Sutherland left Arnold's office with Defries. Outside they were met by a sudden rush of people, who seemed to come out of Sutherland's last dream. He staggered under the impact of Benjamin and Susannah leaping onto his chest, laughing and hugging him. Right behind was Heera and the blue jay, Punch, who flitted about the astonished Scotsman's head. Laughing and embracing his children, Sutherland was jubilant as they cried out, "Pa! Welcome back! We missed you, Pa!"

Through a daze, Sutherland saw Ella, standing near a two-horse carriage. She was wearing a beautiful yellow gown, and her hair was pinned up. How radiant she looked! How wonderful to see her at last! Sutherland's children eagerly piled onto Peter Defries, who guffawed and greeted them as though they were his own family. Owen walked slowly toward Ella, savoring the sight of her as she came to him.

When they were close, she rushed forward, throwing herself into his arms. For a long while both were too lost in relief and gladness to speak.

"Ah, my husband," Ella whispered at last and drew back to look at him; she did not say he was so very worn and shabby, for now he was in her arms, and looked full of love. "It's Sunday, and they'll say it's a scandal that we should kiss on the Sabbath."

Sutherland smiled, weariness draining from him. "We haven't kissed."

With that, she pressed against him and kissed him with all her might, and he crushed her close, neither caring who might be watching. The kisses were fierce, then they relented and became tender. Ella smiled and laughed through it, keeping her eyes closed, as though she feared to open them and find it was only an illusion.

After a lingering moment they parted to take a breath, and Defries led the children past them to the waiting carriage. The crowd that had been fondly watching the reunion moved on, the women misty-eyed and the men admiring such a handsome group.

Sutherland, his arms around Ella's waist, said, "I don't have very long...."

"I know," she said, touching her finger to his lips. "General Arnold sent a messenger as soon as you arrived." She sighed.

He saw her sadness, but they agreed it was good they could be together at least for a short time.

Ella squeezed his arm. "Dr. Franklin sent word that he'll come to our apartment tomorrow morning; until then, you're all mine ... mine and the children's."

Thanks to Peter Defries, who wearily demanded that Benjamin and Susannah take him out to show how Punch assaulted cats, and then drive with him to a public house for a real meal, Owen and Ella were left alone most of the day.

They spent it in each other's arms, and because Owen was so exhausted, he slept deeply when they were not making love. Late in the afternoon he awoke, alone, and lay there listening to the pleasing sounds of Ella cooking dinner. Evening was coming on, and light fell softly through the bedroom window.

Sutherland hardly knew this place, though it had been his family's home for half a year. He had slept in this four-poster bed only once before leaving for Quebec. It was a real luxury compared with the cots and pallets of the campaign. Now at last he was home, listening to Ella in the kitchen, lying here like a successful fur merchant with the northwest at his feet. He closed his eyes, wondered how long he had been asleep, and dozed off until Ella awakened him with a kiss.

Through a haze of lamplight, he looked up and ran his

fingers through her golden hair. "Where are the children?" he asked.

Ella smiled. "That's why I woke you. They're trying to get Peter out of the carriage. He fell asleep three hours ago, when they were riding through the countryside, and now they can't wake him up."

Sutherland chuckled and kissed his wife. Soon he was down in the street, bundling the enormous Peter Defries out of the carriage and lugging him upstairs over his shoulder. He carried Peter into the apartment and laid him on a mattress in Benjamin's room. Immediately Defries rolled onto his side and curled up.

The Sutherlands had a quiet, cheerful dinner by candlelight, and the evening passed. Before long, the children had gone to bed, and Ella and Owen retired as well. Owen felt he could sleep a week, and with Ella again in his arms, he fell into a deep, untroubled slumber, blessed with the tender warmth of Ella's body.

Ella, too, would sleep as she had not slept in all these months. What was still to come she could not tell, but at least Owen was safe and once more beside her, as he should be. She lay there, thinking about those years of peace and harmony, prosperity and happiness. How many times had she slept with him? How many times had they made love? When would they again enjoy the simple pleasures and happiness of marriage? She did not ask for much—only for Owen and their children to be by her side.

Then Jeremy came to mind, as he so often did. She would write him a letter and leave it with the Devaliers, to be delivered after the loyalists retook Montreal. Yes, the rebels were beaten here. She had to admit that. The revolution was in jeopardy. In a few months they might all be under arrest, or ruled by a military garrison quartered in every city and village of America. If the rebellion failed, then so would the Sutherlands.

The British advance from Canada might be the first step to ultimate rebel defeat, but the Sutherlands and their friends would fight to the bitter end. If they had to, they would flee to the distant west, to the fabled Shining Mountains. Ella and Owen had discussed that possibility, for they would never be imprisoned or humiliated by a victorious British Parliament.

To herself she whispered, "Beaten for now perhaps, but not yet defeated. No, not yet." She stroked Owen's black, curly hair and kissed his closed eyes. "We'll go on, my love," she said. "And on and on."

At ten sharp, Benjamin Franklin came, alone, to meet with Sutherland. The renowned statesman had visited Ella several times in his two weeks in Montreal and had become fast friends with the children. Benjamin was his namesake, and Franklin took special pride in that, offering the boy an open invitation to come and visit him, wherever in the world he might be. To Susannah, Franklin was like a wise and kindly grandfather, and he doted on her, saying she reminded him of his own daughter, Sally, when she was young.

From the moment Franklin arrived, the children chatted excitedly, and Punch fluttered in and out of the window. The bird took to Franklin, even hopping on his shoulder during tea.

The old statesman sat in a comfortable rocker, a cup in one slender hand, a piece of Ella's cake in the other. He was large of girth, of medium height, and he wore no wig, instead letting his gray hair grow long and stringy, falling to his shoulders. His coat and waistcoat, though of the best broadcloth, were old-fashioned, in the plain, brown style of the Quakers, and his breeches and stockings were also brown.

Utterly unpretentious, Franklin did not seem at all like the man to whom leading scientists looked for advice, just as American politicians looked to him for approval. The heavy weight of revolution rested upon him more than upon anyone else, save for George Washington, and the portly Pennsylvanian seemed old and frail to anyone who did not reckon with the strength of his heart and the brilliance of his versatile intellect.

When the conversation drifted to matters of war and revolution, Owen sent the reluctant children, along with Heera and Punch, to the market. When they were gone, Franklin said he agreed that Canada could not be defended and that the army should withdraw, intact, immediately. He had supported the removal of Wooster for incompetence, and he esteemed General Thomas highly.

"We must hold Ticonderoga and Lake George and the Mohawk Valley until winter," Franklin said, rocking slowly to the rhythm of Peter's snoring from the other room. "I'm leaving this city in a week or less, and I regret that my delegation to the Canadian French must be deemed a sorry failure."

He sighed deeply. It had nevertheless been well worth the effort, he said, because he enjoyed being a tourist. He regretted, however, that the loss of the lower Saint Lawrence meant that the entire northwest, save for Fort Pitt, would be again open to British domination.

"I'd hoped we could launch an invasion toward Detroit from Pitt at the same time that a force moved up the Great Lakes from Montreal." He eyed Sutherland over his bifocals. "And I'd recommended you to command the expedition from Pitt; but now that all must be called off, and we have to retreat just to stay alive."

Sutherland said, "With all the fresh troops I see coming up from the colonies, I'm sure we can hold Albany if we withdraw methodically, and perhaps by next spring we'll be able to influence Parliament to make terms. Surely the British can't afford a war of the magnitude that would be needed to overwhelm the colonies; already they've hired thousands of Germans from Hesse, and that'll put a hole in the royal purse! If the British try to beat us to the ground, the lives spent, the business ruined, the political careers destroyed would be more than any Tory could stand."

Franklin ruminated, rocking, his lower lip stuck out as he thought about that. After a moment, he said, "I fear the pride of the king and Parliament has been badly damaged by our American impudence; and the British army has been whipped too often, and too badly over here to agree to disengaging without first giving our noses a good bloodying—"

Ella blurted, "But any who think they'll do that easily are underestimating us, just as they did at Bunker Hill! That's partly why we're in this war to begin with! Don't

British lords yet realize Americans will never stand to be oppressed the way poor commoners are in England?"

Sutherland agreed. "If they push for a wider war, they'll get more than they bargain for, whether they win or lose."

Franklin nodded slowly. "They've already refused to accept congressional petitions for a truce; now that they have such a huge force on the move, they won't make peace until their honor—their dratted, brittle British honor—has been fully satisfied! At whatever cost in British lives, and in American lives!"

Normally, Americans considered themselves British subjects, and Franklin's clear distinction here was a pointed declaration that there was indeed a marked difference between Americans and Britons.

"If we lose Canada," Franklin said, almost in a whisper, "then there's little left for us, save to fight for our own honor, and for the best terms we can make. But we must hold New York Province! We must!"

Sutherland spoke up suddenly, his eyes alight. "There's one more card we can play, and that's one that the entire world will consider with the utmost gravity."

Franklin peered intently at him but said nothing. It was Ella who voiced what they all were thinking.

"Declare America's independence of the empire!" She heard those words as though someone else had said them. They hung in the air, echoing in their minds, with the most momentous significance.

After long reflection, Franklin held up his empty plate to Ella and said with a smile, "I never imagined a political philosopher with such foresight would also have the talent to bake such delicious raisin cake, Mistress Sutherland."

The hushed conversation ended with a discussion of Bradford Cullen. A year ago, at Sutherland's suggestion, Franklin had done what he could in Congress to keep Cullen from gaining too much influence with Whigs in the northwest and north. Yet even Franklin could not prevent the wealthy Cullen from buying the support of many rebels who were impressed by his riches and hungered for what Cullen could buy for the war effort.

Ella explained why she believed Cullen had profited illegally from manipulating shipments of food and government supplies. When she told how Cullen had refused to send cannon to the siege of Quebec, Franklin shook his head sadly and grumbled that there was no more time for a full investigation in Canada.

"I'll do what I can to keep the man under observation while I'm here, but when I depart for Philadelphia . . ." He began to think hard, brows knitting. He took a long breath. "Perhaps there is something I can do."

Sutherland said, "It's my expectation that Cullen will become a loyalist as soon as he can, and it'll cost us much if he has the chance to betray us somehow; I'd try to prove my case against him if I didn't have to leave the city this very afternoon."

Ella felt those last words as a stab to her heart. So did Peter Defries. From the bedroom, he groaned and complained in a sleepy voice that he was just dropping off to sleep, and why did they have to go again already?

Franklin said to Sutherland, "Be assured, my friend, that while you're traipsing around the northwest, I'll be scheming to counter Bradford Cullen. He won't find it easy to help the British, if that's his game. I have no hard evidence of Cullen's treachery, but I trust your judgment."

With that, Franklin got up, went to the bedroom door, and rapped the head of his cane on the doorjamb. He knew Peter, and called to him:

"Rise and shine, Mr. Defries. Before I eat up all the raisin cake! And what's this Owen tells me about you running to sea in search of treasure ships and papaya gin? Wake up, my boy! What is papaya gin, anyhow?"

Sutherland and Defries took leave of Montreal late that afternoon, and with them went Bill Poole, the Connecticut blacksmith they had met on the Quebec road. Having stayed in Montreal, Poole had reenlisted as an aide to Arnold, a fellow New Haven man. When he heard Sutherland was back, he requested to join the scout.

They rode overland, then went with a supply bateau across the Ottawa River to the fort at the Cedars. This strongpoint stood on the north bank of the Saint Lawrence, just west of the mouth of the mighty Ottawa. Between here and Montreal, brawling rapids surged for miles downriver, making any crossing difficult. The best place to cross for a British expedition approaching Montreal from the west was over the Ottawa, near the Cedars. From there, a large force, such as the one expected from Fort Detroit, could descend on Montreal from the north, and could cut off its supplies and communication with the rest of Canada.

The three friends had a rough but safe trip, with much to talk about as they traveled in the bateau. In Montreal, Poole had aided many rebel soldiers whose enlistments were up, or who were too ill to stay in Canada. Thanks to the money Sutherland had given him, Poole had been able to acquire a small fortune in Continental dollars, which would go a long way to feed and clothe men traveling home through the lower colonies, where continentals were worth their face value.

Poole had left the money with trusted friends when he rejoined Sutherland. He had even managed to do a bit of trading in Montreal and had accumulated some money to be sent to his wife in New Haven. Poole had asked Ella Sutherland to see that his own money went home soon, in case he was caught up in a confused retreat from Canada.

Owen was glad to find that Poole was back in the bloom of health, ruddy and physically powerful. He had a blacksmith's incredibly strong hands and arms; his barrel chest was the largest Sutherland had ever seen, larger even than Defries's. A high-spirited fellow, he was quick to raise a song with the Canadian boatmen navigating the bateau across the Ottawa. Soon he and the Canadians were trading songs, though their lusty melodies were hardly heard above the river's roar. Sutherland and Defries sat in the back, among bales and barrels lashed to the deck, and tried to catch up on some lost sleep as the sturdy vessel leaped and swayed through the spraying, foaming water.

Eventually they landed at the rebel positions, which were bounded by substantial defensive works. There was a square earthen redoubt, as well as a stout wall of wooden pickets. Two fieldpieces were mounted to ward off attack from the west, and the interior of the earthworks was stacked high with ample supplies and munitions. The troops were stolid Hampshiremen, dependable and hardy, much like the frontiersmen of the northwest, though they were more farmers than hunters or traders. Their colonel, Timothy Bedel, was said to be a good officer who had fought against the French and campaigned in the northwest during the Indian wars of the sixties.

After reporting to Colonel Bedel, Sutherland wasted little time in the post. He and his two friends immediately prepared to set off to the west. Few scouting parties had been bold enough to rove very far, for rumor had it that scores of Indians were on the hunt for rebel prisoners and were stalking every patrol. There had been only two or three actual brushes with the enemy, but Sutherland could see that Bedel was uneasy in this outpost. The colonel told Sutherland that as many as three thousand Indians might be on their way from Detroit.

Sutherland said that was impossible, for it would require many more months and incalculable quantities of trade goods for the British to persuade so large a force of Indians to take the warpath for the king. Bedel was unreasonably nervous, Sutherland thought as he and his friends walked out of the fort at the Cedars. Although the place was very defensible against Indians and a small number of Redcoats who had no cannon, Bedel and his officers did not seem at all sure of themselves. Perhaps it was because of the bad news from Quebec; but whatever it was, these four hundred troops at the Cedars had leaders who did not instill confidence.

## chapter 16

# DANGEROUS COUNTRY

Bradford Cullen sat at his desk in the small office at the rear of his house, a pool of lamplight illuminating a letter he was reading. Behind him Auguste, the butler, awaited his master's decision.

Though Cullen was eighty or more, his hands were steady, his senses sharp. His health could have been better, and his continual wheezing suggested some inner ailment, but the man was in complete command of himself. The letter he held trembled ever so slightly, but not as a result of his old age. His hands shook because of anger.

Cullen tossed the letter with disgust on the desk and sat back so that he was out of the brightest lamplight. "Is the rogue waiting outside?"

"Just so," the butler said. "His moccasins are muddy, his clothes torn! I ordered him to garb himself decently and return, but he pushed right past me and came in, without wiping his feet, declaring that Governor Carleton himself had sent him! Imagine! An English governor sending such a rabble as emissary! It's uncivilized! We French would never do it!"

"The French lost the last war. Too civilized, perhaps." Cullen's jowls worked as he pondered what to do next.

Auguste bared his teeth in a silent look of contempt for his employer—a man who never missed a chance to insult the French. Cullen even required Auguste to speak English.

Cullen wheezed and licked his gums. A spy with a message from Governor Carleton at Quebec had to be received; but what rancor it caused in him that the spy should be this man, of all people! Cullen would rather speak to an Indian—to an African slave—than to this man, who had been such a bitter enemy.

He muttered, "How things change, Auguste. How they change, and what bedfellows we get in wartime."

"Indeed, sir, indeed." Auguste eyed Cullen with guarded loathing. The butler despised all British and Americans, but nowhere in Canada could a butler of Auguste's abilities and standards find a more prosperous master than Bradford Cullen. The Frenchman cared nothing for Cullen's politics—in fact, he was not sure precisely what they were. All that mattered was that Cullen throve, and Auguste with him.

Suddenly there came a flurry of raps against the door. "Papa! Do admit me! Hurry, Papa! It's almost time!"

Auguste let in a squat, thickset woman in her late thirties, wearing an enormous wig and an expensive, gaudy pink gown that did nothing to enhance her broad figure. Linda Cullen was the merchant's only child, his treasure. No one else could have barged in like this at such a moment of wrath, when Cullen was about to swallow some of his pride and meet with a man he hated.

"Papa, Papa!" Linda wailed in a high, nasal voice, running to her father, hands fluttering, her expression woebegone. "You must tell me, please—which side does the patch go on, left or right?"

She held up a tiny heart-shaped black facial patch. Cullen squinted at his daughter's stubby fingers.

"I can never remember!" Linda gasped. "Right or left? In Boston we were loyal, and I think it had to go on the right cheek; but now we're rebels, and they wear patches on the left . . . or is it the other way around? Oh, Papa, all this changing and coming and going is positively horrid! I never know what to do or say to anyone unless I know their position, and Mama says we're sitting the fence for now, so—"

"Dearest," Cullen said firmly, "please bridle your emotions until our Auguste is on his way with an errand for me." Cullen looked at the butler. "Tell the rabble out there that I'll see him in a moment, but first I'll have a word with my daughter." Auguste bowed and departed, closing the door.

By now Linda was close to tears. Cullen patted his daughter's hand and found the beauty patch sticking to his palm. With difficulty, he unstuck it and handed it back to Linda.

"Papa, I just can't tell anymore what I should do or say, or on what side of my face to wear this patch! My birthday ball is in less than two hours, and still I haven't been able to get a straight answer from Mama! She says she doesn't know what we are anymore, and insisted I ask you. Papa, are we rebels or loyalists? Is it right or left? I have to know! You see, there's a handsome bachelor—"

"Linda! Linda, my dear child, I know how difficult all this has been for you—heaven knows it's been difficult for me! But you must be patient, for these delicate political matters—"

"But, Papa, the ball is tonight! Back in Boston when you joined the rebels, you said be patient, for you were not sure we'd always be rebels. And you promised we could live in Philadelphia until the loyalists were driven from Boston. But Montreal! All the best people here are loyalists or papist French who don't even speak English! Now I have a grand birthday ball, and what'll they say if I wear the patch on the wrong cheek? It'll be a scandal!"

"Don't wear a patch at all, then!"

Linda was horrified, her eyes wide, mouth open. "What? Oh . . . oh, Papa! Do you think I'd shame our family name by appearing in public so stupidly out of fashion? Oh, Papa! How can you ask such a sacrifice of me?"

At this Cullen could stand no more, and with a slap on the table he forced himself to his feet and began to stamp about the small office, thudding his cane on the floor.

"Don't you see that we all have to make sacrifices?" he

said. "Don't you see that I have to make sure my final choice is the right one? Don't you see that those patches and those fine dresses and this grand ball are all paid for by your father's prudent decisions? Linda, my daughter, I can't tell you whether your patch should be Whig or Tory! I don't even know whether *I* should be loyalist or rebel! Never mind your damned patches!"

"Oh! Papa! How can you speak to me like this? How can you be so unfeeling of my distress?" She snatched a silk handkerchief from her sleeve and pressed it to her face, bawling and sobbing.

Cullen at last went to his daughter and put his hand on her shoulder. "Child, must you wear a patch?"

That got a long groan, and Linda wailed harder. Cullen quaked with anger. All the weight of his ambition hung on this very same decision: rebel or loyalist. Already, Helen Cullen, his elderly wife, was barely on speaking terms with him because of Linda's prolonged misery and because they had come to Montreal as rebels entering a society of wealthy loyalists. How was Linda ever to snare a husband if the only bachelors in the city were of the other political persuasion?

Cullen sighed and muttered, "No one understands these things better than I do. No one realizes what it takes to succeed in this turbulent world! No one!" His voice rose, and he shook his cane. "I just want to do some business, that's all! The hell with this damned war! The hell with Whigs and Tories! Why doesn't someone start winning or losing so I know which side to join? I hate the indecision, and I hate how it's making you so miserable, Linda, my child."

Linda managed to stop crying, and after a little while her father sat down heavily in his chair.

"Perhaps," he said as gently and as pleadingly as he could, "if you wore the patch in some manner of compromise ... I don't know exactly, but I'm sure you'll think of a pretty and attractive way."

That was the best he could do. With one final sniff, Linda decided to be very brave and left the office. Cullen sat in silence, the only sound his slow wheezing. He had come a long way in this past year. Other wealthy men had been ruined when they declared themselves loyal and were driven out by rebels, but he had cunningly seen which way to go after the astounding rebel defense at Bunker Hill.

Last year he had been sure Quebec would fall and the entire northwest would be captured by the rebel Congress, and he meant to be instrumental in dominating the western lands. Just in case something went wrong, however, he had maintained a secret correspondence with Governor Carleton in the citadel, pretending to be a British agent.

Now Quebec had held out, and the British were on the march. It was over for the rebellion, and he had to extricate himself from the losing side. Thanks to his crafty wisdom, Carleton still believed him a loyalist at heart and now had sent this emissary. Cullen had to be careful, nevertheless, that the rebels did not discover his duplicity and have him arrested, perhaps executed.

There came Auguste's familiar knock, and the butler entered, followed by a black-haired, burly man in buckskins. Into the light of the desk lamp strode Jacques Levesque, and from the first moment it was clear to Cullen that the man still despised him from their conflict ten years earlier. Back then Cullen had tried to have him hanged as a renegade, but Owen Sutherland had interceded with the British governor to have Levesque pardoned. The enmity between these two men could never be bridged, and it showed in the handsome Frenchman's surly expression.

Levesque was weary, dirty from days of hard travel, and wearing clothes that had seen much use. He carried a knife and tomahawk at his belt, but had left his rifle outside. Auguste remained in the room, near the door, with a loaded pistol in his own belt.

The French *voyageur* sat down without any greeting, and Cullen touched Carleton's letter of introduction.

"Tell me why you've come," Cullen said.

Levesque's face was pinched, his eyes dull at having to deal with the likes of Bradford Cullen. Yet Levesque knew Cullen could assist in the defeat of the rebels in Canada.

"The British have already landed at Quebec—thirteen thousand troops. Carleton wants all loyal subjects to prepare the way for the return of king's rule here." It obviously pained Levesque to say the rest. "In return, he's offering you an important place in governing the fur trade in the northwest."

From his shirt Levesque drew out another letter, bound in ribbon and sealed with Carleton's stamp. Tossing it in front of Cullen, he said, "The terms are detailed there. You are to see to it that supplies for the rebels are diverted, lost, or destroyed. You are also to prepare the loyal *Anglais* and French to establish a new commercial system, and to reopen trade with the northwest, and to root out all rebels who might try to turn their coats and pretend to be loyal."

Cullen's face shone, his small eyes gleaming with greed. Levesque was a complete contrast, dour and bitter.

"Hear me well, Cullen," the Frenchman said softly. "Should you betray the loyalists, or should you remain a rebel after this, I will personally hunt you down and cut your throat."

Cullen scowled, but did not waver. With a sudden guffaw, he let his anger at this threat melt away. Anger was replaced by exquisite joy at being offered so important a position. Now that loyalist victory was certain, he could not be in a better position for profit. He let his head go back and laughed heartily, as though Levesque had just told a charming joke.

Then he said amiably, "Go on, Jacques; do not trouble yourself about killing me! My man there will supply your every need—clothes, food, money, a whore."

Levesque nearly sprang at him, and for just an instant fear came into Cullen's face. But the Frenchman recovered quickly. Breathing fast, he rose and said, "I'll take care of myself. I'll not come back here again. I have other work to do. When you write Carleton, tell him you prefer he send another messenger, because you don't like using one who'll kill you if you look at him the wrong way."

With that, Levesque stormed out, nearly knocking the startled Auguste down as he went, banging the door against the wall. Cullen seethed. He ought to have Levesque murdered. But before he could say anything, there came the sound of running down the stairs. His skinny wife, Helen, appeared, her wrinkled face contorted.

"Oh, no . . ." Cullen buried his face in his hands. "What is it, Mrs. Cullen?"

Helen Cullen was dressed for her daughter's birthday ball, and her conservative brown clothes suited her fussy, birdlike manner. Her bony fingers were locked before her withered breast. In a dry, throaty voice, she panted, "Mr. Cullen, I'm sure I don't know . . ." She noted Auguste and hesitated. The butler bowed and took leave of them, discreetly closing the door. Helen leaned on the desk. "Mr. Cullen, I don't know what you said to our child, but whatever it was, it's made her into a clown, a positive harlequin! A . . ." Her mouth trembled, as if she would weep. "A village fool!"

Cullen was too pleased with the British offer of alliance to become upset as his wife continued. "Mr. Cullen, our child insists—and I mean insists—she insists on wearing her patch on her forehead, right between her eyes—"

Cullen leaned back, smiling, much to the dismay of his wife, who fumed that he should care far more than he did about their daughter's future.

"Silence!" Cullen slammed the table, and Helen jumped in fright. "Please, Mrs. Cullen, do not think I'm not concerned about the girl's well-being." Then a sly smile came over his face, and he said with a wink, "This time she wears the patch on her right cheek—the loyalist cheek! Hah! Yes, and you, too, my dear!"

"I?" Helen touched her right cheek. "I? Wear a patch? On the Tory side?"

Cullen chuckled and nodded. "The government's troops are at Quebec! And the governor's made me a handsome offer."

Helen thought about that a moment. Once again her husband was changing sides. This time, however, she knew it was for good. With eyes half closed, she whispered, "It's the prudent choice."

She drifted out the door, fingertips on her right cheek. It was against her Puritan upbringing, but she had to admit

that a patch would be quite pretty. Especially on the Tory
cheek. After all, she had never believed the rebels would
win. Oh, for a brief while it was not so very clear, but now
that Bradford Cullen was sure, Helen would rejoice for the
sake of the king. All would be well.


Sutherland, Defries, and Bill Poole journeyed through the
woodlands and swamps west of the Ottawa River. This was
a settled, peaceful country of rolling hills, farms, and woods,
but its serenity was deceptive. It seemed to know nothing
of the war, yet the enemy must come through this territory.
If Redcoats with loyalists and Indians made an attempt to
attack the city from the west, these pretty green hills would
be where the rebels must stand against them.

As he and his friends moved along ridges and through
the treelines between *habitant* fields, Sutherland guessed
that any regular troops would be from the Eighth Regiment
at Detroit. No doubt he would know some of them. The
Indians would be coming from that country, too, since so
many were massed at the straits.

The three scouts roved as far as thirty miles west of the
rebel strongpoint at the Cedars. Almost four hundred New
Hampshire troops garrisoned the strong earthworks there; it
would take at least a thousand attackers to menace such a
stout post. So great a force of Indians or loyalists could not
yet be raised to supplement the few hundred regulars scattered throughout the northwest, and Sutherland did not believe Henry Hamilton could break through to the east.

Yet Hamilton would no doubt try. There was always the
threat of several hundred Indians and loyalists being mustered into parties hitting hard against rebel supply lines, or
waylaying reinforcements on the way to Montreal. Thus
Sutherland and his friends searched the farmlands and
swamps for any sign of an enemy force. Once their numbers
were determined, the Hampshiremen at the Cedars could be
ready with a strong defense.

During this scout, Sutherland and Defries became fast
friends with Poole. He was a cheerful fellow, fond of practical jokes, even if played on him. He took great interest

in Peter Defries's stories of papaya gin and treasure ships in the Caribbean, and swore to join him on a privateer. Poole had less effusive moments when, at the campfire, he spoke softly and fondly about his children and the splendid blacksmith shop he had to give up in order to join the rebellion.

It was in nightly camps that Defries and Poole grew to admire each other, and Sutherland watched them become like brothers as they played at dice and told tall stories, Defries ending each evening with a twangy tune on his jew's harp. It was always the same melody: "Revolutionary Tea." Defries liked it best and thought he played it flawlessly. No one told him otherwise.

Defries also adopted the habit of lying back with a pipe while Poole snoozed and Sutherland used firelight to enjoy Oliver Goldsmith's novel, *The Vicar of Wakefield,* often reading aloud humorous passages to the delight of his friends. At the end of every evening, when the campfire was burning low, Defries never failed to softly recite the ditty:

> A pipe, a book,
> a quiet nook,
> a fire—at least its embers;
> a dog, a glass,
> 'tis thus we pass
> the hours one remembers.

It was an unexpectedly peaceful interlude, this scouting trip. The war might be raging to the east; the rebellion might be tottering at its very foundations; but these three men developed a close companionship as they searched for a trace of the elusive enemy and prepared for the impending battle.

On May 15, a Wednesday, Sutherland spotted a band of fighting men at a farmhouse nine miles west of the Cedars. He, Defries, and Poole were on a low ridge above a pretty valley dotted with French farmhouses, fields, and ponds. Unseen, the three men observed this little group of six Indians and some whites in buckskins. Was this a raiding party, or was the main body of troops in the woods close behind?

While Defries and Poole watched from the hillside, Sutherland made his way alone toward the cottage, determined to learn what he could. There was little time to waste, for the Cedars defenders had to know what was coming their way. The land he crossed swiftly was cut by thickets, with old haystacks on the edge of the fields. Keeping low, Sutherland moved from tree to stack, and then to a small barn. The day was cloudy and gray, the wind blowing hard, and the sound of rustling leaves and buffeting branches muffled his approach. He had left his rifle with Defries and was armed with his claymore, tomahawk, and dirk. There were workhorses in a corral nearby, but they were unmoved as he slipped carefully alongside their fence. He hoped to take one man prisoner and interrogate him. It was a bold plan he worked out while lying behind a large pyramid of firewood, stacked in the French Canadian fashion.

There were three whites in all, lounging in the yard of the farmhouse, sitting on stools brought out by the French farmer. They were smoking pipes and talking, while the Indians were thirty yards away, near the barn, lying about on piles of hay just thrown down for the cattle.

The Indians were all Senecas, easily recognized by their shaved heads and round skullcaps, as well as by the wooden armor on their chests. They looked fierce; their faces were painted black and red, so Sutherland knew they were prepared for killing. Two of them wandered beside a thicket that separated the farmyard from the cow pasture, probably to answer the call of nature. These were Sutherland's prey. He quickly scurried to his right, toward the thicket. Darting behind a wagon, and then into the bushes, he was unseen. It was common for Indians not to post a guard, but Sutherland was surprised the whites had not—at least he thought there was no guard.

Once in the bushes, he lay in wait as the two Indians approached. One went into an opening about fifteen yards away, and the other—a tall, almost pretty young brave with hard, cold eyes—came closer to Sutherland. Finding the opening that Sutherland expected him to use, the warrior ducked his head to push under the thorns. Sutherland met him with a wicked thud from the back of his tomahawk. Stunned, the Indian fell heavily to the ground, face down.

Acting quickly, Sutherland cut rawhide thongs from the Indian's leggins to truss his hands. Then he stuffed a wad of leather bullet-patches and a handkerchief into the man's mouth to prevent a sound if he recove. 'd too soon. Sutherland dragged the Indian from the bushes, coming out the far side. He threw his prisoner over his shoulder and ran behind the thicket, along the edge of the cow pasture. Sutherland moved rapidly, as though the heavy Indian were no weight at all. It would not take long to get to the ridge where Defries and Poole waited. He came to the end of the bushes and turned the corner, stopping and crouching low, for from here he had to run toward the haystacks, across a meadow of about a hundred yards.

It was then that he saw Manoth.

The Seneca war chief was the party's lookout. He was walking slowly near the woodpile where Sutherland had hidden. Though not acting particularly suspicious, the Indian might have sensed something, for he carried his long rifle at the ready, and was looking about. The man on Sutherland's shoulder stirred. Sutherland laid him down and gave him another blow to quiet him. Now, how to get across the field without being spotted? Sutherland wished he had his own rifle; it would have been worth the risk to shoot the swine Manoth down and then flee, gambling that he could get away. It was a perfect opportunity going to waste, but bringing back information about the approaching force was more important.

He watched a moment longer, hoping Manoth would turn away, but instead the Seneca walked slowly toward the end of the thicket, where Sutherland knelt behind a rail fence. Soon Manoth was only fifteen yards away. Sutherland had both claymore and tomahawk out. If the Indian came any closer, Sutherland would jump him from behind, kill him, then escape.

"Otchaka?"

The call came from a little ways off, apparently from the warrior who had been walking with Sutherland's prisoner, and who now missed his companion. Manoth heard it, too, and trotted back along the bushes toward his tribesman. This was Sutherland's only chance. He sprang to his feet and threw the Indian over his shoulders, then dashed across the field toward the haystack. From the farmyard he could not be seen, but if the Indians searching for the missing man happened to look his way, they would spot him for sure.

Sutherland ran hard, listening for a shout of warning. He came closer and closer to the haystack, the body jouncing on his shoulder. Still no cry from the enemy. The sun broke out of the clouds just then, spilling light on the meadow, as though to betray him. He hunched low, reaching the stack without a shot being fired or a cry going up. Behind the haystack he threw down the warrior, who grunted with the fall and came awake. Immediately Sutherland was on him, the sharp dirk at the man's exposed throat. Helpless, the Indian at first showed terror, then steadied himself, prepared to die in silence, as a warrior should. Otchaka was disoriented, not knowing his companions were just a hundred yards off and would be alerted by his scream through the gag. The prick of the blade on his jugular did something to unnerve him as Sutherland demanded, in rapid Seneca and French, to know whether there was a force following this scouting party.

The Indian shook his head; he was determined not to speak. Sutherland had no time to waste. He took a twist of rawhide and lashed it about the man's neck. Then he ripped out the handkerchief and leather, keeping the garotte tight enough to prevent the Indian from crying out.

"Speak, Seneca, or you'll die like a strangled dog, not like a warrior! I'll not slay you as I would a man, with my dirk, but I'll kill you with this thong, and you'll never join your forefathers in the land beyond the sky!"

The Indian's eyes went wide. He tried to struggle. No warrior could die by strangulation, for that prevented the soul from escaping the body—a fate worse than death for a fighting man. To stop the struggling, Sutherland half-twisted the knot, and Otchaka began to turn blue. Kicking and writhing in silence, he did try to scream, but Sutherland

was throttling him too effectively for that. Relenting just a
bit, Sutherland again demanded information. The man's
tongue was sticking out, eyes popping from his head. Otchaka must have thought he would die anyway, whether he
spoke or not, for again he shook his head, though this time
less adamantly.

Then Sutherland said, "You are the prisoner of Donoway,
adopted son of the Ottawa and sworn enemy of your kins-
man, Manoth. I am known for keeping my word, and I give
it to you now. Speak the truth and you'll not die. Lie, or
do not speak, and—" He gave the thong a persuasive twist,
and the Indian stiffened, choking.

Otchaka nodded once. Sutherland released the pressure.
In a quick series of questions and answers the Scotsman
learned that eighty regulars of the Eighth Regiment, along
with a hundred Canadians and American loyalists, were
marching alongside three or four hundred Indians, mostly
Iroquois. They were not far off and meant to surprise the
post at the Cedars.

When the curt, guttural replies were finished, Sutherland
asked whether Jeremy Bently was with the force, and the
Indian glared fiercely, then spat to the side, showing his
hatred of that name. Sutherland wanted a clear answer, but
before he got it, there was an outcry by the farm. He glanced
around the side of the haystack and saw Manoth with four
other Indians standing at the end of the bushes, where he
had lain in concealment with his unconscious prisoner.

To keep Otchaka from crying out, Sutherland tightened
the noose again and watched. Now the Senecas were coming
on, following his trail across the meadow, Manoth in the
lead. They would cover that hundred yards quickly. There
was nothing else for Sutherland to do but release his half-
choked victim. He leaped up and sprang away. Immediately
he was spotted, and a rolling series of war whoops went
up. These were mostly young men in pursuit, but Sutherland
was strong and still very fast, even though he was in his
forties. He gave a wild Highland yell of defiance and flew
over the meadow, making for the ridge where Defries and
Poole lay in wait.

Running fast, but not at top speed, Sutherland tried to

put some distance between him and his hunters. Glancing back, he saw the entire party of scouts was on his trail, coming on strongly, the Indians yelping and shrieking. At the same time, he noticed a white man spring up on a barebacked horse that was brought by the *habitant* from the corral. It would be a chase, but Sutherland was sure of himself. Dashing through that ankle-high grass, he made good time, keeping the same sixty yards between himself and his first pursuer—Manoth.

Sutherland's heart leaped, for before the hour was out he would come to grips with this adversary at last. He and his two friends could take on nine men, that was certain, especially when he led the enemy into a trap. Otchaka was shaken up, and Defries and Poole would shoot down the men behind Manoth. That would scare off the rest long enough for Sutherland to find a way to lure Manoth into a final duel. If he became too involved with Manoth, Defries or Poole could hurry back to the Cedars with word of the enemy approach.

The ridge was close now, and in another hundred yards Sutherland would swerve and sprint up to its crest, where his friends lay in ambush. He looked around to see how many warriors were in the lead. Four, including Manoth: not too many to handle, and their loss would reduce the odds quite well.

As he turned back to run for the ridge, he heard a long roar, as if the wind had suddenly turned into a tornado and was coming after him. He looked back, and nearly staggered in his stride to see the edge of the distant forest come alive. Warriors flooded from the trees, all of them whooping and shouting like devils, pouring across the field, at least four hundred of them—all after him. Sutherland was astonished, and he sprang ahead, knowing his plans were foiled. These young, eager warriors saw a chance at a scalp, and they came surging out of concealment in the woods. They were a colorful, painted, feathered wave of savage humanity, scampering about three hundred yards behind Manoth.

Sutherland knew now he could not lead the enemy toward his friends. He raced alongside the base of the slope, not daring to look up to where Defries and Poole lay behind some boulders, lest the Indians see and guess the whites were there.

"Don't shoot!" he gasped to himself, but knew he had better conserve his wind. Already his side ached, but he ran on, despite the pain. He looked back. Manoth was only fifty yards away. How Sutherland would have liked to stop and take him on, but he was lost if he even misstepped. When he looked back he also saw that the rider on the white ploughhorse was slow to get onto the meadow, because the rickety gate was closed. It would be a little while yet before the horseman closed in.

Putting on a burst of speed, Sutherland pulled away from Manoth, who was running fast despite a slight limp. His long legs covered huge lengths of ground. The Scotsman pounded along the base of the ridge, not up the slope toward his friends. The ache in his side passed, and he stretched his legs freely, gaining a second wind. Now he would give them a run. His only chance was to outrun them all, and that might take twenty miles. He would not run toward the fort, but cut to his left, away from the river.

Then Sutherland realized the leading Indians behind Manoth seemed to be bearing off, up the ridge. That gave him a shock. He feared Defries and Poole would be trapped. Had the Indians seen them move? Now Manoth was closing again, but the other warriors were indeed going up the slope. They could not long have matched the pace of their leader and Sutherland, but it was unlike Indians to give up a chase so soon. Then the main force of Indians also cut away, charging up that ridge. Sutherland's heart sank. Now it was for him to warn the fort. He cut right, making for the river, which he would follow to the Cedars.

The Scotsman raced on, longing to rejoin his friends if they had to shoot it out. After a little while, hurrying up and down wooded high ground, he again broke into the open, where sunlight was hot and glaring. Sutherland ran up a long, grassy slope and into the trees. He looked back. Only Manoth was in sight. Pausing, Sutherland touched his hatchet. If Manoth came alone, Sutherland would take him. But what had happened to Defries and Poole? His mind was tormented with fear for them.

Then there was a shout to his left, on another wooded ridge. The horseman galloped into sight, through a gap in the trees. It was Lieutenant Mark Davies, dressed like a woodsman and riding well, less than two hundred yards away. If Sutherland stopped to fight Manoth, Davies would be upon them, and he carried pistols. If Sutherland were beaten, and Defries and Poole killed, the garrison at the Cedars would be lost, Montreal would be exposed, and his family endangered. There was far more than personal revenge to consider now, and Sutherland broke away into the depths of another line of trees. A moment later Manoth crashed in and pushed through the woods, but it would take Davies some time to find an opening for a horse in the thicket. Sutherland leaped out the other side into a field of corn stubble.

His lungs ached from months of inactivity at Quebec, and his legs were not as springy as they once were. Sutherland was feeling older than he wanted to admit, and his body would not perform as it had to if he were to get away. He pushed himself harder, but it seemed the ground passed beneath him at the same speed. Behind, Manoth gave a whoop of triumph, for he was catching up. By now the Indian had tossed aside his rifle, but he carried two pistols at his waist. The giant was close enough for Sutherland to hear his bells tinkling. Davies suddenly burst from the underbrush, driving his thundering mount across the field, to cut off Sutherland.

Directly before the Scotsman was a *habitant* farmhouse, barn, and sheds. There were people moving there, and he decided to avoid it because they might take Manoth's side and shoot at a suspected rebel. Swerving to the right, he broke through new thickets and sprinted out across another field of corn. He gave it all he had, but those tinkling bells were always close behind, gaining on him, a step at a time. The thickets had frustrated Davies on his horse, but now there were no more in sight for nearly a thousand yards. Sutherland was running through the soft, boggy ground of a moor, grass as high as his waist. Even the wind blew hard against him, as though to aid Manoth.

There was a pistol shot from close behind. The ball sang

past his shoulder, and he saw that he had been nicked. Blood ran down his chest from a wound that burned at his neck. On he ran. Then came the thud of hooves, closer and closer. A fierce war whoop from Manoth. Sutherland could feel them right at his back, and his spine prickled. The horse blew loudly, hooves hammering at Sutherland's heels. The moment was upon him. He could not outrun them. His legs were leaden. He was about to turn—

The ground dropped away abruptly, and it was all Sutherland could do to keep from stumbling. He was running downhill, and there before him was the broad Saint Lawrence, pounding in turbulent, white rapids, surging against the shore, less than forty yards ahead. The horse was so close he could feel it snorting. Davies shouted. Sutherland swerved to the left, cutting away from the animal's path. A pistol rang out. He caught a glimpse of Manoth running on the same side of the horse as he was. Davies steered his mount toward Sutherland, momentarily shouldering the Seneca aside, knocking him off stride.

Sutherland gained a few yards on them. He made for the river, lifting his numbed legs high, his side and chest aching for want of breath. He strove with all his might that final twenty yards, but the horseman was there again, hooves drumming. The animal was just behind, and Sutherland thought he heard the cock of a pistol. He dropped to the ground. A hoof struck him, and the animal stumbled. The hoof had bitten into his back, but he leaped up again. Davies was rolling, the horse on its back, legs kicking, whinnying in terror. Manoth?

The Indian was bearing down, ten yards away, pistol out. Sutherland plunged to the left and cut toward the river. The bank was there, two steps away. Manoth fired. The bullet grazed Sutherland's left thigh, and his leg flew out from under him just as he dived headlong into the white, foaming water. Borne away like a stick of driftwood, he whirled into the churning, raging rapids that sucked him under as pistols cracked and bullets whizzed past his head. Breathless and exhausted, Sutherland could not fight back, could not resist the terrible pull of the Saint Lawrence as it pounded against the rocky shore.

He tried to surface, went under, and surfaced again. He grabbed for driftwood that skimmed by, but missed. He drank gushing water, was rammed against boulders, and was thrown left and right in the current.

The rapids were full of floating debris, a whirling, surging mass of driftwood that surrounded him and crashed and thudded against him as he fought to swim, to keep breathing, to get back to shore. One of these tangled masses of branches swept over him, drove him under for what seemed like the last time. It left him drowning in a gray, airless world of foam.

Sutherland sensed it was finished with him. It was almost peaceful once he considered his death as a reality. He did not know if his eyes were open or closed. He was losing all sense of how long he had been underwater. It almost did not matter.

Then he saw Ella's face. He wanted to be with her. He would not give up. He must surface, must gasp air before he inhaled too much river water and drowned. With a tremendous effort he grappled for a handhold on the drifting branches overhead, but they slipped away, torn from his grip by the force of the water. Spinning and rolling over and over, he felt himself blacking out. He would not swallow water! He would not surrender without fighting to the last ebb of consciousness! He clawed and raked at the twisted branches above him, grasping a handhold, losing it, and being dragged along, faster and faster. He must have air! He kicked his feet, desperately trying to reach the lighter gray of the surface, but logs smote him, jammed him between them, as if bent on killing him.

He got a long, slender branch in his hand, but it yielded, sinking, and would not let him get to the surface. Yet he refused to let go. It was all he could catch. He went deeper, the branch going with him. He fought, fought blindly, instinctively, and held that skinny branch, held it even though it sank with him. He clutched it fiercely with both hands, pulled it against his chest, his aching, bursting chest, and would not let go, though he would surely be dead in the next moment. Seemingly with a will of their own, his legs kicked for the surface, struggled through that swirling, icy foam. He was so close, so very close to air. He could almost see sky through the water, but that slender branch refused to save him, and it was pulled away, almost yanked out of his hands. It was as though the branch had snagged somewhere, and now was moving backward while everything else in the river poured furiously, mercilessly, in great torrents downstream, toward the devouring rapids below.

Sutherland craved to bellow in rage and frustration, and tried to thrust his being upward, upward and into the air. His one force left was an iron will to survive. He kicked and drove upward, pulling hand over hand along that branch, refusing to let the river have him. Not yet! He kicked and kicked again, and the branch held. It gave him a direction, gave him hope, and the slightest chance to pull himself up, up, up. Slowly, stubbornly, he kicked with all his might. The surface was inches from his face, only inches...

But it was too late. The river gushed and pushed at him, and his lungs gave out. They exploded from within, his breath bursting into water, water pouring into him. He choked and could not breathe. He went black and let go of the branch.

*chapter* **17**

# FRIENDS LOST

There were faces above him, lean, weathered, grim faces, looking down from far off, asking whether he was alive. Asking whether he was becoming conscious.

There was a blue sky behind those faces, with high, drifting clouds. The air was warm, and it was dry. The air.

Owen Sutherland lay, alive and breathing, on a bed of straw, surrounded by young New Hampshire farmers in the rebel regiment commanded by Colonel Timothy Bedel. The slender branch had been snagged close to shore, and when he gave out, he had been swept hard against the land, cast up, and left lying unconscious on rocks. Sentries from the rebel fort had found him and taken him back to recover or die.

Dazed, and in pain from the neck and leg wounds, which had been firmly bandaged, Sutherland forced himself to sit up. The men watching him knew he was their scout, and knew he must have been in action to wind up half drowned in the river. They helped him get to the commander, a Major Butterfield. Colonel Bedel was away meeting with friendly Indians.

Sutherland was so feeble that he hardly noticed what

Butterfield looked like; but when he told the officer about the approach of the enemy, the man paled. For a few seconds Butterfield stood as though frozen stiff. Sutherland did not care about the major's obvious fear, because his mind was on Peter Defries and Bill Poole. Neither had been heard of.

But at least these Hampshiremen, four hundred of them, would be saved. The Indians, Redcoats, and loyalists did not have the strength to take this post. It was likely they would surround it with scalping parties, then move on the countryside around Montreal, to ravage supply trains and harass fleeing rebels. But with so strong a detachment fortified in their rear, the marauders would return westward before long, lest they be trapped and destroyed by rebel reinforcements.

Word had to get to Colonel Arnold right away so that reinforcements could be mustered. Sutherland resolved to go to Montreal along with a couple of soldiers carrying dispatches from Butterfield. Colonel Bedel would no doubt return quickly to prepare a defense.

Exhausted, Sutherland ate a little, then cleaned and oiled his claymore while letting his clothes dry. He prepared as though in some sort of dream. Weary, and weak from loss of blood, he moved sluggishly, though he tried to go as fast as possible. After an hour he departed with Butterfield's messengers, who rowed with him across the Ottawa River and took horses from there to Montreal.

All the while, Sutherland worried about Defries and Poole. Were they alive? Had they been captured? Had they escaped? Could anyone have escaped four hundred Indians pursuing them across open fields? Sutherland had. So could they.

At Montreal, Sutherland reported to Arnold, who rapidly assembled a reinforcement of one hundred and fifty men, many of them getting out of sickbeds to march to the aid of the Hampshiremen. Sutherland was relieved that his duty was done, and made his way home while Arnold scraped up more men and weapons to defend Montreal. There was little enough of either, although troops were coming in each day, marching up in high spirits from the lower colonies, or drifting back, wounded and ill, from the army camped down the Saint Lawrence at Sorel and Three Rivers.

From the first, Sutherland could tell there was a bad feeling in the air. Many rebel soldiers looked like tramps rather than disciplined troops, and they were as antagonistic to the French as the French were to them. The city had too few organized rebel companies under arms, and too many hungry, stray soldiers. More than once Sutherland saw an altercation, with a soldier being chased by a shopkeeper or housewife who was left crying, "Thief!" Many rebels looked lost and forlorn, and bitter with their lot—underpaid, underfed, and expecting a defeat.

Yet there were other soldiers, disciplined and clean, who tried their best to police the town. They were too few, however, for most men in shape to fight were immediately sent downriver to General Thomas, or to meet the new threat from Detroit.

But all dark thoughts left Sutherland as he realized he was so near to being with his loved ones once more. With hope, he plodded on through the crowded street. His claymore was his only piece of equipment left. He was bent, nearly broken by his ordeal, but infinitely grateful to get back to Ella, even if it meant she would be upset to find him like this. When he reached the apartment, the downstairs door was open, and he went in. It seemed to take all his strength to climb that narrow flight of steps, but he would not cry out for help to his family, lest that truly cause them anguish.

Step by step he made his way upward, pulling himself along the handrail. The memory of that slender branch came to him, and when he closed his eyes, he could hear the pounding white-water, could feel its terrible force trying to kill him. He broke out in a cold sweat, and his arms and legs trembled from the strain, but he reached the top, went to the door, and knocked as firmly as he could. He whispered Ella's name. Dizziness and nausea nearly overcame him. He licked his lips and took a long breath, then knocked louder. Composed, recovering from the climb, he again called Ella's name. He knocked again, without answer. They must be out.

A key was always left above the door, on the molding, and he used it to let himself in. To his dismay he found the furniture covered with sheets, the place empty. They were gone.

Could it be true? Had they really left the city?

Moving as quickly as he could to the table, he found a letter from Ella, bound up in white ribbon. With shaking hands and pounding heart he opened it, sat down, and read. It was dated that same day, and Ella had written the time: ten in the morning, just two hours previous. He devoured that letter, reading swiftly.

My darling Owen,

It is not possible to remain in the city, because if we do not depart immediately with the next military convoy, we'll have to wait a long time before the next families will be able to go in a large group.

At night there is much chaos and looting, much confusion and fear among our people, so we and our friends are leaving before matters become worse and the children are endangered. I've sent a letter to General Arnold to inform you as soon as he sees you again, but I don't know when he will have a chance to read it. Everything is happening at once, and very soon I fear the conveyances will all be commandeered by soldiers on the run. That is why we have to go now, before the panic sets in.

Ella wrote that Benjamin Franklin had also left the city before escape was impossible. Then she gave her husband the best news: Franklin had ordered Bradford Cullen to come with him to Albany, thus preventing the man from turning his coat when the British finally reached Montreal.

Dr. Franklin said it was the express wish of Congress to have Cullen come to Albany posthaste, and despite Cullen's protests, Dr. Franklin would not hear of leaving the man "in peril." I watched it all from my carriage, which at Dr. Franklin's suggestion was parked near Cullen's residence, and it was delightful to see the protesting, fuming Cullen, his prune-faced wife, and doleful daughter being bundled into carriages. All the while Dr. Franklin was encouraging them with sweet exclamations of concern for their welfare.

As the good doctor sat in his own carriage, he continuously spouted sayings of Poor Richard to the moaning Helen and Linda Cullen. "Come, come, ladies," Dr. Franklin cried, with a genial smile. "Time is an herb that cures all ills!" And "Do not sorrow for what you leave behind, ladies, for you do not possess wealth, it possesses you!"

Sutherland could hear Ella laughing as he read this, and he chuckled himself to think that Cullen had been thwarted by none other than Ben Franklin. If Cullen was unable to reach loyalist forces in Canada, he would have to continue to support the rebellion. Still, Sutherland was sure the man would take the first opportunity to abandon the war's losing side.

Sutherland read on for more news of his family. The letter explained that Ella's party would go to the Mohawk Valley, and there find a safe place to live and wait for Owen to join them. He admired Ella's resourcefulness for having sent the pelts she had purchased down to the Frontier Company warehouse in Albany, shipping them with a military convoy. It hurt that his family was gone—two hours too soon—but perhaps it was for the best.

We'll be found at the Oneida village of Oriska, and I'll not go on to Albany without you. Only if danger is imminent will I go, and if so, I'll leave word. We'll be safe with Mel and Hickory, Angus and Matilda, and along with us will go the Greys, James Morely, and Sally and Tom. Tom has been serving with the troops downriver, but suffered an arm wound that is slow to heal. He longs to return to the fight, but General Arnold wants to send all the wounded out of the province for their own good.

So you see, we'll be numerous, and able to defend

ourselves against chance encounters with small parties of the enemy. Do not fear for us, my love, though I fear for you. Come back to us soon, and remember how much we love you and miss you.

Ella

Though he felt empty, Sutherland accepted this. There was nothing else to do. How he wished he could have them all at his side right now; but it was good they were gone to safety at last. He could not want it otherwise.

Staggering to the bedroom, he sat on the sheet-draped bed and began to remove his sword and moccasins. Then he felt the world darkening, his senses drifting, and he collapsed into a deep and dreamless sleep, forgetful of everything and everyone.

That sleep was interrupted by a loud knocking. Sutherland awoke suddenly, thinking it might be Defries. He hurried from bed and cried out his friend's name as he threw the door open, but instead of Defries, there was a trim, young Connecticut ensign, who presented General Arnold's compliments and said, "The general has invited you to join him on a relief expedition to the Cedars, sir; it's requested you come immediately."

Sutherland rubbed sleep from his stubbly face and knew he needed more than he had just had. Stepping wearily back into the sitting room, he asked the boyish officer what time it was. It was only three o'clock.

"I'll be no use to the general if I don't get a decent rest, ensign; I've been here only two hours."

"Two hours, sir?" The officer knitted his brows. "General Arnold ordered a constant watch posted on your apartment, sir, and I or my men've been outside your door for nearly two days, and you haven't stirred once in that time."

Two days. A foul mood came over Sutherland. In former years he could have endured the last adventure and recovered with a few hours' sleep. But now even two whole days would not suffice.

He muttered, "We get old too soon."

Scratching his grizzled chin, he told the ensign he would

shave and clean up, then go with him to Arnold. As he poured water from a pitcher into a basin, he asked for the latest news.

The soldier was very professional and cool. "The Cedars post has fallen without a fight."

Sutherland swayed, shock coursing through him. The Cedars fort was strong! A few British regulars and five hundred Indians and loyalists could never take it without a prolonged siege!

"Butterfield was in command in Bedel's absence, sir. He surrendered without resistance, and the enemy have taken the entire garrison. All four hundred men."

The ensign did not know why the fort had given up, but it was a grave disaster, with more than a quarter of the troops in the region lost as captives.

"There's more," he said, and this time his voice cracked, his lips trembling. He tried to maintain composure, and took a shaky breath. "General Arnold sent one hundred and fifty reinforcements before we heard of the post's capitulation, and...and they were ambushed, overwhelmed, and near fifty are dead..."

Sutherland could not believe what he was hearing. When the man lost control and tears came into his eyes, Sutherland steadied him with a hand to his shoulder.

"Forgive me, sir..." the ensign said. "But the Indians butchered the wounded, and...my brother...was killed. Mr. Sutherland, I'm afraid we've heard a friend of yours died, also."

Sutherland did not move, but waited, hardly breathing.

"Bill Poole of my colony, sir. He was...he..." The soldier turned, fists clenched, and pushed his forehead against the wall. "He was tortured to death, roasted, and...the savages...they—"

Sutherland groaned. He needed to hear no more. He could hear no more, not at all. He knew what the Indians had done to Poole. He knew they had cannibalized him, as was their custom with brave enemies, whose courage and power they were determined to assimilate. Poole was dead, and Defries was missing. Perhaps Peter was with the five hundred captives and still alive. Perhaps.

Owen Sutherland was not a praying man, but he went to the window facing the street and leaned on the sill. He closed his eyes to pray for the safety of his closest friend. *At the very least, Lord, let Peter have a quick death.*

At Fort Detroit it was the final day of the greatest Indian council ever held by the British. Though many warriors, most of them Iroquois, were already with Davies and Manoth in the advance against Montreal, other Indian nations were still coming to Fort Detroit for a parley and had been arriving steadily for weeks.

At the first spring thaw, Lieutenant Governor Hamilton had sent runners out in every direction, and this morning the fort was mobbed with Indians who had come from as far as a thousand miles away.

For days, the entire region around Detroit had been infested with brash young warriors eager to prove their valor against the tough white settlers on the frontier to the eastward. Indians wandered through orchards and newly planted fields as though they were on their own lands, and settlers who ordered them to leave were often met with surly looks. There was little trouble, though, thanks to the experienced management of Lieutenant Governor Hamilton.

Hamilton had been generous with gifts and honors to each delegation of chiefs and warriors as they came to announce their arrival. In order to avoid quarrels or outbreaks of violence, he had laid down strict rules of conduct. Today, after four days spent listening to important chiefs making speeches, Hamilton would address his guests.

As Jeremy Bently stood looking out a window of his new hospital, it seemed that the entire world throbbed to the sound of tom-toms and rang with the laughter of excited Indians touring the fort and settlement. Though early in the day, it was already quite hot, and Jeremy was opening shutters and windows. Inside the warehouse hospital it was breezy and comfortable, because of the high ceiling and many new windows recently cut into the walls; and unlike most hospitals, there was no smell of vomit, excrement, or infection.

Jeremy's first patients, the captives from Manoth's raid,

had long since left; now most of the injured and ill were local folk. But even though few war parties were attacking the frontier and bringing back prisoners—thanks largely to Hamilton's restraint, Jeremy knew—the hospital was nearly always full.

Jeremy spent much more time at the fort these days as he abandoned other concerns in order to work at the hospital. Already he was highly respected in the northwest for his astonishing powers of healing, as well as for his kindness and knowledge of human nature. Though he was a young man, people much older respected him, and both whites and Indians came to him for all sorts of advice.

The hospital profited somewhat in this time, but only thanks to Gwen's selflessness and the aid of Lela, Angélique, Annie, and other volunteers who gave unsparingly of themselves. The hospital never charged patients who could not afford to pay, and as a result Jeremy often received chickens, venison, pelts, honey, or beads for his services. When he was paid in cash, it was anything from sound British sterling to worthless continentals offered by rebel captives, or Spanish pieces of eight or Hudson's Bay Company tokens—both common currency in the colonies.

Frequently his thanks was simply a handshake, an embrace, or a promise to plow his fields the following year. Never before had he met so many folk, and never had he felt better about his choice of profession than he did in that first half of 1776.

As for Gwen Hardy, she worked every bit as hard as he, and was just as well-loved by the people who came for help. Gwen was emotionally strong—so strong that often she amazed Jeremy. There were nights when he longed to go home to Valenya, but Gwen was called away to help deliver a baby, and he would stay at the hospital and wait for her to return.

She, Annie, and Cole Ross still lived with him at Valenya, which they had made their home, much to Jeremy's satisfaction. Ross was a clever and honest trader who earned himself a place in Dawson Merriwether's firm. Annie was pursued by the most eligible officers in the post, and she seemed to enjoy it, although Jeremy could tell she had more than a soft spot in her heart for him. As for Gwen, she and Simon Clancy often kept company, though no engagement had been announced. Clancy was in love with her, as anyone could see—anyone but Gwen, it seemed, for she sported lightly with him and never quite allowed him to press his suit too fervently.

Jeremy enjoyed watching Gwen and Simon together, for they were an attractive couple. He did not exactly encourage their relationship, but he was so busy with his work, and so conscious of the emotional wound he felt from the death of Penelope, that he did not admit to himself that Gwen was more to him than merely a brilliant nurse. It usually turned out that Annie and Jeremy were together at balls and parties, while Simon and Gwen attended as a couple. But Jeremy escorted Annie more out of good manners and affection than out of any deeper feelings.

Jeremy was not about to forget his love for Penelope, and would not court Annie Ross, even though she had made it clear she would be pleased to marry him. Annie was not overly forward, but everything about her whenever they were alone together told Jeremy all he needed to know. Indeed, Annie was very beautiful, very appealing, but he was not sure she really knew him. It was clear she wanted a husband with a promising future; but did she really want him, or the man she expected him to become?

As these thoughts went through Jeremy's mind, there came a rap at the hospital door. Gwen got up from the desk, where she had been writing notes about the response of patients to certain medicines. Opening the door, she saw the baker she and Jeremy had operated on some months earlier.

The man came in, carrying a beautiful plumcake. He touched his forelock to Gwen, and then to Jeremy, who had busied himself cleaning needles used to stitch minor wounds.

"I come to thank ye," the fellow said to them, and handed the cake to Gwen, who acepted it cheerfully. "See here, look what I can do!"

The baker twirled on the leg that had been worked on, and ended with his feet and hands apart, a look of jubilation on his face. Then he laughed and spun round again. He pumped Jeremy's hand and once more bowed to Gwen, who sniffed at the delicious aroma of the cake.

"Thank ye! Thank ye for savin' me from that butcher Sennet!"

"Now, now," Jeremy said. "Sennet's not a bad sort; just treats folk the way he was taught to treat them."

"Well, that may be. Maybe he ain't a total flop, for he's sellin' an Indian rejuvenator concoction that I bought a bottle of—calls it *elixir parasennetus,* and I say it works! Tastes something queer, it does, but it's a rejuvenator! Ask my wife! She gives it to me by the soupspoonful!" He winked gleefully. "Your slicin' and his elixir have made me a new man! Another baby due this winter!"

After he went out and closed the door, Jeremy and Gwen chuckled happily and walked to the stove at the far end of the warehouse. There they sliced a bit of cake and had a cup of tea. As usual, they hardly talked, for it seemed they knew each other's thoughts. These days they were together for long hours and underwent frequent strain and hardship side by side. They had forged a bond of trust and friendship that made speaking almost unnecessary.

A little later, Gwen returned to working quietly at her desk, and Jeremy began examining a bullet wound in a loyalist frontier scout who had been shot by Virginians while reconnoitering the region around Fort Pitt. The man was hardy and had nearly made it back to Detroit by sheer force of will, though his side had a gaping wound that he had stanched with leaves of comfrey. Some hunting Indians had found him and brought him to the fort.

The fellow was asleep now and recovering. He and Jeremy had spoken often about conditions on the frontier. The scout despised rebel Virginians, whom he called Longknives—the name given them by Indians. He was a native of Pennsylvania, and for years he and his people had feuded and fought with Virginians who claimed the land he had settled. Just before the war broke out the Longknives had succeeded in driving the fellow's folk away, so he had swung to the loyalist side in order to fight Virginia frontiersmen, who, almost to a man, were rebels.

This scout's tale had moved Jeremy, who was angry that

the Congress would permit its supporters to behave so tyrannically, especially when the cry of rebels was for liberty, freedom of speech, and American rights. Adding to his rising bitterness with the rebel Whigs was a letter recently received from Raymond Graves, Penelope's father in England. Once a partner in the Frontier Company, Graves had been severed from the firm last year when Congress declared that commerce with Britain would be stopped until Parliament quit punishing Boston for the destruction of taxed tea in the infamous tea party.

Graves had been a kind and generous father-in-law to Jeremy, and the gentleman's letter was a moving reply to the news of Penelope's death. The letter was laden with grief, yet was admirably restrained. But he blamed American rebels for creating a state of lawlessness in the colonies, permitting pirates and outlaws to rove freely. Jeremy had to agree with him, for even now there were not enough British troops to police the northwest, and outlaws frequently committed outrages against trappers and travelers.

Raymond Graves had served as a captain in the British navy, stationed off the coast of New England, and his letter recalled times during the French wars when he could not provision his ships because Yankee merchants flatly refused to sell, seeking instead higher prices in the illegal trade with French colonies—the very enemies Graves was fighting to protect Yankees against. He said many of those smugglers, now leaders of the rebellion, were ruthlessly profiteering from the war. He added that thousands of decent, moderate folk in America were being ruined by rebels. He had met many who had either fled or been exiled to England, and they all told stories of savage persecution by mobs—persecution ignored by those rebels in authority who were supposed to enforce the law.

Jeremy well knew that tar and feathers, imprisonment, and riding the rail were only a few of the punishments employed by many impoverished rebels who took the opportunity to strike at wealthy, conservative neighbors not active in the rebellion. The letter from Graves had not only reopened the wound of losing Penelope, but it had stung Jeremy's sense of justice. He had known that rebels abused all who would not bow to their heavy-handedness, but the letter from Graves told of actual people Jeremy had met over the years, both in America and in England. None of them deserved the misery and the brutality all had suffered.

As Jeremy bound up the sleeping scout's wound, the door opened, and he turned to see Lieutenant Governor Hamilton enter. The officer, magnificent in his uniform, carried a large bundle under one arm. Jeremy presumed it was a present for Indians, for he knew Hamilton was on his way to make a final speech to chiefs gathered in the fort's council house.

As the officer and Jeremy shook hands, the pounding of the drums outside seemed louder, forcing itself into Jeremy's mind, against his will.

"I brought these, Dr. Bently," Hamilton said, and held out the bundle, which Jeremy took. "I hope I'm not being presumptuous in making this offer, but I have so many of these, you see, and I thought the hospital could use a little brightening up."

Hamilton spotted Gwen across the room and bowed politely, smiling as Jeremy unwrapped the fabric covering the package. Gwen approached and greeted Hamilton, who said he hoped they both would think well of this small token of his affection and respect for their work.

Gwen exclaimed, "Why they're beautiful, Your Excellency!"

She took from Jeremy one of six pen-and-ink sketches, each twenty inches on a side, and beautifully framed in maple. This one was a sketch of the straits, made near Ile Bois Blanc, or "Bobalo," as the British ear heard the French pronunciation. The others were all excellent renderings of settings near the fort, including the old gristmill where Jeremy liked to wander.

"The last is for you, Dr. Bently." Hamilton beamed with satisfaction when Jeremy held up a fine sketch of Valenya, then grinned and shook the officer's hand.

"You've done Valenya justice, sir. Indeed you have!"

Gwen came to Hamilton and said, "You've been so very kind to us. Without you we could not have opened this hospital."

Hamilton bowed again, then said he had to be about his business. To Jeremy he said, "I came here with an additional purpose, Doctor: I would like to have you attend my speech to the Indians today. I would like you to hear what I say, what I ask, and what I require of them in their service to our country."

Jeremy thought a moment, then nodded. "You believe, I assume, that you'll prove the honor of your motives. Very well, I'll come. But be assured that I know the Indian mind as I know my own, and I can tell when a speech-maker intentionally whips them into a frenzy."

Hamilton gave a half-smile and said, "That, my friend, is why I want you to see for yourself. I yet have hopes of enlisting you."

"I know."

He and Hamilton departed, leaving Gwen in charge of the hospital. It would be a lengthy speech, as all speeches to Indians were supposed to be, and there would be long replies; so Gwen made arrangements with her assistants to cover Jeremy's duties until tomorrow.

As he left, she whispered, "Don't join the army."

He would have smiled at that, but Gwen seemed almost serious.

Hamilton received a hundred leading Indians in the Detroit council house, which was a rough-timbered building near the parade ground. Jeremy sat at the officer's left hand, Tamano beside him. A council fire burned in the center of the interior circle, which was composed of the most important chiefs. Additional rings of Indians formed behind them until the building was completely filled by glistening, sweating dark bodies smeared with bear grease and paint, decorated with feathers, furs, and beads. Half a dozen white and half-breed interpreters adorned like Indians stood nearby to address the tribes in familiar languages.

Rum and tobacco were passed around to be ceremoniously consumed, and everyone sat in grave, contemplative silence for at least an hour. At the proper moment, Hamilton rose and stood before the waiting Indians. He wore a blanket of pure white over his uniform, and on his right arm was an enormous belt of black and red wampum beads—the colors of war. He held that arm out, and the belt dangled to the ground, for all to see.

"Children of the king!" Hamilton began, in a booming voice that at every pause was followed by the quick words of the interpreters. "I bid you welcome, and speak to you by order of the king, our great white father across the sea!"

In his other hand he held aloft a large mug of rum, then called for a drink to the king's health. The Indians shouted in chorus, "Ho! Ho!" and kegs were passed around to refill their cups. All the peoples of the northwest were represented there: Iroquois, Mingoes, Ottawas, Chippewas, Potawatomies, Miamis, Hurons, Illinois, Sioux, Shawnees, Delawares, Kickapoos, Winnebagoes, Sac, Fox, and Menominees. They had come to be honored and presented with gifts; they had come to hear what the king would do with the fur trade; and they had come to see what their fellow Indians would do with respect to the civil war in the east.

Most of all, they had come to ask what the king would do to protect them from the armies of the rebels, who hungered to possess the Indian lands.

After the Indians had drunk a long and potent toast to George the Third, Hamilton cried out, "My brothers, look upon this mighty war belt—the mightiest ever seen in the world—and know that it has been sent to you by the Iroquois, the People of the Longhouse, whose fearless warriors have set their feet on the path of war to protect their lands and your lands from the ravages of the Longknives and the *Bostonnais*.

"My own people, the *Anglais,* are the brothers and allies of the Iroquois, and we fight alongside them to destroy the armies of the *Bostonnais,* to drive them back into the sea, and to purge the colonies of their madness and their lust for your country!"

Hamilton described British victories and made a sharp distinction between *Anglais* and *Bostonnais*—this second term being a traditional Indian name for their age-old enemies in New England: Bostonians. He made the same distinction between *Anglais* and Longknives, as the Indians' southern antagonists were named because of their hunting knives. Hamilton made it clear that the hope of the Indian lay in the defeat of all rebels who coveted Indian hunting grounds—a fact that Jeremy could not deny.

He knew that many rebels were fighting the king mainly because they were after northwestern lands, which the British government had refused to open to settlement. He also knew that the Indians' sole protection against these rebel settlers was the British army, which had promised to supply the tribes with powder, ball, and guns.

Beside Jeremy, Tamano sat grim and quiet, listening to Hamilton promise to stand by the Indians whenever the rebels came to take their lands, as he assured them they soon would do. When Hamilton's flowery speech ended, the chiefs whooped and shouted in agreement, while soldiers went among the Indians, handing out gifts of cloth, medallions, and hand mirrors. Small mirrors were prized possessions of Indian warriors, who loved to preen and paint themselves before ceremony or battle.

Tamano did not cry out for rebel blood as did the others, but he leaned over to Jeremy and said, "Hamilton speaks straight; no one else will defend us but the Redcoats—at least until the Redcoats do not need us anymore."

As Tamano said this, Jeremy caught the eye of one of the shouting braves, whose smile vanished abruptly as he met his friend's gaze. It was Little Hawk.

Meanwhile, Tamano was saying that the Indians knew that many leaders of the rebellion were wealthy land speculators. Tamano said he had kept a close watch on treaties being enacted between whites and those chiefs who were willing to sign anything in return for bribes. Jeremy was astonished by the Chippewa's knowledge of white conspiracies to get hold of Indian lands, but then he realized there were many colonials in the northwest who were opposed to these speculators and informed the Indians thoroughly about all that happened.

"We do not hate the settlers," Tamano said to Jeremy. "They are simple folk, like us. We hate the rich white men who buy this land and make fortunes selling it in small pieces to the settlers. It is the rich men who send the settlers over the mountains to fight us. And who wins? Not the settler. Not the Indian. The rich man wins, when the Indians are weakened. He wins when the house of the settler is burned down, or when the bloodied farmer gives up and resells to him, or when the land is abandoned and becomes his again."

Tamano even knew the names of the greatest of these land companies: the Indiana Company, the Grand Ohio Company, the older Virginia association called the Loyal and Ohio companies. These groups had purchased millions of acres in Indian country, either from the colonial governments they themselves influenced, or from unscrupulous Indians who had no right to sell.

"Our chiefs know the rebel general Washington has claims on our country on the Ohio, and even Franklin is after lands here. We know the famous woodsmen like Boone and Clark are not frontiersmen looking for farms, not long hunters, as they would pretend, but surveyors paid by the rich men to come and spy out our best lands."

Jeremy wondered when whites in the East would stop thinking of Indians as ignorant, heathen savages and begin to recognize them as the astute statesmen who had been capable of manipulating both the French and British governments over the years, maintaining a delicate balance of power. With little military strength, they had been able to hold on to their own country in the face of tremendous forces, which, like the waves of an ocean, lapped at their borders.

Soon Indians would have to fight to protect their homelands, Jeremy knew, and he did not blame them. Sitting there, with drums throbbing, men springing up to dance, chant, and sing, Jeremy saw the chiefs in an entirely new light. They all knew the odds were against them, even with the aid of Hamilton, yet they were determined to fight, not just against warlike settlers, but against the wealthiest, most powerful men in America and the armies those men commanded.

Again he was smitten by the insistent rhythm of those drums, caught up by their strength and magic. Perhaps it was his years with Indians that charged him with an inner fire, but for just an instant he wanted to spring up and dance with them, as he had often danced with them before as a brother and friend. He felt a deep hostility toward the rebels, even though among them was his own family.

When it was all over, Jeremy was impressed. Despite his original conviction that an Indian army could not be managed without causing great suffering in the Whig settlements, he almost began to believe that Hamilton and his subordinates might control Indian attacks.

The lieutenant governor firmly told the chiefs that no war parties were to go out without first being authorized, directed, and assigned white advisers. Futhermore, he said, there was to be no wanton slaughter of women and children, and even in the case of males, these were best captured, not killed. Hamilton offered no scalp bounty, but promised to reward military success and to buy all captives from the Indians when they were brought to Detroit. These captives would be permitted to live near Detroit until the war was over.

The chiefs solemnly swore to Hamilton's conditions, and although Jeremy knew there would be indiscriminate slaughter on both sides from time to time, he was convinced the Indians were sincere. They were even willing to carry reams of handbills, to be posted along trails and at watering places. These handbills said all persons who came to Detroit or other British posts to declare themselves loyal to the king would be helped to resettle. Those who agreed to bear arms "in defense of His Majesty against Rebels and Traitors . . . shall receive His Majesty's bounty of two hundred acres of land. God save the king."

The first few war parties would go out in a month, and would strike at the Virginia and Kentucky forts. To the northeast, around Fort Niagara, Iroquois were cooperating in the recapture of Montreal. Later, they would advance eastward against the Dutch and German settlers along the Mohawk River. The Mohawk was a gateway to the northwest, an arrow pointed at Albany, the most important rebel city in the northern theater of war.

• • •

Sutherland went on fighting. The expedition to save the troops captured by Davies and Manoth was a success. Arnold had hastily collected every man who could at least lean on a musket, gathered whatever could float, and dashed up the north bank of the Saint Lawrence, crossing the Ottawa River. Though he had only four hundred men, he caught up with the retreating enemy and harried them, for they were encumbered with five hundred prisoners.

Davies had prepared a defense against Arnold by digging in on an island in the river, but the indomitable general swore he would attack them unless they gave up their captives. Davies warned Arnold that if they were assaulted the Indians might go into a murderous frenzy and massacre every rebel captive. In reply, Arnold boldly promised to slay every last Indian, loyalist, and Redcoat if the prisoners suffered any further abuse. Already, the mutilated remains of four prisoners, including Poole, had been found by the rebels.

Intimidated by Arnold's resolve to launch a bloody attack, Davies relented and signed articles of parole, by which the prisoners were given up and his own force was allowed to withdraw back to the northwest. It was a daring rebel triumph pulled out of a humiliating defeat. To Sutherland's profound disappointment, Peter Defries was not among the captives, and no one seemed to know where he was. Sutherland hunted for him for two weeks, but without success.

In June, at Arnold's request, Sutherland again went eastward to join the rebel army in its defense of the Saint Lawrence against the enormous British force moving up from Quebec. By now the thirteen thousand British troops—including German mercenaries, American loyalists, and Indians—had accumulated a vast amount of war supplies and equipment and were preparing to toss the weak rebels aside in an advance on Montreal.

Arnold was upset that the rebel high command still intended to meet the British in an open battle instead of fighting a cautious but fierce withdrawal that would cost the enemy heavily and delay their advance into New York. General Thomas, dying of smallpox, had been replaced by a Hampshireman named John Sullivan, a brassy, overconfident fellow. As reinforcements, General Sullivan had been able to bring only six regiments from Washington's army at Boston. Joining with the ragged survivors of the Quebec campaign, they made only five thousand in all fit to do battle. And already many of the fresh troops were falling ill from smallpox and dysentery.

It was folly for Sullivan to risk his entire army against an enemy almost three times his size—an enemy that was not suffering from hunger, disease, lack of equipment, or inadequate supplies.

Like many others, Sutherland had grown sour and angry with the army. He had sickened of political commanders such as Sullivan—men who would waste troops by rashly throwing them into impending disaster on the Saint Lawrence. But Sutherland was determined to do whatever he could to help his fellow foot soldiers. He cared nothing for high political ideals now. All that mattered was the army's survival.

*chapter* **18**

## A SOLDIER'S FATE

"They call her a boerhound," said Gwen Hardy as she sat with Jeremy on a grassy knoll overlooking the straits and Valenya. Between them cavorted a frisky light-brown puppy—very large for two months old. She had floppy ears and immense paws that told she would be a large dog. "I bought her from a Dutch Jewish trader who came up the Mississippi—his name was Klein, I think. He had a whole litter with him."

"Jacob Klein? He's an old friend of the family. Was he in Capetown?"

"That's what he said," Gwen answered, playfully tossing the floppy-eared pup onto her side and grabbing at her muzzle. "In southern Africa they also call these dogs lion dogs, he told me. Look how a ridge of hair runs the wrong direction along her spine."

Jeremy agreed, stroking the boerhound's short, sleek coat. "She's a beauty! And she'll be big enough to whip a lion. What'll you name her?"

Gwen did not know. She lay back on her elbows, looking very pretty in a light gown of green, her hair pinned up elegantly. She gazed across the straits, which were blue and shining in the summer sun. Boats sailed tranquilly back and forth. How peaceful it was here at Valenya, far from the dusty turmoil at the fort. Directly below them, at the foot of a long, windblown slope, were the seven standing stones, dark against the water. The house was down to their right, near the shore, and to their extreme right was the young apple orchard Ella Sutherland had planted. It was doing very well, with every tree in leaf. Next year, or the following at the latest, there would be fruit.

On this Saturday in early July, the two friends were taking a day of rest from the hospital, where Lela and Angélique were on duty. Fortunately, few Indian raiding parties had come in with captives lately, owing mainly to the firm rule of Henry Hamilton.

As Gwen tussled with the puppy, Jeremy's thoughts drifted to the war. He knew that other than the force of Indians with Manoth and Davies, there were only four or five authorized bands roaming between Detroit and Fort Pitt. No full-scale Indian war had yet been loosed on the frontier, but Hamilton had asked the nations to be ready. Thousands of Indians had agreed and had already departed for home, pleased with Hamilton's terms and with his generous treatment. It was hoped, Hamilton had told Jeremy, that no major Indian campaign would be needed at all, for the word from Montreal was that the rebels, weak and disorganized, would soon be driven all the way back to Albany.

Jeremy was becoming increasingly set against the rebels and all the suffering they had caused. More and more he wondered whether the ideals of liberty and equality were really the goals of those men who led the insurrection. His own family were honest idealists fighting for what they thought was a just cause, but many in the Whig party were simply after power.

Lying on that grassy, windblown knoll, with the sun warm on his body, Jeremy dismissed these somber thoughts. The air was dry and clear, and a strong breeze hurried through the grass all around them, flitting the fabric of his beige shirt and breeches. The boerhound was lying with her muzzle on his chest. Gwen was good company, he thought, as both of them absently caressed the pup's smooth back.

He looked down the slope to note how Valenya was

blossoming. The house had been repainted, and the barn was being rebuilt. Cole Ross had supervised much of the work, and Jeremy was grateful. He himself was at the hospital almost constantly these days, too often having to neglect Valenya and the affairs of the Frontier Company.

The fort's hospital was becoming indispensable to the people of the region, who now came to it at the rate of several hundred a week. Henry Hamilton often came to offer medical supplies, food, new linen; the man was indeed doing his best for the people of the northwest.

Week after week Hamilton had restrained warriors who wanted permission and supplies to travel south to raid frontier settlements. With great ceremony he had awarded presents and medals and bestowed honors upon the chiefs—and then persuaded them to return home. Now that the war was going well for the British in Lower Canada, there was no need for thousands of Indian irregulars fighting for the loyalists. Yet Jeremy thought of how Hamilton's name was already loathed in the colonies by folk who believed he was buying scalps of whites, heedless of age or gender.

Suddenly the boerhound snatched up Jeremy's hat and scampered away. With a shout he pursued the pup, which bounded and leaped in excitement as Jeremy tried to catch her. Gwen laughed, and Jeremy yelled that she should help, since it was her dog.

"No, she isn't mine!" she cried with a giggle. "She's yours! She's a gift!"

Jeremy laughed and dived for the dog, but missed. "I'm delighted, but what's the occasion?" He dived again and caught his hat, which the dog refused to give up. She snarled and tugged, her rear in the air.

Gwen said, "Just . . . just out of friendship. That's enough, isn't it? She's yours if you can manage her!"

Jeremy grappled at the pup's head and shoved her down roughly, but still she would not let go of the hat. Finally he picked her up and trotted back to where Gwen sat. The pup squirmed out of his arms and brought the hat politely to her, dropping it, torn and wet with saliva, in her lap. Gwen giggled again and bit her lip.

"Oh, my goodness, pup, you are making a problem of yourself! Shall we call her Problem?"

"No," Jeremy replied, collapsing beside her to examine his ruined hat. "Indians believe a name makes you what you are. Let's use something more innocent."

They puzzled over a name for some time, yet none was good enough. Jeremy finally mentioned that sailors called one another names of the places they came from, so he and Gwen ran through such ideas as Africa, Boer, Capetown . . . "How about just Cape?" Jeremy asked. "How's that, pup? Shall we call you Cape? Let's see."

He stood up, teased the dog with his hat, and got her springing and jumping for it. At last he let her have the hat and began to chase her around. When the pup became too wild to catch, Jeremy yelled, "Here, Cape! Come, Cape!"

It did no good. The pup ignored him and raced about the slope, the hat flopping in her mouth.

Turning to Gwen, he said, "There, you see how she knows her name? She just needs to learn to obey; but she knows her name all right!"

Gwen laughed and pointed. Jeremy turned, and there was Cape, sitting obediently right behind him, offering the hat.

"Cape!" Jeremy exclaimed. "You do know your name after all! What a dog!" He reached down for the hat. But Cape yelped and sprang away, once again flying over the knoll, proudly carrying the tattered remains.

"Hah!" Jeremy laughed, nodding. "I like her!" He looked at Gwen, a light coming into his eyes. "Very much." He went to his knees and took her hands, holding them warmly as they both smiled. "You've given me a perfect gift, Gwen, and as usual I can't thank you well enough."

She drew him toward her. "You can kiss me." She smiled mischievously. "I'll not ask for anything else of you, Jeremy; just your friendship." Now Cape lay between them, tongue hanging out, brown eyes big and friendly.

Jeremy leaned to kiss Gwen lightly, and felt his heart racing. The kiss was soft, tender, and Gwen closed her eyes. After a longer moment than expected, Jeremy moved back, still holding Gwen's hands, and her eyes fluttered open. Both of them smiled, like youngsters sharing their first kiss.

Just then there came a shout from near the house, and they saw Dawson Merriwether and Cole Ross approaching on the path, both obviously in high spirits. The couple ran down to meet them, the puppy frolicking after a butterfly in the long grass. Merriwether clapped Jeremy on the shoulder, declaring that Montreal had fallen to the British and loyalists.

"The trade route's reopened, my lad!" Merriwether cried. "In another month or two we'll have shipments coming and going as before! The trade with Britain is on again, and we can get back to business!"

Jeremy was relieved. Life would return to something like normal out here. It seemed his hopes would be fulfilled, and Hamilton would not have to send Indians out after all. Though Jeremy worried about his family and ached to know where they were, he said nothing of this to the others, lest he dampen their enthusiasm. Annie came running up, and she hugged Jeremy eagerly, then Gwen.

It was then that Jeremy realized Gwen was showing no enthusiasm for any of this. Instead, she strolled away, her head down, Cape at her heels. Merriwether and Ross went stamping off toward the house, clapping each other on the back, declaring they would all toast to victory at last. This left Jeremy and Annie together, watching Gwen walk slowly to the apple orchard, with the pup still chasing butterflies.

Jeremy observed Gwen a moment, hardly feeling Annie's hand on his arm. Then Annie sighed and shook her head.

"Poor misguided cousin," she said softly.

Jeremy glanced at her, then back at Gwen. "What's wrong with her, Annie? Why is she so gloomy?"

Annie pursed her lips and brushed a wisp of auburn hair from her face. "You'll have to ask her that; but I don't think she'll tell . . . nor will I."

Jeremy looked directly at Annie, who said plainly, "We have our secrets, and I gave my word to Gwen not to reveal this one." Then she brightened and said, "Come on to the house. I'm baking a delicious peach pie that's nearly ready.

Gwen'll come down soon enough; she goes through these moods, you know. Come! I know how you love peach pie, and I made it especially for you."

He looked at Annie and then at Gwen's back. He wanted to call out, but Annie tugged his arm. Perhaps Gwen needed to be alone, he thought. If she wanted him along, she could have asked, and he would have gone—peach pie or no peach pie.

As the long summer days passed, Jeremy had more opportunity to enjoy Annie's company, and she was always full of good cheer and chatty news. Gwen was with him every morning and afternoon in the hospital, and perhaps they began to know each other too well. Their conversation was usually of the ill and dying, of the sadness and pain that they saw too much of. Thus, when Jeremy was with Annie, away from the hospital, it was like enjoying a fresh spring breeze, light and airy. They spent many hours sailing or riding together while Gwen was with Lela, who had become her close friend, or with her suitor, Simon Clancy.

On a warm, clear Sunday afternoon in mid-July, Jeremy and Annie went boating downriver toward the abandoned mill for a picnic. Cape went with them, taking up nearly half the canoe.

Annie sang most of the way to the mill. For all her misgivings last winter when she arrived, she now blossomed out here in the wilderness. Annie had many friends, and plenty of men were eager to court her. A number of fine ladies—wives of officers and merchants—always made her welcome. In all Detroit, there was no one more loved than Annie Ross, and no one had a bad word to say against her. She never complained, never gossiped, and always looked for what was beautiful in things. Now and again Jeremy thought she ought to be more realistic about life, less fanciful and naively optimistic. Yet he cared for Annie—how much and in what way he was not really sure—and was always at ease with her.

They spent the afternoon in the shade of a willow near the pond, she reading poetry, he writing in a journal he had kept since returning to Detroit. Annie had found a wild red rose to put in her hair, and she looked lovely in a white taffeta gown. Jeremy, who also wore white, was growing a beard, which was yet thin and shone almost golden in the sunlight. Annie did not care for the beard, saying it was uncivilized, but she could not persuade him to shave. It bothered her enough that Jeremy refused to wear a wig, as was proper, but sporting a full beard was almost more than she could accept.

As he wrote in his journal, Jeremy half heard Annie read a poem by William Livingston, titled "The Choice of a Rural Life," lauding the solitude and beauty of untroubled life in the country.

> Let ardent heroes seek renown in arms,
> Pant after fame, and rush to war's alarms;
> To shining palaces, let fools resort,
> And dunces cringe to be esteemed at court:
> Mine be the pleasures of the rural life,
> From noise remote and ignorant of strife...

Jeremy mused, "William Livingston, is it? He was a member of the Continental Congress, representing New Jersey—" Annie gasped, shocked that she should enjoy the poetry of an important rebel. "And as for ardent heroes, Livingston knows all about seeking renown in arms, for he's now brigadier general in command of New Jersey's rebel militia!"

"Hypocrite!" Annie declared loudly, letting the book fall to her lap. "Oh, I so wanted to read to you the beautiful passages about his vision of an ideal wife!" She became somewhat wistful and perused those lines, absently curling a lock of hair around a finger. Then, unbidden, she read them anyway, in a soft and breathy voice.

> I'd reign the happy monarch of her charms;
> Oft in her panting bosom I would lay,
> And in dissolving rapture, melt away...

Annie released a long and lingering sigh, then murmured, "Rebels can't all be bad if they have such tender emotions, Jeremy."

"No, not all bad, most of them," he said, and closed his journal, wiping the pen dry with a rag and putting it into a leather carrying case with ink, sand, and paper. "But their philosophies don't always match their actions. It's terrible what's happening to law-abiding loyalists and even moderate folk in the colonies who refuse to bend to the tyranny of local rebel committees of safety. But they dare not protest, for if they do they'll be thrown in prison or exiled, if not pilloried, or have the tops of their ears cropped . . . yes, they're even executed."

His anger rose as he told what he had learned of life back in the colonies, where those accused of being loyalists were imprisoned, blacklisted, and stripped of all civil rights. They could not vote, practice law or medicine, teach, hold office, even preach in church. Most on these blacklists were not allowed to travel more than a mile from their home, nor could they have a lawyer represent them in court, where they were often and viciously tried, sued, and fined.

Annie said, "I heard there was a South Carolina man thrown in prison and stripped of all he owned just because he named his dog Tory—meaning that a Tory's life was a dog's life." Abruptly she stood up, and her expression changed. "But let's not talk of these sad things on such a beautiful day. Why don't we take a stroll around the pond and see what those French boys are catching over there?"

Soon, walking along with Annie made Jeremy calmer, and as they passed the three children fishing, they exchanged a cheerful banter. Jeremy began to feel better and took Annie lightly on his arm. Cape loped ahead, around the pond.

"When we return to Montreal," Annie said later, lifting her skirt slightly and whisking it like a fan as she walked, "there'll be a need for physicians there, an even greater need than out here, because so many of our wounded will surely be sent to Montreal to recover."

Jeremy said simply, "There'll always be doctors down there, because there's money to be made; but up here there won't be many doctors for years and years to come. Besides, I like it here."

"Oh, yes," Annie said, with a slightly bored sigh, "it's beautiful and rustic and so on out here, but . . . well, Jeremy,

I believe I for one could never be completely happy always living on the frontier. I mean it's so much more exciting down in the cities, and we could go anywhere we want from there: simply take a ship down the river and pop over to New York Town, or Philadelphia, or even to London."

"We?" Jeremy asked, cocking his head and half smiling.

Annie became just a little coy and also smiled. "You and I." She walked on and gently caressed an orange lily with her soft, long fingers. "We'd enjoy Montreal so." She whirled prettily until she was suddenly in his arms, and he held her close. The light of passion was in Annie's eyes as she gazed at him, her face close to his, lips parted slightly. "Wouldn't we? Wouldn't we be ever so happy there...so blissful? Wouldn't we?"

Her eyes closed. Jeremy felt a surge of physical desire as she pressed against him. How long had it been since he had kissed a woman the way Annie was ready to be kissed? She moved her lips closer, not caring that across the pond the French boys were staring, eyes wide.

Jeremy took a breath and said, "Annie—"

There came a loud shout from down in the gully of the stream that led to the straits. Startled from their embrace, the couple saw Tamano standing in a canoe, waving. Leaving Annie breathless and swaying, Jeremy dashed to him, knowing something serious had happened.

Agitated, Tamano shouted, "Come quick! Your friend Weston is hurt bad! Just brought in! Rebels got him! Gwen sent me to get you! Come quick!"

Almost forgetting Annie, who was hurrying across the grass toward them, Jeremy scrambled down the bank and into the canoe, Cape bounding in after him. He was shaking with fear for his friend, who Tamano said was gravely wounded. Annie gave a little scream to wait for her, and Jeremy impatiently shouted for her to hurry. When she heard what had happened, she gasped and began to cry. Jeremy grabbed her and put her in the center of the canoe, then knelt in the prow.

In the next moment, Jeremy and Tamano were thrusting the craft downstream toward open water. Tamano said Gwen

Hardy was trying to keep Weston alive at the hospital.

"It does not look good," Tamano said glumly. "They scalped Weston. Left him for dead."

They reached the hospital in the fort just as the main body of Davies's force arrived at the landing. Despite the loss of their prisoners, the men were glad to be home, and jubilant at having humiliated the rebels at the Cedars.

With the sound of their singing in the background and the fort coming alive as folk pressed out the water gate to welcome back their fighters, Jeremy rushed into the warehouse. Annie hesitated at the door, unable to go in, afraid to see the horrible condition of her friend. She stopped abruptly, hands to her face. Cape whined and nuzzled at her skirts. Immediately Cole Ross appeared from the building and laid an arm about Annie's shoulders. Then she broke down, weeping uncontrollably, and Ross led her away. Cape lay down at the door to wait.

The atmosphere was hushed inside the hospital. The twenty or so patients occupying cots in two long rows were quiet, aware that Weston's life hung in the balance. The air smelled of lye soap and fresh paint.

Rushing through the room, Jeremy found Weston on a bed at the far end of the hospital, in a quiet corner. Around him were a few Iroquois Indians, tall and regal in their warrior capes and feathers. These included the Mohawk chieftain Joseph Brant, who with his men had brought Weston in after finding him lying in a thicket on the island where Davies's force had prepared to defend itself against Arnold. It appeared that some rebel rangers had landed on the island at night and had captured and scalped Weston. At least that was what Davies had said after the Mohawks brought the wounded officer to him.

Jeremy shook with fury to see his unconscious friend's grotesquely fallen face, a fresh bandage around his head. "Oh, Richard, my poor..." He knelt there, surrounded by Indians, the most downcast of these warriors being Brant.

Chief Joseph Brant was a burly man, with strong features, keen, intelligent eyes, and a handsome face. As the leading war chief in the Six Nations of the Iroquois, he held a title that the Seneca Manoth longed to own. Now Brant watched Jeremy lean over Weston, who was sickly pale, scarcely breathing.

After several minutes, Jeremy stood up and managed to thank the men who had rescued Weston.

"You did well to swathe his head so, but was the wound treated first with any cleaning agent?"

Brant said, "It was not we who did this bandaging, Doctor, for our poor work is not as expert as this." Brant had been a divinity student at an Anglican school in Connecticut, and his sister had been the mistress of the late, powerful Indian agent, Sir William Johnson. The Mohawk's English was impeccable, his manner proper and gentlemanly. He was even a member of the Freemasons, and had translated the Anglican prayer book into the language of the Mohawks.

Jeremy was trembling with emotion as he said, "I hope whoever did this bandaging knew enough to clean the wound. . . ."

"It was done, Jeremy." He looked around, and Gwen was there. She looked tired and wan, but was calm and spoke slowly. "I have seen to the wound. There is . . . there is nothing else we can do but pray, I'm afraid."

Jeremy's expression became one of fear and dismay, as if he were trapped, unable to breathe. He dropped to his knees beside the bed. Nothing they could do! He knew Gwen well enough to believe Weston's survival was out of their hands now. If he lived, it would not be their ability that saved him.

He looked up at Gwen, then to the insensible Weston, and then to her again. Gwen knelt at Jeremy's side and took Weston's limp hand. Jeremy took Weston's other hand— it was so cold—and also gripped Gwen's; her hand, too, was cold. Weston was resting as best as could be expected, his heart beating regularly, though weakly.

A soldier must always be prepared to fall in battle, but to suffer like this was a terrible thing, especially at the hands of men who professed belief in human dignity and regard for life. Without rising, Jeremy questioned Brant and learned that the rebels had made a bargain for the release of their captured men. In return the Redcoats, loyalists, and Indians were to withdraw unmolested. Brant said Weston had been attacked soon after the rebels had signed the agreement with Davies.

"Scum!" Jeremy hissed and his fists came up, quivering. "Low dogs! This is not war, it's murder!"

Gwen touched his arm, and he again gripped her hand; her other hand covered his to keep it from shaking. Jeremy felt tears come, and his breath was quick and short. But then he thought of Gwen's welfare, for she had been on duty all day, and the hour was growing late.

"You should rest," he told her, but she refused.

"Not yet; I can't leave him just now."

They stayed on their knees a few moments longer. Then Jeremy got up stiffly and asked Brant how this had happened. Brant did not know, for whoever had done this deed had been stealthy, as cunning as an Indian, and swift.

"This officer was struck from behind, Doctor, and that means his attacker must have slipped through some of my warriors, who were posted nearby; they're good men, sir, and not the sort to let an enemy through easily. This one must have been a devil."

Jeremy sighed and agreed. "A devil, indeed, to crack his skull and take his sclap, yet not—" He found it hard to say "kill him." Whoever had wounded Weston had purposely not slain him, but left him for dead, as if to prolong his suffering. It was only chance that Brant had discovered him. A kind of madness welled up in Jeremy, and he abruptly strode out of the hospital, not knowing where he would go. He stamped off, cursing under his breath, damning all rebels, damning the revolution and Congress, and damning all who had upset the peaceful lives of decent, honest people. Cape yelped, then loped after him, confused and eager to play; but her master went off quickly, and the dog followed at a distance.

Before long Jeremy found himself on a western block-house, high above the fort, staring into a brilliant red sunset over the forest. He had wept tears of anger, tears of sorrow, and his mind had whirled and turned over a hundred possibilities for his future, a score of paths to follow. There was no clear answer yet. Somehow the horror of civil war that was causing so much agony in America must be brought to an end quickly. Somehow he had to do whatever he could to help prevent further useless slaughter. Even though the rebels were losing the initiative, there would probably be another half-year of fighting before the rebel cities were taken and their troops crushed. He was certain it would be no longer. It must not, could not be longer!

Jeremy prayed the rebels would sue for peace, make terms before more lives were wasted. Surely even his own mother and father must see that their idealistic cause was lost.

He heard Cape whine on the ground below, and there came a sound on the steps. Jeremy turned to the hatchway to the blockhouse, and partway through it came Gwen Hardy. She gazed at him a moment, as if asking whether she should join him. In the fading light, her eyes were shadowed, and she looked weary. Jeremy reached over to pull her up, and she went with him to the palisade that faced the sunset.

They stood quietly together, the dying light casting reddish hues over their clothes and blond hair and glinting in their eyes as they stared westward. It was some time before they spoke. The sun was nearly down. Jeremy said they should get back to Richard's side, but Gwen replied that Tamano and Lela were watching him.

After a while, she asked, "Is this blockhouse where your mother and Owen Sutherland first knew they were in love?"

Jeremy looked around at that, surprised she should know. Then he recalled that Gwen's friendship with Tamano's wife, Lela, had probably led to her learning much about the Sutherlands. Lela's sister had been Owen's first wife.

"Yes, it is. It's a beautiful place, if you look westward, not down at the fort." Leaning over the pointed stockade, he felt a cool breeze lift and blow in his face. "I used to come here with Owen when I was a boy, and he would tell me stories about the Indians, and about their spirits and manitous." He wistfully considered those days.

"Happier times?" Gwen asked.

Jeremy shook his head. "Not in every way, for then we

were surrounded by fifteen hundred bloodthirsty warriors—
the fathers and uncles of those now encamped about the
fort—and they meant to get in and massacre us all."

They went to the other side of the blockhouse and looked
over the fort, which was in darkening shadow. Lamps and
candles glowed in the windows, and people with lanterns
passed here and there. Beyond the fort were the cooking
fires and ceremonial fires of the tribes that had come to
meet Hamilton, and from that direction rose a distant, steady
throbbing of drums. It seemed Jeremy noticed those drums
for the first time, although they had been sounding constantly ever since springtime.

"They're celebrating the victory over the rebels at the
Cedars," he told Gwen. "If Hamilton wanted to, he could
send a thousand men on the warpath tomorrow, and the
frontier would be laid waste in three months."

Slowly the blanket of darkness deepened, and Jeremy
and Gwen stood listening, feeling the soft wind, and thinking. She was against his side, touching him with her arm,
though not intentionally. Simultaneously, they became conscious of it and looked at each other. In the last light of
sunset he saw tears on her cheeks. Putting his arm over her
shoulder, he drew Gwen close and kissed her forehead. She
sniffed and sighed and pushed her face against his shoulder.

"I can't believe civilized men would do that to Richard,"
Gwen whispered. "I can't believe the men behind the rebel
cause would do such a thing."

Jeremy knew well that whites were often as brutal as
Indians in warfare, especially whites who had fought in the
wild and knew cruelty to an enemy as a normal condition
of battle. Even Indians had a sense of honor in war, he said;
he had learned that Joseph Brant had prevented Manoth
from murdering other rebel prisoners, and by so doing had
further earned the Seneca's ill will. Gwen replied that the
high ideals of the rebellion were totally against all cruel
methods of fighting, and that the attack on Weston was not
typical of rebel warfare.

She said, "I can understand Hamilton being compelled
by the government to send Indians against settlers, but why

would rebels wantonly murder an officer—"

"He's not dead!" Jeremy snapped, squeezing her shoulders roughly.

Gwen shuddered and apologized, moving away from him, but Jeremy drew her back and put both arms around her. She was crying now, for the sake of the dying Richard Weston. Jeremy did not deny that their friend was, indeed, dying.

There came a sound at the ladder, and they turned to see Annie Ross watching them. Annie was flustered and hurt at finding them in each other's arms, and she apologized hastily.

"Come up," Jeremy said to her, for she was halfway through the hatch.

But Annie shook her head once and began to go down quickly.

"Annie!" Jeremy called out. She did not reply.

They heard her running away, and then her footsteps were gone. In the distance, dogs barked. Below, the night watch walked past, calling out, "Nine of the clock, and all's well."

Jeremy and Gwen stayed in each other's arms, her head against his chest as he stroked her hair. He was sorry Annie had become so upset, so obviously jealous. She had no reason to be jealous, for he and Gwen were only friends, after all. As he held her to him Cape whimpered, wanting to come up with them.

An hour later they returned to the hospital, where Lela and Tamano were watching over Weston. There was no improvement in their friend. If anything, he was weaker.

Gwen methodically changed the bandage by the light of a lamp, and Jeremy saw how the scalp had painfully been cut away in a circle, around the forehead and above the ears. Weston's handsome features had been made grotesque, because the muscles of his head and face had gone limp, with nothing to hold them to his skull. It was too late to stitch him up and make those muscles tight again, as sometimes was done. The injury had been incurred weeks ago, and scab had formed in some places, new skin and open sores in others.

Lela and Tamano left for the night, and the lights of the hospital were snuffed or dimmed. Gwen slept an hour or two on another cot, and Jeremy put his head down on the desk. After a few hours, only the sound of patients breathing and snoring was to be heard. Jeremy found it difficult to sleep, and often he went to Richard's side, talking softly to him, trying to wake him up, bring him back to consciousness.

At one point, Jeremy observed Gwen's beautiful face in slumber. He could have looked at that face forever... but she awoke, and gazed back at him. She was so easy to look at, as though she were somehow a part of him.

"I suppose you are," he whispered to her, and she sat up, wondering, leaning on an elbow, her long, golden hair spilling down over her arm. She did not know what he meant, but she did not speak.

It was then that Weston half opened his eyes and made a sound. Jeremy thrilled, seeing a glint in those eyes, as of consciousness. With a gasp, he leaned forward and asked his friend to speak. Gwen hurried to Jeremy's side, and they watched, transfixed, as Richard's lips moved slightly. He breathed almost unintelligible words.

"...jour—journal."

In a whisper, Gwen asked him to repeat what he had said. Both she and Jeremy knew Richard had kept a diary, but it had not been brought in with him by the Iroquois.

"Where?" Jeremy asked softly. "Where is your journal, Richard?"

"...took...it—" The words were unclear, garbled.

"Who?" Jeremy asked, excited that the officer was coming around. "Who took it, Richard? The ones who did this to you?"

"Yes." Weston breathed shallowly, weakly, and his eyes flickered closed. "Yes..." he whispered, saying a name Jeremy could not hear. "...took it. Jer— Find..."

Suddenly, Richard was hardly breathing. With a cry, Jeremy pushed on his chest and shook him, fear mounting.

He called his name, once, twice, and then again, over and over.

"Wake up! Richard, please wake up! Richard!"

He was not breathing.

"Richard!" Jeremy moaned, feeling that same inner ache, that gnawing pain that had nearly torn him apart when Penelope died. Richard had been like a brother, and now he, too— "All because of this damned rebellion!" Jeremy hissed. "Because of treacherous, hypocritical rebels! Richard! Please, Richard! Try! Try to live!" It was no use.

Jeremy was trembling all over as he knelt there, fists clenched. Gwen slowly drew the sheet over Richard's face, tears running down her cheeks.

In a voice loud enough to waken the patients and cause a baby to cry, Jeremy declared, "Those rebels did this; this and everything else! They're the fault of Penelope's death! They've caused me to lose my family! Their misguided rebel lunacy has ruined my life!"

Then Gwen was kneeling with him, embracing him fiercely, with all her might, squeezing as though to prevent him from blowing apart.

"Shh," she whispered. "Hush, my Jeremy. Hush."

Now it was for him to weep, and for Gwen to comfort him. She stroked his head, and he knelt there with his arms hanging, forehead on her breast. The baby stopped crying, but in the distance there rose a louder throbbing of drums as warriors went into a wilder dance of triumph. Then there came the sound of several drunken soldiers staggering past, singing and laughing, insulting all rebels, and promising the gallows for any who dared defy the king. Gwen trembled at that but kept trying to calm Jeremy.

As they knelt in the faint lamplight, they heard the drunks sing the familiar soldier's song, the one General Wolfe was said to have sung the night before he died, victorious, capturing Quebec from the French. Though the voices were blurred and thick, Jeremy knew the song well, and it ran around and around in his mind, even when the drunks had drifted past and were gone.

Why, soldiers, why,
Should we be melancholy, boys?
Why, soldiers, why,
Whose business is to die?

Jeremy whispered to Gwen. "I don't know why any of this has to happen to our people, but one way or the other...one way or the other I'm going to—" He stopped himself and crushed Gwen against him, and her arms went around his waist as she sank so close to him that it truly seemed they were one.

*chapter* **19**

# SENECA VENGEANCE

Jeremy Bently could not find Richard Weston's journal, though he questioned everyone who might know something of its whereabouts. Hamilton knew nothing, nor did Lieutenant Mark Davies. Jeremy spoke to nearly every Redcoat from the Cedars expedition, as well as the volunteers, but none knew exactly how Weston had been slain, or what might have happened to the journal.

Manoth and a score of Indians were still out, falling upon undefended farms. This angered Hamilton, because he had directed all the Indians to come back after the campaign; he did not want independent raiding parties causing havoc. He had sent Joseph Brant out with Mohawk warriors to order Manoth back to Detroit, to prepare for another campaign. The next offensive would be under direct orders from the British high command in Montreal.

Meanwhile, after Weston's death Jeremy spent even more of his time at the hospital, often working there long past dark. Since the night on the blockhouse, he and Gwen had forged an unspoken bond of respect and trust, much stronger than simple affection. Both knew something had changed between them.

Annie, too, could see the depth of feeling the couple

shared. Although she might have felt jealousy, she knew Gwen was not scheming to entrap Jeremy, and was certain the couple's mutual affection had grown out of their work together. Annie suspected that Jeremy was not yet over the death of his wife and therefore would not allow himself to fall in love with anyone. Before long, he would discover that Annie was the one truly meant for him. Until that time came, she would be patient and would not give in to jealousy, though it flared up frequently. She was determined to prove herself of such noble character that one day Jeremy would fall headlong in love with her.

Actually, Jeremy thought of little else but the war. He steadily grew to loathe the very name Continental Congress, accusing all its delegates and most of its supporters of being corrupt and hypocritical. The rest, like his parents, were misguided idealists whose hopes for a new America would be dashed.

He spent more and more time with Henry Hamilton. The two became fast friends, with a common interest in Indian affairs and natural philosophy—and whist. Cole Ross and Dawson Merriwether usually made a foursome at cards, and the conversation almost always turned to the war. Listening to Hamilton, Jeremy came to understand how precarious was his position as commander of Detroit.

For one, Congress was managing to sway some Indian tribes and the French toward staying out of the conflict instead of joining the loyalists. The region of the Illinois River in particular was the scene of growing rebel intrigues. Despite the rebel setbacks in Lower Canada, Virginians were settling along the Ohio River and were journeying west to the Mississippi then northward to the Illinois as rebel ambassadors. The isolated French residents and their Indian neighbors did not know what to think when brash, well-armed Virginians boasted of the omnipotence of Congress. There were no British regulars in the Illinois, no one able to convince the folk there that these Virginians were merely trying to scare them into withholding support from Hamilton.

Rumors raced through the northwest of a huge army of rebel Americans gathering at Fort Pitt for a major thrust at

Detroit. These lies frightened the French and Indians. What
was true, however, was that rebel settlers were building
forts on the Ohio Valley frontier of Shawnee and Delaware
country, and these could serve as staging areas for invasions
of Indian lands. While such threats were held over the heads
of Indians and French, the Virginians offered friendship in
exchange for their neutrality.

One Saturday evening in July, Hamilton was at Valenya,
having come with Merriwether for dinner and a game of
whist with Jeremy and Cole Ross. The sky was still light
as the four men sat on the veranda enjoying glasses of
brandy. A card table stood in the common room, where
Annie played the spinet and Gwen sang a cheerful air.

The men on the veranda smoked pipes and sipped brandy
as they listened. The mood was tranquil, and the evening
could not have been more beautiful, but the silence was not
one of contentment, for all were thinking of what Hamilton
had just said about the growing disaffection in the Illinois.
If that region were lost, then communication by river to
New Orleans would be cut off—and the *habitants* and Indians would be compelled to join the attackers, in all like-
lihood.

Smoke puffing from his mouth, Hamilton said quietly,
"To make matters worse, the Spanish troops in Saint Louis
also have designs on the Illinois, and might soon close the
Mississippi to us completely."

Jeremy knew that Spain was a lackey of Bourbon France
and might threaten British claims in the northwest. After
the last war with England, France had not only lost the
northwest, but also had ceded to Spain the vast lands west
of the Mississippi, including the village of Saint Louis.
Though weak, Spain might present a danger if her agents
worked to help shake the allegiance of Illinois *habitants* and
Indians.

Merriwether's gloomy voice broke the silence. "All these
Indians have been coming in as our allies, but if they think
we're weak, they'll turn on us like dogs."

Cole Ross could not understand. "But how could they?
It's clear our troops are winning in Lower Canada and soon

will defeat the rebels once and for all. Why would the Indians think twice about supporting us?"

"They'll always want to believe suggestions that we can't win," Hamilton replied. "They've always shifted allegiances, choosing whichever white side rose to superior power. If the war drags on, they may be persuaded that the rebels will mount an assault to destroy them. That's why we absolutely must capture Albany before winter. Then, with another fleet coming to capture New York Town itself, there'll be no rebellion next spring."

"But what if our troops don't take Albany?" Ross asked. "If they're stopped before winter, will that mean our Indians and French will spurn us?"

"Not immediately," Hamilton replied, his face grave. "But they'll waver..."

Jeremy interrupted: "Not if they're promised that the government will launch a general frontier war next year." He added that victories over frontier rebels would raise Indian spirits and promote enthusiasm for a strong alliance with the king. "But as Mr. Merriwether says, if the tribes detect weakness, they'll slip away in droves and might never come back—"

"Unless to attack us," Merriwether added. In the sudden silence, he got up to pour another round of brandies.

"That would be the irony of ironies," Hamilton said, with a weary, humorless chuckle; then he became even more sullen. "If the rebels heard that Henry Hamilton's red-skinned allies were turning against him, they'd have a good bellylaugh!" He accepted the brandy, drank it down quickly, and asked for another. He was slightly drunk, and a hint of bitterness came into his cool blue eyes.

"Do you know what the rebel propagandists are calling me, gentlemen? Perhaps you do. Perhaps you're all too kind, too sincere as friends even to ask whether I resent the insulting name. Yes, rebel speech-makers and pamphletscribblers have a name for me...a colorful epithet that'll become part of history just because it's so colorful."

He drained his next brandy, and Jeremy suggested they go back inside to resume their whist game. Ross and Merriwether agreed, getting up, but Hamilton sat, unmoving, a scowl on his refined face.

"They call me 'Hair-buyer'!"

He said this through clenched teeth, and glared across the broad straits, seeing nothing. The others self-consciously shuffled their feet, looking at each other. Hamilton took a deep, shaking breath, and slowly let it out.

Jeremy said softly, "Those who know you will never believe such a lie." Not forgetting that he himself had once been guilty of such a slur, Jeremy was furious with the rebels, who would stoop to destroying the character of a man as decent as Henry Hamilton, if it served their purpose. Months ago Hamilton could have sent a torrent of destruction down upon the frontiers, if he had wished. He could have unleashed fire and death and torture across two thousand miles of forestland. It was Henry Hamilton alone who restrained Indians eager for scalps and glory.

Jeremy was brought back to the present by those cool blue eyes staring at him.

"Those who know me won't believe it," Hamilton agreed. "But many others shall; and for as long as I live, this stain will mark my reputation!"

Trying to cheer him up, Jeremy said, "It'll all be forgotten once the war is over and the histories are written."

But Hamilton simply stared for a long, heavy moment, making Jeremy uncomfortable. Then the officer said, "It all depends, my friends, on who writes the history of this civil war: rebels or loyalists."

"Winners write the histories the way they want them!" Ross cried out. "Truth or lies!" He urged them all to go inside, where the women were still making music.

Hamilton got up a bit stiffly with a long, exasperated sigh. "So they do, Mr. Ross. Truth or lies."

Owen Sutherland was a weary man, in company with three other weary men, paddling a canoe up a silent, placid stream in Iroquois country. The stifling heat of July bore down on them as they fled, defeated, from Canada. The birch boat cut through open water swarming with mosquitoes; the paddles dipped and rose, glittering in the sunlight as the men struggled to leave the memory of death and slaughter far behind.

By now Montreal was in British hands, and not a single rebel soldier was at liberty in all Canada. Five thousand rebels and hundreds of loyalists and king's soldiers lay dead. Most of the rebels had died of smallpox or dysentery, and hundreds more would die on the long road or in sickbeds at home, their families watching helplessly.

From Montreal, Benedict Arnold had conducted a tenacious defense of the Saint Lawrence Valley, making possible the escape of the ragged remnants of the northern army. Escape had been the only possibility, for a rash attempt at counterattack by fresh rebel regiments under other generals had been trapped and mauled by the British at Three Rivers. Sutherland had fought there alongside Anthony Wayne's Pennsylvanians. Even now, sitting in the stern of the canoe with three Mohawk Valley German farmers, he could still hear those booming cannon. He could not forget the screams of rebel wounded, their curses and pleading for help. Even now, with eyes open for any sign of an Indian ambush on this lonely stream, he could not get the memory of the Three Rivers battle out of his mind.

The rebels had been too cocky. After being repulsed in an attack on British positions, they had turned on the enemy and formed ranks in the shelter of trees. Panting, sweating, many of them wounded, two thousand grim rebels had watched as the British and their allies massed in the fields, as if for an attack. Sutherland could still hear those bagpipes skirl, could see the kilted Highlanders, now his enemies.

The rebel leaders expected the British to make a stupid frontal assault, as at Bunker Hill—to come straight ahead and be cut down like ripe hay. Sutherland had warned Anthony Wayne and Matthew Smith they were wrong to expect such insanity, but he had been rebuffed. He had respected the raw courage of the green rebel soldiers, but had been sure it was wrong to stand and fight, madness to try to stop thousands of disciplined troops. He had known it as those hundred drums rolled and rattled, and had known it when the enemy infantry stopped short and let the cannon be wheeled into position. Then ships in the river had sailed close to shore, and the cannonade had begun. While the British and their allies watched, their guns hammered the rebel positions hour after hour, throwing shot, shell, grape, and canister into the hidden American lines.

Sutherland had stood, waiting for his turn to fall, as had they all, as bravely as any of the world's best-trained soldiers. Iron had whizzed through the trees like a plague of locusts, with leaves, branches, and men falling all together. The massed British and German guns were like thunder overhead, but there was no direct Redcoat attack. The Redcoats simply watched as rebels died under those merciless, battering guns.

When the main body of rebel troops had at last been ordered to withdraw, Sutherland had stayed with Anthony Wayne's rearguard and had fought hour after hour, day after day, all the way up the Saint Lawrence, finally reaching Montreal and rejoining General Arnold. The general, in charge of saving what was left of the rebel army, had directed Sutherland to take dispatches down to Fort Stanwix.

Stanwix was a weak post guarding the portage between the upper Mohawk River and streams flowing westward. Nearby was the Oneida village of Oriska, where Ella and the others were waiting. After turning over the dispatches, Sutherland was at liberty to arrange his personal affairs, and he intended to rejoin Arnold for the autumn campaign against the anticipated British thrust toward Albany.

As Sutherland sat in the canoe, paddling up Wood Creek on the last leg to Fort Stanwix, he wondered what would become of the embittered Benedict Arnold. No one could deny his fierce courage and brilliant leadership; his troops loved him and would follow him into the jaws of hell. But there were too many officers who hated him, usually because he would not overlook their incompetence. Benedict Arnold was a genius in war, but he was not a smooth gentleman who earned the admiration of other smooth gentlemen. Sutherland only hoped Congress would allow Arnold to go on fighting, for during the next critical months a British advance on Lake Champlain would strike like a lance at Albany. Sutherland meant to find Ella and his family, see they were safe, and then rejoin Arnold for the defense of Champlain.

As he canoed with these Valley Dutch—as most whites in the Mohawk were called; its loyalist Scots and Scotch-Irish had fled to Canada—Sutherland frequently passed signs of Indian war: burned cabins, fresh graves, and small groups of refugees heading eastward. The handful of white families who had lived on the borders were haggard and afraid. Some of their folk were wounded, others struck dumb with the memory of horror, all of them hungry and impoverished.

They told of marauding Senecas who had attacked in the night or murdered farmers working in the fields. Although this band numbered no more than twenty, its trail of destruction was abominable. Sutherland counted at least ten farmsteads burned out, and three families had been butchered, including infants. At the outbreak of the rebellion, neutral whites here had stayed on their lands, not fearing an Indian attack. But their confidence that Indians would respect their neutrality had been shattered suddenly, with a horrifying, bloodcurdling shriek and the unexpected stroke of a tomahawk.

Fort Stanwix, the nearest military post, could not defend these folk, because Congress had not sent enough troops or workmen to strengthen its defenses. When Sutherland arrived with his dispatches from Arnold, he found the fort in the same miserable state as last year. The Continental officer in charge took his dispatches and offered a night's rest inside the fort's palisades; they were broad, a hundred yards on a side, but most were rotting. Only thirty rebel troops were posted here, and although trained regulars, they were too few to police the region.

Sutherland declined the invitation to stay; he must push on to Oriska, where his family waited. It was then that he heard the worst news yet. The young officer did his best, but there was no easy way to say that three days earlier a community of whites living near the Oneida village had been attacked by the marauding Senecas.

Sutherland was stricken with horror. The downcast officer shook his head, saying, "We heard about it, and I sent a squad out immediately. . . . I'm sorry, Mr. Sutherland, but the whites were driven out, and some were killed."

"Who?" The Scotsman's eyes were wild with fear and anger. "Who died? Who? Where are the others now?"

"I—I don't know. My subordinate has not yet written his report, and at the moment he's out on patrol—"

Dashing from the soldier's office, Sutherland snatched up his rifle and gear. He shouted at two young Oneidas fishing in the river, and offered them a few pieces of eight. Soon they were all paddling in great haste downriver to Oriska. Sutherland was stunned; he might have come too late. Anxiety rose as he rapidly questioned the two paddlers. They explained that the Senecas under Manoth had passed through, abusing peaceful Oneidas for their support of the rebels and promising to come back one day and destroy the entire tribe. Then Manoth had attacked the whites near Oriska and burned down the new church.

Almost afraid to ask, Sutherland stroked fiercely with his paddle, and then had to say, "Who died?"

The Indian sitting in the prow of the canoe turned to observe Sutherland, aware that the famous Donoway had close relations among the group of whites. The warrior's eyes were intense, and with much feeling he said:

"Sorry to tell you, Donoway, but the minister and his wife trusted too much in their God and tried to persuade Manoth to go in peace; they now are lost to my people, and we are sad, for they were good to us, and kind."

Sutherland stopped paddling, and he closed his eyes. Matilda and Angus Lee's first real church had cost their lives. He would miss them very much.

After some time, as forested riverbank and stretches of tall Oneida corn passed by, he forced himself to ask the rest of this tragic tale. The older of the two Indians, who sat behind him, said the other whites had been forced to flee for their lives. He did not know exactly where.

"Albany?" Sutherland asked, and again paddled hard, feeling a driving urgency to get on with the chase. "They must have gone that way, for it's the safest!"

"No," said the second Indian. "The bad Senecas all followed the trail that way, tricked by Oneidas who told them

the whites took that direction; your people are heading
southwest, away from the murderers. Donoway, the terrible
Manoth is sworn to rub out these whites. The terrible Manoth will pursue them to the ends of the earth."

At Oriska, Sutherland took leave of his canoemen at the
lodge of the village chief, to whom he briefly paid the
customary respects. Then he went alone toward the ruined
chapel, which stood on a hillside a few hundred yards away.
The village had been noisy when Sutherland had first arrived, but the people fell silent as soon as they heard he
had come to find his family and friends.

Oriska was not a village of bark lodges and dirty hovels;
instead, like many Iroquois communities, it was mainly log
cabins with cedar shingles and, in some cases, puncheon
floors. Sutherland had been here years earlier and had been
impressed by its prosperity. Today, however, he was too
full of worry, his mind tormented by fear, to pay much
attention to the neat houses and well-tended gardens.

A little way out of the village, he saw the blackened
spire standing, like some ancient pine. The spire had survived and now seemed to be a monument to man's cruelty,
rather than a symbol of God's love. The rest of the church
was a collapsed mass of charred beams and clapboard. Sutherland's emotions surged as he strode rapidly forward. Crows
flapped away from the fenceposts of a cornfield, and a rabbit
scampered across the track. The neighborhood was deserted,
as if the Oneidas could not bear to come here and view what
had been done.

Heart pounding, a sharp pain shooting through it, Sutherland saw the two grave crosses, side by side, in a little
plot surrounded by a new white picket fence. He whispered
the names of Angus and Matilda, threw his gear aside, and
fell to his knees, leaning on the fence. Removing his hat,
he lowered his head. There he prayed and wept, unaware
of the present or the past.

Then someone was behind him. He was about to whirl and
spring at whoever it was, but there came a voice he knew —
a gravelly voice both old and strong.

"Donoway, it is my people's profound sorrow to have lost the good minister and his lady."

Sutherland turned to face a bent, skinny old man who had a blue trade blanket over his bony shoulders and wore the round cap with an eagle feather that was common to Iroquois dignitaries.

"Joe Onayote!" Sutherland exclaimed, standing up to shake his hand. "You know what happened? How can I find my people?"

Onayote was the aging uncle of Hickory Webster; he was a wise, thoughtful man, highly regarded for having been a valorous leader fighting against the French. His face was long and wrinkled, his eyes set deep and glittering in his weathered, dark complexion. The sorrow of which the Oneida elder had spoken was real, and in their handshake was mutual condolence.

"Let us sit, Donoway, for my sore old bones do not allow me to think when they must stand." They went to the shade of a great maple tree and sat there in silence awhile. Sutherland shared a pipe with his friend, and the two men spoke briefly of their journey the previous year through the Mohawk Valley, when Sutherland had been helped by Onayote and had first tangled with Manoth. Onayote well knew Manoth hungered to take revenge against Sutherland's people, and had misdirected Manoth's party so that Ella and the others could flee southward. Manoth had not yet come back, so perhaps he was still searching for the whites in the wrong direction.

After some contemplation, Onayote spoke again. "My niece, Hickory, is taking your folk to the country of the Tuscaroras, our Iroquois brethren. Tuscaroras are like us Oneidas; they want to remain neutral in the white man's war. They do not love loyalists, nor do they love Manoth's killers. Your people will be hidden with them until your arrival. There they will be safe, as long as Manoth cannot find them. But if he does, the Tuscaroras can do little, for they are peaceful and know not the ways of war."

Onayote said he had been expecting Sutherland, and last night had a dream that the Scotsman had survived the debacle in Canada. Indians had great respect for dreams and faithfully and solemnly tried to interpret whatever was indicated in them.

Onayote said, "And I have had another dream and in this dream a giant snapping turtle is pursuing a smaller turtle, who is protecting his kin, but the giant snapping turtle is too powerful to be stopped by the smaller turtle.

"More I have seen, but could not understand, for it is not given to me to be a reader of dreams. I have seen a wolf attack the giant turtle, and then there was a flash of fire. I awoke and could see no more, yet I know this: Manoth is the snapping turtle—for he is of the noble turtle clan of the Seneca."

Sutherland nodded. "And I, aged one, am also a fighting turtle, with a shell that protects family and friends." He showed a mark on his chest: a green turtle, tattooed there when he was adopted by the Ottawas.

"Perhaps," Sutherland continued, "if you had seen more of that dream, you would have seen the destruction of the giant turtle."

Onayote nodded slowly. "Perhaps." Then he gazed directly at Sutherland and said, "I will guide you myself to the country of the Tuscarora."

Sutherland thanked him for his offer, but said such an overland journey was too hard for Onayote, much of the ninety miles being rocky hunting trails.

"If you direct me on my way," Sutherland said, "I will find my people and lead them to Albany."

Onayote said he would insist on being the Scotsman's personal guide. "My bones will not think of the work, Donoway, if I tell them they will learn the meaning of my strangest dream."

They set off that night, riding Onayote's horses. The trip would take five days if all went well; they should arrive at the Tuscarora village soon after Ella's party got there. They planned to move fast, seldom resting for more than an hour, for it was always possible Manoth would discover Ella's route. Even now he could be following swiftly, eager for blood.

• • •

The days were sweltering, nights damp and heavy; mosquitoes and blackflies tormented them and their horses. After two days of riding along winding, hilly forest trails, they left their mounts with an Oneida family, then walked for two days over trails too steep and narrow for horses. Next they borrowed a canoe from an Oneida hamlet and paddled down a lively, deep river.

Sutherland thought this elm-bark craft heavy and unwieldy compared to the graceful birch boats of the Algonquian-speaking peoples to the north and west. Yet the canoe served well enough, for this stretch of water had few troublesome rapids and required little skill. Instead of kneeling, Onayote stood in the rear quarter of the boat, paddling in the Iroquois way.

Throughout their journey, the two seldom talked. Sutherland, preoccupied with thoughts of Ella and the children, hardly noticed the beautiful country. The river led through steep gorges, between high hills overgrown with dense forest. Here and there were small communities of Tuscaroras, the weakest of the Six Nations, and a people who wore white-man's clothes. The men even clubbed their hair like whites, and women wore bonnets against the sun.

On the way, Sutherland and Onayote asked questions of the Tuscaroras and were told that Ella's group had recently come past in two canoes. Not stopping long, they had been very secretive about their destination. Sutherland was glad to hear they were cautious.

Early in the evening two days later, he and Onayote beached the canoe at a quiet Tuscarora hamlet, set between sheer hills where a smaller tributary came down from the forest. From here they would go on foot for the last three miles, to a second village deep in the woods. Sutherland was excited; the journey was nearly over and he would once again be reunited with his loved ones.

The headman of this first village was a youngish fellow, stocky and polite of manner, but Sutherland thought he seemed strangely nervous. Pulling the canoe ashore, Sutherland asked about Ella and was told she and the others had passed yesterday. All were well, except for one woman about to have a baby, worn out by the hard journey. This worried Sutherland, for Sally Morely was not due to give birth for almost two months, and to bear a child prematurely in this wild country was extremely dangerous, both to mother and infant.

Also, Sutherland knew there must be some reason the headman was so tense. As old Joe Onayote climbed stiffly out of the canoe, hailing the dozen Tuscarora men who had come to greet him, Sutherland glanced around at the cluster of eight log huts. All was not right, and he moved casually to Onayote, saying softly, "No children or women in sight, old one."

Onayote was also casual, and lifted Sutherland's sack of twisted tobacco from the canoe. Though neither man suspected the unarmed Tuscaroras, they knew an enemy might be watching, ready to spring from ambush. They also knew that to take rifles from the canoe might start something too soon.

Speaking quietly to the headman, Onayote said, "If there is a threatening Seneca here, my son, be assured you'll be protected, for this is the mighty Donoway, of whom you have heard. Do not let us fall into the hands of an enemy, my son, or lasting dishonor will be upon you and your folk."

"Noble Onayote," said the headman, taking a deep breath, "have care how you move, for there are three armed Seneca watching from behind the canoes." A little ways off, at the edge of the creek, several canoes lay on racks, another on the ground, all upside-down. Sutherland did not look directly that way, but out of the corner of his eye he discerned a faint movement, as of a feather flickering; or perhaps it was the play of light upon steel.

Onayote suddenly laughed aloud, calling for drink and holding up the tobacco. Sutherland followed his lead, and together they all went into the uneasy headman's cabin.

When the dangerous Donoway was out of sight inside the cabin, Otchaka and his two friends slipped in a crouch along the edge of the creek, making for the canoe of the Scotsman and Onayote. Just a few minutes earlier, Manoth had posted Otchaka here to watch for Sutherland's approach, then had moved off up the creek with fifteen others, headed for the secluded hamlet where Ella and her group were thought to be.

Five days ago, the marauding Senecas had returned to Oriska, angry that they had been tricked. Although it was forbidden for Iroquois to attack one another, Manoth had threatened to slay the Oneidas if they did not reveal the truth. When a coward among the Oriska Indians confessed that Donoway had come through on his way to find his people, Manoth soon learned all he needed. He had set off with his men, and by running hour after grueling hour over a shorter, though brutally hard route, he had reached this hamlet just before his hated enemy, Sutherland.

After slaying Ella's group, Manoth meant to await Donoway's arrival, but he had not thought Sutherland and old Onayote would have come so soon. Their arrival had startled Otchaka and his men, who had threatened the Tuscaroras not to warn Sutherland.

Otchaka and his men concealed themselves near Sutherland's canoe. When the Scotsman came out of the cabin, he would walk right into an ambush. Otchaka had not fired, lest his shooting warn the other whites upstream and upset Manoth's plans for a surprise attack. Furthermore, to slay the noted Donoway by use of a tomahawk and war club would be a far greater honor than killing from cover. Otchaka found shelter behind a bush near the water, and his companions hid farther up the bank. Out of sight, they waited.

Indians were known for patience, and Otchaka and his two concealed companions were no exception. Normally they would have waited hours in silence for a deer to come close enough to their hunting blind. But even five minutes dragged when it came to stalking the formidable Donoway.

Otchaka lay in long grass behind the bush, staring at the house of the Tuscarora headman. He expected Sutherland to come out soon. Surely if the Scotsman were so anxious to reach his family, he would come eagerly to his canoe and be easily ambushed. Otchaka was certain these timid Tuscaroras dared not warn Sutherland that Senecas were here; at that moment, smoking and eating must be going on inside the cabin. Each minute that passed brought Manoth nearer to Ella's group.

Otchaka lay under bright, hot sunlight that made him even more uncomfortable. His two friends had chosen better spots twenty yards to his left, hidden in cool shade.

Otchaka was so restless that he did not realize that the men of the hamlet were now no longer to be seen. There were only a few dogs to the left, near the creek, scampering and barking after something beyond Otchaka's two friends. The dogs apparently were scaring up a muskrat or a rabbit, and their yelping grew louder as they trotted nearer to the hidden Senecas. It was not until the village headman came from his lodge and shook a stick at the dogs, yelling for them to be off, that the animals ran away from whatever quarry lay in the thicket nearby.

Otchaka watched the headman glance nervously about the hamlet, then duck back into the low doorway of his lodge. Everything became so still that the Seneca had the unexpected, unnerving sensation of being watched—as though he were the hunted, not the hunter. He felt for the scalping knife at his side, and his fingers ran over the fresh scalp that hung from his belt. He touched metal, and looked down to see the pair of broken glasses he had taken as a souvenir to go with the scalp of the white minister from Oriska.

The glasses were a good trophy, a funny prize that he would wear when he got back to his village and told the tale of how he had made a fool of the dying minister, of how he had put on the man's glasses, mocking him so wittily that it had caused even the grim Manoth to laugh—

What was that sound?

Otchaka had heard a dull thud to his left, near where the other two men were hiding. They ought to be more quiet. His stomach had knotted from the sudden start, and he became angry with himself for behaving so much like a shaky novice warrior, like a boy in his first real fight. This was not Otchaka's first fight at all, for he had been at Manoth's side all the way from Detroit. He had fought the white farmers in field and cabin, had shot them down at the plow, and had run in on them with only the war club against their flintlocks.

How he had proved himself brave in these past moons! How he had slain them, had drunk their blood, and—

This time Otchaka began to think something was wrong. There had been a muffled groan from where the nearest of his companions lay in hiding. It was then Otchaka noticed, with a heart suddenly pounding, that the village dogs were lying on open ground not far off, gazing right at him, heads cocked, ears up. Now and again one would whimper, or perhaps growl low, obviously watching something . . . someone.

To his right, stone clattered on stone. Otchaka sprang around. But this was a ruse, he knew: a thrown rock to distract him, to make him turn that way. He would not. An enemy was coming from the left, he was . . . he was almost sure. He glanced at the cabin. No movement there.

Softly Otchaka called out the name of one friend. There was a soft grunt of acknowledgment. Then a rock splashed near the creek's edge, again at his right. He whipped around involuntarily, crawling backward on all fours, just in case someone was about to spring. Donaway had a reputation: it was said he was as good as the best Indian in stealthy killing. But he had not yet come out. Otchaka would have seen him.

Otchaka called to his friend again, this time a little louder than he should have.

There was no reply.

He became afraid. He wanted to scream his friend's name, to charge for the lodge where Sutherland was feasting and break in, club and knife slashing.

But he did nothing. His advantage was in ambush. Every Indian knew cunning was worth ten times more than reckless courage. He must wait until Donoway showed himself and came unsuspectingly toward his canoe.

But why did Otchaka feel so alone? Why were those village dogs still staring? What did they see? What was behind—

"Seneca!"

# chapter 20

## AMBUSH

The Indian was so frightened that he bodily left the ground and lost his grip on the war club. He wailed and fumbled for it, catching hold of the handle. But he was too late. Owen Sutherland's heavy claymore came whistling down and chopped the club away.

Otchaka rolled backward, scrambling to his feet, coming up with knife and tomahawk. Sutherland stepped forward slowly, deliberately. The Seneca shrieked for his friends, but there was no answer. The people of the village were moving out of their lodges, fascinated by the drama. The Tuscaroras had not betrayed Sutherland when he had slipped out a back window of the cabin and taken on the Senecas one by one. Joe Onayote, too, was there.

Sutherland said, "Your two friends are bound. They will again be conscious in a few hours. Put down your weapons, and I'll—"

Just then Sutherland saw the glitter of the metal frame of Angus Lee's bifocals hanging at Otchaka's side. Beside the frames was the minister's half-dried scalp. Sutherland began to shake. His eyes went wide and fixed on that scalp. His claymore presented before him, he suddenly was breathing heavily, almost violently. He had intended to take the

Seneca prisoner, but rage, madness, surged in him, erupted.
He roared with a fury that caused women and children to
cower and the men of the village to stare in astonished
fascination.

The claymore came alive, gleaming in the sunlight. Sutherland seemed a giant, a murderous, malevolent beast with
death in his eyes. He struck, and Otchaka screamed, bringing up the tomahawk in desperation. It was smashed from
his hand, and the sword cut the Indian high on the chest,
driving him backward, the scalping knife falling to the
ground. With a fearful groan, Otchaka lay trembling, a
shallow cut on his chest beginning to ooze blood.

Though he was brave, he had never before seen such
raw animal savagery in an enemy. Helpless, Otchaka was
not ready to die. He begged for mercy.

But Sutherland raised the claymore and bellowed again.
The stroke fell. The Indian howled in terror.

Then it was Sutherland howling, a cry of rage and frustration. The claymore blade abruptly stopped its fall, inches
above the victim's head. Steel quivering, Sutherland screamed.
Otchaka gaped, but made not a sound. Sutherland fell to
his knees, eye-to-eye with the the Seneca. He sought to
strike again, but he could not. He released a keening cry
of despair for the memory of the dead Angus Lee. But it
was this memory that stopped him. Lee would cry out for
mercy. And Sutherland's own knowledge of right and wrong,
his honor, stopped that bloody swordblade, inches from the
cowering Otchaka's horrified face.

In a shout of fury and inner agony, Sutherland roared,
"No! I cannot kill even you like this!" He let the sword's
point fall to the ground and glared at the wounded Seneca,
who was so astonished and afraid that he thought an av-
enging manitou possessed this white man. In a brief moment
of breathlessness, Sutherland shook all over, fists clenched.
Anger and sorrow, revenge and mercy, evil and good, all
battled for dominance within him.

If any man deserved to die, this man deserved to die.
But to slay him in cold blood, as Otchaka had slain so
many—Sutherland simply would not do it.

Otchaka's nervous eyes flitted back and forth, from Sutherland to his fallen tomahawk. He needed but one opening, one instant. Sutherland, still trembling with the force of his volcanic emotions, looked up at old Joe Onayote. That was all Otchaka needed.

"Donoway!" Onayote yelled in warning. But the tomahawk was in the Seneca's hand, swinging round, backhanded, in a short arc that ended with a vicious thud against Sutherland's right side. The Scotsman grunted in pain and at the same moment grappled with the Indian, snatching the tomahawk free and killing Otchaka with one hard blow to the skull.

The Tuscaroras shrieked for joy and ran to Sutherland, who swayed, then fell forward into the sinewy arms of Onayote, who was helped by the headman.

"How bad?" Onayote asked the dazed Sutherland as they carried him to the headman's cabin. Blood was running from Sutherland's side, and ribs surely were broken. The lung might be punctured, but so far no blood was coming up through his nose or mouth. He was more in shock than severe pain just then, and cried out that he must go to find his people.

"Soon," Onayote replied. "But you'll bleed to death if you don't get bound up first. How bad is it?"

"Don't know," Sutherland groaned, and as they laid him on bedding in the cabin, pain began to come, sharp and violent, worse with every breath. "Don't know, old one! But fix me up...fix me up quick." Sutherland began to lose consciousness. He could not see. He heard the rapid, excited voices of Onayote and some squaws who had hurried into the cabin to treat him.

Sutherland knew great agony. He could hardly breathe. It must not be over for him, not this time! He must not even pass out. Not yet; not with Ella out there, and Manoth closing in on her. He had to go! He must!

"Stay down, Donoway!" Onayote shouted over the clamor of the Tuscarora women. Then, abruptly, everything was quiet. The Indians were all listening, and so was Sutherland. From the distance came gunfire, shot after shot. Manoth had found Ella! His attack had begun! Sutherland tried to go, but he was weak, and the Indians would not let him up. Joe Onayote kept shouting, "Not yet, Donoway! Soon! Not yet!"

A packhorse was shot and whinnied in terror, rising on its hind legs and falling with a crash to the ground, where it kicked away its life. Men were shouting, guns banging, bullets flying around a small, sunny clearing beside the creek. The shrill war cry of the Senecas rang out in the forest, and as the other five packhorses fled, their hoofbeats were loud on the stony trail leading upstream to the next village.

Ella knew it was Manoth, because she had seen him when Tom, Jeb, and James had opened fire, ambushing the unsuspecting Senecas. Ella had hoped Manoth would be hit, but he had not gone down. Two of his fifteen warriors had been shot, however, and now lay dying beside a log bridge over a small brook that emptied into the larger creek.

Ella was inside an abandoned cabin in the center of a clearing, not far from the village where Owen Sutherland lay wounded. The old cabin was rotted, with only three sides still standing, but it was good shelter for Ella, Sally, Mel, Hickory, Lettie, and Susannah. Outside, the other men and Benjamin were hidden in a clump of bushes, exchanging fire with the Indians concealed in trees beyond the log bridge.

Less than an hour ago Ella's party had stopped here and made a campfire. They had paused short of their destination—the next village—because Tom's wife, Sally, could go on no longer. She was in the final stages of labor, and the baby would come at any moment.

Though still suffering from his arm wound, Tom Morely was a skilled frontiersman and had posted James to watch the trail they had just come along. Manoth had led his men up the trail, thinking the whites were already at the next village, where he would simply walk in and have them at his mercy. But James had spotted the Senecas' approach and had given the warning. It was Manoth who was surprised, but he had the advantage of numbers and mobility. The white men had to stay on the defense to protect their women and especially Sally, who could not be moved even if escape were possible.

Sally Morely lay, breathing hard, on the cabin floor, a bed of balsam branches and blankets underneath her, a pan of hot water at her side. Lettie Morely was watching over her and tending the fire, while Ella, Mel, Hickory, and Susannah stood guard with pistols near a window facing the log bridge. Heera lay nearby, commanded by Ella to stay quiet. The exposed side of the cabin faced the far end of the clearing, where the trail continued toward the next village. The three walls still standing were a solid defense against an approach from the river and the trail crossing the log bridge.

From the cover of bushes overlooking the log bridge, Tom, Jeb, and James were firing at the Indians, while Benjamin quickly loaded and reloaded extra rifles, passing them to the men and receiving empty ones in return. Gunsmoke hung heavy and dingy yellow in the hot, humid air, the acrid stink of sulfur fouling a soft breeze that drifted along the surface of the stream.

Inside the cabin Ella saw to it that Sally was comfortable and reassured her all would be well. Sally smiled wanly, squeezing Ella's hand. A bullet sang through the cabin, making them wince.

"The baby's not coming just yet," Sally said, her face perspiring, eyes a bit glazed. "But . . . very soon."

Lettie spoke softly and wiped Sally's face as Ella hunched low and moved away to the window. She tried to see their men in the thicket, but could not. She did notice the blue jay Punch, however, flitting and diving from branch to branch. Ella was sure the jay would be near Benjamin. She feared for her son, hoping he would not be too rash in this, his first battle. The boy had missed the fighting at the Oriska church, because he and Susannah had been off with her, picking berries with some Indians. They had been able to escape when their friends came running from the village, having been warned of Manoth's approach by Joe Onayote. Unknown to any of them, the Lees had refused to go when warned and had stayed behind in the hope of persuading Manoth not to attack anyone.

Ella's thoughts returned to the present as Susannah came to her side. They peeped through a chink in the logs, searching for some sign of the enemy.

"There are at least a dozen more," Susannah said. "They seem to be in those woods beyond the brook." She pointed to the tree line sixty yards away. "But they can't get across the clearing without our men shooting them down."

Ella said, "I'm afraid they'll try something more wily— maybe slip through the trees on the slope beside the cabin, to come in from behind. They're probably doing that already. It's lucky we have Heera to warn us."

Hearing this, Mel came to her side, just as a bullet ricocheted through a chink and whacked into the far wall. He looked out at the tree line across the brook, taking note of where the white men crouched. "The woods on the left are on a steep incline," he said. "The Indians might climb up to fire down on the exposed side of the cabin. I'd go up that way myself if I had a few of my grenades—that'd give them a smart check." Ella knew these were like small cannonballs, weighing a few pounds each and filled with black powder. When their fuse was lit, they could be hurled at an enemy, to explode and send bits of metal in all directions.

"But my bombs're all on that poor packhorse lying out there; I'd be dead if I made a move to get them."

He looked indecisive for a moment, then a kind of fire came into his eyes, and through clenched teeth he said, "I will get 'em!"

"Husband!" Hickory cried and grabbed him before he could dash out the open door. "You do not run so quick; they will shoot you!"

"I must!" Mel declared, shaking her off. "If not, those devils out there'll slip up on us in the darkness!"

Indeed, there was only an hour of good daylight left. The Indians had to be beaten back before that, or before they gained the high slope. Otherwise, the male defenders would be isolated and picked off, one by one, until only the women and Mel were left in the cabin. Hickory knew he was right.

Throwing off his tricorne, Mel quickly kissed his wife. Then he rushed out the door, heading the thirty yards across the clearing to fetch the satchel with the grenades. It was on the dead horse, in plain sight of the Indians, another thirty yards off. The women stared wide-eyed as Mel scampered away. Immediately he was met by gunfire. With a loud cry he spun and went down hard.

Hickory screamed and raced out for him. The Senecas were reloading, and the whites in the thicket must have seen what was happening, for they immediately opened fire to cover the Oneida woman as she frantically dragged her husband back to the cabin, blood rushing down his left temple.

In this brief lull, Susannah Sutherland knew there would be no second chance. She flew out the cabin door, blond pigtails flapping, bolting past Ella and Hickory, who were dragging back the unconscious Mel. Ella screamed Susannah's name, but the girl darted for the packhorse. Some of the braves had reloaded, and the first Indian shots skipped at Susannah's feet, one cutting through her skirts. She kept running, her head ducked low, as more lead zipped past.

She stumbled and fell, then scrambled to the packhorse. Protected by its body, she worked feverishly to unstrap the satchel. Lead whizzed past her head. Finally she freed the leather bag, but the bullets buzzed close. The Indians had the range, and as soon as she moved, they would shoot her. Yet she had to run.

"Stay there!" yelled James Morely from the bushes twenty yards off. "Stay, girl, until I say go back." He shouted something to the others, and they all held their fire, waiting for the right moment—the only moment Susannah would have.

She lay panting behind the dead horse, the mingled smell of blood and sweat strong in her nose. She held the heavy satchel ready and watched James. Across the clearing, she knew, the Seneca rifles were all aimed at her. This was no time to let her imagination work, though. She must rise above fear.

Suddenly James shouted, "Run, Susannah! Run now!" He sprang from the bushes, dashing across the clearing toward the two dead Senecas near the bridge. Scalping knife held high, James screamed a triumphant war cry.

The plan worked: to save their comrades from being scalped, the Senecas concentrated fire on James. Simultaneously, the whites opened up to cover him and Susannah, who was struggling back to the cabin, the weighty satchel slung over her shoulders. Just before entering the door, Susannah turned and saw James stagger and go down, hit, near the bridge.

"No!" she shrieked and stopped her own flight. "No, James! No!" Strong hands grabbed her and dragged her inside the cabin. She shrieked with horror as Hickory and Lettie held her from running to help her friend. Dashing to the window, tears in her eyes, Susannah saw James dragging himself away toward the larger stream, where he crawled into a thicket and disappeared from sight.

Then a Seneca warrior darted from cover, carrying pistol and tomahawk, heading for the bushes that concealed James. Susannah screamed as the whites tried to gun down the Indian. Bullets whined, kicking up dust all around the man, who zigged and zagged like a rabbit. Unharmed, he leaped into the thicket, and Susannah howled at James to watch out.

Tom Morely suddenly broke cover and began to run to his brother's aid, but the Indians had been waiting for this, and he immediately went down in a hail of gunfire. Though terrified for him, no one in the cabin dared shout Tom's name, lest the woozy Sally be shocked to hear it. In the next moment, Jeb ran from the bushes, a lumbering, slow target, spared only because the Indians were reloading.

Then one brash young warrior with a musket came sprinting out of the trees to get a better shot at the ponderous Jeb as he hurried to Tom.

"Jeb!" Lettie shrieked, hypnotized, unable to look away as the Indian drew a careful bead. "Lordy, my Jeb! Jeb!"

There was a crack of a rifle. But Jeb kept running. The Indian was down. Someone had picked him off, but who? Was it Benjamin?

Ella pressed near the window, searching for a sign of her son. Then she spotted him, standing right in the open, brandishing his rifle and threatening any other Indians who might run out to shoot Jeb. Two more shots came from the

Senecas, but by now Jeb was dragging Tom behind a nearby fallen tree. Both were too far away, however, to help James, who was somewhere in the thicket near the stream, along with a Seneca.

After a few bullets flew close by, the reckless Benjamin took cover. His small size had made him a difficult target. Now he was the only one left in the nearer clump of bushes, and the others were down by the bridge. Mel lay semi-conscious on the floor of the cabin, his forehead swollen and bleeding from where the bullet had grazed it.

Ella and Hickory were at the windows, ready with pistols, while Lettie and Susannah tended Mel, wrapping his head in torn petticoats and trying to revive him. Sally was bravely silent as she went into a strong contraction; then she began to call Tom's name softly.

Outside it became quiet. Tom and Jeb were lying behind the log, both without rifles. No one knew what had become of the wounded James or the Seneca who had gone to take his scalp. Manoth was up to something. That was why it was so quiet.

Just then there came a cry of pain from the thicket where James had crawled for cover. The women shuddered, and Susannah threw herself into her mother's arms, weeping.

Tom began screaming in anger, and Jeb was holding him back, keeping him from throwing his own life away. Ella expected that the other Indians would make a decisive move now that the whites were so weakened. If they charged the clump of bushes, Benjamin had no chance.

Ella watched in fear. Hickory came to her side; trembling, they stared out the window, searching for the enemy, wondering what would happen next.

Lettie was talking, and Ella turned to see her finish binding Mel's head. Ella asked what Lettie had said, and the older woman replied that she wanted Susannah's help for a moment.

"Where is Susannah?" Ella asked. Then terror shot through her like cold steel. "Susannah's gone! So are the grenades! Susannah! No! Susannah!"

Ella dashed to the open side of the house and looked up the wooded hill. She caught a glimpse of the girl vanishing into the woods. In the name of heaven! She was trying to do what Mel had planned. She meant to outflank the Indians and heave grenades down from the high ground! This was madness.

Ella began to run from the house, but there came such a heavy burst of fire from the Senecas that she had to duck back inside. The Senecas were not firing at the cabin, however. They were blasting away at Benjamin's concealment, ragged volleys of bullets cutting through the bushes. Apparently the Indians thought there were more whites in there and meant to pin them down, for in the next moment three Senecas scampered into the clearing, carrying tomahawks and war clubs, running straight for Jeb and the helpless Tom.

Meanwhile, Ella shouted for Heera to follow Susannah, and the eager dog bounded away up the hillside. Then she turned back to the window and desperately fired her pistol, and so did Hickory, but the range was too far. On the left, two other Indians, these armed with rifles, were running toward Benjamin's clump of bushes, one of them hopping as the boy's bullet narrowly missed. This was it! Ella frantically reloaded, knowing there was nothing she could do to stop the warriors—nothing at all.

"Run, Benjamin! Run!" she screamed, and Jeb Grey yelled the same as he rose with only a hunting knife to face the three men coming at him and Tom. War clubs were whirling, and Jeb stood like a strong old tree, facing certain death. As the burly Indians approached, they shrilled their battle cry and moved to surround him. He was ready to take them on.

At the last moment Lettie grabbed a hatchet from Hickory and, with a wild shout, raced out to stand by her husband. Hickory followed with a pistol. Ella prepared to protect the others. At that moment, Benjamin again burst from his hiding place. Instead of fleeing for the cabin, however, he, too, raced to Jeb's side, getting off a desperate shot that missed. Yanking out his own tomahawk, he yelled as his father had taught him to yell: a shrill, wild shriek. He came on as though he were a seasoned warrior, not a child going to his doom.

When the three Indians were almost upon Jeb, he, too, gave a roar and leaped ahead. Then a rifle cracked from somewhere, and the leading Indian fell backward hard, shot in the chest. The second Indian had to spring, off-stride, over his fallen comrade, and Jeb went for him, ducking under the awkward swing of the war club. He grabbed the Indian's waist and drove him down, his shoulder crushing into the man's chest. The third raised his club and rushed to help his companion. Jeb was done for, it seemed. Then suddenly Benjamin was there, and the Indian dodged sideways, losing his balance, as the boy's whisking tomahawk grazed his chest. The Indian quickly recovered, however, and made for Benjamin. Lettie dived into the fray with Jeb, and Hickory charged toward the Indian going for Benjamin, just as the warrior's club struck the boy a glancing blow and sent him sprawling. The screaming Hickory was on top of the warrior, grabbing at his club, but he swung an arm savagely at her and knocked her to the ground. The two Indians with rifles were coming on fast, just a few yards away. Her opponent joined them to face Jeb.

With Lettie's help Jeb had killed his enemy, and, along with her, got up as fast as he could. The two Indians with rifles were taking no chances, however, and as they approached they presented their weapons to fire.

The next shot again came from somewhere else, and one of the two Indians went down, a bullet in his chest. The second was so startled that he stopped short and gaped about in a terrified search for the unseen marksman. He spotted movement in the thicket where James Morely had concealed himself, and fired wildly. It was then that Owen Sutherland bounded from that same thicket. Though blood soaked his shirt, Sutherland swung his claymore like a madman, and both remaining Indians backed off, war clubs ready. They were no longer so eager for a fight.

All at once, loud cries came from the tree line, and the rest of the Senecas jumped out, Manoth at their head. The Indians were confident that the whites had spent their final effort, even with Owen Sutherland by their side. Manoth paused a moment, and so did his men. He scowled in contempt and triumph when he saw how Sutherland was swaying, blood darkening his shirt in a large stain that went all around his torso.

The Indian leader grinned and moved forward, casually, deliberately, the small bells on his leggins tinkling. Revenge at last was his. The shame Owen Sutherland and Jeremy Bently had heaped upon him soon would be wiped away in the blood of Donoway and his family and friends. There would be such a harvest of scalps today as would do the greatest warriors of the Senecas proud. Manoth would be remembered as slayer of the mighty Donoway.

"I will eat your heart, Donoway!" he shouted in Seneca. Sutherland made no reply. "And your loved ones will suffer at my hands before they die."

Sutherland was groggy, but the heat of battle kept him at the ready, beside Jeb, Lettie, Hickory, and Benjamin. Tom had a knife, but that was all, and he, too, waited, lying on his side, his left shinbone broken by a bullet. It would not begin hand-to-hand, however. The Senecas with Manoth were already bringing their rifles to bear, to shoot from close range before attacking with tomahawks and war clubs. The Indians were thrilled, laughing and joking among themselves. The two confronting Sutherland were excited, ready to strike as soon as their companions came to them. It was nine men with guns against Sutherland's party. Already Manoth was thinking about that new ostrich plume for his cap.

He reached up and yanked out the broken red feather, which would be replaced with one to remind him of this exquisite moment. He tossed the piece of feather over his shoulder, and it floated down . . .

Instantly the world shook, as a savage blast of gunpowder smote the earth among Manoth's men, sending them sprawling, recoiling from the concussion and flying shards of iron. Another grenade came bouncing down from the hillside, its thunderous explosion even more devastating than the first. Indians shrieked, screamed in agony, and collapsed in bloody ruin.

Manoth bellowed, kept his feet, and whirled just as a third black grenade with a hissing fuse fell in the midst of his shattered warriors. Those who saw it shrieked in panic and scrambled away, pushing one another over in their terror. Manoth dived to one side, behind a wounded Seneca who was kneeling with hands to his injured head. This man saved Manoth's life, for the third blast sent iron splinters into him instead of the war chief, who immediately sprang to his feet, shock and madness in his expression.

At that moment, the two astounded warriors confronting Sutherland's party leaped around and scampered for their lives toward the creek. Other Indians were struggling to rise and run, and Manoth stood among them, as if made of stone. Blood ran down his tattered leggins, and there were several deep wounds on his chest and arms. He gaped at Sutherland, who raised the claymore to his waist and began to advance.

"Owen!" cried Jeb Grey, seeing how feeble he was. "Not now! He's not hurt that bad!"

Sutherland did not reply. He hardly heard Jeb, though he sensed Ella might be shouting from the cabin. He kept on toward Manoth, who was shaken and confused. The Indian carried no weapon, but a war club lay by his feet. His companions were fleeing, shouting in terror, some writhing in pain on the ground, others lying still, in awkward positions of death. Manoth picked up the club and hefted it. Sutherland would not stop. He was twenty yards away, each step bringing him closer. He did not see Jeb pick up a rifle and, from Benjamin's ammunition, quickly begin to load it. If Owen went down, so would Manoth.

The two fighters were ten yards apart. Manoth did not move forward. He looked less sure of himself than he had earlier.

Sutherland gave a flick of the sword-tip as he came on. A few more paces and they would begin. The Indian's eyes suggested doubt. Perhaps it was Sutherland's condition that shook his resolve, for the Scotsman's body was covered with his own blood, yet still he advanced. The claymore moved side to side as though it had a will of its own, glittering in the last rays of sunlight.

"Manoth!" Sutherland said, his voice powerful, without the slightest fear. "Come to me, Manoth! Come and show me how you can die."

Sutherland continued slowly forward, claymore at the ready. Manoth's eyes were fixed on him. For a moment the Seneca seemed to move slightly backward. Sutherland tensed and the sword went above his head, beginning to whirl, as fighting Highlanders whirled their steel. It was a wickedly fascinating gyration that caught light and sound and seemed to give power to the bloodcurdling howl that came from the Scotsman's innermost soul. Sutherland was amazing, terrifying to behold.

Claymore and war club. To the death. It was now.

Then Manoth moved, without a sound, save for the tinkling of bells. He ran. With two enormous bounds back into the trees, he was gone, leaving Sutherland standing in surprise. The claymore stopped whirling. The Highland yell became an echo against the hillside.

Then all that could be heard were Manoth's bells, faintly jingling, long after he was out of sight.

There was nothing Owen Sutherland could do about it. He nearly collapsed, and leaned on his sword, head bowed in pain and exhaustion. No one could pursue Manoth or the other Senecas who fled, some of them still splashing waist-deep across the larger stream, praying a grenade would not be hurled at them. The killing was over, as far as Sutherland and his haggard friends were concerned. The weakened Scotsman stood, held up by his claymore, and out of the trees on the hillside ran Susannah and Heera. Sutherland's heart leaped to see her.

The girl was bewildered to view the bloody carnage her grenades had made, and she fell into her weary father's arms and began to weep. Sutherland stroked her hair; he was on the verge of passing out from loss of blood.

"Susannah, lass," he murmured. "Susannah."

Lettie was in Jeb's arms, and Hickory was attending to Tom, who would be all right. Just then the blue jay Punch dived down from high in a tree and landed on Benjamin's shoulder, hopping about and squawking angrily at the world.

"Oh, Papa," Susannah sobbed, her face buried in Sutherland's chest. "You're finally here! But . . . but James is in those bushes! Papa, I'm afraid the Indians got—"

Sutherland could hardly stand, but he pushed the girl back and squeezed her shoulders, saying gently, "He's alive, lass; only the mosquitoes are troubling him now. I waded up the creek and got to him before that Seneca did. James'll need his hip fixed up, but otherwise he's all right. Go to him, lass."

With that, Susannah gave a little cry of amazement and pushed into the thicket to find James. Benjamin came to embrace his father and help him stay on his feet. Heera sniffed at Sutherland, whining at the smell of fresh blood. Jeb and Lettie got under the woozy Sutherland's shoulders and eased him down to sit on a large rock, saying they would take him to Ella in a moment.

From inside the cabin, Ella had seen all this. Terror had become breathless relief. Owen was back at last. Now she had some peace of mind. Though she knew there were many wounds to tend and that this small triumph would not be accompanied by jubilation, she was sure a way through everything could be found now that the Sutherlands were together again. From behind, Sally gave a long, delirious groan. Ella sensed that the moment of birth was upon them. Though Ella's beloved Owen was so close, she put off going to greet him and knelt at Sally's side. Sally was on her back, knees bent, eyes shut; Ella had hot water and cold water in pans nearby.

"Have faith, my child," Ella said. With a cold towel she wiped the sweat from Sally's face, then kissed her closed eyes. "I know, it's all like some strange dream, and it seems impossible it's happening to you, but you'll be fine..." Ella spoke words of encouragement to Sally and told her to relax, to think about the child, and let nature bring it forth into the world.

Lying nearby, Mel was still barely conscious, but the bleeding from his head had stopped. The others would be back in before long, and the way Sally looked, they might find the newborn babe already at the mother's breast. Ella was nervous, but she had been a midwife before, and so had Lettie, who would be here directly. Ella wished Lettie would come quickly, before matters became too pressing. Sally groaned again and again, trying to catch a breath and push the baby out.

In the clearing a breeze lifted, blowing away the smell of black powder. To Ella the wind sounded fresh and clean, almost musical, as though there were bells tinkling nearby.

Sally came through another deep contraction and momentarily lay breathless, gathering strength for what Ella thought would be the final push. Ella was thrilled and nervous all at once.

Except for the sound of the wind, it was strangely silent. Even the birds had stopped singing. Only that musical tinkling could be heard. Indeed, it did seem to Ella like small bells—closer now, as though the wind or her weary mind were playing tricks. It came from beyond the cabin wall, on the side nearest the forest.

Ella was distracted, uncertain what she heard, but when Sally groaned loudly, a long and lost moan of concentration that Ella recognized as the climax, she spoke softly to her foster child. "Come on, now, Sally, my dear one! Come on! Bring it home to us! Yes, let us have the baby, for it's time! Yes, my dear brave Sally, here comes the baby—"

She heard those tinkling bells, moving slowly along the side of the cabin, toward the open wall, but she paid little attention. The baby's head was showing now. Sally was convulsed in the tremendous effort to deliver. Ella felt fear. She wanted to shout for Owen, but she dared not alarm Sally lest something happen to the child, whose head was out, Ella's hands cupped to receive it. She had to stay there. She had to take the baby by the head and from the mother.

"Ella!" Sally moaned, her face contorted with effort. "Ella, it's coming! It's coming—"

"Yes!" Ella cried in answer. "Yes, my darling! Keep pushing."

Manoth stood over them, his ugly face almost inhuman in its cruelty. He had a moment in which to kill, before he was discovered. He savored that moment. Ella felt someone there, but the newborn babe was almost out.

"My baby!" Sally cried in joy and effort. "Yes! My baby!"

"Yes," Ella gasped, and the infant was born, head first, a wrinkled, red, wriggling little boy, already crying.

In the instant Ella laid down the baby, she glanced back to see Manoth raising his club. Ella shrieked and threw the pan of hot water over her shoulder. It scalded him, and she turned and dived right at his chest, hitting hard enough to throw off his blow. He gave a hissing growl and grabbed her by the hair, wrenching her brutally under control, club again coming up. Ella kicked and screamed. The baby was crying, Sally moaning. Manoth exulted in victory. Ella fought to get free, but he had her. The club moved swiftly.

Through the door came a blur of snarling and snapping white husky. Heera bit fast on the club arm, stopping the weapon's fall, driving the surprised Manoth back, though the Indian kept hold of Ella. So powerful was Manoth that he would not release the club, even with the jaws of a husky shaking his forearm, pulling him to his knees. Manoth howled and raged, more fierce than the dog, wrenching the growling animal back and forth as though it were a puppy at play. Then Manoth threw down Ella and yanked out his scalping knife, his blade aimed at the dog's neck.

There came the fiery blast of a rifle. Manoth fell heavily backward, struck by the point-blank force of a bullet, which caught him on the forehead. He was dead instantly, eyes open, staring at the sky. The baby was crying loudly.

White-faced, Benjamin Sutherland stood in the doorway, astonished at his perfect aim. Even from only fifteen feet away it had been a difficult shot, at a moving target and with the battling husky in his way. Now Heera came to him and rose up on hind legs to lick his face. The boy was weak in the knees, absolutely amazed at killing the mighty Manoth.

Then Ella was laying the baby on the dazed Sally's breast, and saying she had a beautiful, noisy son. In the next moment, Lettie and Jeb came running through the door and rushed to Sally and the babe. Ella rose and embraced Benjamin, who absently dropped his rifle to the floor. Just outside the open wall, Owen Sutherland stood, his rifle no longer ready, though he, too, had been about to shoot Manoth. He was gazing with admiration at his young son, who looked back at him, not knowing what to think.

In came Susannah, rushing to her mother and brother to embrace them. All the Sutherlands joined in a tight group, standing in silence, grateful to be alive and together. The baby was crying, and so were Lettie and Hickory—for joy. Outside, where they had been left in the panic to save Ella, Tom Morely shouted for someone to drag him and his brother in so they could see the boy. Mel stirred and mumbled that there was a baby crying. When Hickory came to him, he took her hand and fell into a deep, restful sleep.

# chapter 21

# INDEPENDENCE

Dusk settled, and the wounded sat or lay on the floor of the cabin, while Susannah and Hickory bandaged them. Lettie cooked supper over a fire outside, and Sally fell asleep with her son suckling at her breast, her husband by her side. The Sutherlands were out in the light of the campfire; Owen was leaning against the stump of a tree, his clothes changed and clean bandages wrapped thickly around his chest. The bleeding was stopped, but ribs were broken and he had taken a deep puncture wound; he would not be able to return to Arnold very soon. That problem was for tomorrow, however. At the moment he was inexpressibly glad to be with his loved ones, who would have to be taken to safety before winter set in.

Just then a cry came from back down the trail. There was a scramble for weapons, but then Joe Onayote came in sight, tramping rapidly toward them, shouting and waving his arms. As a member of the Iroquois League, he was forbidden to take up weapons against other Iroquois, but old Onayote was overjoyed to find his friends alive and learn that Manoth and his marauding Senecas had been destroyed. After congratulating Sutherland, Onayote turned

341

and cried in a shrill, wavering voice, a signal to whoever was down the trail behind him.

"We heard the shooting, but did not know the outcome," he said. "A friend who is coming wanted no Seneca surprises, so I told him to wait until I called." Onayote said the surviving Senecas had freed Sutherland's two prisoners back at the first village, and all were now fleeing northwestward to their homes.

"Today's loss was heavy for the Senecas, and I fear this conflict is driving us Oneidas and Tuscaroras away from them. This civil war of yours will be between more than just whites." He looked gravely at Sutherland. "Soon Senecas, Onandagas, Mohawks, and Cayugas will join to subdue their brothers, the Oneidas and Tuscaroras." The others listened, aware of how vulnerable the two small nations would be. "If the war goes on, then by next spring our forests will be filled with Indian raiding parties and with the troops of Congress and the king. Our beautiful rivers will run red with the blood of whites and Indians alike."

"You speak straight, wise man," Sutherland said, glancing at Ella. "These are bad times for us all and for our cause. But we cannot surrender—not yet. Not while there is still breath left, and the glimmer of hope!"

Ella tried not to be downcast as she knelt beside Owen, a cup of mint tea in her hands. She stared into the fire, then looked through the smoke at Onayote on the other side, wrapped in his white blanket. The old man was again staring back at the trail, but Ella did not think of it, for her heart was so heavy. Perhaps Owen had hope, but she could not say there was even an ember of hope in her heart. Unless the British in Canada were stopped this autumn, they would march right to Albany. But who could stop them, and with what?

Onayote shrilled again toward the trail, and in reply there came a strange yet somehow familiar twanging sound, a sort of plunking...

Sutherland sat straight up, despite the pain. "Could it be?" he gasped. The twanging melody was indeed "Revolutionary Tea"!

"Peter!" he roared. He tried to stand but could not, and

felt a brutal, stabbing pain in his chest. Still, he overcame that awful hurt to bellow again, "Peter Defries! Peter, is that still the only tune you can play?"

With a lusty whoop of happiness, Peter Defries came thundering out of the woods and into the camp, arms spread wide, a broad grin on his boyish face. He was wearing tattered clothes and reeked of sweat as he embraced them all, laughing and congratulating them on having come through without his help.

"Lord knows I owed Manoth a few licks!" he shouted in his carefree, high-spirited way. "He had me prisoner for three long days and worked me over good enough to make a pincushion jealous! But I couldn't get here in time, though I near ran all the way from Oriska—and ain't ate mor'n two oxen all the way! Whoopee!" He would have thumped Owen, but held off, seeing his friend's feeble condition. Instead he smacked the grinning Hickory on her broad shoulder, for she could easily take it.

Soon they all sat down to a hearty meal, including food brought by the Tuscaroras downstream. Defries related that he and Poole had been captured by Manoth's men near the Cedars, when Sutherland had nearly drowned. Poole had been cruelly murdered by Manoth.

"Could've been me," Peter said glumly, "but Manoth wanted to keep me alive awhile, so he could slice me up back in his village, boasting that I was the right hand of the great Donoway, or some such Injun-talk."

But Defries had been saved by the timely arrival of Chief Joseph Brant, the most powerful leader of northwestern Indians loyal to the king. Defries and Brant had been boyhood friends, and the Mohawk had interceded with Manoth to spare the prisoner's life. Arguing that the British were against all torture of captives, Brant had pressed Manoth hard, even repeating the direct orders of Henry Hamilton to turn prisoners over to the loyal authorities.

Finally the Seneca had been compelled to bow to his superior, who had even threatened to lay his case before the Iroquois council. "I guess Brant knew Manoth wanted to get hold of his rank, and Brant saw this as a chance to enforce his authority."

Eventually Defries had been sent by Brant to Fort Niagara, and there imprisoned by the British. He had escaped from jail three weeks ago, running from his loyalist guards while out on a work detail chopping firewood. It had been a hard and dangerous journey, but Defries knew the region well and had finally made it on foot all the way to Fort Stanwix. Upon hearing of the distress of the Sutherlands, however, he had immediately rushed to Oriska. There he had borrowed a rifle and ammunition and pushed on through the forest in pursuit of his friends in Tuscarora country.

"Looks like you didn't need me," Defries said, stretching out his legs before the fire, as though they ached in every joint and muscle. "If it wasn't for the other news I got to tell you, I might figure the whole danged trip down here was worthless."

Defries paused just long enough to get almost everyone's attention—all save Benjamin, who was fast asleep. Sally and Tom were listening from the cabin, near the sleeping Mel.

"We ain't British no more. That's right, we're full-blooded Americans, pedigreed, dyed in the wool, the genuine article, and God save the Congress of these United States! Long may they rule!"

Defries was grinning to see the others so thunderstruck at the news that for months they all had hoped to hear. Defries savored the moment, and with a pleased chuckle he said, "That's right, as of July second, these thirteen colonies are free of England! Congress voted it that day. All we got to do now is make it stick!"

He pulled a folded paper from inside his dingy shirt and gave it to Sutherland. It was the *Pennsylvania Gazette,* which Defries had picked up at Fort Stanwix. On its front page was the text of the Declaration of Independence, approved by Congress on July second, as Defries had said, and signed on the fourth.

"Free!" Sutherland murmured, and gazed at Ella's amazed and happy expression. "Nothing'll ever be the same again! The whole world will look at the rebellion differently. Free! If we can hold out, England's enemies will surely back us! If France and Spain believe we can make it stick, we have a chance!"

Agitated, he tried to get up, saying, "I've got to heal! I've got to join Arnold! We have to hold Champlain, Albany...."

But Sutherland's wound was more serious than he knew, and this abrupt effort and sudden emotion made his head spin. He felt Defries and Ella catch him, and he knew he was unable to help anyone. They laid him down.

"Free!" he cried out. "We're independent states, and we *will* make it stick! We'll never be anyone's colonists again! We're free, Ella!"

The next morning, with Sutherland slightly feverish, they held a council around the fire. Defries said he intended to go to Albany to bring his family away, in case the British broke through Arnold's frail defenses.

In fact, the fall of Albany seemed only a matter of time, unless some miracle delayed the British advance. If Albany was still in rebel hands when cold weather set in, the enemy would have to withdraw to Montreal and wait until spring to invade again. Right now, however, Albany was a ripe fruit, and Defries thought it safest if their families were elsewhere for the next half year.

Sutherland agreed. He believed there would be a rebel invasion from Fort Pitt toward Detroit next year, and he wanted to join that march. His injuries would prevent his campaigning until spring, and until then his family would be safest in a settlement farther westward, midway between Pitt and the Mohawk Valley.

"Maybe I'll be able to help in one place or the other next year if there's a major Indian outbreak. Meantime I'll heal, and we'll all be together and safe."

Ella said they should buy or rent homes in Pennsylvania, perhaps in the Wyoming Valley; they still had plenty of money. A rebel financier in New York Town owed them for furs he'd bought last year, and he would likely buy the pelts Ella had just shipped to Albany. They could draw on the financier's credit if they needed funds. Furthermore, even though the flight from Oriska had been hasty, they had brought all their hard cash, mostly British sterling. Thus they would not go cold or hungry this winter, and next year would have enough to go either to Albany or Philadelphia to resume their trading company's affairs.

Tom Morely rose up on one elbow and said, "If there's Indian trouble next year, our guns will be welcome anywhere in the northwest. But the Mohawk Valley's where the British're sure to attack. Maybe we should go to the Mohawk and live with those settlers."

Defries said, "I don't know, Tom. Valley Dutch're not given to speaking much English—though you'll like 'em once you get to know 'em. But I think you'll find more empty cabins in Pennsylvania. In the Mohawk, the rebel folks're staying put for now."

Defries said hundreds of loyalist families had abandoned their homes in northeastern Pennsylvania and fled to Niagara—the guards he had slipped were two such Tories—and he added that the rebel settlers in that region all spoke Connecticut, but that was close enough to English. Their elected officials would be able to sell confiscated homes immediately.

"Besides," he added, "women and children and wounded men ain't going to be much help to anyone this fall if the British come through the Mohawk."

So it was decided. They would go westward to the Pennsylvania mountains and sit out winter there. They would regain strength and prepare for the springtime war that undoubtedly would break over them if the rebels held out until then.

After a few days' rest in the Tuscarora village, Defries headed back to the Mohawk River with Onayote; from there he'd go to his family at Albany.

For Sutherland, this reunion with his friend had been all too brief. As he and Defries shook hands, then got into canoes for journeys in opposite directions, they promised one day to be united once more.

They pushed off into lapping, quiet water, and the aching Sutherland lay in the center of an unwieldy elm-bark canoe bought from the Tuscaroras. Benjamin was in the prow, with Punch on his shoulder; Susannah and Heera were next; and behind Sutherland, Ella paddled in the stern. The Greys, the Morelys, and the Websters followed in two other canoes. Far in the distance, Defries's mouth harp could faintly be heard.

Sutherland struck up a cheerful chorus of "Revolutionary Tea," and his family and the others—though Mel, Tom, and James were also hurting—all joined in. For now, the war was far away, and their destination was a tranquil winter haven in the hills. But next spring, come what may, they would rise to fight again.

On a blistering hot August morning, the news that Congress had declared the thirteen colonies independent of Britain came to loyalist Detroit by schooner.

Immediately people gathered in knots and small groups to bombard the crew and passengers with questions. The news was hard to believe, for everywhere the rebels were being defeated. Still, dismay and concern sent folk hurrying through the fort to tell others. One enterprising newcomer from Niagara had brought scores of copies of the revolutionary *Pennsylvania Gazette* to sell on the streets. An astonished Gwen Hardy bought one and rushed back to the hospital.

She dashed past surprised patients and burst into the small operating room Jeremy had recently set up. He was donning a white linen apron for a bloodletting. The patient was waiting nervously on a chair outside the door.

Jeremy laid the apron aside and sat down. As he read the account of the declaration, his hands shook with rising fury. At first he could not believe it possible. But then he realized things had been moving steadily this way all along. He hardly noticed Gwen's excitement as she read over his shoulder. Yes, he thought, he should have expected this. Had not thousands of copies of *Common Sense,* written by the rebel firebrand Thomas Paine, been snapped up by colonial readers? Jeremy had read Paine's "Plain Arguments for Independence" with shocked anger; he knew that even many leading rebels were set against declaring full colonial independence. And what with the rebels' dreadful defeats in Canada, it bewildered Jeremy that Congress would dare declare the colonies free of Britain.

Jeremy read aloud: "'unalienable rights . . . life, liberty, and pursuit of happiness'!" With a scoffing laugh, he said, "Where's the pursuit of happiness, life, or liberty for those honest folk who disagree with rebels? They're thrown into the Simsbury mines in Connecticut and left to rot!"

Gwen noticed their patient was at the door, listening. She asked him to come back tomorrow, and the man, relieved, hurried away. She closed the door and listened to Jeremy read, absorbed by the beauty and eloquence of these words; she thought them so simple, so direct, and yet so brilliantly perfect.

"'. . . whenever any form of government becomes destructive of these ends, it is the right of the people to alter or abolish it.'"

Again Jeremy made a sound of derision, and Gwen was brought back to the present, as from a trance, to hear him say, "Who are the people, then? The bullying rebels, or those who are cowed and driven, lied to and manipulated for the sake of a few wealthy, unprincipled men—"

"No!" Gwen cried. "No, Jeremy, can't you for once put aside your blind hatred and see? This declaration is speaking the truth, explaining what is naturally best for human existence! The people have the sacred right to choose government; kings are not divinely placed over us! It's the right of all Americans, and it's our duty to choose governments that treat us as freemen, not as so much colonial rabble, fit only to fatten the purses of pompous British lords!"

At first Jeremy was startled, then abruptly angered by Gwen's support of the declaration. He flung the pamphlet to the table and glared at her.

"Am I to understand you're a Congress supporter?" he said in disbelief.

"If I were that, and only that, Jeremy, I would not be living out here!" She stared right back at him, filled with both powerful emotion and uncertainty. "I support the cause of my country! The government of Britain and its king do not! We are Americans first, British second! If we were considered by Britons as equals, and had all the rights to which we're entitled as British, I'd oppose Congress! But, Jeremy, can't you see that the only hope for a happy and prosperous America is liberty, separation, independence from British chains? We have to turn our eyes westward, not toward Europe! We're destined to create a whole new people—not British, not French or Negroes or Indians, not colonists, but free Americans!"

She would have said more, but cut herself off when a shadow came over Jeremy's face. He seemed to stare right through her. Gwen moved against him, took his hands in hers, and looked closely at him.

Disappointment was in his voice. "I cannot believe you really mean what you're saying to me. . . ."

He was so upset that he might have raged, shouted, and stormed away, leaving her alone—but he could not. For all the anger and astonishment that swept through Jeremy, there was another emotion gripping him, holding him steady, an emotion that was more powerful than fury, yet harder to understand. His face was mottled with the heat of inner turmoil, but his eyes were touched with love. Jeremy Bently knew at last exactly how he felt about Gwen, but he did not know what to do or say next.

"You," he almost whispered. "A Congress supporter. Gwen, to think that after all this time . . ." He drew away from her and went to the window, to stare out at the confused people swarming in the streets. They were hurriedly reading pamphlets or chattering angrily, none of them sure what it all meant, or where it would lead. Nor did he; not at all.

When he turned to face Gwen, she saw the sorrow and hurt in him.

With great effort, he said softly, "Gwen, I love you."

She wanted to run into his arms, but caught a breath and restrained herself, closing her eyes. A tear escaped and ran down her cheek. She could not hold back her own overwhelming feelings.

Then he was near her, taking her in his arms, gently embracing her with an intimacy she had never felt before. She spoke his name, and found peace, if only for an instant. And so did he. There was nothing else in that moment, nothing but their love.

Jeremy looked down into her eyes. He did not yet kiss her, lest they become lost in a passion they later might blame as being too desperate. How could he dare love her now, in these times? How could he not?

He said, "I want to understand it all."

"And I— Oh, I don't care! I just know I love you, Jeremy."

Her arms went around his neck, and they kissed, softly, gently, passion pouring through them. Suddenly he brought her against himself so fiercely that she gasped with the force of it and held him close with all her might.

"I want you so," she whispered, "but I wasn't sure at all what I felt until now! Until now! How could I have not known?" She gave a laugh and shook her head slowly. "This moment should be joyous, heedless of everything but our love."

"It is!" Jeremy exclaimed, kissing her cheek and forehead. "It is!"

Breathless, she asked, "What . . . is?"

"This moment is joyous!"

"It is!"

"Full of love! Ah, Gwen, you make me feel brought back to life—at last!"

She kissed him, closed her eyes, and said, "It's all mad and foolish, but it can't be any other way! I don't want to let go of you ever again!"

There were voices out in the hospital, people calling to Jeremy to discuss his opinion of the Declaration of Independence. The lovers were rudely wrenched from their intimacy. They looked at each other, searching each other's eyes.

Then Jeremy took Gwen's hand and said, "Come on!" He pulled her toward a back door.

"Where?"

"To the old mill! Come on! I want to change your political—" He stopped short, and she was warmly in his arms. "I want to change your life, Gwen Hardy!"

They kissed quickly, and then rushed out. Running along the promenade inside the fort's palisade, they headed for the water gate and a canoe. Cape scampered out from under the porch and gave a yelp, bounding after them.

In that tumultuous, clamorous fort, they might have gone unnoticed, but there was one person who always took note whenever Gwen and Jeremy were together: Annie Ross stood by the door they had left open in their haste. She was devastated. Annie had been about to enter when she heard them speaking. She had immediately heard too much.

An hour later, the lovers were alone at the millpond, lying in the long grass, hidden from view. Above, clouds drifted peacefully through a blue sky, and swallows flitted and dived, as though celebrating the freedom, the joy this young couple shared at that moment. Soon Gwen lay asleep in Jeremy's arms. He was awake, watching swallows play, observing the clouds. It was as if the clouds were all new, for they had never before been quite so appealing. Cape lay contentedly at their feet.

The weights of war and politics were put away for now, almost forgotten under that summer sky and those lazy clouds. After everything that had gone before, all the heartache, uncertainty, and buried emotions, it was no wonder Jeremy exulted. Tomorrow would bring whatever it must; he would rise above it. This was a new world, a new beginning. When he had to confront the old world, he would do so head-on, knowing that he had almost everything. Almost . . .

"Tell me something," Gwen asked, awakening and snuggling close. Taking a long breath, she asked, "Do you really think all leaders of the rebellion are unworthy hypocrites, cheats, and scoundrels?"

Jeremy sighed with exasperation, for this was the last thing he wanted to think about just then. He pushed her gently back, so she lay on her own left arm, gazing at him with those soft, lovely eyes. She was spent, satisfied with love, but the inner strength, the potent fire that made Gwen Hardy what she was, would not permit her to lapse too far into daydreams—not yet. Jeremy recognized that. A soberness crept over him. It seemed the swallows were only noisy now, and even the wind and clouds were moving too fast, for a storm darkened the western horizon. Cape sat up, as though to hear the reply.

Jeremy pushed up on an elbow. "I thought we'd have today, at least, to court, to make love, but you simply cannot let go of the world, can you?"

She bent to his hand, kissing his fingers. "I can. Forgive me. Never mind." She lay on her back and looked upward; with a moody sigh, she muttered, "Anyway, I know what you'll say."

Though he admired and respected her, appreciating such frankness, Jeremy was annoyed. His troubled heart surged with mixed emotions—all those emotions combining with one greater emotion: a love for Gwen that was strong, complete.

He lay back beside her and, after a pause, said, "If it were easy to sort out the right and wrong of this war, I'd have put on a soldier's tunic by now. In any case, I thought it all could be settled soon. I never thought our people would wage full-scale civil war.

"Listen, Gwen, I don't say British colonial government is better than anything Congress could give us; but the upheaval, the misery Congress has created is bound to grow worse." He shifted to his side and took her hand. "There are thirteen colonies declaring for independence, and each despises the others as much as loyalists despise rebels. What do you think would happen if Britain ever gave up those colonies?

"There will be constant wars—one bloody conflict after the other. At least half the colonies claim the northwest; it would take a miracle to make peace among them in parceling out the wilderness. Already Virginians have fought Pennsylvanians over the Ohio, and Yorkers have fought with Hampshiremen over disputed lands near Lake Champlain."

Gwen squeezed Jeremy's hand. "But there is no other way, Jeremy; we have to find our path. We are a new land, a new nation, and we can't fear what might happen. One thing is very clear: Britain will always keep us down—"

"That's not clear at all!" Jeremy declared loudly, sitting up. "British folk don't tar and feather countrymen who don't agree with them! It's the lawlessness unleashed by Congress that's created America's misery today! Congress has permitted the rule of the strong over the weak! The colonies are now suffering under an unjust tyranny that no amount of idealistic phrases and high hopes will wipe away. Oh, Gwen, let's not talk of this today, because for me this is not a matter of abstract philosophic banter. I lost my wife and my best friend to this lawlessness. My family's divided by it. Sometimes I think you don't understand!"

"Do I not?" she cried sharply and sat up, straightening her dress. "Do I not understand your suffering? Well, Jeremy, I feel your pain, and I have good reason to oppose wealthy loyalists and their government with all my heart, because it was loyalists who destroyed my poor parents. It was the 'better sort of folk'—as loyalists like to call themselves—who cheated and abused my mother and father until they were driven to poverty, shame, imprisonment, and death."

He lay back to take her in his arms and calm her, and she put her head on his chest, managing not to cry. "There are two sides to every war, Jeremy Bently, and my side is as righteous as yours! My side has its good and bad, as does yours—but it's my side that has the true idealism, the inspiration that will make it triumph!"

After a moment, he said grimly, "It's not words or ideals, but deeds that count, and your Congress has caused untold suffering. I oppose it, and I'll fight it if need be."

She ran her fingertips over her lips. "I pray it will never come to that, my love."

He kissed her, and she melted into his enfolding arms. "Gwen," he asked, kissing her, "how can you love such a stodgy, conservative—"

She kissed him hard, and put her hands behind his head, drawing him against her trembling body. "For now," she whispered, kissing him back, "I'll pretend it's all a dream. And in dreams, anything can happen."

# *chapter* 22

## LOYALIST SOLDIER

Nearly everyone was delighted to see Gwen Hardy and Jeremy Bently so much in love—everyone, that is, save Simon Clancy and Annie Ross.

Simon spent a few days stumbling drunk. Then he spent another few days somewhat less drunk, enjoying the company of a lusty French maid. After a few more days, merely not quite sober, but still with the same company, Simon began to accept Gwen's love of Jeremy.

Simon eventually set his course in another direction. At first he made up his mind to sail away to Cathay or Russia next spring, if only the Frenchwoman would go along to keep him company. She refused. Employing her own powers of persuasion, she tried to convince Simon that everything he really desired was right here in the northwest.

As for Annie Ross, she became cold to everyone. With each passing summer day, her unhappiness at losing Jeremy grew more bitter. Gwen had not seemed to be a serious rival; now, unexpectedly, Gwen had won Jeremy. Annie felt the pain excruciatingly deep within. Gwen deserved her affection no longer, was actually an enemy.

Annie was one of the few loyalists in the settlement not in high spirits late that summer. The ineffective Declaration of Independence was forgotten. The repulse of the rebels from Canada had reopened the trade route eastward, and in September the British captured New York Town. George Washington's army had been decimated, and rebels were rethinking the fighting abilities of Redcoats. The confident and numerous rebel amateurs had bravely taken on the largest invasion army ever assembled by Britain and had learned a terrible lesson, being driven across the Jerseys by swift-moving British and German shock troops.

Strategically the defeats were disastrous for the army of Congress. The middle colonies were nearly cut in two; the next step, an invasion from Canada toward Albany, would sever New England from the rest of the colonies. The end of the war seemed simply a matter of time.

It gave Annie Ross no comfort. Instead, she regularly sought arguments with Gwen over the smallest things, even saying her cousin was not carrying her weight in household duties at Valenya, was too full of herself, reigning as a revered "princess of healing" at the hospital, while Annie was compelled to slave thanklessly, doing the work of two women at home. Trying to appease the distraught Annie, Gwen labored to exhaustion at Valenya as well as at the hospital; but her best efforts were of little worth as far as Annie was concerned.

By October, Annie had convinced her father that they should no longer stay at Valenya, in view of the scandal caused by Gwen's open romance with a man living under the same roof. For his shattered daughter's sake, Cole Ross sadly agreed to go. Late that month, Annie, Cole, and Gwen moved into a rented cabin just downriver from the fort.

Perhaps it was for the best this way, Jeremy thought, as he sat in Valenya's quiet, empty common room one windy night. He had tried more than once to soothe Annie's distress, but had failed. She said he was vain to presume she cared one whit about him. Lately, she had even begun to encourage the advances of Lieutenant Mark Davies, Manoth's ally.

Frowning, Jeremy listened to the mournful song of the north wind blowing through the seven standing stones. The German clock ticked loudly, and Cape gazed up from where she lay near the fireside. Jeremy knew it was time to plan a wedding, no matter what difficulties he and Gwen had to work out.

They had not yet made any definite decisions, but it was an unspoken understanding that they would face, together, whatever came their way. They wanted to bring their turbulent emotions under control, and they both hoped Annie would eventually accept their union and wish them well. Also, they were trying to come to terms with their contradictory political beliefs in order to find a meeting place, a compromise from which to begin life as husband and wife.

Their stands on the rebellion were so strongly opposed that both wanted to agree on other points before marrying—where they would live, and what they would do if rebels invaded the northwest in force. But to deal with such cold and painful matters in those first intoxicating weeks of love was impossible. Their passion was so overwhelming that they shut out the rest of the world and hardly noticed the passage of time—save when they were apart.

Thinking about the joy of those past weeks made Jeremy smile, and he got up, going to the spinet. He touched a key, striking a clear, chiming note. This instrument reminded him fondly of his mother and Owen Sutherland. Jeremy wished his relationship with Gwen could be as uncomplicated and as fulfilling.

And why shouldn't it? Their cooperation at the hospital was certainly as happy as ever. When working, they both remained professional, detached; yet when they were alone together, they were blissfully lost in love.

He and Gwen had spent many an afternoon at the old mill, and early mornings often found them galloping over meadows on the bluffs above the straits. In the evenings, they strolled beside the river. Cape, as ever, gamboled merrily at their side wherever they went. In those swiftly passing weeks, the world had been kept out of their relationship. Now the lovers had to come back to reality and make the next step.

Jeremy went to the window, to gaze out at the night. Cape wagged her tail once, anticipating a walk. They went outside into the strong wind, which was refreshing and exhilarating. Soon Jeremy stood near the shore, listening to that wind blow between the standing stones. He breathed deeply, knowing now more than ever that the time had come to ask Gwen's hand.

Life was too uncertain, the world too dangerous a place to waste their chance for happiness. No one could tell when America again would be at peace, so they had to take what they could of love, nurture it, protect it, and allow it to grow stronger, more enduring than hatred.

Late the following afternoon, Jeremy asked Gwen to go with him to the millpond, where they could talk about their future. As they left the hospital, arm in arm, Gwen was half anticipating Jeremy's proposal. With Cape loping on ahead, they huddled together as they hurried along the promenade, against a biting wind sweeping in from the straits.

Near the water gate, a dozen or so soldiers and sailors were shouting and cursing, some of them shaking fists.

"Looks like a brawl," Jeremy said. Seamen and soldiers were always eager to fight, even without reason. Cape hesitated as Jeremy and Gwen came up to her. An old, grizzled trader went stamping past, and Jeremy asked what was the matter.

The fellow gave a snarl and raised a fist. "Damned Arnold's stopped our invasion fleet on Lake Champlain! That's right! With some leaky gunboats and a few cobbled cockleshells, he stopped the Royal Navy! Stopped 'em cold!"

Jeremy was stunned. A setback in the campaign meant the rebels would win time to stockpile arms, reorganize an army, and keep going. "How could they? How?" he cried to the man, who swung around and shouted in reply.

"Don't ask me; I ain't no high-and-mighty officer! But if you want to know what I think, I say Arnold's sold his soul to the devil! He deserves to be burned at the stake, like they did to his kind in the old days!"

Gwen gripped Jeremy's arm, her eyes alight, and he feared that her enthusiasm might be seen by these others. A growing mob was furiously reviling Arnold and the rebels, who had stopped the powerful fleet carrying the British army from Canada to invade Albany.

"A pox on 'em rebels!" the old fellow shrieked. "Ask these Jack Tars here—" He indicated the sailors answering questions from the dismayed Detroiters. "They just came up from Niagary. Won't be no more invasion till next spring! A pox on 'em rebels! They got the devil's own luck!"

Another man yelled, "Sold their souls, they did!"

"Should be strung up!" roared another. "Hangin's too good for devil rebels and their supporters!"

Fierce anger erupted in a din of shouts and whistles. "A pox on rebels! Kill 'em all!"

"Kill the traitors!"

Gwen was trembling, unable to remain there, and Jeremy began to hurry her away from the surly crowd. What would these people do, he wondered, if they knew Gwen's sympathies? He was afraid for her, afraid she might lose her own composure and shout back at someone; but most of all, it hurt to hear those people call for rebel blood, and he knew it also frightened and pained her.

Just then, Jeremy stopped short when he saw a familiar face glaring at them. Lieutenant Mark Davies, twenty feet away, stood fit and splended in his scarlet and white uniform; he was leading a guard detail of Redcoats. Jeremy felt hatred flow from the man, who had a triumphant scowl on his thin face. Davies was looking at Gwen as he moved toward them.

"Hang all rebels!" Davies cried, so loudly that Gwen suddenly saw him staring at her. "Yes, and their sympathizers, too! Hang them all for the low dogs they are!"

Jeremy put himself between Gwen and the approaching officer, confronting the man squarely. Did Davies know about her? How could he, or anyone else, know she supported the rebellion? Impossible! But Jeremy felt the man's evil just then, and a crackling heat between them nearly bursting into violence.

"What do you want, Davies?" Jeremy demanded through the noise of the mob. "Keep back from Mistress Hardy, or I'll call you out!"

The officer stared at Gwen and said with a sneer, "You'll not call me out, Bently, for if you do, I'll expose the treachery of your sweetheart."

Jeremy raged, about to spring; but then he realized what Davies was saying. Somehow the man knew Gwen was not loyal to the king, and he was willing to use that knowledge to hurt her.

Jeremy pulled Gwen away. She was wide-eyed, her face pale but defiant.

"Do or say anything to harm her," Jeremy warned, "and you'll be a dead man, Davies; and when they hang me, I'll come find you in hell!"

Gwen pulled Jeremy's arm. Davies was smiling, hands behind his back. The shouting mob moved away, collecting more loyalists, getting more rowdy.

"Have a care, Bently," Davies hissed. "Don't blame me if everyone is beginning to talk about the disloyalty of your woman; be grateful I don't arrest her now—and you with her!"

Jeremy restrained himself. It would be folly to assault Davies now.

"It's too late to challenge me," the lieutenant declared haughtily. "The damage to Mistress Hardy's character has already been done." He stared at Gwen, his eyes hard and cold. "Would you deny that you are a rebel sympathizer? Everyone's seen how you fawn and coddle these prisoners we bring in."

"Enough!" Jeremy was close to attacking.

With a snort of scorn, Davies casually turned his back, calling to the soldiers, who strolled away with him, following the mob. Did the soldiers, too, know she favored the rebels?

Jeremy was shaking with fury, and as they hurried with Cape from the fort, he asked how Davies could know. Gwen, fighting back tears, shook her head, saying she wanted to get away from the fort.

Soon they were at the millpond, surrounded by a solitary, chilly November scene of grays and dull whites, of bare trees and withered grass. They stood close together, leaning against the willow tree. By now Gwen had finished crying, but sensed the worst was ahead for her.

Jeremy said, "Your true friends will protect you, my darling." He kissed her lightly, and she took a deep breath.

"You must not become involved," Gwen replied. "My life might now be ruined here, but I will not permit you or any of the others to be hurt! I stand my ground! I'll not deny what I know to be right!"

Jeremy was at a loss. He loved her; somehow they would come through the war together. Their future would be happy when all this pain was put behind them.

He said so, then lifted her chin and gazed into those beautiful blue eyes. "Gwen, I want you as my wife."

Gwen's eyes closed. She tried to speak, but her emotions overwhelmed her. Opening her eyes, she took Jeremy's hands, shivering. He moved closer.

"I'll never cause you to suffer, Jeremy! You cannot ask me to marry, not now."

"Gwen!"

"No! Can't you see? We can't marry now . . . not after—"

He kissed her hard, and she embraced him desperately, then more tenderly. "We don't know what will happen. So many of our folk love you—"

"But so many despise all rebels, and once they know, they'll hate me, too, cast me out, threaten me! But I won't let you be destroyed because of me! I won't!"

She moved away, head bowed, to stand in the wind at the edge of the pond. He followed, put his hands on her shoulders.

"Gwen, we'll go away . . . we'll go to the West Indies . . . anywhere you'll be happy."

"And you?" She turned, touching her fingers to his lips. "Where will you be happy, my love? London? Montreal? No; only here. You can do so much good, especially during this war. Jeremy, I'd never be happy unless you were."

"Gwen!" He kissed her again, and held her tightly. "Marry me! Marry me now! I don't care—"

She pushed him away and shook her head, hands still on his chest. "I love you too much! Don't ask me to make you pay the price I'll have to pay!"

"Gwen! I can't go on without you as my wife. I'm asking you to marry me. The rest we'll resolve however we must. As a woman you'll not be imprisoned by the authorities if you give no cause. And I'll protect you—"

"Stop!" she said. "Please, Jeremy, give us both time! Please! Let me think what I have to do...." She moved against him. "But know, my darling, how much I love you!"

Standing in the biting wind, they kissed, and for a moment were one again. Both knew they could not live and work here without being married. They also knew it was too late to stop the tale from spreading. Gwen would be an object of hatred. And whoever befriended her would be hated for sharing her beliefs, or at least for giving comfort to an enemy—an enemy whose cause was stubbornly refusing to be defeated.

Jeremy had no idea what to do next, but he knew he would never let her go.

That night the north wind brought snow to the straits, whistling and swirling around the house at Valenya, and in the morning Jeremy awoke to the storm's gray light. He lay there, thinking about Gwen, about her peril, and how she had refused his proposal. He did not doubt she wanted to marry him, but he knew she would not easily abandon a decision she believed was right. In this case, Gwen would staunchly refuse to involve Jeremy in the trouble that would surely come her way.

In the distance the wind howled through the standing stones, a melancholy echo of his own emotions. Lying there, he heard a banging; a shutter must have come loose in the wind. He ought to get up and latch it before it smashed a pane, but his mind was so distracted that he lay a while longer, Gwen on his mind. It was only when he heard his name called that he realized that someone was knocking at the door—it was Annie!

He leaped out of bed. Drawing on his robe, he hurried to let her in, amazed to think she had crossed the choppy, wind-lashed straits, apparently alone. Annie almost stumbled in, wet and freezing, and Jeremy helped her to the common room, where the stove was still warm.

She was pale, shaking with cold, and looked very distraught. As she sat before the iron stove, rubbing her raw, red hands, Jeremy realized tears were running down her cheeks and that she was having difficulty trying to speak.

"What is it?" he asked, crouching, and taking her icy hands. Her cloak, wet with sleet, fell from her shoulders, and she shivered despite the warmth of the room. When she was slow to reply, Jeremy went on. "Annie, why have you jeopardized your life to come here? Calm yourself, and tell me what's wrong."

"Ah, Jeremy," she sniffed and awkwardly wiped her running nose, her voice wavering. "How could I have been such a witch? I've hurt you and Gwen, but I didn't mean to let it go this far...Oh, Jeremy, please forgive me—"

"Annie! What's happened? Is it Gwen?"

Annie buried her face in her hands. Afraid for Gwen, Jeremy grasped the woman's wrists to get an answer. Annie began to cry and fell forward into his arms.

"She's gone! Gwen went away last night!"

"What?" Jeremy moved Annie back, aghast.

Annie quickly went on. "Last evening, some men...some drunks...came to our house—" She swallowed and tried to steady herself. "They...they shouted things, ugly things, about Gwen, and about you—"

"Who was it? Davies?"

Annie shook her head vigorously. "No! Not him! I don't know who. But there'll be others, and it'll be far worse than I...than I had intended."

"You? It was you who told Davies about Gwen's stand?" Jeremy saw how sorry Annie was, yet he was so furious that he nearly threw her back in the chair as he leaped to his feet. "Where is she? Quick! Tell me! Help me now, Annie!"

"I don't know! After those men came, throwing stones and shouting those foul things at her, she locked herself in her room and would not come out. You see, she knew I was the one—Oh, Jeremy, can't you see? I didn't mean to harm her, or to make her leave us. It all got out of hand...and I don't really know how," she wailed.

"Here, Jeremy, she left you this." Annie gave him a sealed letter. There had been another note, for Annie, forgiving her and telling her not to blame herself for anything.

Jeremy tore open his letter and sat down, trembling with rage and fear. Gwen wrote that she had gone away with friendly Indians, toward winter hunting grounds, where she would have the time to think. She would see to the village's medical requirements until springtime, and could do much good out there—but she did not say where.

> Do not try to follow, and do not worry for my safety, Jeremy, for I am with friends. Also, please understand that I have gone away to give both of us time to think about what we must do, either together or apart.
>
> I love you with all my heart, my dearest friend, and therefore you will comprehend why I cannot marry you now. After all that has happened, I know even more certainly than ever that your life and mine cannot yet become one. If you care for me, Jeremy, let me go, and do not try to change my plans, I beg of you. I shall return in the spring.
>
> Until better times, keep well and think fondly of me, as I shall often think of you.
>
> Gwen

In despair, Jeremy leaned forward, elbows on knees, forehead in his hands. Outside the storm raged even harder. Though Gwen and her companions would not get far that day, they would already be impossible to track. It would take weeks, perhaps months to find her. Furthermore, it was her fervent request that he not pursue her.

With sinking heart, Jeremy realized that he must not go after her. He had to respect her need to be away from him and from the hostility at Detroit. She would come back. By spring she would know what she must do. As for himself, he, too, would step back, to contemplate what had to be done.

Annie's soft voice broke his reverie. "My letter said that she'll write, to assure us she's well. Jeremy, perhaps... perhaps it's best she be somewhere safe."

Jeremy rose and drifted to the window, to gaze out at the sleet blowing gray and dismal over the straits. The storm did not look like it would soon abate; crossing to Fort Detroit just then would be foolhardy.

"Perhaps," he replied quietly. "But we won't know until springtime." He sighed and leaned on the windowsill, forehead against the cold glass.

Annie clucked her tongue and shook her head. "Gwen's so headstrong!" she said. "So very, very stubborn!"

Jeremy closed his eyes. *Yes,* he thought, *she is headstrong. That's one reason I love her so much.*

"It's unbelievable how quickly the balance of power changed over the winter," declared Henry Hamilton one sunny March afternoon, as Jeremy Bently paced back and forth in the officer's headquarters, listening. The officer's tone was matter-of-fact. "I've been informed by my superiors that no fewer than thirty-five French government ships have embarked for America, loaded with munitions, uniforms, food—yes, even with hard cash to support Washington's growing army."

Hamilton was seated at his desk, a pile of dispatches before him. These had just come from Montreal and London with the dismaying news of the rebels' tenacity and their surprising ability to wage war in the jaws of defeat. Jeremy had called on Hamilton to discuss enlarging the hospital, but the news in these dispatches took precedence.

Pacing the room, Jeremy stared moodily at the floor, hands behind his back. Many things were on his mind, including nervous anticipation that Gwen Hardy would soon be returning. By now he knew she had gone with Tamano and Mawak and their families, heading to a distant Chippewa village near Michilimackinac. Despite winter weather, Jeremy and she had exchanged several letters, delivered by trappers and traders. Those letters professed love for each other, yet did nothing to decide their next step.

Also in Jeremy's mind were anxious thoughts of the developing war. Washington's fugitive army had turned at bay and astonishingly defeated government troops at Trenton and Princeton. Then the elusive Virginian had escaped to safe winter quarters in the mountains of New Jersey. As Hamilton had just said, it was not only the incredible rebel victories that were so significant, but also the fact that Washington's army had recovered from its smashing defeat at

New York Town. Now men from every colony flocked to the rebel standards, and the French were blatantly financing and supplying the forces of Congress.

Pausing to face Hamilton, Jeremy said, "How can you remain so calm? If the rebels carry off one more major victory, I fear France will enter the war openly, and that'll prolong the fighting for years!" He began pacing once more.

After gravely considering this, leaning back in his chair, Hamilton replied. "On the other hand, if we soon inflict a telling blow, the French will think twice about risking war with us." He made a clutching motion with one hand. "But we must have that decisive victory, posthaste."

"Take Albany!" Jeremy cried aloud, waving his arms. "What's stopping Burgoyne's regiments in Canada from marching down to Albany, then going right down the Hudson to join the main army in New York?"

Hamilton smiled, taking a dispatch from the pile and handing it to Jeremy. "Here, my friend, is precisely that plan of attack. As you may see for yourself, it is so obvious, and so unstoppable, that there's hardly any need for secrecy. I can confidently say it will make my own operations in the Ohio and Illinois that much easier, if not altogether unnecessary." He went on to say that General John Burgoyne was to advance through the Champlain Valley toward Albany. Another expedition, mainly Tories and Indians, commanded by Lieutenant Colonel Barry St. Leger, would sweep eastward from Niagara along the Mohawk Valley, joining Burgoyne at Albany. "Furthermore," Hamilton said as Jeremy read, "a third attack, from General Howe down at New York Town, will advance up the Hudson simultaneously. I can disclose all this because there will be no effort made to keep it confidential."

Jeremy jubilantly cried that this was the best plan yet to end the war once and for all. In that instant, however, he thought briefly, and with a twinge of regret, about his family—as so often he had thought of them over the winter. He prayed they would not be caught in this powerful vise. Nevertheless, it had to be done, and the rebellion stopped immediately, before the French became full allies of Congress and widened the brutal civil war further.

Hamilton added that Congress must be getting worried about a major Indian campaign opening against the frontiers that season, because many lies had been spread by rebels in European periodicals concerning the management of Indians by the British. He laughed with unconvincing irony as he gave Jeremy a copy of what appeared to be a well-known American newspaper, the *Independent Chronicle* of Boston. Complete with advertising, local news, and even an almanac and weather report, the paper was an artful fraud, printed to be distributed as propaganda. On the top of the first page was a report of rebels capturing a loyalist man carrying bales of human scalps totaling one thousand, on his way to the British governor general at Montreal.

With a mixture of amazement and shocked anger, Jeremy sat down to read this blatant, gruesome lie. How could anyone in America believe this article? It seemed genuine in form and style, but Jeremy knew no such bales had ever been received at Detroit, and could not conceive it to be the case at Montreal: forty-three scalps of Continental soldiers; ninety-eight scalps of farmers, some marked with triumphal designs to indicate whether the victim had stood and fought or had been killed at night; eighty scalps of women; one hundred and ninety-three boys' scalps; two hundred and eleven . . . Jeremy could not finish.

"Why, this is horrible, despicable!" he cried, throwing the newspaper onto the officer's desk. "Bare-faced, cunning lies! What's the meaning of such slander?"

Hamilton explained why rebel propagandists—Benjamin Franklin was suspected—were willing to stoop to such falsehoods: These reports turned the British public against its own army and Parliament, and also served to excite wavering Americans to fight for the rebellion. And Hamilton did not have to tell Jeremy who suffered most from such lies. As the main planner of Indian activity against rebel frontiersmen, Hamilton himself was the one accused of approving wholesale slaughter, of paying handsomely for such bloody trophies.

Even though a rebel invasion of Detroit now seemed unlikely, this year of 1777 had already seen brutal fighting between parties of Indians and whites on the Ohio frontier. Hamilton, Jeremy knew, was doing his best to keep his raiding parties under British command, but with the remarkable stubbornness of the rebels, he had finally been commanded to attack the frontier settlements to force the inhabitants to flee. Pennsylvania, Virginia, and New York would be compelled to send troops to protect their frontiers—troops that could not be spared from other theaters of war.

This spring would see the largest Indian assaults yet begin to take shape, and no one was more worried about the behavior of Indians than Henry Hamilton. After a year of barely holding them in check, Hamilton had to obey orders to send out the northwestern warriors. Other Indians would be employed with Burgoyne's and St. Leger's armies moving toward Albany.

Seeing Hamilton accused of heartlessly unleashing an indiscriminate Indian scourge, Jeremy boiled with resentment. He was groping for something to say to solace the downcast officer when there came a knock at the door. Dawson Merriwether entered, and Jeremy was taken aback to see the normally jovial fellow so changed. Hat in hand, clothes rumpled, and his appearance unusually unkempt, Merriwether sat down between his two friends. He seemed fragile and bent, showing his age.

After a moment, Merriwether drew a shallow breath, turned his hat over and over in his hands, and spoke in a sobbing near-whisper.

"Matilda's gone."

Jeremy started, and Hamilton leaned forward over the desk, concerned for Merriwether. Neither could say anything to soothe their friend.

Hamilton's expression changed from sympathy to one of profound distress as Merriwether slowly told that a letter from Owen Sutherland had related how Manoth had murdered the Lees. Jeremy could hardly bring himself to look at the lieutenant governor, for anguish was painfully evident on the man's flushed face. Word had already come to Detroit that Manoth had been slain in a fight with rebels, but nothing had been reported of the brutal rampage that had preceded the Seneca's death. This letter, relayed by several Indians through the wilderness, told everything Manoth had done.

When Merriwether paused to compose himself, Hamilton hoarsely offered his condolences and said, "To know that Indians who should have been under my control did such a thing... Mr. Merriwether, I truly share your burden, and must... and must accept the responsibility—"

"Please, Your Excellency," Merriwether replied, weakly lifting a hand and dropping it to his lap again. "Please do not blame yourself." The Virginian shook his head and stared at the floor, eyes filled with tears. His shoulders shook with the effort to stop crying. Two years past, his wife had been murdered by mob violence, and now Matilda was dead.

Jeremy, yet unable to speak, abruptly got up and once again began to pace. He was as furious as he was sorry to lose two more dear friends to all this killing. *So much pain! So much hardship!* He had to do whatever he could to stop it. He could remain neutral no longer.

Sadly Merriwether finished his tale. Hamilton again offered his most heartfelt condolences. Then Merriwether took a stained and wrinkled letter from inside his waistcoat and handed it to Jeremy, saying Owen and Ella had sent this one for him.

Jeremy's hands trembled as he accepted the letter. Before he opened it, he faced Hamilton.

"It's my duty... to my country, Your Excellency, to help put an end to all this misery!"

Hamilton watched as Jeremy fingered the letter, then slipped it into a pocket. With great resolve, Jeremy looked directly at the officer before speaking.

"If that commission as surgeon major in the regulars is still available, sir, I'll accept, on the condition that I be permitted to accompany the army advancing from Niagara to Albany."

There was a profound silence in the room. Hamilton's expression was controlled, but he was obviously moved by his friend's offer. Both the lieutenant governor and Merriwether were aware of the turmoil raging inside Jeremy

Bently, and knew this decision meant a tremendous inner struggle had at last been resolved.

Hamilton stood up and offered his hand, saying softly, "It is my honor, sir, to accept your services in the name of our king and country; may our strength and courage be sufficient for the difficult duty that lies before us."

Merriwether, too, gripped Jeremy's hand, and with a tear in his eye he said, "We can't bring back our loved ones, son, but at least by our loyalty to the king we can prevent many others from losing what they hold dear. Let us pray that for them it's not too late."

# PART THREE

# Frontier War

*chapter* **23**

# THE BRITISH ADVANCE

The thaw of 1777 was slow in coming to Detroit. Ice lingered late into April, keeping canoes from coming down from Fort Michilimackinac. Jeremy Bently waited anxiously for Gwen's return, and every day he walked along the straits, peering out at the glossy, buckled ice that refused to let the northern waterways run free.

Eastward, the route across Erie was clear, and the detachment Jeremy had joined would soon depart to join St. Leger's army. But the Detroit River, Lake Saint Clair, and Lake Huron were so locked that the spring canoe brigades carrying furs were already two weeks overdue, still not in sight by the first of May. So he waited, watching the ice shift ever so slowly, ever so reluctantly, as if to torment him.

In the past few weeks, the hospital had taken most of Jeremy's time, for he was preparing friends to manage it as best they could in his absence. These included Lieutenant Lawrence Sennet, who was by now less enthusiastic about amputation; the trader Jean Martine, to handle business affairs; and his daughter, Angélique Levesque, to see that the place always was clean and well-kept. Her husband, Jacques, had recently returned to Detroit to enjoy a brief reunion with his family before he, too, would go out with the army.

Throughout this time Indians were coming in for the campaign, soldiers were preparing to depart, and civilian volunteers were excited that the final blow was about to fall on the rebels who had caused them so much grief and ruin. Detroit would send several hundred men to Fort Niagara to join St. Leger with more hundreds from New York, for the push along the Mohawk Valley. Everyone was eager to get going.

Except Jeremy Bently. He ached to see Gwen first, longed to talk with her about what they would do after the war. He knew she would be very upset that he had chosen to join the army, just as he was sorry she would not put aside her support of Congress. He so much wanted to explain that his motives were in the best interests of all Americans, that the sooner the war was over, the sooner Americans could begin to heal the wounds and rebuild their homeland.

Gradually the ice broke, slipping downriver into Erie in smaller floes. Fur canoes began to arrive from the north, and every morning Jeremy would be on Valenya's landing, Cape at his side, watching. But Gwen did not come in time. At last Jeremy had to depart with a flotilla heading for Niagara. He left a letter for Gwen with Dawson Merriwether, who would keep watch over Valenya while Jeremy was gone.

On that sunny, warm spring morning, Jeremy donned a magnificent new scarlet uniform, with white breeches, black boots, and gold buttons. He was even obliged to wear a military wig, which had two curls, as befitted an officer, rather than the one curl worn by rank and file. He felt especially uncomfortable in the wig, but Annie Ross had admired it, saying how wonderful he looked in his uniform, particularly now that he had shaven his beard. Annie was so impressed that she did not suggest he powder the wig to make it extra white.

Hamilton had not required Jeremy to be in uniform or to change his daily routine in the weeks before the detachment embarked. Now, however, the entire force, armed and equipped, was gathered on shore beneath the fort's palisades, receiving tearful but proud good-byes. Among them, Surgeon Major Jeremy Bently, of the Eighth Regiment, attracted the eye of every woman on the shore. Annie Ross and her father were there, holding Cape on a leash. The dog whined as Jeremy knelt and said good-bye. As he stood and kissed Annie's cheek, she could not hold back tears, yet she said she would tell Gwen how anxiously he had waited for her.

Jeremy took leave of them and climbed into a two-prowed whaleboat. With the crowd on the shore shouting and singing, waving handkerchiefs, hats, and whatever else they could, the expedition pushed off. Jeremy was unexpectedly in company with Lieutenant Mark Davies, who made a point of ignoring him. Jeremy did not care, however; he would later change boats, for it would not do to clash with the officer on this campaign. Jeremy was determined to see it through without unnecessary problems, then resign his commission and return to civilian life.

As an American who had enlisted in a British regular regiment, Jeremy knew he would be the most despised object of rebel scorn. There was nothing a rebel hated more than another American serving in a regular British uniform, as many hundreds were doing. Though nearly twenty regiments of American loyalists had already been raised and equipped, the rebels hated to admit the magnitude of the organized opposition from loyalists. Rebels had taken to calling all enemies British, ignoring the fact that many serving the king were native-born Americans.

Americans, British—the distinctions were often absurd, Jeremy thought as he shifted in his seat near the stern, trying to make himself comfortable in the cramped boat. Why, one of the top British commanders, Sir Henry Clinton, was an American, born in Newfoundland. Other British commanders—Hamilton, Burgoyne, Cornwallis, Gage, Howe—had spent much of their lives soldiering in America. Like thousands of other Redcoats, many ranking officers had American wives and American-born children.

On the other hand, some of the foremost rebel leaders were British-born or were former British officers, including General Horatio Gates, field commander of the northern

army; General Charles Lee, an important subordinate to
Washington; and Richard Montgomery, who had died at
Quebec. Also, Jeremy knew, huge numbers of rebels, like
Owen and Ella Sutherland, had come from Britain.

As the sail of his whaleboat filled with wind and thrust
the sleek craft out into choppy waters, he gazed back upriver
for some sight of Tamano's birch canoe, with the familiar
orange sun painted on its prow. But his last hopes faded as
the riverbanks slid past, a rush of fresh green color, dotted
with purple and yellow flowers. Gradually Fort Detroit passed
out of sight around a bend in the river. Jeremy prayed Gwen
would wait for him, and would understand.

As the boats funneled between a crowd of low islands
with rocky shorelines, the excited, confident fighting men
cried out to one another, and soon many were singing a
lusty new version of an old English song titled "The King's
Hunt."

> The hunt is up, the hunt is up,
> And it is well-nigh day,
> And George our king is gone a-hunting
> To bring his rebel to bay!

The song went on, loud and cheerful, with "George"
being substituted for the original King Harry, and "rebel"
taking the place of deer.

Seated in the bow of Jeremy's whaleboat was Jacques
Levesque, who had beamed to see his friend finally in uniform. For hours the Frenchman sang tune after tune with
the others. The loudest singer of all was the Irishman Simon
Clancy, also in Jeremy's boat, a volunteer boatman for the
coming campaign.

Close by swept a birch canoe full of Ottawas in ceremonial paint and feathers, all chanting a tribal paddling
song, thrusting rapidly, trying to lead the entire flotilla,
heedless of proper military decorum. In the stern of that
canoe was the Sioux Little Hawk, who whooped in excitement as he passed Jeremy, receiving a grin and a touch of
the tricorne in salute.

Jeremy was with many good friends and knew virtually

every white man in the force, as well as those Indians who lived on the straits or visited regularly. He had grown up with most of these men, and most felt as he did: the war must soon be won, whatever it took. Some whites were soldiers in scarlet uniforms, but most were civilians who had managed to dye a hunting shirt green, or else had been fitted out with one of the new green loyalist tunics recently arrived from Montreal. They were a bold and cocky bunch, full of camaraderie and certain they would run the rebels all the way to the sea.

Jeremy still felt strange in his uniform, much of which Annie Ross had sewn. He felt the gold braid, the fine scarlet broadcloth, and touched the glossy black tricorne on his head. For a moment, he wondered how all this had come about.

Taking the letter from his parents out of the medical bag lying near his feet, he read it over for the twentieth time. The letter was full of reassurance that they were well and cared for him. By now he knew every word and was no longer disappointed that they had declined to reveal their precise residence. It was to be expected that they would try to persuade him to abandon Detroit and meet them at Philadelphia or New York, that they would say they were fighting for peace, just as he now was.

But it had taken some time to accept the fact that they would not tell him where they were living. They could not, lest the letter be intercepted and lead to Owen's arrest or death.

Yet such things had to be expected in a time of civil war, when even the closest of friends could be cruelly divided, forced to fight one another in the name of righteousness, in the name of peace.

Benjamin Sutherland felt good, as any boy of twelve would feel, after proving himself an excellent hunter. Throughout the winter and spring in the Wyoming Valley, Benjamin had joined his father on many a hunt into the hills and woods surrounding the two cabins occupied by his family and the others in their party. Since Owen Sutherland had not fully healed from his brutal wound until February, much of the

burden of hunting had rested on Benjamin's shoulders, and
he had done very well indeed.

With his father's advice and guidance, Benjamin had
mastered stalking and tracking skills, learned how to control
his excitement until the best shot was possible, and developed the uncanny knack of anticipating where to find game.
Everyone had depended on him, for Tom and James Morely
were still recuperating, and Jeb Grey and Mel Webster were
inexperienced hunters. Benjamin had kept them all fed that
winter, and now, late in May, he was returning with his
father from another successful hunt. A fat doe was slung
on a pole between them, and a turkey hung over his shoulder.

Sutherland had offered to carry the heavy bird, for he
was as strong as ever by now, but Benjamin had to prove
his own increasing strength. Though the turkey was cum-
bersome, he managed it for miles, and soon they approached
the pretty clearing where the cabins stood.

Walking behind Benjamin, the pole on his shoulder,
Sutherland thought proudly of the lad's accomplishments
that winter. Like Benjamin, everyone else in the group had
labored hard to keep them warm, fed, clad, and protected
throughout the cold months. The weather was balmy now,
the hilly forestlands of the Wyoming Valley bursting with
leaf and blossom. Sutherland no longer had pain at his side,
and the ribs had healed. Now and again breathing still hurt
him, though, especially in raw weather.

Striding along, Sutherland smelled woodsmoke from the
cabins and heard Heera's bark. Overhead, the blue jay Punch
flitted through trees, having accompanied the two hunters
on their three-day journey through the Wyoming Valley.
There were many scattered farms in the region, with large
tracts of land having been cleared during the twenty-five or
more years that whites had dwelt there. The section Sutherland had chosen for their winter quarters was heavily
forested, with only a small plot for a vegetable garden.

The former owners of the homestead had been loyalists
from Connecticut, just starting out in this country. They
had fled to Niagara last year, and soon afterward the Sutherland group had rented the rude log dwellings from the

Whig committee of safety, which was responsible for regional government.

The hunters were nearly at the end of the leafy trail, greeting Heera, who barked and bounded up to welcome them. Sutherland thought with satisfaction of how the rebels had persevered, binding up their wounds and fighting on. And they had emissaries like Benjamin Franklin across the sea, working to arrange alliances and win the financial support Congress needed.

While rebel armies had suffered heavily in the two years of civil war, Congress's privateers were vigorously—and profitably—attacking British and loyalist shipping. Dashing across the seas in sleek, incomparably swift American-built ships, these bold adventurers had cut deeply into the commerce of the empire, capturing vessels from the Caribbean to the South Atlantic. Sutherland thought fondly of Peter Defries, who had sent a letter from Albany early that spring, saying that if it were not for the threat of another British invasion from Canada, he himself would already be on his way southward to become a privateer.

Sutherland grinned to think of Peter and wondered when they would meet again. These cabins in the Wyoming Valley were between the two nearest theaters of war: New York and the Ohio Valley. Sutherland had read accounts of both regions, had spoken with travelers and exchanged letters with friends at Fort Pitt in Philadelphia. Clearly the coming months would decide the war in the north, where Defries would be fighting. At the same time, Britain's Indian allies were breaking out in Kentucky and on the Ohio, driving rebel settlers out by the thousands.

Down in Kentucky, only Boonesborough and Harrodsburg were still occupied by rebels, virtually without women and children, who all had been sent east for safety. Dozens of other frontier communities had been abandoned because of Indian raids since winter. Parties of whites had been ambushed on the Ohio, hunters caught and tortured to death, and isolated settlers were disappearing all the time along the borders of Indian country. But the Wyoming, with its own bloody history of Indian massacre, had been quiet so far.

Over the past months Sutherland and his men had joined with other settlers to patrol Indian trails, search for signs of war parties, and keep watch on the Iroquois, a day's journey to the north. To the southwest, Shawnee, Delaware, and Miami raiders had struck hard at the Ohio country and Kentucky, but northward the Iroquois had been quiet all winter, allowing the Sutherland group to rest, if not to relax.

Giving Heera a playful shove, Sutherland heard the cheerful sound of violins as Sally and Mel played a jig together. It was time for the midday meal, and the work in house, garden, and woods must have come to a halt. Sutherland felt glad to be home, even if these were no more than sorry shacks, compared with Valenya. He and his friends, though they longed to go back to the straits, were making the best of their new quarters. Sally and Tom had been busy keeping bees, and had even made maple sugar that winter. Ella had planted the flower seeds she had bought from a peddler who had passed through selling trinkets and smallgoods early that spring.

As Sutherland and Benjamin came into the clearing, they waved to Lettie, who was boiling clothes in a huge cauldron in the yard. The howling of Sally's son, Timothy Owen Morely, could be heard, a homey though raucous sound.

Sutherland recognized the fiddling tune—"Revolutionary Tea"—and hummed along as he and Benjamin hung the doe from a tree limb. It was time to decide his next direction, before the summer fighting began in earnest: northward to Albany, or westward to Fort Pitt. He knew, by now, the proposed rebel invasion of Detroit from Pitt would not happen that season, for the Indians were too active and Congress could not spare the troops. Every rebel was anxiously watching the British regulars to the north and in New York Town—forty-five thousand in all—and awaiting the inevitable offensive.

"Pa!" As Punch landed on his shoulder, Benjamin raised a hand for Owen to listen. "Is that a jew's harp I hear?"

Indeed it was, and no one could plunk "Revolutionary Tea" quite like Peter Defries. Sutherland whooped and ran toward the cabins. The music came to an abrupt stop, and there was an answering whoop as Defries bounded around the corner to hug Sutherland, lifting him off the ground.

They exchanged hearty greetings as their friends gathered round to welcome Owen and Benjamin back from the hunt. Sutherland asked why Defries was not with Arnold up on Champlain.

"He doesn't have enough rum. Anyway, he's asked me to serve in the Mohawk Valley and in Iroquois country," Defries went on, as they all walked toward stools and chairs set out in the clearing. Ella was carrying Timothy, who had stopped crying, and Hickory came over with Susannah, who had been taking a lesson in the Oneida language.

Defries told Sutherland about the expected invasion by St. Leger—"Sillinger," he pronounced the name—leading British, loyalists, and Indians through the Mohawk Valley. The Albany Dutchman said the Iroquois League had been torn apart by the civil war, and the Oneidas and Tuscaroras were ready with three hundred warriors to fight on the rebel side.

"But our spies say Sillinger'll have at least a thousand Injuns, lots of 'em from Detroit. With Sillinger's thousand regulars, Tories, and Hessians, the Continental troops we got at Stanwix ain't enough to stop 'em."

Fort Stanwix had been strengthened and, with nine hundred defenders, was a stout place now; but if the enemy surrounded the post, it could be starved out, for most of the Continental troops were north of Albany, waiting for Burgoyne.

"When Sillinger moves, it's up to the Mohawk Valley farmers to muster their militia and help the troops at Stanwix," Defries said, as Sutherland accepted a mug of spruce beer from Ella, who stood at her husband's side, listening. "They could use a scout if you got nothing better to do this summer."

Sutherland glanced at Ella, whose expression was impassive. She shifted the baby to her other arm, saying nothing. Yet he knew she regretted his having to go again. Drinking some beer, Sutherland said to Defries it was important he stay with his family lest the Indians break out into the Wyoming Valley. But before he finished speaking, Ella touched his arm.

"If the Mohawk Valley is lost to the rebellion," she said calmly, "then we in the Wyoming will surely be attacked next. I know what must be done, husband." He put his hand on hers.

Defries said slowly, "There's something else you should know." Thinking a moment, he went on, eyes narrowing, one big hand in a fist on his knee. "Bradford Cullen's up to something; don't know what exactly, but he's moved his whole family, kit and caboodle, out to the Mohawk Valley—not the safest place for a rich rebel to settle down."

It was one thing for struggling farmers to hang on, tooth and nail, to their Mohawk Valley homesteads in the face of Indian danger, but there was no apparent reason a wealthy man like Cullen should place himself in such a precarious position. Defries said Cullen had bought one of the finest Tory homes in all the valley and now lived exposed to the imminent invasion.

Scratching his jaw, Defries said, "If anyone was to ask me, I'd reckon Cullen was getting in good position to bolt to the other side."

Sutherland agreed. "And to bolt before all the other secret Tories jump on the wagon; Cullen wants to declare himself loyal before it's too late to be recognized as a man who was loyal before the British began to win the war."

Sutherland turned to his wife. "I'll be back by autumn, Ella." She said nothing, but handed Tim to Sally. Then Owen gripped Ella's hand and, looking around at the other men, said, "I think it best you all stay here to protect our folk." They concurred, and he thanked them.

Then James Morely, who still limped from the bullet that had broken his hip, spoke up: "Before next winter, friends, I mean to travel to Philadelphia to sound things out. I think the Frontier Company should engage directly in foreign trade."

There was a muttering of surprise and excitement as James explained that he believed the partners should invest their funds in foreign commerce. Direct trade without British middlemen would be an entirely new proposition, a field wide open to Americans, who hitherto had been forced to trade only with British empire ports. The others heartily endorsed James's ideas. Only Susannah was silent at the news that James was to leave them.

Defries cried that they should also back and outfit a good privateer. "If we did it right," he said, slapping James on the back, "we could make a fortune in the Caribbean trade, just by loading up with papaya gin!"

Fort Oswego, on the southern shore of Lake Ontario, was a traditional meeting place for whites the key Indian tribes living along the northerly routes from New York into the northwest. For decades Indian councils here had announced British policies.

This summer, Oswego again was crowded. The broad and spacious vale between two grassy, fortified knolls was mobbed with tents and Indian lodges, while above on the high ground the Union Jack flew over freshly reinforced earthworks and new gun batteries.

The camp was dusty and dirty, and a raucous din arose from restless drunken Indians, bitter drunken loyalists, and sullen drunken French boatmen. By now, they all would rather be somewhere other than with this stalled, sluggish military gathering.

Jeremy Bently was quartered in a large tent on the weed-grown parade ground of a ruined fort that had not been used since the French and Indian wars. He was hot and bored, though they were all fed well enough, and able to come and go quite freely in boating trips on Lake Ontario. Twice already Jeremy traveled to the islands where Weston had been scalped. Jeremy had sought the officer's missing journal—which he hoped might have been discovered by a French or Indian resident—but without success.

By early July of 1777, the mixed, polyglot army being collected at Oswego represented all the various folk of the northwest, New York Province, and Canada. Their leader, Lieutenant Colonel Barry St. Leger, ranking officer of the British Thirty-fourth Regiment, was a veteran of twenty years' service in the eastern colonies. This was his first independent command, so it was understandable that he was slow and careful in planning the advance toward Stanwix, fifty miles to the east. St. Leger had no experience in handling the mercurial Indian warriors, who required countless gifts and long speeches to humor them, and who ate enormous quantities of government food—so much that the army could barely supply them. Jeremy had watched St. Leger awkwardly trying to please the Indians, and it was plain he was ill-prepared to accept or deal with the temperaments of his half-naked allies. Though St. Leger was generous enough, showering the tribes with trinkets, ammunition, and medals, Jeremy remained doubtful that the Indians would be dependable in a pitched battle. Joseph Brant and his Mohawks could be counted on, as usual, but the others included too many brash, boasting young men eager for glory but unused to war. These too often were troublemakers and thieves, dangerous to everyone when drunk and surly when sober. Recently St. Leger had tried to set off eastward for a new staging area, and after making what he thought was a stirring speech to excite the warriors, he had given them each a generous gift: a quart of rum.

The Indians had immediately fallen drunk, a thousand at once, and for days they had refused to march. Plans were delayed, troops movements changed, but finally the force of two thousand was preparing to move. Then came exciting news of General Burgoyne having easily taken Fort Ticonderoga up on Champlain, and this gave everyone renewed heart. It was expected that by September the two armies would meet in Albany, joining Howe's force advancing up the Hudson. Thirty thousand regular and loyalist troops would mass at the confluence of the Hudson and Mohawk rivers, ready to continue their conquest, with no rebel force anywhere strong enough to stop them. Jeremy had no doubt that the last days of the rebellion were at hand.

Such high hopes helped Jeremy to endure these dog days in camp, a time of very hard and tedious work for him. There was plenty to keep a physician busy, tending the ills of a two-thousand-man-army made up of such different and often hostile men.

During this muggy, hot summer, he had written two more impassioned letters to Gwen and sent them to Detroit, but no answer had come. That he did not hear from her was frustrating and distracting, adding to his worries. He had learned Gwen had been in Detroit by May, for a letter from Dawson Merriwether had assured him she was well, though exceedingly downcast. By now, though, Jeremy had no idea even if she was still at Detroit.

Jeremy had other matters on his mind, such as the health of the men in this camp, many of whom were close friends. Sickness was always a threat to a military campaign, and Jeremy was ever active in seeing to it that the Detroit force kept their bivouac area clean, free of filth or garbage. He also insisted they drink only fresh stream water. Overall, his companions were among the healthiest in all the army, and they cheerfully responded to his demand for cleanliness. The only person not interested in Jeremy's efforts was Simon Clancy, who for some unknown reason spent most of his days down in an encampment of civilian camp followers, who dwelt in tents near the lakeshore.

There were women with this party, the wives, daughters, and sweethearts of soldiers and volunteers, so Jeremy understood that the genial Irishman naturally would prefer the company of females, a number of whom were without men for one reason or another. Yet it troubled Jeremy that Clancy had become so abruptly distant from the friends with whom he had journeyed east. Simon seldom shared mess with Jeremy's detachment and apparently had lost interest in doing anything at all with the volunteers. He did not go boating, play at ball games or other competitions, and even seldom drank with his mates. All Simon did with the others was to sleep in his assigned tent. Jeremy did not much approve of Clancy's behavior, but did wonder about it from time to time.

One Sunday afternoon, after being six weeks at Oswego, Jeremy lay on a cot in his tent, the sun beating down. He was half asleep when there came a tapping on his tent pole. It was Little Hawk, one of the few Indians who did not drink, and, as ever, a close confidant of Jeremy's. He was modestly dressed, without war paint or battle gear, and entered to sit on a cot. Jeremy sat up, and they exchanged greetings, but he sensed some discomfort about the Sioux.

Little Hawk wasted no time in handing over a sealed letter, saying in Chippewa, "It was given to me by one who

said it was given to him by another, who said . . . and so
on. I don't know where it first began its journey, but I can
tell you it's from Gwen Hardy."

Thrilled and surprised, Jeremy tore open the seal. There
was no address, no date:

My dearest Jeremy,
    After all this time, I am not to be forgiven for not
writing to you and telling you my heart, but as you
can imagine, there has been a deep sorrow within me
ever since I learned you were with the British army . . .

Jeremy read on quickly, and Little Hawk left the tent
without making a sound. The letter poured out Gwen's
disappointment that Jeremy had volunteered to serve the
Redcoats, but it sent her prayers for his safety. Gwen made
it clear that their relationship was impossible now because
he was in a British uniform. Jeremy was shaken and sorely
hurt. He read on.

    Perhaps I am not strong enough, or perhaps the
events of our times are too powerful for both of us,
but when all is said and done, it is necessary we bid
each other farewell. Perhaps if you had been there to
meet me at Detroit, you might have persuaded me
otherwise, but after searching the depths of my soul,
I find that the answer is always the same. We cannot
build where there is no foundation, no cornerstone
save uncertainty and enmity. For your own sake, dearest Jeremy, go on and forget the sorrow, but please
never forget, as I never can, the brief, if dreamlike,
joy we once shared.

                        Gwen

When the army marched that month, Jeremy was a dark
and brooding man. During the hard struggle toward Stanwix, the dense wilderness of Iroquois country held no obstacle too difficult for him. He moved hospital tents, loads
of baggage, and assistants up rivers, over hills, and through
dank swamps with a relentless, driving resolve. St. Leger

himself often commented on the hospital corps and how it was a mighty example to the rest of the army. Even the hardy German artillerymen pushed themselves to greater exertion to prove they could travel as well and as efficiently as the grim Dr. Bently's medical unit.

Jeremy had not yet given up ever finding Gwen again. He still had the hope that when the rebellion was defeated this autumn, their wounds would heal, and together they would remake their lives back in the northwest. The balm of their powerful love would be more than enough—love and hard work. First war, then peace, then renewal of his relationship with Gwen Hardy.

# chapter 24

# THE CAPTIVE

So the rebels have made themselves a new flag, thought Jeremy Bently as he stood by the freshly hayed yellow fields. He watched the red, white, and blue standard ascend its flagpole above Fort Stanwix. It was dawn on the fifth of August, a Tuesday, two days after the arrival of St. Leger's army at the rebel post.

There had been little rebel resistance so far, but Stanwix held a garrison of nearly nine hundred regulars, and the walls were far stouter than anticipated. The fort appeared a squat, hulking mass, its ramparts extending a hundred yards on a side, with bastions at each corner.

Jeremy was quartered south of the fort, his three hospital tents pitched on the western bank of the Mohawk, where the river turned sharply northeastward, flowing almost under the earthen bastions of Fort Stanwix. He was in an encampment of three hundred loyalist volunteers, most of them from the Mohawk Valley, and many related to rebel militiamen who were said to be mustering downriver, preparing to march and attempt to lift the siege. Jeremy's camp was a neat arrangement of thirty tents set on both sides of the rutted Albany road, which ran down to the Oneida village of Oriska a few miles distant. There the road crossed the river at a ford, then proceeded through the valley for more than a hundred miles to Albany.

In company with Jeremy's group of loyalists were a few hundred Indians from the northwest, and another force of Indians—mainly Iroquois—was camped across the river, in the bulge of the Mohawk's eastward bend. The main body of St. Leger's army, including the British and German regulars and most of the artillery, was on the far side of the besieged fort. That was just fine with Jeremy, for it meant he would not have to observe the strict deportment called for when among regulars, nor would he have to share mess with Lieutenant Mark Davies.

As Jeremy stared through the glaring sunlight of what would be yet another hot day, he was joined by Simon Clancy and Jacques Levesque. They stood in silence, listening to the rattle of snare drums and the whistle of fifes from inside the fort.

"They're proud of that flag," Clancy said, his comment followed by a steady bang of rebel cannon fired in salute. "We took a prisoner yesterday who said we'd soon see the new flag of the United States of America, according to what the high-and-mighty Continental Congress decreed the official pattern should be."

"It is not bad," replied Levesque, rubbing his beard and nodding at the standard. It had thirteen red and white stripes, and a dark blue field in the upper corner with a circle of white stars. "They must be proud indeed to waste powder saluting it like that; but it will not fly for long."

The three of them were already sweating, their throats parched, for the heat was stifling. It had not rained in weeks, and drought had baked the ground until it cracked. The air was humid, the sky dull, yet it would not rain.

Jacques Levesque was acting as St. Leger's premier scout, and often gave his friends privileged information. This morning he said St. Leger expected the fort to hold out no more than a few days.

"They've already declined twice to surrender," Jeremy said. "What makes him so sure of a quick capitulation? And what about the valley's rebel militia on its way? I've heard there are eight hundred or more of them."

As the salutes ended in the fort, Levesque, his voice suddenly hard, said that the Indians and local Tories would ambush the rebel militia the very next day.

"They'll be snared near the ford at Oriska, and we'll send them packing—them that live." Levesque looked around the camp at the loyalist troops, who were seeing to weapons, bundling private possessions for storage, and packing food for a couple of days' fighting. "There is a hatred between our men and the rebel militia that is worse than the French have for the English; never have I seen anything like this before. I have heard stories from these men, how they have been run out, ruined, friends and family jailed or executed on the spot. . . ."

Clancy concurred that he was sure the loyal troops and Indians would do their worst on the approaching militiamen, most of whom were former neighbors of the loyalist troops from this valley. And many of these former neighbors had engaged in bloody feuds for years before the war. With so much hatred on both sides, it promised to be a hard battle.

All about the camp the Indians were also preparing, painting themselves for what Jacques said would be a large-scale ambush. Hand mirrors flickered in the low sunlight. Vermilion paint laid on beside black and white stripes turned already grim-looking warriors into images of devils. Even the handsome Sioux Little Hawk, who saw Jeremy watching his artistry, seemed incredibly ugly as he posed and grimaced in his mirror. As he hesitated, red fingers near one cheek, and nodded to Jeremy, his hideous face became transformed momentarily into the face of a clown, flashing a broad and easy grin.

Then there came the dull roar of artillery from St. Leger's encampment beyond the fort. Mortar shells whistled down into Stanwix, exploding with distant thuds, kicking up dirt on the ten-foot-thick earthen walls bolstered by logs. Loyalist and Indian sharpshooters climbed trees and began to open fire on the defenders. Fervor stirred the blood of the Indians, who began to whoop and chant, dancing and brandishing weapons, playing at war with one another, warming up for the real war to come.

St. Leger now had opened the killing part of the siege,

and his guns played steadily on Stanwix, without much being done in reply. From the start, Jeremy could see that the British guns had little real effect on the outpost, which was very solid and could scarcely be damaged by cannon fire. It was too strong for a frontal attack; the only alternative was to starve out the defenders, or terrify them with the declaration that they were doomed to surrender sooner or later. Levesque had told Jeremy that St. Leger's first requests for surrender had warned the defenders that the Indians might break loose and rampage out of control in a bloody rush down the valley. Still the rebel commander had refused to give in.

Levesque said grimly, "The loyalists still living in the valley are ready to rise, and when we take Stanwix, they will get their arms and join us."

Jeremy said he thought most of the loyalists had fled the Mohawk months ago. Levesque replied that there were still hundreds who were angered by rebel oppression.

"And there are a few others who have recently moved into the valley because they want to be close to our army and join us as soon as they can." He spat and ground the spittle into the dust. "Some of those so-called loyalists I would rather not have on my side! Pah! You know one— Bradford Cullen!"

Jeremy was disgusted to hear Levesque say there was a high-level British plan to get Cullen behind the loyalist lines before long. Levesque was to meet him in the Mohawk Valley and spirit him and his family westward past the rebels. Once Albany fell, Cullen would surface as a leading loyalist ready to take the reins of government.

"Cullen has money," Levesque remarked, cradling his rifle as he prepared to go. "Our side needs money, so I have been ordered to guide him to safety." As he left he called back, "If I knew where Owen Sutherland was right now, I might forget my orders and help my old friend catch a turncoat. Bradford Cullen! Loyal? Pah! He is loyal only to himself, and now he sees the end is near for rebels, so he is making a slippery change!"

When Levesque had gone, Clancy turned to Jeremy, saying he would go with the loyalists on the ambush. Then

he handed over a letter, asking that it be opened only if he
did not return, or was too badly wounded to speak.

The Irishman was not apprehensive, but his eyes were
troubled as he smiled. "You'd not forgive me, and I'd not
rest in peace if you didn't know what's in this letter." Then
he shook hands, clapped Jeremy on the shoulder, and went
off with Levesque. The advance detachment would be followed that night by the other Indians and most of the Mohawk Valley loyalists. The others remained in camp during
the day to keep the rebels in Stanwix from realizing that so
many men had left. It was risky military practice to split
one's force, as St. Leger was doing, and to allow the enemy
to see an encampment left virtually unprotected.

That evening the Continental flag over the fort was lowered to the rattle of snares, the boom of cannon, and the
blare of what sounded like a regimental band. Jeremy came
out of the hospital tent and stood in the gathering twilight,
surrounded by moving shadows and fireflies. Silently, the
men were now departing for the ambush. It was as though
the camp were haunted by a host of specters.

Jeremy was smoking a pipe, and as men he knew slipped
past his tent, he wished them luck. In reply they made
comments about the heat or mosquitoes, or told him to sleep
well because tomorrow he would be busy. The campfires
in sight of the fort were kept burning, but only a dozen
sentries were left behind, to guard tents filled with valuables,
clothes, and possessions.

In a clutter of lean-tos and tents near the river, where
the women and black slaves were living, it was as busy and
noisy as ever. Observing the place before going back inside
his candle-lit tent, Jeremy felt the urge to go down there
for a stroll. He wanted company, and the main camp was
deserted and lonely.

Instead, he put out his pipe and went to bed, knowing
that there would certainly be much work for him and his
staff of twelve the next day.

That hot night, as he tried to sleep on his cot, Jeremy
thought of those strong young fellows now slipping along
forest trails toward the battle who would be dead or maimed

by this time tomorrow. As for the rebels, it would unfortunately be even worse.

The next morning was hotter still. Jeremy stood watching the Union Jack being raised and saluted over in St. Leger's camp. It was defiantly answered by the rebel stars and stripes going up. The enemy band played and their cannon saluted, despite a steady bombardment that began from the British mortars. As the morning wore on, Jeremy would have been languid, bored by that sultry, mosquito-plagued heat, but for knowing that at this very moment men were fighting hand-to-hand a few miles away.

The sweltering morning dragged by in that empty encampment, where only a sentry or two and occasional women from the camp followers were to be seen. Even the desultory British cannonade fell silent, as if St. Leger assumed that the imminent defeat of the approaching rebel militia would force the fort's surrender without further expenditure of powder and shot.

At noon, Jeremy was at the small desk in his tent, writing in his diary. As always, he thought of Richard Weston and wondered what his dying friend had been trying to tell him. But it was no use; Weston's journal probably would never be found.

Finished, Jeremy closed the book and went outside, into the heat. To his surprise, the sky in the west was incredibly black; great storm clouds towered high on the horizon, racing toward the camp. Watching with fascination, Jeremy absently nodded to three young women camp followers who walked quickly past, heading for the commissary tent near the edge of the hayfield. They were nervous about the weather, and two of them greeted him with warnings that he would get wet if he stood there much longer. The third woman, whose face was hidden by a hood, softly urged her friends to hurry, and they scampered away, leaving Jeremy gazing at the darkening sky.

With astonishing speed the clouds came over, and the wind suddenly picked up, bellying the canvas of the tents, which strained and pulled on their shrouds. They were clearly

in for a fierce blow. As he hurried into his own tent, rain
spattered noisily on the canvas. At the last moment he decided to take a look outside to check whether anything
should be brought under cover. A blast of lightning met
him, and it was suddenly as if night had fallen. Horses
whinnied in fright, and the wind gusted hard, knocking over
a plank table near the commissary tent and even sending
Jeremy off-balance.

As he struggled to keep his feet, other people shouted
and ran for shelter. Everyone was drenched in seconds, and
the rain pounded the earth as if the sky had opened. As
Jeremy gathered up some kindling and tossed it into an
empty tent for the evening's cook fire, he nearly bumped
into the three women, who were hurrying back through the
encampment.

The rain was so hard that it blinded them, and Jeremy
called out as the first two hurried by, saying they should
come inside. But they did not hear him, for lightning struck
on a hemlock with a deafening crack and splintered the
treetop. Gasping in fright, the pair scampered away. The
third woman, her head covered by the hood of her cape,
hesitated a moment. Then the lightning blasted again, and
she began to run, only to trip over Jeremy's tent stakes.

She went down hard, and he dashed out to help her up.
Struggling in the slippery mud, he lifted her to her feet,
asking whether she was all right. The woman said nothing,
but nodded, trying to pull away from him. Her face remained
concealed until, at the next flash of lightning, her hood fell
away. Jeremy was staring at Gwen Hardy.

Her head running with rainwater, she stared back at him;
both were unable to speak or to move. Thunder boomed
fiercely, and rain pounded them. Without a word, they were
in each other's arms, holding on with all their might.

"It was the only way I knew to get back to rebel country,"
Gwen said, as she sat forlornly on Jeremy's cot, her clothes
soaked, hair stringy and hanging over her shoulders. Jeremy
was standing at the tent flap, gloomily leaning on the pole,
listening. "I know it's dangerous, but I could stand Detroit
no longer—without you—and I made up my mind to get

back to my home north of New York Town before it falls to the . . ." Her voice was weak as she said, ". . . the enemy."

It had been an hour since the storm began, and rain still poured. During that hour, Gwen had explained how she had been so distraught at his joining the army that she had left Detroit and come eastward. At Fort Niagara, she had caught up with the camp followers of St. Leger's army, intending to travel with them and take the first chance to slip away and get back to her former home, where there were relatives to aid her. She said Simon Clancy had helped her after she met him in Oswego—she having arrived there on the heels of Jeremy's detachment from Detroit.

"Simon was kind enough to keep my secret from you and from the others in my group; to them he pretended I was . . . his woman."

Jeremy looked around sharply at that but said nothing; as far as he knew, the Irishman had slept with the soldiers every night.

As if in answer to an unspoken question, Gwen said softly, hardly audible over the pounding rain, "Simon's like a brother, Jeremy. No more." She looked down at her hands in her lap. "After what you and I shared, how could he be anything else?"

Then Jeremy was kneeling beside her, hands on her shoulders. He had the urge to kiss her, but restrained himself, because it was all too confused.

He asked, "Why didn't you stay and wait for me to come back to Detroit?"

"You know why," she replied, almost coldly, though her lower lip trembled. She looked away. "Please don't ask again."

He got up. "All right." Going once more to the tent flap, he half noticed that the rain was letting up. "I'll not ask you again." Then he whirled. "But, Gwen, if we had anything at all worth remembering—"

"Oh, Jeremy! We did!" She almost stood, but sat back and shook her head, then stared blankly at the ground.

He said, almost breathlessly, "Then promise me you'll at least let me watch out for you until this campaign's over."

She nearly shouted, "Jeremy, I won't stay with your army

all the way to Albany! I have to get away before then! Can't
you see I don't want to watch what might befall my people?
I've got my pride, too!"

That hurt him, but he could not insist. After a moment,
he won her promise to remain with the army until she was
safe from being caught between Indians and rebels. Jeremy
would then help her flee southward toward New York Town.

"Ah, Gwen," he said, bending over to take her hands as
she looked up at him with those lovely blue eyes. "Whatever
you want, I'll do for you."

She rose, hands on his chest, fingers touching the scarlet
tunic. "You'll not give up this uniform."

Like a dagger, he felt that in his heart. He sighed, lips
tight. Gravely, he said, "I've given my word, and will not
be released from it until I see this campaign through; but if
you'll give up openly supporting your cause, perhaps we
can try again; perhaps in the Illinois, where you're not
known and the war is not so close . . ."

She was looking away even before he finished. She drew
an unsteady breath and said quietly, "None of it is simple."
Then she looked at him, and the passion between them was
so strong that they hardly heard the three successive cannon
shots from the fort. Gwen moved against Jeremy, lips close
to his. "Nothing is simple, Jeremy; nothing but . . . this . . ."

They kissed, and in that moment the memory of blissful
days in autumn, days when they had discovered their love,
swept over them. In that moment they were no longer sad,
no longer angry, but lost in love—a love transcending all
else. Their love could be cut in two and separated, with
miles and politics between them, but could not be overcome
by their world's madness, nor stilled by cool reason and
practical sense.

They held each other close, never wanting to let go, yet
knowing they must soon part. The rain had stopped, and
they felt a cool breeze waft past, as if the world had been
refreshed and soothed by the storm.

She said with a sigh, "How I ached all these weeks,
seeing you from a distance; yes, every day I saw you, though
I thought at first it was only by chance." She gave a laugh

and put her head against his chest, and he stroked her hair. "Not by chance at all, for I wanted to see you, to touch you once more."

After a brief time of silence, Jeremy became conscious of voices outside and the sound of many footsteps running by. He tensed; something was wrong in the camp, but before he could move there came the triple shrill of a military whistle. Roughly releasing the startled Gwen, he rushed to the tent flap, throwing it open. Suddenly a bayonet flashed before his face, and he ducked back just in time. There was a shout of anger, and two burly Continentals in blue uniforms charged into the tent, cursing, and driving Jeremy backward as Gwen sprang up and screamed in fright.

Jeremy's sword hung at the rear of the tent, and he went for it as the Continentals shouted, "Surrender or die!"

As Jeremy reached for the weapon, one of the soldiers lunged forward, stabbing with the bayonet, narrowly slicing through his tunic. His attempt for the sword was nearly fatal, but the rebels were blocked by Gwen, who shrieked for them to stop. Almost at the same instant she threw herself at Jeremy before he tried again for his sword.

The rebels were wild with excitement. "Go on!" one yelled, jabbing his bayonet at Jeremy. "Get your steel! Give me a good reason to stick you!"

The other man menaced with a growl, "Don't need a reason. I'll kill him myself."

Just then more blue-clad soldiers barged in, halting the confrontation. Holding Jeremy at bay, a lieutenant quickly searched for documents or other valuable information. Jeremy boiled with anger as Gwen kept hold of his arm.

He heard the rush and shouts of rebels dashing through the camp. A few scattered shots sounded, but there was hardly anyone left behind to resist.

The daring sortie of more than two hundred volunteers from Fort Stanwix had happened so fast and with such precision that Barry St. Leger in the main British encampment could do nothing about it. While St. Leger organized a futile counterattack that was driven back and stalled by the rebels,

Continentals plundered the loyalist and Indian encampment, taking much booty but finding few prisoners, for everyone else had escaped or was still fighting at the Oriskany ford.

Jeremy Bently was trussed, hands behind his back, and led away. Gwen stayed at his side, frantic and afraid, and was allowed to come along, for she declared she was his woman. As wagonload after wagonload of captured gear, food, and personal possessions rumbled away, the couple were hurried to the fort. Even before Jeremy and Gwen reached the drawbridge, five captured battle flags from the loyalist encampment had been run up the staff—beneath the Continental flag, which fluttered proudly above them.

Gwen stayed with Jeremy the whole way, and both of them were treated politely by the rugged, lean commander of the assault—Lieutenant Colonel Marinus Willet, a hawk-faced Long Islander of middle age, with cool blue eyes and a quick, decisive manner. Learning Jeremy was a physician, Willet had seen to it that his medical equipment was kept intact and taken for storage to the fort.

At the last moment on the drawbridge, just before they entered the gate, Willet stopped Gwen and said in a kindly, quiet voice, "It may be, my lady, that you'll be safer if you remain without the walls, in company with your own people; I cannot promise safety if St. Leger should overpower us and allows his redskins free reign."

Jeremy agreed, urging Gwen to depart while she had the chance. Willet offered her an escort back to the loyalists under a flag of truce, but Gwen did not waste a moment making her decision.

"I'll stay."

She was gazing at Jeremy as she said this. Suddenly there came a whistling and the shout of "Mortar!" They all ducked low as British shells began to fall among the column of troops withdrawing from the sortie. Jeremy and Gwen quickly followed Willet into the fort, which was a simple, cramped affair, with log barracks buildings, shingled roofs, a small parade ground, and thick earthen walls with openings for cannon to fire out.

Immediately, as Willet entered, there arose a mighty cheering from the mob of Continentals and civilians, who

doffed hats, shook muskets, and shouted their compliments
to the officer and his returning, jubilant men. Some folk
jeered at Jeremy, others simply stared in curiosity. A few
insulted Gwen, but she lifted her head, refusing to respond
or show the slightest fear.

The couple were led away to the tiny headquarters of the
fort's young commandant, Colonel Peter Gansevoort, a fair-
complexioned, pleasant-looking fellow. He was the model
of a correct Albany country gentleman, both polite and
considerate from the first, personally untying his prisoner's
hands. He offered chairs to Jeremy and Gwen, and sat down
himself behind an uncluttered desk; then, quickly but politely, he questioned Jeremy about his background and role
with the expedition. All the while, Willet stood off to the
left.

Seemingly satisfied with Jeremy's curt answers, Gansevoort said he would be confined in a small room now
used by two ensigns of a Continental regiment. It was not
much, but better than most officers in the fort could boast.

"You see, sir," Gansevoort said with a smile, "we Americans can be just as accommodating to British prisoners of
war as any British officer would be to a captured gentleman;
I hope one day you'll return to your homeland with a kind
word for American officers and their courtesy."

Jeremy glanced at Gwen before saying, "I'm sure before
this unfortunate conflict is over there'll be many a Briton
with new respect for the American fighting man, Colonel;
as for myself, I've always had such respect, for I'm an
American myself."

Gansevoort's eyes widened and he stood up immediately,
face reddening. The older Willet was unperturbed, but Gansevoort became agitated, almost furious. "A loyalist! In that
case, sir, you'll have no lesson in American courtesy, for
I have none to waste on traitors such as you!"

Jeremy also stood up, fists clenched, much to Gwen's
anxiety. "I ask nothing from you, for nothing can change
my opinion that you and your kind are leading my people
down the path to certain destruction, simply to feed your
own selfish ambition! You're no more a true patriot than
I—"

Willet stepped between them, calmly speaking to Jeremy, telling him to have a care in what he said. At this, Gansevoort slowly began to recover. Then he spoke to Gwen.

"As for you, mistress, you'll find a place to sleep among the women and children in a barracks, if they'll put up with an American woman who's the sweetheart of a loyalist."

"Colonel!" Jeremy cried out, Willet keeping himself positioned to prevent Jeremy from losing his head and attacking Gansevoort. "Mistress Hardy's been my nurse, but she's no part of this expedition! Despite her remarkable abilities as a nurse, she shares the misguided opinions of your own kind, and if you're any sort of gentleman at all, you'll see to it she finds her way safely home, to join other ardent supporters of your rascally—"

"Jeremy!" Gwen blurted, knowing he was about to insult Congress. "I mean, Dr. Bently! Please do not describe . . . That is—"

Gansevoort raised a hand, sighed, and asked everyone to sit down. Taking his own chair, he thought a moment, then asked Gwen if she was actually a Congress sympathizer. With a nod, she said it was so. But she would not beg this man to believe her, nor to treat her any differently than he would treat Jeremy.

Gansevoort glanced at Willet, and commented on civil war being just as much an affair of the heart as was love, and just as hard to fathom. Then he ordered Jeremy confined.

At the last moment, as Jeremy was being led from the room, the heartsick Gwen touched his hand. She did not care who observed, or what they thought of it. They spoke of love with their eyes, and then Jeremy was taken away.

Willet and two sentries escorted Jeremy across the busy parade ground toward the guardhouse. Cannon and mortars were firing steadily from St. Leger's batteries to the north, and though the ominous whistling of shells was nerve-wracking, Jeremy could see that the bombardment had done little damage.

As they walked, Willet said, "For that girl's sake, sir, I'll keep it quiet that she has a loyalist sweetheart, and I'll explain simply that she'd been your nurse, and now longs to go home."

Jeremy thanked him as a sentry opened the door to the small, dank cell in a log guardhouse. Despite the rainstorm that had cooled the air, the cell exuded a rank odor and tremendous heat. Indeed, the entire fort stank from dampness, overused latrines, and from the acrid smell of gunpowder as sharpshooters and guns fired occasional replies to St. Leger. Stanwix was jammed with more than a thousand folk, most sleeping in sheds or outside. Nowhere, however, was it as foul as in this guardhouse.

As he glanced about the fort before entering the cell, Jeremy asked Willet, "Can you feed them all for another two weeks? Your clever little sortie won't stop St. Leger, nor will your farmers in the valley militia."

Willet nodded once, his expression impassive. "You had best hope we can't hold out, Doctor; for if we do, you'll soon be on your way to the Simsbury mines for the rest of the war."

With that Willet motioned to the cell, and Jeremy ducked low to enter. The small door was closed behind him, leaving his world black, save for a tiny window in the door. There was no one else inside, and after a blind search with his hands, Jeremy found it was only four feet wide by eight long, hardly enough room to lie down and too low for him to stand. Immediately, the heat was oppressive, the air stale, and he began to sweat profusely.

As he sat down in a corner, Jeremy thought of all he had heard of the dreadful Simsbury mines in Connecticut, where loyalists captured in New York Province were shipped for confinement. He knew those mines were as cold and black and wet as this cell was hot and black and stifling. It would take considerable strength to survive even a year in Simsbury, and it was nearly impossible to escape.

Then Gwen was in his thoughts. For a fleeting, unguarded moment, he hoped Stanwix would hold out, if there was danger of an Indian massacre. That was a mad thought! He shook his head, leaning forward, arms on his knees.

"A mad thought for a mad world," he muttered. He might have laughed at the irony of it, had not Gwen's peril been all too real.

*chapter* **25**

# REBEL AND LOYALIST

Time passed slowly in that cramped cell. Days dragged on, through fitful sleep and listless waking hours of muggy heat. Jarred by the steady thump and shudder of British artillery fire, Jeremy was left alone, day after day. Outside, people passed back and forth, chattering, shouting, even laughing, speaking about food and water and weather, and about the despicable loyalist prisoner.

Jeremy was seldom offered food, and then no more than a bit of old bread and some tepid water. But he rapidly consumed it, for he was ravenous and dry. Whenever the guard opened the door, Jeremy drank in the fresh air as if it were cool rain falling on a desert. When the door was shut and bolted again, he languished in the corner, listening to the scuttle of small creatures along the walls, wondering how long Gansevoort would keep him here, and what was happening with Gwen.

Night passed into another sweltering day. He was constantly running with perspiration, nauseated from the loss of fluids, and very hungry. The crusts of bread and the little water did nothing to satisfy him. Steaming day and another night, and then another, broken only by the brief feeding and the sounds of the passersby. He was not allowed to go outside, not even to clean his chamberpot. The cell was putrid, but after the seventh day he hardly cared. He kept track of time by daily scratching a notch into the wood of the small window in the door.

The British cannonade was a steady, dreary thunder. Along with the rebel color guard—its band and cannon salutes each morning and night—the guns told Jeremy that the siege was still going on, and there was no reason to think St. Leger would lift it. But after nine miserable days passed, Jeremy wondered why there had been no massive bombardment or a sharp assault to weaken rebel resistance.

On the tenth day, to Jeremy's amazement, Gwen came to the cell window and called in a low, anxious voice to him. He clambered to his feet; dizzied by the effort, he nearly fainted before he got to the window to speak with her. The sentry and Colonel Willet were at hand to listen, to prevent any conspiracy from taking place. Gwen had pleaded to talk with him, but until now had been forbidden, obviously to aggravate his punishment as a loyalist.

"There's been a terrible battle near Oriska," Gwen said nervously. "The Indians and loyalists ambushed the Mohawk Valley militia, but so many were killed on both sides that there's no saying who won."

She said more than two hundred and fifty rebels had died on the field, and far more were carried home seriously wounded. The loyalists and Indians had lost a hundred and thirty dead, many of them leading chiefs, with as many wounded. After the battle, rebel scouts had slipped into the fort, to report that the Mohawk Valley militiamen had withdrawn downriver, but that another force of eight hundred Continentals was on the way from Albany, commanded by General Benedict Arnold.

Jeremy gave a dry laugh and said through the iron grate, "If you've come to raise my spirits, woman, you've not done very well."

Gwen ignored his resentment and touched his fingers, which were at the grate. Through the opening he saw the grief in her face.

"I'm sorry," she said, voice catching, "but I thought you'd want to know something . . . anything."

"And you?" he asked, his words sounding thick and dull. "Are you all right?"

She nodded quickly. "I'm helping as a nurse in the infirmary; I asked whether you might be permitted to come out and aid the doctor here, but—" She cut herself off, realizing that once more she had brought up a subject which could only agitate him.

Jeremy muttered, "I understand; they don't want the dirty hands of a loyalist touching their sacred patriotic wounds!"

"Don't!" she exclaimed, louder than intended. Then more quietly, she said, with a shaking voice, "Please don't, Jeremy; I think they'll let me bring better food to you soon, and perhaps they'll let you out for air if only they realize you've suffered enough.... But if you irritate them—"

He smashed the door with his fist and grabbed the grate to shake it. "Irritate them? Yes, I'll irritate them, and worse, when I get back with the army again!" He was nearly mad with strain and fury. "I'll make them think twice about abusing loyalists! I'll make them—"

Her hand, soft and cool, was again on his fingers and he abruptly stopped his tirade. Looking at Gwen through bleary bloodshot eyes, Jeremy let go of her fingers and shook his head. He said gruffly she should go now, before her own reputation was further tainted by continued association with a loyalist prisoner.

He was gazing at her, trying, but unable to look away. He heard Colonel Willet quietly agree with that last remark. Angrily, Gwen blurted that she did not care what anyone thought, and coming close to the window, she declared:

"I don't understand the meaning of any of it anymore! But I know I love you, Jeremy, and I'll always love you. And I believe with all my heart that one day we'll be together, somehow, some way! I believe it! Do you? Do you?"

Shock coursed through him, and his heart pounded to hear this. He stared at her, and she at him, waiting, anticipating a reply. He nodded. "I must believe it, Gwen; I must, for I can't live without you."

A shell whistled down and blew up not far away, turning a cart on its side and throwing shards of iron and splinters in every direction. Willet urged Gwen away from the cell, for the next few mortar rounds were sure to fall near the same place, as they always did. Jeremy watched them go, the glare of sunlight hurting his bleary eyes. Gwen stumbled away, looking back, until she was lost from sight around the corner of a log building.

From then on, Gwen was permitted to come to Jeremy for ten minutes each morning. She brought him decent food and drink, and they spoke of small things, not of war or of their loyalties. She told of the children in the barracks, how they had become used to the shelling and went on cheerfully through it, playing checkers or chasing hoops and balls. The rebel doctor in the fort was suspicious of women nurses, but he had allowed Gwen to change bandages and cleanse wounds. Whenever she liked, she could help care for women and children.

The days passed, sweltering and exhausting, as though Jeremy had labored without rest in harvest fields. He was always fatigued, by now insensible to the stink of his cell, and forever thirsty, no matter how much he drank. The only ray of relief was Gwen's appearance, which soon was permitted twice a day for half an hour, morning and evening. She told nothing of the war, but often would read poetry, or an old newspaper story that was nonpolitical. She leaned against the door, Jeremy on the other side—he sitting by now, for he was too weak to stand. He did not complain, for he knew the rebels were trying to break his spirit. He would not give in.

The regular thump and boom of British cannon fire gave him hope that St. Leger would soon force the fort to surrender. He knew food must be scarce, and being aware of the certain success of Burgoyne far to the east, the people in Stanwix would have to admit they were beaten, with further resistance impossible.

One morning he counted the notches, hardly paying attention to loud cheering going up all through the fort. He was so weak that it was difficult enough to count, let alone listen. When he reached the last, and seventeenth notch, he realized it was August 22. For three weeks Stanwix had held out! That was twice as long as St. Leger had anticipated. Jeremy had to concede these rebels were brave and tough enough.

As he turned to sit down in his corner again, he was startled by a clatter at the lock, followed by a blinding flood of daylight as the door was opened. Unable to see, Jeremy obeyed an order to come outside. Neglecting to pick up his scarlet tunic from the corner, he put an arm over his eyes and stumbled into the fierce sunlight.

Then someone was close to him, embracing him. Who? British? Had they taken the fort at last? He blinked and cleared his foggy mind, trying to see, to make out who was there.

"Jeremy, son!" said Owen Sutherland. It seemed like a dream. "Jeremy, my lad, it's me. Come on...it's over now."

In dazed astonishment, Jeremy gasped his stepfather's name, struggling against collapse as his knees nearly buckled under him. He wanted to stand straight, and a helpless anger welled up in him at appearing so feeble before Owen Sutherland. As best he could, Jeremy steeled himself, managed to stop blinking against the glaring light, and peered at Sutherland.

"Pa, how did you come...?" He swallowed, but his throat was parched, and he found it difficult to speak. "What's over? What do you mean?"

Sutherland's face was shadowed, grave, and Jeremy saw pain, perhaps grief there. Sutherland put Jeremy's arm over his shoulder and began walking him away from the cell. Willet and some guards followed close behind. Jeremy was stunned as his stepfather said St. Leger had fled and that the entire British army was retreating through the forest.

"How?" Jeremy muttered, almost to himself. It had seemed impossible that the rebels could have done anything to counter the combined invasions. "How, Pa? How?"

Sutherland spoke softly, for only Jeremy to hear, as they made their way across the parade ground, where a few people were stopping to watch, most others continuing their raucous celebration of victory.

"The Indians lost too many men fighting the valley militia. Then General Arnold sent his agents amongst them, spreading rumors of the approach of thousands of Continentals... as many as the leaves on the trees. The Indians believed it, became afraid, and lost spririt. They ran out on St. Leger, and without them he was too weak to go on with his offensive."

Jarred, and sick at heart to hear such news, Jeremy wanted Owen to say no more of this. As they went through a low doorway into a cool, dark building, he asked almost in a whisper: "And Ma? The young ones? How are they? Where are they?"

"They're in the Wyoming Valley, and they're well," Sutherland replied. "They miss you." He helped Jeremy into a chair. Willet and the guards left them alone in the room, and as Jeremy's eyes became used to the dimness, he asked further about his family and friends. All the while his distraught mind spun from exhaustion, dismay, and disbelief, after everything that had happened. The campaign to win the war was not going according to British plan. The rebellion might not be beaten after all, at least not this year.

Guessing Owen must be thinking the same things, Jeremy was determined to warn his stepfather that the British would not let minor setbacks shake their resolve to fight. His groggy mind was clearing, and he braced himself to get up, intending to declare proudly that the rebels dare not allow their hopes to rise because of the defeat of St. Leger. He had chosen his words, and began to stand up in order to say them properly. But his legs were stiff; they would hardly move. His head began whirling so that he started to sweat, and his stomach turned.

He could not stand. All those days in confinement had taken their toll, and though his loyalist spirit was strong, Jeremy Bently's body was sorely weakened. As Owen tried not to watch, Jeremy sat there, head in hands, muttering over and over, "Don't delude yourselves, rebels. Don't delude yourselves...."

A few hours later, Jeremy and Owen sat at a table in another room. Jeremy had washed, put on clean clothes, and had been brought food. Eating slowly, his hands shaking from his ordeal, he knew it would take months to recover from his imprisonment. But there would be no chance for that at Simsbury mines. This room would be his temporary quarters until the transfer, according to Colonel Willet. Since the British had fled, there was no reason to keep him in close confinement.

Though Jeremy's mind was clouded, he had learned by now that Sutherland had been with the main body of troops ambushed at Oriskany, and he had taken several minor wounds on arms and legs. The ambush had at first been successful, Sutherland told Jeremy, trapping eight hundred surprised militiamen, who had courageously stood their ground. That bloody battle had lasted four hours, interrupted by the tremendous downpour that had temporarily stopped savage, hand-to-hand combat. The outnumbered rebel militiamen had held on long enough to prevent complete massacre, however, because word of Willet's sortie had drawn Indians and loyalists from the field in an unsuccessful effort to save their possessions.

The mauled valley militia then had withdrawn painfully, dragging home their wounded. It had been a stalemate. The rest Jeremy knew—that the loyalist Indians had lost their ardor for fighting and had believed Arnold's rumors of a Continental advance. Most had then left for home, so the whites had no choice but to retreat as well, leaving only a few scouts and a handful of stalwart Mohawks under Joseph Brant still in the region.

As Sutherland told all these things, the glum Jeremy ate slowly, listening, finally muttering that he believed Jacques Levesque was still with Brant as well. Sutherland passed over this, saying:

"I'm told by Colonel Gansevoort that if you swear to a parole, you'll be allowed to go back to Detroit; but of course you must promise never to take up arms against the states again." He paused, looking as fresh and strong in his buckskins as Jeremy looked haggard and tired in his white blouse and breeches. "Otherwise, I fear it's Simsbury." He leaned forward. "Don't throw your life away, laddie."

Jeremy slowly shook his head. "I'll not agree never to fight rebels again, Pa." He raised his eyes to look at Sutherland; he knew his stepfather would understand and respect the motives of honor and loyalty that compelled him not to accept a parole. "I believe in my cause, as you and my mother do in yours. Our world may be changed forever as you'd have it, Pa, but if I deny all I believe in, what use has any of this fighting been? What use the dying and the ruin?"

Sutherland was angry. "If you won't think of your own life, think of Gwen Hardy, who loves you! Yes, I've talked with her, and you'll be wrong to let her go! Think of her! Don't think of a king, or of a lost cause that's being swept under by the inevitable tide of change! It's Penelope Graves who taught you to love England, not a king who'll take your blood, your body, and your very soul, Jeremy. Our people will have liberty! Sooner or later! A new age is upon us, Jeremy, and even kings can't hold it back."

Getting up as abruptly as he could, Jeremy pushed himself away from the table. Swaying slightly, then regaining his balance, he turned to Sutherland.

"I'm not thinking of a king, but of all the good folk who've been destroyed by your war for liberty, Pa. You know why I'm in the British army, and you know my reasons are as strong to me as yours to you, and never mind bringing Penelope into this! Yes, I love Gwen Hardy, and she loves me, but what sort of husband would I be if I turn my back on what I believe is right? I'm no Bradford Cullen, no weathervane who shifts allegiance at the whim of the political breeze!

"I've good friends on my side, whom I'll never betray, though your rebels lock me in a mine to die! For all that Gwen and I love each other, we cannot pretend we live in a dreamworld! I have my duty, just as you do. Let the Cullens of this world turn their coats—I never will!"

"Wait!" Sutherland demanded, raising a hand. "Why do you speak of Cullen now? Is it true what we've guessed, that he's come to the valley to join the loyalists?"

Jeremy would not answer, though he cared nothing for

Cullen. He would not reveal the secret Jacques Levesque had shared, and he told his stepfather he would say no more about it.

Sutherland thought long and hard, and then smashed his fist on the plank table.

"Levesque! Yes! That's it! Levesque is still in the valley because he has to lead Cullen westward!"

Sutherland leaped to the door, and when Jeremy asked where he was going, the Scotsman turned, his expression fierce.

"If you won't accept parole for your own good, maybe we can force you at least to accept freedom!" He began to go, then stuck his head back in the door. "Think about Gwen Hardy! She's a fine girl, and if you weren't so pig-headed, you might see how lucky you'd be to have her by your side! Life'll go on beyond this war! Think on that!"

The door slammed, and Sutherland was gone. Jeremy sat down wearily on his bed, which actually had clean sheets. He settled down again to wait. He had no idea what Sutherland had in mind. He longed to see Gwen, but Sutherland had told him she was downriver in company with Peter Defries, helping care for hundreds of wounded rebel farmers.

There was nothing for Jeremy to do but wait.

That night, Joseph Brant's Mohawks slept in their secluded camp in the forest not far from Fort Stanwix. They had given their all in the failed campaign, had fought bitterly at Oriskany, lost many good men, and had prevented the militia from breaking the siege. Now they were angry at having been let down by St. Leger, who was unable to keep the other Indians fighting.

By now the Mohawks had learned to their chagrin that Arnold's reinforcements totaled fewer than a thousand and were not as numerous as the "leaves on the trees" described in the rumor that had swept through St. Leger's camp. Like the whites, Brant had not believed the rumors, but he had been unable to convince the war-weary, sullen Indians of the northwest and the other Iroquois. St. Leger had hastily fled after his Indians, even leaving papers and writing desk behind. The only organized loyalist fighters still in the area were Brant's men, including Jacques Levesque and the Sioux Little Hawk.

Brant intended soon to drive fast down the valley, to dash past the advancing Arnold and to do what his Mohawks had promised they would: unite with Burgoyne for the capture of Albany. Perhaps St. Leger could not complete the mission, but Brant and his courageous followers would do it, or die trying. First they needed to rest here, to gather strength before they sprang onto the hunting trails that wound through forest and glen, all the way to Albany.

The Mohawks had posted several guards around their hidden camp. The rest were deep in slumber, secure enough to sleep well for at least one night before their march began. Long before dawn, however, they were astonished to be awakened by a loud voice. They sat up all at once, to see a white man, who had slipped into their encampment like a ghost, standing brazenly before their fire, hands on his hips.

One of the younger warriors—a guard who was ashamed at having been outwitted—gave a shriek of fury and leaped up with a tomahawk. But he was driven back by Brant himself, and in the next moment the Sioux Little Hawk was standing beside the white man, clearly ready to protect him. Levesque also appeared as Brant faced Owen Sutherland, who offered his hand, if not in friendship, then at least out of respect.

"I have come to council with Brant and Levesque," Sutherland began, surrounded by dark and hostile faces whose eyes glittered in the firelight. "I have come to ask that they save one who is a friend to them and to others in this group; one who is my son."

Two days later, as Jeremy finished a breakfast of mush, cheese, and tea, Lieutenant Colonel Willet entered and asked him whether he was well enough to travel. Jeremy said he was, and Willet motioned for a servant to carry in the scarlet tunic and white smallclothes, all of which had been washed;

even Jeremy's wig had been cleaned and powdered, as if it had never gone through a campaign and then been imprisoned with him for three dismal weeks.

Jeremy got up, feeling strong now, and thanked Willet, who said, "Please be ready to leave the fort within an hour."

Jeremy could not help but ask, "Simsbury?"

Willet's narrow face and sharp features broke into a pleased grin. "That depends on whether Owen Sutherland has done what he tells us he's done. But we'll soon see."

Jeremy was confused, but before Willet left, he asked about Gwen. Willet said she had not yet returned from downriver, and Jeremy's heart sank to think of again departing without a chance to say good-bye.

It was then he remembered the letter Simon Clancy had given him before the Irishman left for the ambush. Jeremy searched through the pockets of his tunic, wondering whether someone had inadvertently washed the letter. But there it was, apparently taken out for the washing and put back unopened. He unfolded it and read it at the window.

Clancy wrote that he feared Gwen would be unprotected if he fell in the battle. Thus, the letter told everything about her being with the army's camp followers.

> . . . she is the grandest lady I have ever come across, Doc. If my Irish luck should run out, and you are compelled to read this, then please listen to common sense and marry her before you lose the best thing that could happen to any man. She does not need much courting when it comes to you, boyo, so just speak your heart, as I know you feel it. Tell Gwen you love her, Doc, and don't let her get away without a fight.

Jeremy laid the letter aside and felt that he must talk to Gwen. He had to see her, though he was sure Gwen would never come back to the northwest—not as long as he wore the scarlet uniform. And he meant to wear it until the war was over.

A few hours later, in a bright clearing near a babbling stream west of Fort Stanwix, a carriage stood, unlimbered, its team of horses nowhere in sight. Nearby were its three passengers—two well-dressed women and a fat, bewigged gentleman. The gentleman was angrily shaking his cane at an Indian who sat unmoved on a rock, his arms crossed.

"You can't do this to me!" cried Bradford Cullen, at the same time batting at a large fly pestering him. Immediately, his wife, Helen, and daughter, Linda, began to whine and wail that the solemn redskin must listen to reason.

Cullen roared that the women should be still, and they huddled together in fright near the carriage, while the merchant implored the Indian to believe him. "You can't take me prisoner!" Cullen wheezed. "Why, I'm on your side! I'm a loyalist, just like you! Great white father my great white father, too! Understand? *Comprenez-vous?* We're loyal, I tell you!"

The Indian grunted but did not look at the fat merchant, whose fine gray clothes were stained with greasy sweat. "That is what they all say," the Indian finally replied, speaking slowly. "When we catch 'em rebels, they all pretend to be good Tories." He scowled, uncrossed his arms, and brandished a coup stick that looked like a shepherd's crook decorated with scalps and feathers. "You be my prisoner now. No more talk!" The stick whisked under Cullen's nose, and he shrank back toward his anguished wife and daughter.

Despite her discomposure and the hardships of a journey begun before dawn, Helen Cullen was still immaculate in a brown riding outfit. She clutched at Linda, who was like a wilted pink flower against the deep greenery of the surrounding forest. Both women were pale with terror, but Cullen urged them to be calm, for this Indian was obviously waiting for friends to arrive. There surely would be white loyalists with the party, and Cullen could explain everything. He would also ask the whereabouts of that rascal Jacques Levesque, who had got them into this terrible mess.

Guided by Levesque, the Cullens had departed from their home in the valley before the first light, driving their two-horse carriage along a bumpy trail through a swamp, and out the other side beyond rebel pickets at Stanwix. Soon the journey would be easier, going by canoe downriver to Oswego, then by bateau to Montreal. Until half an hour ago, the Cullens had been jubilant, relieved that their plans to join the loyalists were at last going smoothly. For months Cullen had been an active British spy in the Mohawk Valley, and all that time he had expected someone to arrive and lead him away to loyalist country.

Now they were on their way, but not long ago Levesque had unexpectedly stopped the carriage in this clearing, insisting that a wheel was damaged and would have to be repaired immediately. Though Cullen had angrily protested that surely it could wait another few hours, Levesque had unhitched the team, let the animals graze nearby, and proceeded to jack up the wagon and remove the wheel.

The women naturally had been extremely nervous and had complained to the agitated Cullen that they must push on before General Arnold's troops came along to ask what was the matter and prevent escape. What it was that had frightened off the horses Cullen still did not know, but Levesque had gone crashing down a trail after them, shouting and clapping his hands, as though he meant anything but to calm and catch the beasts.

Then—and Cullen shuddered to recall the terrifying moment—this big Indian, who somehow looked so familiar to him, had stepped out of the woods. In good English the redskin had declared they were all his prisoners, to be taken back to Oswego as captured rebels. As unsettling and annoying as this insolence had been, Cullen had not been worried, because officers in the British high command would eventually verify his loyalty and release him.

But things had not gone smoothly. For one, the Indian had not taken them anywhere. He had sat down on a boulder, rifle and coup stick across his knees, and ordered Cullen and the women to wait. For another, Levesque had not returned with the horses.

Now a whole hour had been lost—an hour in which all Cullen's protests and pleadings had done nothing to move the stubborn, pompous Indian. Cullen had even offered the man money, but for some bizarre reason this strange Indian had flatly refused. As Cullen mopped his brow with a handkerchief, now and again slapping at that troublesome fly, Helen came to his side and whispered that she feared for

Linda's maidenhead if they were caught by rebels roving the woods.

"Should they know we're escaping," Helen muttered, so that Linda, nearby drying her eyes, could not hear, "they'll surely take revenge on the poor child before carrying us back to their fort! Please do something, Mr. Cullen, before she and we lose all we have in the world!" She touched a carpetbag lying on the ground at her feet; it contained a fortune in British sterling that would buy Cullen into any society in America.

Cullen shook off his wife, struck at the annoying fly, and declared in a low voice that no rebels would guess what he and his family were up to. "Anyway, there are loyal men in these woods, too, and with a bit of luck, they'll run across us first."

Yet Cullen knew this region was again fast becoming rebel country, and when Helen gave a squawk of terror, gasping that strange men were coming, his face turned ghastly white. He stared openmouthed at a tall figure in buckskins who moved out of the trees and stopped to observe them. Then came another man, and Cullen groaned with despair, for even though his eyes were poor, he recognized the blue tunic of a rebel Continental. His former assurances to Helen not to worry were abruptly forgotten. He almost whined, "We are undone, Mrs. Cullen."

"No!" Helen cried out, just as their Indian rose to face the newcomers. "There's a British soldier there! Look!"

Cullen saw the flash of scarlet across the clearing, then made out a Redcoat in full uniform. Giving a squeal of joy, he clapped his fat hands together. Presuming these were loyal troops with a rebel prisoner, he waved his cane and stamped toward them, calling out, "Friends! Here we are! Friends!"

But the Indian grabbed his arm and pulled him back, then held out a white handkerchief as a flag of truce. Cullen blustered that it was safe, for these were obviously loyalists and Redcoats. The Indian told him to shut up. A white flag was waved by the other party, which, to Cullen's relief, began to move slowly toward them across the clearing.

Cullen thumped his cane into the earth and declared,

"Now, my dusky fellow, we'll have this straightened out once and for all!" He began to advance, the women following close behind. "Come, ladies, we'll soon be on our way to—"

But then Cullen saw that Owen Sutherland was beside the Redcoat officer. And on the other side of the Redcoat was Marinus Willet from Stanwix, a man well known to Cullen. The merchant staggered to a stop, his wife and daughter bumping into him from behind and chattering with annoyance, demanding to know what was the matter. To his horror, Cullen knew precisely what was the matter, and what Levesque had done. Sutherland's group came forward, and Bradford Cullen began to hiss fervently at the Indian:

"No! I'm loyal! No! I'm no rebel! No! You can't— You mustn't! I'm loyal, I tell you!"

"They all say that," Little Hawk replied, trying to keep a smirk off his face. "You lucky, though; you to be exchanged."

"Exchanged!" shrieked Helen Cullen, her cry echoed by Linda, who hurriedly fumbled at the patch on her right cheek, trying to stick it to the left side, the rebel side, as at the same time she somehow kept her mother from fainting away.

By now Bradford Cullen knew disaster could not be avoided. He dared not protest further, lest Willet and a soldier driving a pony cart hear him and become suspicious. Then he recognized Jeremy Bently as the Redcoat officer— and suddenly knew the Indian was the one he had seen before hobnobbing with Sutherland. The Scotsman had bested him again!

Marinus Willet stepped forward, bowing deeply to the women, touching his hat to Cullen, who could scarcely bring himself to look at the officer. First, Willet addressed the Sioux, his voice clipped but correct.

"As you earlier arranged with Mr. Sutherland, we have brought Dr. Bently to you, and now, as agreed, we'll accept charge of Mr. Cullen and his family."

Cullen was red in the face, but he managed to master himself enough to clear his throat and bow in return to Willet.

"I can't tell you how grateful we are," Cullen rasped, still not meeting Willet's eyes.

The rebel officer gestured to the women, offering them a seat in the waiting pony cart, saying, "Forgive the inconvenience of our humble transportation, ladies, and be assured we'll send a team of horses and a driver to recover your carriage; in the meantime, I pray neither of you has suffered undue embarrassment or harm in being kidnapped from your home by our enemy."

"Enemy?" Helen almost shrieked, losing composure, and her rubbery face began to work until her husband gave her a scathing glance of warning. Willet seemed not to notice Helen's near hysteria.

Linda, meanwhile, still could not get the facial patch to stick, so she held it against her cheek, trying to smile adoringly at Willet.

Bradford Cullen said not a word to Willet, but glared at Owen Sutherland, who paid no attention. The Scotsman was shaking hands with the wan, downhearted Jeremy Bently, wishing him a safe journey.

"No one knows what will become of us," Sutherland said. "But I pray we'll never meet on the battlefield, my son."

"As do I," Jeremy replied, handing over a letter he had written to his mother, along with several other letters for his friends down in the Wyoming Valley.

As Owen and Jeremy spoke, Cullen and his family were led to the waiting pony cart, which would take them back to Stanwix. It would not be a pleasant or a comfortable ride. Once again, the Cullens were to be counted as rebels.

Sutherland, though sad for his stepson, was pleased that the exchange had worked out so well. Unfortunately, he had no indisputable proof that Cullen had planned to turn his coat—the merchant would no doubt swear he had been kidnapped—but that proof would come eventually. For now, Jeremy's safety was all that mattered.

As the merchant and soldier helped the distraught women get aboard the cart, Willet said Jeremy was now free to rejoin Little Hawk.

"You have three hours to get out of the region, and then

you'll be liable to capture once again." Willet and Jeremy shook hands. Jeremy was not on a military parole, so he was not bound by any oath requiring him never to fight against Congress forces. This affair was a direct exchange of prisoners, and as far as Lieutenant Colonel Willet was concerned, a British surgeon was a worthy trade for a rich, prominent rebel. What good would Jeremy Bently be, rotting in Simsbury mines? And the rebellion had great use for Bradford Cullen's influence and fortune. As Willet bade farewell, then mounted a horse tethered to the cart, he said loudly that Cullen should reconsider his residence and move down to Albany, where kidnappings were far less likely.

Cullen grumbled something in reply, climbed with the driver's help into the straw-covered cart alongside the women, and scowled at Sutherland. The Scotsman looked back and winked, causing Cullen to shout at the soldier who was tossing the carpetbag and luggage aboard, telling him to hurry.

After the cart jolted noisily out of sight, Willet riding behind, the clearing became quiet until Little Hawk, with a joyful hoot, sprang into Jeremy's arms, nearly knocking him over. Though weak and still despondent, Jeremy grinned wanly and clapped his friend on the back. At that moment, out of the woods dashed Jacques Levesque, greeting Jeremy, then pumping Sutherland's hand. Jeremy set Little Hawk down and watched Levesque and Owen, seeing the ache they shared at being enemies. The war was too big for all of them, and was growing in its might and oppression. No one could have foreseen that it would go on and on like this. Jeremy knew this might be the last time they all would be together in a brief moment of peace.

Levesque and Sutherland exchanged remarks about good and bad luck in the past campaign, ending with wishes for a safe journey and expressions of affection for each other's family and friends. Then Sutherland turned to Little Hawk, and they gripped forearms as the Sioux said, "I saw you at Oriskany, Owen; I almost shot you."

Sutherland held his shoulders, both men grim. "And I saw you, my friend. I saw you lower your rifle. . . . One day I'll repay you. Tell me, is Clancy alive? I saw him fall."

Little Hawk said the Irishman had been wounded in both legs, but would recover. And Lieutenant Mark Davies, who had been fighting near Little Hawk, had also gone down, seriously wounded, the Indian said. Then Little Hawk forced himself to be cheerful and clapped the downcast Jeremy on the shoulder, saying, "Welcome back, soldier! Come on! We'll ride Cullen's horses all the way to Oswego!"

Jeremy took a deep breath, gathering himself. Yes, it was time to go, but he longed to see Gwen. He had not said enough to her. Perhaps, he thought, even if she were in his arms right now, he would still not be able to say enough, never be able to say what she truly meant to him. How could he say that, and then say good-bye?

He reached into his tunic and took out a letter, handing it over to Sutherland. "This is my . . . my farewell to Gwen Hardy. It's not how I would have wished to bid her farewell, but—"

A gruff voice from the woods bellowed, "Then say what you want to say, and say it right now, Doc!"

Peter Defries lumbered out of the trees to give Jeremy a massive bear hug. Saying that he had heard at Stanwix about the prisoner exchange, Defries whirled Jeremy around and placed him down neatly in front of Gwen, who was standing at the edge of the clearing, her eyes wide. Jeremy stared at her, amazed and thrilled all at once. He ran toward her in a rush that she met with open arms.

"Oh, my love!" Gwen cried, and hugged him.

He crushed her close, saying her name over and over and over, not even noticing as the other men moved away to let them be alone.

Jeremy had never felt such stormy emotions. How he wanted this woman! Gwen was in his arms as if a part of him, as if her heart were beating with his and he knew her very thoughts. Neither spoke as they stood together in that peaceful glade, sunlight streaming over them. Their eyes were closed, and for as long as they could hold that fierce embrace, the war had no meaning. Jeremy knew nothing save the warmth of Gwen in his arms, a feeling he would not forget for as long as he lived.

After some time, they drew apart just enough to gaze at each other, Jeremy's arms still around Gwen's waist. He saw the tears in her eyes, then felt the force of his own sadness rising in him. Still without speaking, they stood back a bit, holding hands. Jeremy's mind was filled with words of love, but there was no need to speak, for she felt the same as he did.

He leaned forward and kissed her gently. He felt her fingers tremble as they lightly touched his cheek, and he kissed her again.

Finally he said, almost hoarsely, "I'm grateful to have seen you once more." He squeezed her hands, and she gripped his tightly, as if to keep him from going. He said, "Owen will see you safely on your way back down the Hudson. . . . You'll be home soon, Gwen." He looked down at the ground, seeing nothing.

Gwen had tears in her eyes, about to cry as she looked at him. Slowly she shook her head, and breathed, "Is that all you want to say?"

He gave a sound of despair. "Is that all?" He squeezed her hands. "No, Gwen, that's not all! I want to say come with me! Come with me, and we'll start over! Come with me, and we'll go to the Illinois, and I'll serve there, where there is no fighting, and where you'll be able to live as my wife, and the war won't touch us! That's what I really want to say! That, and so much more."

She caught her breath, closing her eyes momentarily. As if with tremendous inner effort, she declared, "Then say it!"

He stopped short. "Say it?"

"If it's in your heart!" She looked at his pale, exhausted face, seeing in his eyes how much he loved her. "Say what's in your heart, Jeremy Bently, for I've searched my own heart again and again, and there's only one certainty. Only one certainty that matters—I love you! Whatever may come, I want to be your wife!"

Then they were locked in an embrace that was no longer a farewell, but a beginning. Gwen was laughing and crying, and Jeremy squeezed her against himself so hard that it almost took her breath away.

"We'll make it work!" he said, kissing her hair and forehead, then her lips. "Nothing in all the world'll stop us, Gwen!"

"Nothing!" she exclaimed, kissing him back. "We'll never be parted, my darling, not really parted, no matter what happens. How I love you, Jeremy!"

"And I," he said, full of joy, holding her back a little so he might see her beautiful face. "And I love you even more than I knew, until this very moment." Again he kissed her, and she put her head against his chest, releasing a long sigh of contentment. No matter what they would face in the years to come, they knew it had to be this way. They were meant to be together, for the rest of their lives.

From a distance, Sutherland saw them embrace, and he smiled.

Peter Defries, who was chatting quietly with Little Hawk, looked around to see the lovers in each other's arms. He, too, smiled and slapped his thigh. Levesque wiped hard cider from his beard and passed the jug to Defries, saying, "Let us toast to the future of those youngsters!"

Defries downed a swig, handed the jug to Sutherland, and said, "Too bad this ain't papaya gin and we ain't all on some Caribbean island trading lies about what heroes we were back during the rebellion!"

Levesque asked, "Who would own that island? The British empire or the United American States? Ah! Don't answer. Anyway, French-Canadian cider is more potent than this papaya gin you speak of, whatever that is! It is a known fact. Now, *mes amis, allons!* We must fly!"

Defries and Sutherland shook hands a final time with Levesque and Little Hawk. Jeremy and Gwen approached, he with his arm over her shoulders, a joyous look on both their faces. Sutherland hugged his son and wished him all the best, saying, "Take care of your woman, and give us grandchildren, lad!"

Then Sutherland became almost misty as he said to Gwen, "I wish we all could be at your wedding. Detroit would shake at its roots with the dancing!" Trying to smile, but failing, he kissed her on the cheek. "God bless you, my lass. And welcome to the family."

A Special Preview of the
Opening Chapter of
Book 6 in the
Northwest Territory Series

# TRIUMPH

by
Oliver Payne

*On sale in the Spring of 1985
wherever Berkley books
are sold*

# chapter 1

The gray maples were naked against the snow, clattering their branches in a wind that swirled away down the ravine. Evening was coming on. The smell of a storm hung in the air, mingling with woodsmoke rising from a few log cabins clustered at the bottom of the slope.

A blaze of orange flame blossomed in the center of the settlement, and seen from up on the wooded ridge, the fire was a hot, bright flare against the gloomy winter forest. Above the rush of wind in the trees lifted the keen melody of fiddle music, light and carefree. Silhouettes could be seen dancing back and forth around the bonfire as it burned higher, sending billows of smoke into the darkening sky.

On the ridge, where bleak rocks crowded into shadows, a youthful figure knelt, unmoving. Wreathed in dimness, he seemed of stone himself, indistinguishable from his surroundings as he watched the settlement below. Only the wind gave him away, flicking at the eagle feather that hung from his fur cap. In the hollow, where the settlers gaily surged about the bonfire, no one could tell they were being watched. No one would know until it was too late.

Soon, other Shawnee warriors would join him, and before night fell, they would move in, silently, swiftly. By the time the snowstorm began, it would find the scout and his companions satisfied and warm in these cabins. When the storm ended, they would escape with their booty and trophies of war, fleeing on snowshoes through the north-western wilderness, not stopping to rest until they were far away and safe from pursuit, in their own villages....

In the reflection of distant firelight, the Shawnee's eyes glittered, revealing the excitement that coursed through him. He was courageous. He was invincible. He was confident. Before the moon was high, another nest of whites would be wiped out. All the warriors of the Shawnee nation would know of his brave deeds this day.

Then, all around, he sensed the quiet arrival of the others. They were among the trees, the elder warriors drifting in the forefront of the advance. The young scout rose to a crouch and moved down toward the light and the fiddle music. It had begun.

At the edge of the noisy clearing where the cabins stood, a tall, slender man of twenty-two in a bulky blanket coat and a woolen hat took a last look at the people dancing on a plank floor near the bonfire. Bright reddish light glinted over his face, which was boyish and appealing. His dark eyes were large and soft, and a hint of humor glowed in them as he watched his friends celebrate New Year's Day. James Morely was taking a turn on guard, having just re-placed his older brother, Tom, who was already whooping and carousing with his pretty wife, Sally, in the throng of happy folk.

Leaving the sounds of the celebration behind, James con-tinued on through crunching snow up the narrow trail toward the crest of the ridge. All trace of a smile left his face. It did not matter now whether he was rebel or neutral or loyal. For the moment he was the guard of family and friends. If Indians ever struck this settlement, they would not consider a man's politics. They would simply take as many scalps as they could and carry them back to the British fort at distant Detroit, to prove their prowess in battle. King George's officers were rewarding Indians for victories against rebel settlers on the frontier, and no one could say whether a scalp came from a white rebel or loyalist, or from the neutral James Morely.

As he walked deeper into the forest, he felt a sensation up his spine—a feeling that was more than just cold, but less than fear. The ashen woods were gathering about him, but it was still light enough to see some distance through the trees.

Instinct prickled the hair on the back of his neck, but James could make out nothing unusual in the drifting shadows, gray and cold, that filled the maple forest. The settlement's happy sounds faded as he moved farther from the clearing. The party would end before long, for these days folk went inside after dark and stayed there until morning. Too often of late, stragglers had not come home at all, to be found in the morning, murdered by lurking Indians.

A twig cracked behind, and James whipped around, his rifle coming up as he dropped to one knee. Shadows moved, and out of them stepped a slim and delicate figure, silhouetted against the blaze from the settlement. James released an annoyed sigh and lowered his rifle.

"Be you daft or simply touched in that girlie head of yours?" He stood up straight as Susannah Sutherland approached, tramping up the same path he had taken from the cabins. As she came near him, James half smiled. She was a pretty one, even though she was only eleven years of age. Her face seemed to glow from within the hood of the fine green frock she wore. They had known each other all their lives, and he knew she was soft for him—puppy love, his brother Tom rightly called it.

Susannah's voice was hushed as she drew her coat tightly about herself. "You talk too loud for a sentry, James. And you stand up too straight. Pa's right—you should stick to the fur-trading warehouse instead of being our watch."

James became unexpectedly serious at this remark, though Susannah had meant only to tease him in reply to his own barb. James turned and looked into the forest, which was steadily deepening in twilight.

Susannah came closer to him, clearing her throat. One slender hand played with a string of shell beads that hung at her breast, and the other was behind her back, holding a sprig of mistletoe. As James glanced at her, she saw she had hurt him, and she was sorry. James was always too touchy about these things, as if he were not proud of being the most brilliant trader in the country—after her own father, Owen Sutherland, of course.

Trying to change the subject, Susannah again cleared her throat and smiled as coquettishly as she could. She wanted just the right moment to hold the mistletoe over the fellow's head and demand her rightful kiss.

After a few seconds, James let himself look at her again, and her eyes held his. She smiled, and so did he.

"Your pa's right," he said softly, shouldering the rifle. "I'm meant most for business, not for the woods." He glanced about at the forest as the wind picked up. The trees seemed to hiss and creak more than before, but he noticed no danger.

"I feel safe," Susannah said, "knowing you're out here." She was sure the right moment had come, and was ready to reveal the sprig of mistletoe.

James gave a little laugh; still staring at the trees, he said, "You'd be safer if I was alone here, paying attention to the woods instead of listening to you prattle away." He looked kindly at her and said, "Best you go back down there now. I'll keep an eye on you as you walk."

Susannah was disappointed and brought the mistletoe into both hands. "I came to talk to you . . . alone—"

Suddenly there was a crashing in the bushes, and James brought the rifle to bear and cocked the hammer in one fluid motion.

"Don't shoot!" someone croaked. "It's just me! Hold your fire."

It was a familiar voice, and James saw the speaker struggling to get free of a tangle of thornbushes, gasping and groaning all the while. Susannah stamped her foot in the snow, and the hood fell back, uncovering her long blond hair.

"Benjamin Sutherland! You little sneak! You heathen! You skulking, sneaking . . . skulking . . ."

James laughed, uncocked his rifle, and reached to pull the lanky youth out of the bushes, where he had fallen after trying to climb on a rotten limb to eavesdrop on his sister and James.

Benjamin came clambering out of the thorns, half laughing, half in pain, jamming a three-cornered hat back on his head. He said their father had seen Susannah leave the cabins and wanted her brought back immediately.

"I was coming to fetch you just as soon as I got up that tree and spied out where you were...." He eyed James, who nodded in mock agreement. Benjamin was darkly handsome, like his father, and had a ready grin, which he could not contain as he glanced from the blushing Susannah to James and back again.

Susannah did not think it funny and looked in appeal to James, who became momentarily distracted as he turned to listen to the forest.

Susannah grumbled at her brother, "You just want to mind my personal business cause you think—" She glanced back at James, who was moving up the trail, paying no attention. Then she said in a whisper, "Benjamin, you think I'm trying to throw myself at his feet!" Suddenly she remembered the mistletoe and whisked it behind her back. But Benjamin had seen it. He doffed his hat with a flourish, kissed it tenderly, then snickered.

Susannah angrily tossed up her hood, turned on her heel, and followed James. She heard her brother hiss that the snow was too cold to throw herself at his feet, and she should wait until James was ready to catch her first. "About five years from now!"

The girl turned the bend in the trail, out of sight from Benjamin, and found James leaning against a tree, head bowed. At first she thought he was listening to something, for his face was pressed against the bark, his rifle butt in the snow. She hesitated, shoving the mistletoe into a pocket of her coat. Then she became anxious as James gave a groan and the rifle began to fall. She caught the weapon and clutched at his shoulder.

"James!" she gasped quietly. "Heavens! Are you ill! James?"

He let out another low groan, and as he tried to look at

her she saw his eyes were out of focus.

"You're ill!" she declared, hoping Benjamin would come to help. But her brother was not to be seen.

In the distance she heard the happy sounds of music and song. She wanted to get James back down there right away, but he would not go. He shook off her hands when she pulled at him.

"I'm all right . . ." he breathed, "all right . . ." He seemed to be recovering. Straightening up, he swayed momentarily and swallowed hard. Slowly, he shook his head, passed a gloved hand over his face, and muttered again that he would be all right.

"These . . . these spells come on . . . me, now and again," he said weakly, and let his head go back all the way, eyes closed.

Susannah was frightened for him, for she had never known James to be subject to fainting.

"Come down to the settlement!" she insisted, taking his arm. Once more he shook her off and reached with a trembling hand for his rifle.

"No!" He forced the word out, but appeared all right now. "No, I won't admit to anyone that there's . . . there's something wrong with me! Especially not to Owen. I've got my duty, Susannah, and I'll not shirk it!"

"Have you been ill, James?" She pressed close to him, her fingers touching his face. He yielded slightly and gazed into her lovely blue eyes. "You must have a care, dearest," she said.

James smiled and removed one glove; then he held her fingers close to his cheek.

Startled and charmed at the same time, Susannah did not know whether to feel romantic or concerned for his health. "James, if there's something seriously wrong with—"

"No, no." He shook his head. "I've lived with this for years now, and you're the first who's ever seen me take a fainting spell." Suddenly he became grave enough to dismay her. "Listen, Susannah, do you care at all for me?"

"More than I can say!"

"Then promise me—"

"Anything!"

He squeezed her hand harder than he meant. "Promise you'll tell no one . . . ever . . . about this!"

"What? But—"

"Promise!" He brought her fingers against his lips, and she nearly melted with emotion. "If you truly care for me."

"Oh, James!" She was thrilled beyond words. "Oh, James, I do . . . I promise! I'll not tell a soul."

"Never!" His black eyes flashed. "Tell no one, not even Owen, unless I give you leave. Swear it!"

"Never!" Her eyes closed with the intensity of it all, and she kept them tightly shut, whispering with a gush of passion, "Never, ever, ever!"

Then his hand went suddenly limp. She felt the weight of him sink down. "James!" she whimpered. He was fainting again. He was so very heavy to hold up. The rifle struck the snow. Susannah grappled for his waist, trying to ease him down. "James!" They fell together under an evergreen.

Then Susannah heard someone farther down the trail. She glanced back to see several shadows moving through the trees. At first she thought it was Benjamin with others, and knew she must say nothing to give herself away, lest they find James unconscious and his secret be discovered.

"James," she whispered ever so quietly, but he still did not move. She peered anxiously at the shadowy men in the trees. James was breathing evenly, and she prayed he would wake up soon, before anyone found them. Fortunately, they were concealed by bushes all about and might not easily be discovered.

After a moment, when she thought they were alone, Susannah lightly slapped James's cheek. He began to come around, but his face was so pale that it seemed radiant in the gathering twilight. His eyes flickered, and Susannah was swept with relief. She murmured in thankfulness.

Abruptly, there came shouting and the sounds of a struggle nearby. Something was wrong with Benjamin, for it was his voice, though partly muffled. James was not yet conscious, and Susannah dared not rouse him further, lest he cry out and give them away. She knew something was terribly amiss and grasped the rifle, cocking it. She listened, panting with fear, trying to make out where her brother was.

Then she knew, and terror rushed through her. She stood up slowly. Benjamin was near at hand, cursing and growling in a stifled voice, being thrown about in the thickets. Susannah trembled. She could hesitate no longer and moved through the trees, whispering her brother's name, knowing the worst: He was being attacked by Indians.

"Please, God," Susannah whispered, over and over. "Please save him . . . please . . ."

Before Susannah reached him, Benjamin must have broken free, for he let out a bloodcurdling shriek, a ringing shout of warning for all down at the settlement to hear. The fiddle music stopped abruptly, and at almost the same moment Benjamin's fierce yell was cut short by a sickening thud. Susannah was close enough now. She saw a warrior raise a club, about to strike again. She wailed, swung up the heavy rifle, and fired. Instantly she was jarred backward by the weapon's recoil, smashing hard against a tree. Everything went black.

Ella Sutherland knew her son's cry, and in terror she screamed his name and broke away from the bonfire to dash for the opening of the forest path. The others had stopped their dancing and music and for one brief moment were frozen in surprise, firelight playing on them as they watched her fly toward the trail Benjamin had taken.

The instant passed, and as though they had rehearsed it many times, the settlers swarmed away from the firelight, women and children making for the stronger cabins, menfolk grabbing rifles and pistols that were ready to hand. Ella heard voices cry for her to stop, but she forgot caution, ignored the danger, and scrambled into the trees. As she ran and called Benjamin's name, branches tore at her, catching the cotton mobcap and tugging at the linen apron worn across her breasts and tied in back. Her frock flew out as she ran, and her hair fell from where it had been pinned, dropping in straggling blond curls to her shoulders.

Ella had no idea how she could save her son, but she could not prevent herself making this headlong, mad effort to reach him before it was too late. When the first gunshot sounded, Ella cried "No!" and ran even more wildly than before. She was too distraught to hear the clamor of the people back at the settlement readying themselves, nor did she see the Shawnees in the trees, watching her pass—not until three of them rose up and shrieked insanely, painted like devils, black and white and red, steel tomahawks gleaming.

Ella gasped and stumbled, trying to stop before she ran into the first warrior, a swarthy, overweight older man wearing greasy trade shirts and a bearclaw necklace. He whooped and swung his tomahawk. Ella ducked as the ax came down. The blow just missed. In that same instant the rest of the Indians broke cover and opened fire at the settlement. Their ragged volley told that their plan had lost its best element— surprise. Ella snatched at a stick as the Shawnee went for her again. She poked it at her attacker, but he chopped it away with a grunt of anger and lunged at her.

Ella was off-balance, on one knee when the man came in. Her hair obscured her sight, and she cried out in pain as his thick, gnarled fingers grabbed for her, clutching the nape of her neck and jerking her face back so that for a moment they stared into each other's eyes. Ella saw death there. With a frantic effort she scratched and pummeled, and he was furious at a woman so resisting him. In one short stroke, he brought the tomahawk down at her head.

Ella saw it come, but there was nothing she could do to save herself. She crumpled heavily to the snow, her blood spilling out over the old Shawnee's worn moccasins. . . .

*So begins* Triumph, *the sixth book in the* Northwest Territory *series by Oliver Payne. In subsequent scenes, the Indian attack is repulsed, though at heavy loss to the settlers. Ella Sutherland lies near death, and her son Benjamin has been abducted, perhaps killed, by the Shawnees. Barely containing his fury at James Morely for not warning the others, Owen Sutherland vows to his unconscious wife to find their son and bring him back.*

*But before he can set out on his search, two more Indians appear . . . friends, this time, bearing a mysterious package for Sutherland's stepson, Jeremy Bently, who is thought to be a rebel prisoner. It is the bloodstained journal of a British officer named Richard Weston, and its last pages tell an incredible tale....*